Part One

Before

Chapter One

Sunday, February 10

It's happened again, the night-sweating thing. 'Christ, Viv,' Andy announces. 'It's like waking up in a swamp around here.'

I blink at my husband as he climbs out of bed. 'I can't help it. It just comes out of my body while I'm asleep.'

He winces. 'Yeah, well, I'm just saying.'

'But you're not *just saying*, are you? You're telling me off for being a middle-aged woman in the throes of hormonal collapse—'

'It's just unpleasant, that's all I mean.'

He pulls on his dressing gown, tightening the belt with a sharp tug. It's unpleasant for *him*? Well, I'm sorry, but along with the sweats I have a few other issues on my plate right now, such as: mood swings, heart palpitations, irrational outbursts and perpetually simmering anxiety that's ramped up considerably from my usual already signif-icant levels; plus a craving for hefty puddings (which might explain the weight piling onto my stomach), a tendency to cry at the sight of puppies, kittens, calves – any juvenile animal in fact – and more spots than I've been plagued with since I was thirteen years old. Oh, and there are the night fears too, neatly parcelled up with insomnia: about whether I booked my boss's flights for the correct date, and why I am overdrawn so badly, and what's happened to make my hair go crunchy like straw. There's always something to fret about at 4.37 a.m., from the state of the government to the size of my arse – and, failing that, I can angst about my anxiety in general (is it normal to feel this way?). And my husband has the audacity to moan about a clammy bed? For a man, the menopause is a breeze.

'I could sleep in the spare room?' I suggest. 'If it's that bad for you?'

'No need for that,' he says with a martyrish sigh.

'Or book into a special hotel for menopausal ladies with fans everywhere and sympathetic men to tend to our needs?'

He chooses not to respond to this.

'There's not much else I can do,' I add. 'It's not as if I can have a thermostat fitted.'

'All right, you've made your point . . .'

'Although I wish I *did* have a little knob.'

I study my husband's face: dashing Doctor Flint, with those intensely blue eyes and long, long lashes, as lush and curly as if he's been at my mascara. I suspect the majority of his colleagues and patients nurture a crush on him. I'm hoping to detect a glimmer of humour – or at least sympathy for my plummeting oestrogen levels on this drab, grey-skied morning. He just regards me coolly as if I've been sweating disgustingly just to spite him. Considering his lofty position in the medical profession, his bedside manner stinks.

Trying to shrug off my irritation, I shower after Andy and peep into our daughter's room where she is still in bed. She has fine, light brown hair, big blue eyes like her dad's and a wide gappy smile, with two milk teeth gone.

'Morning, Iz,' I say. 'Time to get up, love. Remember we said we'd go swimming today?'

'Oh, I forgot!'

'Let's go before it gets too busy,' I add. She slips out of bed and grabs at clothes from her wardrobe; Izzy won't tolerate being told what to wear. People are often taken aback that Andy and I have a seven-year-old daughter. We are both fifty-two and I am easily the oldest mother at the school gate. When Izzy was conceived we had long given up hope of ever having a second child; there were a couple of miscarriages after we'd had our son, and then nothing more after that. We both had tests, and everything seemed to be in proper working order, but the years rolled by with no more pregnancies.

Andy and I had just accepted that we would only have the one child. Spencer was a brilliant boy, and we didn't feel short-changed in any way. In fact, although we never used contraception, we'd almost forgotten it might be possible for us to conceive again. We certainly didn't expect it to happen when I was forty-four.

When I missed a period I thought it was the menopause starting. But instead, along came Izzy, an explosion of joy for whom I am grateful every single day. Spencer, who's twenty-two, looked a little queasy when we announced that he'd soon have a sibling (although he came round, of course, and he has adored Izzy from the moment she was born). But I guess most teenage boys don't wish to be confronted by the hard evidence that their parents still do it.

We don't much anymore, which wouldn't be so much of an issue, were it not for a more startling aspect of the menopause. More startling, anyway, than the sweating, which I'd expected. But I hadn't anticipated this surge in libido, to the point where I want it constantly and am driven to pawing at Andy in bed like a rampant sex pest.

Aw, Viv, I'm a bit knackered tonight.

I want to get up early for a run, love.

My lower back's playing up again. Pretty sure it's sciatica.

. . . Or maybe lumbago? Yeah, I think it's that.

Ouch! Sorry, I got a twinge when you did that . . .

Such is the loin-stirring effect I have on my beloved. One day *he'll* be desperate, breathing hotly in my ear and I'll be the exhausted/sciatica-bothered one. *Sorry, mate, you had your chance!* The prospect of denying him sex cheers me hugely while I make scrambled eggs for the three of us, and by the time we sit down to breakfast, I have just about forgiven him for his grumpiness earlier.

I even find it within myself to apologise, basically for being a woman, growing older. 'Sorry I'm being so narky,' I say, sipping my coffee. 'It's just horrible, waking up feeling like a slimy reptile.'

He eyes me levelly, this man who is supposed to love me and, by extension, possibly *care* about the hormonal stew I have found myself in. 'I think you'll find reptiles are dry-skinned, Viv,' he says.

6

Chapter Two

First day back after half-term, and Izzy and I are speed-walking to school. I am trying to greet the new week with a positive attitude and forget about how snarky and unsupportive Andy has been lately. Maybe it's work pressures and I should try to be more understanding of *his* needs? I know his job is pressurised, that everyone is overstretched, that working in a major hospital under tighter and tighter budget restrictions is no picnic. And, Christ, I respect what he does.

However, the reptile thing is still niggling me, especially as he added, 'I'd say you're more . . . *amphibious*,' while quirking his left eyebrow in that irritating way that always makes me want to thump him (have I always been this intolerant, with fury simmering just below the surface, or is it a new thing?). Plus, I've noticed Andy using the phrase 'I think you'll find' quite a lot recently, and not just in a reptile context. For instance, we have a worrying fan heater in our bedroom (Andy really feels the cold),

7

which he refuses to throw away, despite the fact that it emits a burning smell sporadically.

He insists it's perfectly safe. Being male, with that x-ray vision all men have, he can obviously see through the white plastic exterior to its inner workings and be confident in his diagnosis. 'I think you'll find it's just the dust inside burning off,' he added, last time I 'went on' about it (i.e. happened to mention that it smelt worryingly close to burning the house down).

'But should there be dust in it?' I asked. 'And, if so, is it meant to "burn off"?'

'It's fine!'

I can see it inscribed on our tombstones: *He said the fan heater was perfectly safe to use.* One more thing to add to the menopausal worries currently piling up in my head.

'Mum, there's Maeve!' Izzy announces, snapping me back to the present as she spots her best friend across the street. Maeve and her mother, Jules, wave to us, and we cross the road to join them.

'Hey, we were hoping to see you on the way,' Jules says as the girls fall into conversation and scamper ahead. 'What've you been up to?'

'Just pottering about really,' I reply. 'How about you?'

'We decided to go down to the caravan at the last minute. I know it sounds mad at this time of year but Erol was determined to get away for a few days.'

Ah, lovely Erol, Jules's husband, who makes no secret of the fact that he adores her and is always festooning her with compliments. She seems to think this is entirely normal, to be expected in a marriage. Maybe it is?

'Bet it was lovely,' I say, at which Jules chuckles. Jokingly, they call their static mobile home The World's

Most Disgusting Caravan although, from what I've seen, it looks pretty idyllic with its faded green decking and hanging baskets, and views of Lake Windermere.

'I'd never say it's lovely,' she says, 'especially now it seems to have developed a leak right over our bed. But we had fun, didn't we, Maeve?'

'Yeah.' Her daughter looks back and grins. 'We built a fire by the lake and cooked sausages on it.'

'Wow, in February?' I exclaim.

Jules smiles. At forty-two, she looks even more youthful than her years with her wiry body and boyish crop. I guess her look would be described as 'elfin.' If I had her hairstyle it would be more 'stout, angry man.'

'You know what Erol's like,' she goes on. 'Never deterred by bad weather. Anyway, it was lovely to be away, especially as I have a pretty full-on time coming up.'

'Plenty of clients at the moment?' I ask.

'Yeah, and I'm starting some new classes too.'

I nod, and a thought starts to form. Before I knew her, Jules was something very important in banking. Burnt out and disillusioned with corporate life, she chucked all that in and now has several strings to her bow: yoga teacher, caterer and . . . life coach. I know Andy regards coaching as a silly indulgence for the privileged few, but, frankly, who cares what he thinks? If I booked a few sessions, perhaps some of Jules's qualities might rub off on me. Perhaps I'd be less . . . *amphibious*.

'D'you have room for any more clients at the moment?' I ask as we approach the school.

'You mean, for someone you know?'

'Erm, not exactly . . .'

'You mean for you?'

'I do, actually,' I say.

'Great! Yes, we can fix something up no problem. Fancy a coffee now, or are you rushing straight off to work?'

'Back to work, unfortunately,' I reply, 'but let's get together soon.' At the school gates now, I turn to Izzy. 'Remember it's after-school club today, won't you?'

'Yeah.' She grins. Maeve goes too; they have toast and honey and are apparently embarking on a mural-painting project in the playground. 'Is my gym kit in my bag?' she asks.

'Yes, love.'

'What kind of sandwiches did you give me?'

'Cheese and pickle.'

'What else is there?'

'Tangerine, cereal bar, packet of Crunchy-Bites . . .'

'Did you pack Woolly?' That's the joke sandwich my friend Penny knitted for Izzy's last birthday, which amused her so much that she likes to bring it to school every day. Every so often I have to wrestle it off her for a gentle hand-wash.

'Of course I did.' I bob down to kiss her as the bell sounds. 'Have a good day, sweetheart—'

'Mum, I'll be late!' She pulls away, inadequately brushed hair flying behind her as she and Maeve charge towards the door.

And so to work, on an unlovely industrial estate to the west of Glasgow, where I find my office phone already ringing. It's my boss calling in a state of distress.

'What on earth made you book this place, Viv?'

Rose is phoning from China. This is why she is shouting. Despite her undeniable intellect, she seems to believe that the further she is from our headquarters, the louder she

10

has to be. Never mind that she could easily have messaged me. Rose prefers to communicate verbally and – with the seven-hour time difference firmly established in her mind – had obviously been poised to call me the minute I'd sat down at my desk.

'It looked fine on the website,' I say. 'I checked out loads of options and thought it seemed like the best . . .'

'You said it was as good as the Larson!'

'Yes, but the Larson was full. Remember I told you?' *And I showed you pictures of this place, of the glass-walled lounge and rooftop infinity pool, which you barely looked at.* We have clients all over the world and, with China being a particularly big market for us, Rose has been to Tianjin on business several times.

'Yes, well, they're in the throes of building works here,' she explains, as if I should have known this, 'and I've been shovelled off into this god-awful annexe.'

'Oh, I am sorry to hear that. Is it comfortable, though?'

'Not exactly. There's a problem.'

I clear my throat. 'What is it?'

'There's . . .' her voice tightens '. . . a pubic hair on the toilet seat.'

For a moment, I don't quite know how to respond.

'Can you hear me, Viv?'

'Yes, yes, I hear you . . .' Loud and ruddy clear! 'Um, could you call housekeeping or something? Maybe they could send someone along to deal with it?' *Or how about grabbing a piece of loo paper and wiping it away by yourself?*

I'm prepared to humour her little freak-out because, in many ways, Rose is a remarkable woman. Our company, Flaxico, might sound like some kind of anti-flatulence medication but it's actually a long-established, male-dominated global food company. Perennially single and child-free, Rose has forced her way, terrier-like, up through the ranks and now presides over our sprawling complex of glass and steel. At barely five feet tall, she favours massive blow-dries and teetering heels and, although the overall effect is a little scary, I admire her commitment to adding height to herself from both ends.

It wasn't part of my life's plan to work somewhere like this. Years ago, I worked in theatre, which I loved. I did various jobs – props, lighting, set building – before working my way up to stage manager. However, the hours were insane, which was fine when I was younger, but less so when I became a mum again at forty-five. So I took a couple of years out after having Izzy. By the time I was ready to return, the theatre company I'd been connected to had had its funding stopped, and I couldn't find anything else. Disconcertingly, it felt like all of my reliable contacts had moved on. To tide me over I took on some temping work here until Rose appointed me as her PA five years ago.

When I'd taken the temp role, I'd had no idea that Flaxico was one of the world's biggest manufacturers of . . . well, *pellets* in fact. They're formed mainly from cereals (corn, wheat, rice) that have been 'extruded' (i.e. forced through a shaping machine). When they leave our factory they look like beanbag filler, or gravel from the bottom of a fish tank, and are what's known as an 'intermediate product'. They are then sold on to other companies to be flavoured, dyed, fried, baked, air-puffed or whatever's required to turn them into the desired savoury snacks, breakfast cereals or pet treats.

So, that's what we are about; hardly artisanal, nothing fresh or even resembling anything you'd actually want to eat. It's basically enormous vats of *stuff* being pumped about. Meanwhile, Rose travels the world, negotiating eye-watering deals with some of the most ruthless individuals in food manufacturing – yet she falls apart at the sight of a pube on a loo seat.

'Could you get onto someone please?' she asks now.

'Yes, of course. Leave it with me and I'll get straight back to you.'

'Thanks *so* much.' When I manage to sort it, Rose calls me a 'lifesaver', which is perhaps overshooting it a bit, but at least she is appreciative of my efforts.

I tell Andy about all of this as we get ready for bed that night – thinking, well, it's funny, isn't it, the pube-in-China emergency? 'So,' I rattle on, 'from a distance of 5,000 miles I finally managed to speak to a human being on the phone – they speak English, of course they do, Tianjin's an international city of something like thirteen million people. Can you believe that? That there are these enormous cities, way bigger than London, some of them, that most people in Britain have never even heard of?'

I clamber into bed. Andy is sitting on the edge of it, seemingly engrossed in the task of peeling off a sock.

'Andy?'

He flinches as if he's only just remembered I'm here. 'Huh?'

'I was just saying, most people haven't even heard of it.'

'Haven't heard of what?'

'Tianjin.'

He gives me a baffled stare. 'Tian . . . jin?'

'It's where Rose is right now.' *I think you'll find it's in China.*

'Oh, is it? Right . . .'

As he climbs into bed, I wonder if this is how it feels to do stand-up and be faced with row upon row of unsmiling faces as your routine bombs. *Maybe it's my material,* you'd think, desperately. *I need to change direction – find something fresh and new.*

The problem is, this is my life. It's the only material I have.

Chapter Three

Thursday, February 14

No Valentine's present − not even a card − but then I didn't get anything for Andy either. This year, we decided 'not to honour Valentine's Day'. As it was by mutual agreement (at least, he suggested it and I couldn't think of a good enough reason to disagree without seeming needy or simply wanting a gift), I can hardly be huffy about it. In fact, I don't even mention it. I just get ready for work as normal, and chivvy Izzy along, pretending it's just an ordinary day.

Until last year, we exchanged cards at least. The fact that even this ritual has dropped off the radar gives me an uneasy feeling deep in my gut, but I try to ignore it as I drive to work.

At the office, a bouquet of red roses arrives for one of the other PAs from her newish boyfriend. That's what newish boyfriends do, I reassure myself as everyone gathers around and makes a big fuss of it. They make these grand gestures; it's almost expected. And an image flashes into my mind of a Valentine's Day many years ago, when I still worked in theatre. I'd just gone back after having Spencer and was working on a production that was proving incredibly tricky to pull together. In the middle of a rehearsal, an enormous, showy concoction of pink lilies and white baby's breath arrived for me from Andy. The entire cast and crew gathered around and cheered, and my face blazed with delight.

To my gorgeous superwoman, the card said.

Another time, Andy had a request played for me on the radio, when people still did that. Further back, when we were still pretty new as a couple, having recently met at an otherwise terrible party, he'd make mix tapes for me and turn up at my door at 2 a.m., a bit drunk and proclaiming love, which I'd pretend to be mad about for about three seconds before pulling him in and hauling him off to my bed.

Back then, we didn't need it to be Valentine's Day to make thoughtful, affectionate gestures. Andy and I sent cards and letters to each other in the post all the time. If he'd stayed over at my flat, and left before I'd got up, I'd often find a sweet or funny note from him, sitting by the kettle. I'd draw silly cartoons to make him smile when he found them in his fridge. It occurs to me now that Valentine's Day is more useful to long-term couples like us, acting as it does as a reminder to make an effort, to consider the other person and make them feel special. But too late for that now, at least for this year. As we are Not Honouring It, there's no night out planned, no treaty dinner, just for the two of us.

Back home after work, I tell myself that this is a good thing as restaurants are always packed on February 14th, and they have those special Valentine's menus, which are actually just their normal ones with 'seduction cocktails' and pink champagne jellies tacked on, as if that constitutes romance. I have almost convinced myself that going out with one's beloved on Valentine's Day is corny and faintly embarrassing (who wants to eat out just because the date on the calendar says we should? All that pressure, jeez!) when Andy announces he *is* going out – *with other people!*

'Just a couple of drinks,' Andy says, kissing me fleetingly on his way out. 'Won't be a late one. Sorry, I totally forgot what day it is. You don't mind, do you?' He pulls a pained expression.

'Of course not.' What else am I going to say? Since V-Day is Non-Honoured it would seem ridiculous to kick up a fuss. I mean, what would we be doing anyway? Watching TV?

An hour or so later, still irritated and listless, I text my friend Shelley to vent that my husband has chosen tonight to meet up with a couple of old mates, but never-bloody-mind. I hadn't realised her partner, Laurence, is away with work. We decide she must come over right away (Izzy is already tucked up in bed, and Shelley doesn't have kids).

It's my full intention to be perky and cheerful tonight. Shelley is a social worker with a barely manageable caseload, and the last thing she wants is for me to be blethering on about how Andy seems to have developed an aversion towards me. But after a large glass of wine, it all tumbles out: how mild disdain seems to be his default setting; how unaffectionate he is generally, and how I suspect he could quite happily never have sex with me again. How there's always some excuse not to do it, and how shitty and rejected I've felt, night after night, to the point at which I have now stopped trying to initiate anything at all.

How I stand there naked sometimes, looking at my middle-aged body with the saggy boobs and wobbly stomach in our full-length mirror and think: Christ, no wonder he doesn't want to do it with me. I mean, who *would?*

'Could it be that simple?' I ask Shelley. 'That, basically, he no longer likes what he sees?'

'Of course it's not that,' she retorts. 'You're gorgeous, Viv. Don't be crazy. If he doesn't realise how lucky he is, he's an idiot.' She pauses. 'It's probably nothing to do with you at all. It'll be his job, I bet. He's probably just tired and stressed, or he's become complacent—'

'Or maybe I had all my quota in our early years,' I cut in, topping up her glass.

'Of sex, you mean?'

'Yeah.'

'I don't think it quite works like that,' she says with a wry smile. She tucks her stockinged feet under her on the sofa and smooths down her fine auburn hair.

'It might. You can overdo things, can't you? Like when you eat too much of the same thing and suddenly you can't stand it.'

'Oh, God, yeah. Like hummus.' She shudders. 'The smell of it makes me want to vomit now.'

'Mine's strawberry fromage frais. Izzy used to love it and I was always scoffing a pot whenever she had one. But once I'd reached that tipping point, that was that.'

'You'd over-fromaged yourself?' she suggests.

'Yep. I could hardly bear to look at it. So maybe that's what's happened, and these days I have a sort of fromage frais effect on Andy.'

''Course you don't,' she splutters.

'Or are my sprouting face hairs putting him off?'

'Don't be ridiculous!'

'But maybe they are,' I say firmly. 'There was a new one this morning – a thick, long wire – like you might find if you took a vintage radio to bits . . .'

'Before they were wire*less*?'

I nod. 'Exactly.'

'I had one of those too, sticking out of my chin. I couldn't believe my own body had made it.'

'And then there are the softer ones,' I add. 'The ones that sneak out, barely visible but definitely there, like little bits of fur. No wonder he doesn't want to have sex when I'm halfway to being a goat.'

'Some people would pay good money for that,' she guffaws.

She does cheer me up, because when you talk about how someone won't do it with you, it seems jokey and ridiculous and easily fixable with 'a chat'.

'You *are* going to talk to him, aren't you?' Shelley asks as she leaves. 'I mean, to find out what's actually going on?'

And I agree that I am.

We're in bed now, and he is engrossed in a weighty psychological thriller. I clear my throat. 'Andy?'

'Mmm-hmm?' His eyes remain fixed upon the book.

'You know all this sweating and stuff I've got going on?' I begin, alluringly.

'Er, yeah?'

'Well . . .' I pause. 'Does it kind of . . . put you off, you know . . . us doing stuff?'

He turns and blinks at me. 'Doing stuff? What d'you mean?'

What does he think I mean? Having day trips at the

19

seaside? 'Doing *it*,' I mutter. 'You know what I'm talking about, don't you?'

Oh God, I am rapidly losing confidence here. This is ridiculous! We've been together for twenty-five years. He held back my hair while I threw up from a bad oyster at his youngest brother's wedding. He has seen me push out two babies. He didn't seem to enjoy it especially, and with Izzy I caught him poking at his phone – but still, it's mad that I should feel shy with him.

'Doing *it*?' he says carefully. 'D'you mean, uh—'

'Yes,' I say, my cheeks burning now.

He frowns at me. 'No, I'm not put off. Why d'you say that?'

Because you're always in too much pain with your raging sciatica, although not so much that you can't bound off to the pub . . .

'I just wondered,' I say flatly.

He turns back to his book, and I pretend to read mine, skimming the same paragraph over and over. Perhaps I'd get along better with *Fantastic Mr Fox*, which I am currently reading to Izzy.

I decide to try another angle. 'Andy, d'you think I should try HRT?'

He gives me a confused look, which I might expect, were he not an endocrinologist: i.e. a doctor who special-ises in hormones *and therefore knows every sodding thing about them*. And not any old endocrinologist either, but an eminent one, who travels the country to deliver lectures on the subject – although not to his wife, obviously. That would be far too troublesome. All this world-renowned oestrogen expert will say on the matter is: 'Oh, I dunno, love. It's up to you really.'

I fall into silence, unable to dredge up a response to

that. Am I being unreasonable? I wonder. Is it crazy behaviour to ask one's husband for advice when the subject happens to relate to his profession? Jules doesn't seem to think so. Erol is a roofer and any trouble they have with their guttering, he has it sorted no problem. When their garage fell into a state of disrepair, he had it demolished and replaced with a spanking new one he built with his own hands.

My eyes are prickling now and I'm aware that I am dangerously close to crying. *Get a grip*, I chastise myself silently. Like Shelley suggested, he's probably just tired and stressed. I should leave it until he's more amenable.

'I'd just like to know what you think,' I bark at him. 'I'm wondering if I should do something about it instead of just accepting all these horrible symptoms, you know? It feels like I'm losing my mind sometimes—'

'Well, yeah. Perhaps you should see the doctor?' he concedes, which has the effect of accelerating my heart rate to the point at which my entire chest seems to be juddering. I *am* seeing the doctor, I want to snap. He's lying here a foot away from me in his stripy pyjamas and he doesn't give a flying fuck.

Andy turns the page of his book, and I glare at him. *Why* won't he help me? Does he want me to dissolve in a pool of anxiety and stress?

As he yawns and places his book on the bedside table, I tell myself to calm down and stop making such a drama of everything. Instead, I read recently, I should focus on the *positive* aspects of the menopause, like being able to enjoy sex (pah!) without fear of pregnancy, and being a wise, mature woman, who is graceful and elegant – as if we are all sodding Helen Mirren with sculpted cheek-bones, still slipping easily into our size ten jeans.

As Andy clicks off his bedside light, and we exchange terse goodnights, I try to reassure myself that he is behaving like any normal man. After all, he works hard at that hospital and the last thing he wants is to be harangued into giving medical diagnoses at home. If he were a chef, I wouldn't expect him to whip me up a fabulous carbonara the minute he'd walked in through the door.

So, our marriage is probably fine. Isn't it?

Chapter Four

Saturday, February 16

But it's not. As it turns out, it's *not fine at all*.

It's because of the stars. That's how I find out. In the city you don't often see them shining so brightly, but tonight you can. They are sparkling entrancingly. It's magical.

It's around 10 p.m. and I'm standing in our back garden, looking up at them, still gripping the bucket from emptying our recycling into the wheelie bin. Remembering the app that Andy installed on his phone, I head back into the house to ask him if I can have a go with it. He was telling me how it can identify constellations when it's pointed at the sky, and tonight is the perfect night for it.

'Andy!' I call out from the hallway.

'In the bath,' comes his voice from upstairs. 'What is it?'

'Oh, nothing . . .' I'd forgotten he'd gone up for a soak. Izzy is over at Maeve's on a sleepover, so it's just the two of us in tonight. Spencer moved out four years ago, when he was eighteen. He dropped out of university in first year – it just wasn't for him, he insisted, and there was no arguing with him – and we were thrown into panic about his future, but he got a job pretty quickly for a company that installs sound systems for gigs. He lives in Newcastle now, in a shared flat with two friends and a varied selection of fungi sprouting from the bathroom carpet. Whenever I ask him what his job entails he just laughs and says, 'Lifting things, Mum,' and ruffles my hair as if I'm a little kid.

I spot Andy's phone sitting on the hall table, take it out to the garden and tap in his passcode. That's weird; it's been his date of birth for as long as I can remember, but now it doesn't seem to work. He must have changed it. I try tapping in the full year – still no luck. Shrugging off a twinge of unease (*why* has he changed it?) I try reversing the six digits of his date of birth. Bingo, that was easy! I'm now in the inner sanctum of my husband's telephonic device.

Having found the app, I hold up the phone, marvelling at the way it names Betelgeuse, Venatici, Perseus; what beautiful decorative names they have. Ooh, there's Mars! This is brilliant. I must get this app. It's a lot more fun than my fitness one that reminds me – scathingly – that I have only done 397 steps out of the recommended daily 10,000.

Ping! That's a text from 'Estelle', which I know means something celestial (I find out later that it's Latin for star) so I assume it's to do with the app. I open it, expecting it to say something like, *Look out for incredible shooting stars tonight!*

Darling baby, it reads, *missing your sweet kisses so much xxx.*

24

I frown at it. How very weird. Perhaps the app is malfunctioning? Or has someone messaged my husband by mistake? A moment later, there's another:

Aching for you sweetheart xxx

Something clenches inside me as I see that it's one of a string of messages. I scroll up and read the conversation:

Andy: *Soon I hope xxx*

Estelle: *When can I see you darling? xxx*

Andy: *It really was baby xxx*

Estelle: *Last time was so special xxx*

The fact that I am reading it from the bottom up makes me wonder again – momentarily – if my brain has tipped upside down and I am misinterpreting the situation. Could this be another menopausal symptom? I'm aware that I can be a little oversensitive, even verging on paranoid. I read on: *I love you baby* (from Andy). Is this some kind of joke? Or – I realise I'm clutching at straws here – could someone have hacked into his phone?

Sweetie, reads another of her messages, *that was the best ever!!!* What was the best? It can only mean sex, can't it? Which means he's done it with someone who isn't me. My heart is pounding hard and I feel dizzy and quite sick. I try, desperately, to think of other things that might be described in that way but can't come up with anything except, perhaps, 'cake'. And I don't think she was referring to cake.

'Evening, Viv!' The voice makes me jump. I swing around to see Tim, our next-door neighbour, beaming at me.

'Hi, Tim.' *Please go away and let me quietly freak out.*

'Everything okay?' Tim – a short, tubby quantity surveyor who's as bald as an egg in his late thirties – gives me a concerned look.

25

'Yes, I'm fine, thanks,' I say, forcing a smile.

He looks up at the sky. 'Aren't the stars amazing tonight?'

'They are, yes.'

'Erm, look, Viv, I'm sorry to be the bearer of bad tidings . . .' My heartbeat accelerates. Does Tim know about Estelle? Does *everyone* know? '. . . but we have rats in the garden,' he goes on. 'Seen them a few times so a council guy's coming round tomorrow to check things out. Is it okay if he has a poke around your garden too?'

I blink at him. 'Rats?'

'Well, yes,' he says, looking regretful now, as if he feels somehow responsible for their arrival. 'And if they're in our garden, they're probably in yours. I don't think they respect boundaries . . .' I watch our neighbour's fleshy mouth moving as he carries on talking, but nothing seems to make sense anymore. I think he's talking about poison, something about rats tending to follow a specific route. All I can think is: *Andy says he loves her. He's sleeping with her. My husband has an entire parallel life with this woman that I've known nothing about.*

'Oh, Viv,' Tim exclaims, looking aghast now. 'I'm sorry. I didn't mean to upset you. Was it something I—'

'No, no, you haven't upset me, Tim. I'm *fine* . . .' I realise I am crying.

'It's just rats,' he adds, brow furrowed in concern as he hurries closer and peers at me over the fence. 'Not ideal, I know, but they're everywhere these days. The guy'll put poison down in little bags, buried in the ground . . .'

I nod, wordlessly, as tears continue to roll down my cheeks.

'Honestly, it's nothing to worry about,' he goes on,

looking quite distraught at the state of me. As parents, he and his wife might be spectacularly ineffective – 'We don't believe in saying no,' Chrissie told me recently – but Tim is a decent, well-meaning man. He's not a cheating bastard of a husband.

'Worse things happen,' he adds as I dab at my face with my sweater sleeve.

'It's not the rats, Tim—'

'Oh . . . ?'

'It's something else.' I glance up at our frosted bathroom window with light coming through it, where Andy – 'Sweetie' – is currently marinating in bubbles, oblivious to my distress.

'Is it, um, anything I can help with?'

'No, I'm sorry, and it's fine – about the rat man,' I blurt out, marching towards the house, thinking, *He can concrete over our entire garden for all I care.*

Inside now, I run upstairs and rap sharply on the bathroom door.

'Still in the bath,' Andy calls out in a jovial tone.

'Could you open the door?'

'Mmm?' The water sloshes. 'Won't be long . . .'

'Andy,' I bark.

'Can't you use the downstairs bathroom?'

'No, I can't.' Fury is bubbling up in me now. I'm gripping his phone so hard it's a wonder I don't crush the screen. I bang harder on the door, at which Andy curses under his breath – but still audibly – then there's more sloshing and ostentatious sighing as he hauls himself out of the water. He opens the bathroom door wearing his dressing gown unbelted and stands there dripping all over our wooden floor.

'What's up?'

I thrust his phone at him.

'What is it?' He gives me an uncomprehending look.

'I read your texts. I read them just now. The ones from Estelle.'

My back teeth are jammed together and my heart seems to be battering inside my chest. Andy hesitates before taking his phone from me. And I know, as a sense of grim resignation settles over his face, that there's no innocent explanation for these messages.

The astronomy app didn't malfunction. No one hacked into his phone. My husband has been seeing this woman, and calling her 'Baby', and our marriage will never be the same again.

Chapter Five

The terrible early hours of Sunday, February 17

The way he tells it, it was a dreadful mistake. Too much drink after a heady day at that conference in Manchester, back in October: 'So full on, Viv. You know what these things are like, especially on the last night when everything's wrapping up.'

October! A whole four months ago! That's sixteen weeks . . . a hundred and, um, a *lot* of days. And, actually, I don't know what 'these things' are like. At Flaxico we don't go away for conferences. We don't even have any. Instead, we have 'ideas days', held in what's known as the lower basement (as opposed to the upper basement), down in the bowels of the earth, perilously close to its fiery core, which is never used at any other time.

There's no shagging at these, obviously. There isn't even any booze; just a dismal buffet sent down to our window-less bunker from the canteen, comprising cress-garnished sandwiches containing something called 'cheese savoury' (i.e. grated cheese and onion bound with generous quantities of mayonnaise) plus small, sticky, factory-made cakes sweating in their cellophane wrappers. But that's not the issue. The real point is, even if I did know what 'these things are like', I can't imagine any situation where I'd have slept with someone else. The naughtiest thing I've ever done in a hotel was pinch an extra shampoo from a chambermaid's trolley.

'Massive night at the bar,' Andy goes on, slumped on our sofa in his dressing gown. 'Everyone all charged up, free drinks all night, things got out of hand . . .' So what better way to round things off than to 'find himself' in someone else's room, rather than in his own? An easy mistake to make, when blundering drunkenly along the corridors. Thank God for the eminent Dr Estelle Lang – whom he'd 'barely known really' – who had pulled him in, removed all his clothing and had frenzied sex with him until it was time for him to stagger, limping, down for breakfast.

Of course, I am making that bit up. Andy just blurts out the bare details – that it 'sort of' happened, though he was so horribly drunk he can hardly remember anything at all. In fact, it might *not* have happened that night. He's really not sure. 'And then,' he continues, but only because I force it out of him, 'we met up, just for coffee, to talk about stuff, and we slipped into this thing, Christ knows how it even started. I'm so sorry, Viv . . .'

His dressing gown is now belted tightly. That's a relief. I don't think I could bear to glimpse his sorrowful wandering penis right now. As for this celestial Estelle, I gather that she is based in Edinburgh, and that's where these subsequent meetings took place. It was easy for him to get away with it. It's a fifty-minute train journey from Glasgow, and he's often invited to lunches, presentations and the occasional evening with his old medical-school mates; events I've been happy for him to go to without me tagging along.

Sometimes, he stays overnight in Edinburgh, supposedly at a friend's place. 'Can't face rushing for the last train,' he told me last time.

The lying shit.

'I'll do anything to make things right,' he says now, wringing his hands as if trying to squeeze all the badness out of himself. He is crying, and I am crying, and we go on like this, shouting and snotting and repeating ourselves, winding up exactly where we started hours before.

At one point I pick up a board game of Izzy's and throw it at him. The lid falls off and tiddlywinks fly out. Both of us scrabble to gather them all up. As dawn creeps into the living room I consider going out for cigarettes. However, as I haven't bought any in twenty-four years, I'm not sure where I'd go. Plus, the alluring shiny gold packaging has been replaced by pictures of diseased mouths and babies on respirators, which would hardly make me feel better about anything, and I seem to remember that they did away with packets of ten so I'd be stuck with twenty, and I'd feel obliged to smoke them all and become addicted again: fagging it up in the back garden, horrifying Tim and Chrissie and their little darling, Ludo, next door. *That* would be more alarming than a few rats!

By the time it's properly morning – we have been up raging and crying the entire night – I have started to grasp at fragments of positivity: like, thank God Izzy was invited to a sleepover at Maeve's last night (how would Jules set about life coaching me out of this?). And: at least Andy seems genuinely sorry.

'I suppose I was just flattered,' he murmurs, 'that a woman like her seemed to have feelings for me.'

A woman like her, i.e. several notches above his slightly overweight, menopausally sweating wife back at home?

'I just got sucked into it,' he adds.

'Could you possibly use a different turn of phrase?'

'Sorry! I'm sorry!'

I glare at him, my nerves shredded, utterly exhausted, yet simultaneously wondering whether I will ever sleep soundly again. 'You said you loved her. Remember, I read the texts.'

'I lost my mind for a bit,' he says, trying to hug me. I push him away. I'm not ready for hugging. It's bizarre to think how much I craved his arms around me, and his kisses, before I found out. 'I'll delete her number,' he adds. 'You can watch me do it.'

'Do what you want. It won't make any difference to what's happened, will it?'

'But it will, Viv.' He holds his phone in front of me, trying to make me watch as he deletes her. 'Look, the number's gone. I swear on my life I'll never contact her again.'

Still Sunday, properly daytime

After our night of madness, naturally I am the one who has to patch up my face in order to try to look normal when I go to pick up Izzy from Maeve's. 'Are you *okay*, Viv?' Jules asks, registering my puffy eyes and ravaged complexion as Izzy gathers her stuff together in Maeve's bedroom.

'Me and Andy had a bit of a thing last night,' I explain

32

quickly. 'I'm sure we'll be all right. I'll tell you all about it another time.' I mean it – I will tell her – but I can't face it right now. I'm not sure if I'd even be able to talk sense.

'I hate to say this, but you look exhausted.'

'Well, yes, I am. But honestly, I'll be okay,' I say, trying to believe it myself. But God, the mess of it. A quarter of a century, we've been together: almost half of our lives. We have our two lovely children and live in a sturdy Victorian house in a leafy area of the Southside. We have plenty of friends, both individually and as a couple, and although I had my gripes, I thought we were basically solid.

How wrong I was. Why on earth didn't I suspect anything? The going-off-sex thing, for instance. *Now* that makes sense. Have I been walking around in some kind of daze?

Thankfully, Izzy doesn't notice anything's wrong – not because my clumsily applied make-up has acted as a successful camouflage, but because she's full of all the fun things she and Maeve have been up to.

'Jules let us make dinner,' she says proudly as we walk home.

'Oh, that's nice,' I say, pausing from trying to count up all the lies Andy's told me over the past few weeks.

What about the last time he was in Edinburgh, supposedly for his mate Colin's fiftieth birthday? And the time before that, when I seem to remember he made a particular effort to look good for a talk in the National Library?

'Mum?'

'Yes, Izzy?'

'I said, d'you want to know what we made?'

33

'Yes. Yes, of course I do.' I take her hand and squeeze it and she beams up at me.

'Stuffed tomatoes.'

'What?' I exclaim. She's terribly iffy about vegetables usually. Even peas can be shunned.

'They're Turkish,' she adds. 'Erol's Turkish.'

'Yes, I know he is, honey. What were they stuffed with?'

'Um, rice, pine kernels, raisins . . .'

My God, a dried fruit component? For a moment, this seems even more shocking than Andy shagging Estelle Lang at the Crowne Plaza hotel. What is it about Jules that enables her to persuade children to enjoy such exotic delights? Then we turn the corner and that awful sense of dread settles back over me. Our house is in view now, no longer solid and safe, a cosy haven, but emitting anguish and doom.

Izzy drops my hand and runs ahead of me, barging in through the front door. I step inside to see her hugging her dad and feel as if my heart could break.

Chapter Six

Six days later: Saturday, February 23

Bizarrely, my previously disinterested husband has become terribly attentive. I suppose I'd almost become accustomed to the way we were, with each of us doing our own thing, inhabiting the same house but not interacting very much at all. It's just the way things were. Now he follows me around the house like a needy dog, trying to nuzzle me and sitting jammed up next to me whenever I dare to sit on the sofa for five minutes. I almost feel as if I should let him out to the garden to do his business.

I know why he's doing it, of course. He's hoping it'll make the terrible Estelle stuff go away. Before all of this, he hadn't touched me for weeks – apart from to pick a crisp off my jumper – so it's unsettling to say the least. Often, I flinch at Andy's touch, and on occasion I've swung around, primed for combat – or to at least pull the emergency cord – as if I've been groped on a train. I've had to explain, very firmly, that I have no wish to have my neck kissed when I'm battering away at the ice that's stopping our freezer door from shutting properly.

As well as being Strokey McStrokerson, Andy has acquired another startling new role: the DIY Enthusiast. The coat hooks I've been asking him to put up for several decades are finally *up*; yes, I know I should have acquainted myself with the cordless drill and done it myself, as any self-respecting modern woman would have. But I didn't, and – hurrah! – I no longer need to trouble myself, as they now adorn our hall wall (exactly where I'd asked him to put them). He has also put up shelves in the bathroom, yet more in our bedroom and hung a large mirror in the hallway; in fact, he has been erecting things all over the house. But not near me, thankfully. Another unexpected development is that he's come over all canoodly in bed. But naturally, my libido was killed stone dead when the Estelle stuff broke, so there's nothing happening on that score. Not that he's being grumpy about his loving attentions being thwarted. On the contrary, he has been extremely pleasant to me, and appreciative to the point of ridiculousness:

Thanks for doing those shirts for me, darling!

Oh, you've washed up? I would've done those . . .

Wow, this so delicious . . .

'It's just an omelette,' I snap. *No need to over-egg it*, is what I want to say – but I don't want him to think we're allowed to be jokey again. I'm still angry, yes – but I also hate the way this whole mess is making me so snarky and bitter, and I wonder if this is me now, for the rest of my life.

Everywhere I look, there seems to be an article on how to 'be your best self'. Now, with Andy firmly on best behaviour, I seem to have turned into the very *worst* version of myself: that of a grim-faced parole officer, unmoved by praise.

'Yes, but you make the best omelettes,' Andy murmurs, gazing at it reverentially as if he might kiss it. 'I've always said that.'

No, actually, I want to remind him, *you're only saying it because you couldn't keep your dick in your pants.* He looks at me across the kitchen table. Izzy – who thankfully still has no idea that anything is wrong – is tucked up under a blanket on the sofa in the living room, with a cold. I get up from my chair to go through to her. I'm still finding it difficult to be in the same room as Andy.

'What's the secret?' he asks, having followed me through.

'The secret of what?' I frown at him.

'Of your omelettes!'

'Do you *really* want to know?'

'Yes, I do,' he splutters, looking hurt.

'He does want to know,' Izzy says, peering at me in confusion, which makes me feel as if my heart is being crushed. 'Why won't you tell him? Are you cross with Daddy?'

'Of course not,' I say with a terse smile as I scuttle out of the room.

I hide upstairs for a while, wondering how on earth we are going to get through this. We are doing our best to manoeuvre around each other, somehow managing to do the normal things that couples do, like cook dinner and watch TV and, of course, all the usual stuff with Izzy. All week, we've talked plenty about Estelle – long after Izzy's gone to bed, obviously – as I've tried to drag every detail out of him: whether she's married (yes), has children (no) and how successful she is in her field ('Fairly,' he admitted, reluctantly, which clearly meant: *extremely*).

It's the length of time it's been happening that's the toughest thing to handle. It means they were 'carrying on' (such an old-fashioned phrase!) throughout Christmas, when I'd thought everything was fine and normal with us. But now I realise he was probably thinking about her when he carved the turkey. She'd have been on his mind when he and Spencer played a tipsy game of Jenga together, and when he hugged Izzy and told her the Christmas card she'd made him was 'the best one I've ever had'.

How could he *do* this to us?

Naturally, I have googled the shit out of this woman. As I'm hardly sleeping anyway I've taken the sensible option of sitting up half the night, staring at pictures of her speaking at conferences and sitting on panels of Terribly Important Doctors.

She is attractive in that cool, thin, almost transparently pale kind of way: lightly freckled with challenging green eyes and rod-straight fair hair that hangs, wig-like, at her chin. If she were a sales assistant in a clothes shop, you'd take one look at her and decide you'd be better blundering around, trying to find the right thing in your size, rather than asking her for help. And you'd be too scared to ask to try anything on. You'd decide you're probably too fat anyway and leave without buying anything, muttering a meek 'thank you' as you left the shop.

So yes, she is thin. Of course she ruddy is. I imagine she's tall, too; she has that lofty look about her, as if she 'carries herself' well, whereas I merely barge about. However, I can't find any mention of her height anywhere, and when I ask Andy he just groans, '*Please*, Viv, can we stop this now?' and leaves the room.

I do manage to find out her age, though. She looks way younger than me – early forties at most – but, horrifyingly, it transpires that she and I are the same age. Fifty-bloody-two with the skin of a peach! She looks natural, too – not obviously Botoxed or weirdly stretched as if she's had her skin hoisted up behind her ears. I can't decide whether she is ageing incredibly well or I am crumbling at a terrifying rate.

'I just want us to be happy, like we were,' Andy says, looking exhausted when I try to grill him on this. 'What can I do to help us get over it?'

The trouble is, I don't know.

Sunday, February 24

But my friend Penny does. 'Make the most of it,' she says. 'All those household tasks you've wanted doing? Get him onto them right away.'

I had to escape the house today – I literally can't bear being around Andy – and was grateful she was around. It's a sharp, blue-skied afternoon, and I'm helping Jules out by looking after Maeve for the day. As the girls scale the climbing frame, Penny details how I should put my husband to work as a handyman; a 'strike while the iron's hot' sort of approach.

'But he's done everything already,' I explain. 'I found him the other day, prowling around actually looking for jobs that needed doing. There's not one lightbulb that needs changing. He even pumped my bike tyres without being asked. He *washed the skirting boards*. There's literally nothing left to do.'

'How about the garden? Didn't you say you want to start growing veg?'

'Yes, but—'

'Then get him started,' she insists.

'It's too early, Pen,' I say.

She looks quizzical. 'You mean you're not ready to talk?'

'No, it's too early to plant veg.'

'Yes, but he could start digging things over, preparing the ground . . .'

I laugh, despite the awfulness of it all. As if a ready supply of rocket will make everything all right. 'Penny, I don't care about that anymore.'

'But you were so keen,' she insists. 'You said—'

'Yes, before I found out about this woman!'

'Oh, darling. I'm so sorry this has happened to you.' As she squeezes my arm I look round at her kind face, pillarbox-red lipstick on as always, ash-blonde hair tumbling around her shoulders in bouncy waves. Despite being almost two decades older – Penny is seventy-one – she's not remotely maternal with me. If anything, I find our age difference refreshing as, whatever I'm going through, there's a pretty good chance she's breezed her way through it and emerged, if not quite unscathed, then laughing throatily with a G&T clamped to her hand. So far, I have managed to keep my own booze consumption to a reasonable level; at least, reasonable for someone who's been lied to and humiliated.

We first met right here, Penny and I. Back then – five years ago – Izzy and I virtually lived in the park, a five-minute walk from our house, and we'd started to notice the lady who often wore dazzling bright colours when she walked her little black dog. We began to look out for her and, of course, she was delighted when Izzy made a fuss of Bobby, her schnauzer-poodle cross ('He's a schnoodle,' she explained, to Izzy's delight). After a few weeks of chatting we'd exchanged numbers so we could meet up. I started to look forward to seeing her.

With her prim accent and crackly laugh, Penny seemed both earthy *and* grandiose. I soon learned that she'd been a fashion model in London in her teens, featuring on magazine covers and dancing in the Top of the Pops audience in a home-made crocheted dress. A mother at twenty-two, she had taught herself to pattern cut as a means of making a living once the modelling work had dried up. Whilst working in a typing pool by day, she started making clothes at night to sell at Portobello Road market – 'My ponchos are collectors' items now!' she told me proudly – and eventually opened a tiny boutique back in her home city of Glasgow. Her talent and charm had attracted investors, and more shops opened. Throughout the latter half of the Seventies she presided over a popular, hugely influential chain of boutiques, called Girl Friday – the Topshop of its day.

She's turned serious now. 'What *are* you going to do, d'you think?'

'I honestly don't know.' I glance down at my scuffed boots poking out from my jeans. Penny is wearing a quilted red jacket with a fur-edged hood, a calf-length blue shimmery skirt and tan brogues.

'So he's promised he'll never contact her again?'

I nod. 'Yeah, that's what he says.'

'D'you believe him?'

'I don't know what to believe.' I glance at the girls who are huddled together, engrossed in chatter in the rope nest on the climbing frame. Bobby is snuffling around the bushes close by. 'But I suppose I have to,' I add.

'You mean, you have to believe him, or you have to stay with him?' She looks incredulous.

'Well, both.' I know how feeble this must sound. Apparently, Penny had kicked out her husband before their son Nick's first birthday. When she told me this, she made it sound as if their break-up was as easy as dropping off a bag of old clothes at the charity shop. 'I cleared the decks,' was how she described it in her usual blasé way.

'Darling, you do know Izzy would be fine,' she ventures, not unkindly. 'I know it seems enormous, breaking up when you have a young child. But it can work out better for everyone, believe me.'

I nod, although the very idea of doing that to her makes me feel sick.

'She's a smart, level-headed girl,' Penny adds. 'She'd get used to the idea. Children adapt to all kinds of situations.'

'It would be a massive thing to her,' I murmur. 'She adores her dad.'

'But she must have lots of friends whose parents aren't together,' Penny adds, as if that would make things easier.

'Well, yes, there's a few.'

'What about Maeve's mum and dad?'

'No, they're very much together and blissfully happy.' I fix my gaze upon my daughter's cheery, animated face. I can't even bear to think about turning her life on its head. 'And then there's Spencer to consider,' I add.

'But he's an adult, leading his own independent life!'

'He'd still be upset. I'm sure he thinks me and his dad are pretty solid, you know?'

'Yes, but it's not about them, is it? It's about you, and what *you* want. And look what Andy's done to you.'

'Yes, I know,' I say, unconvincingly. *But we're a family*,

42

is what I really want to say, *and I'm not sure I can throw away these twenty-five years*. Although I'm still angry and hurt, I'm trying to do the right thing here. I don't know how to explain that to Penny without it sounding as if I somehow disapprove that she left her son's dad. In fact I think she was far braver than I could ever hope to be. Right now, I feel terrified.

'Pen,' I say now, 'can I ask why you split up with Nick's dad?'

'Oh, I've told you all that already,' she says quickly.

In fact, she has barely mentioned him, beyond remarking that he was hardly a hands-on father – 'He'd rather have chopped off his own foot than change a nappy' – and started a new life in Canada after they'd split. When I asked if he is still alive, she shrugged and said, 'Allegedly.'

'Well, yes, you have a bit,' I say now. 'But I wondered . . . was there something specific that happened?'

'A final straw kind of thing?' she asks, getting up from the bench as Bobby potters out of sight. 'Well, yes,' she continues, 'there was the soup incident . . .'

'What happened?'

She chuckles. 'I've told you what Brian was like. Big-shot architect, shagging half the office, probably, surrounded by dolly birds, as he called them . . .'

'Was it that? Was he sleeping with other women?'

'Oh, almost definitely,' she says blithely as she clips on Bobby's lead. 'But that wasn't the reason. Everyone in our circle was doing it. It was more how he viewed me, you know?'

I nod, although I don't really understand. The girls run over to us, pleading for ice creams. Izzy takes Bobby's lead as we leave the park and make our way towards the van. 'I mean, these days you'd never be expected to do this,' Penny goes on, 'but back then, men like Brian wanted the corporate wife back at home. You know – the good little woman flapping about in a pinny, rustling up dinner parties for his colleagues . . .'

'Surely he didn't expect that from you!' I exclaim.

She sniggers. 'Unfortunately, he did. You mean, you can't imagine me topping up glasses and handing out vol-au-vents?'

'Absolutely not.'

Izzy looks round. 'What's volly vonts?'

'Little pies,' Penny replies, 'with something like mushrooms inside, in a creamy sauce.'

'Ugh,' exclaims Maeve.

'You didn't make them, did you?' I ask. I have encountered Penny's 'experimental' cooking a couple of times: her 'mango pork' consisting of anaemic-looking chops and sliced fruit in a dish of cider, and a lime cheesecake with the texture of blackboard chalk. She seems to exist mainly on boxed meals from her freezer.

'Of course not,' she declares as we join the small queue at the ice cream van. 'But one day, Brian phoned from his office – never mind that I was up to my neck with a new baby – and said, "Pen, darling, Roger and Cleo are coming over for dinner. Make sure you put together something nice, would you?"'

'What did you do?'

She beams at me. 'We had a big tin of tomato soup so I heated that up. Brian came into the kitchen as I was ladling it into bowls – pretty, hand-painted bowls from Marrakesh – and said, "God, Penny, is that the best you can do?" And I said, "No, don't worry, darling . . ." And I grabbed a lump of Cheddar from the fridge and waved

44

it in his face and said, "I'll put some fucking grated cheese on it."'

Izzy and Maeve are thrilled by this, and it feels like the entire ice cream queue has swivelled to glare at us as we crack up. My God, I am actually laughing. My husband has been shagging someone else, someone far more beautiful and successful than I could ever hope to be – but I can still laugh so much, I'm in danger of falling onto the ground.

I'm so grateful to Penny for stopping me from thinking about Estelle Lang for about ten seconds.

Chapter Seven

Monday, February 25

All day at work, I play over what Penny said: that my kids would be fine, and that sometimes, breaking up works out better for everyone.

But then, Penny's not me. We are entirely different. It's not that I view myself as a better mother; just that I am incapable of being as relaxed as she seemed to be. I'm a worrier and a fusspot, of the belief that I must do my *absolute best at all times,* and that if I happen to get anything wrong I'll be judged and reported and Izzy will be wrestled away from me and put into care.

It sounds mad, but this is the situation we modern mothers have put ourselves in. Parenting Seventies-style was very different.

My dad used to smoke in the car with Mum and me in it, and no one thought that was wrong. Mum once broke a thermometer and gave me the mercury to play with. I loved that mercury like Izzy loves her knitted sandwich! And no one worried about children's nutrition.

It didn't seem to occur to anyone that they might need something called 'vitamins' and 'not too much sugar'. Penny told me recently that, when Nick was about five, he refused to eat anything but butterscotch Angel Delight – *for a whole year.*

'What did you do?' I asked, aghast.

'What could I do?' She shrugged. 'I let him!'

'But . . . what about his health? His teeth? And nutrients?' Although amazed and impressed, I also felt a little outraged on his behalf, even though he's now apparently a fully functioning man in his forties, having carved out a successful career as a documentary maker in New Zealand.

Penny laughed. 'I was running seventeen shops, Viv. We had new stock dropping into these stores every two weeks. I didn't have time to arrange vegetables in little faces on his plate.'

Then there was the time he stripped off his clothes and ran around naked in the library. Apparently Penny 'let him' do that too ('I was *reading*, darling'). I've heard how she took him on fashion shoots where 'the make-up artist or model would play with him'; though, if there was a big social thing, there'd usually be a friend – or friend of a friend – she could drop him off with. Yet, amusingly, there's always an extensive interview procedure before she ever leaves Bobby with anyone. Potential dog sitters are *grilled.*

Another aspect of Penny that I find fascinatingly bizarre is how unbothered she seems about Nick living on the other side of the world. Divorced from his New Zealander wife, he's still showing no sign of returning to the UK. She has only ever showed me a single picture of him – bearded and blurry, possibly taken from half a mile away – and that was because I asked her to.

I find it hard enough with Spencer living a three-hour drive away from us. Maybe that's why, every couple of months, I have a grocery order delivered to his flat.

'Don't they have groceries in Newcastle?' Penny teased me when she found out about this.

I guess the fact is that we are very different, and her insistence that everyone would be 'just fine' if Andy and I broke up is doing nothing to sway my decision. As it is, he keeps on saying he's sorry, and that he loves me, and somehow, we are managing to get through the days. Thankfully, Izzy still seems to have no idea that anything is wrong.

I'm actually quite impressed by the two of us. Our marriage might be in shreds, and every so often I can't help grilling him yet again about his feelings for that woman, and why he did it – those terribly cyclical conversations which lead us precisely nowhere. But despite all of that, we are doing our utmost to keep up appearances in front of our daughter, or whenever we are in the company of other adults.

Whenever we're out and about together, no one would guess there was anything wrong. I'd never have imagined we'd be capable of such Oscar-worthy performances.

Wednesday, February 27

I wake up to two revelations:

1. I have somehow made it to my fifty-third birthday without dying of misery and shame.
2. Culinary treats are being bestowed upon me as Izzy brings me breakfast in bed, comprising thickly buttered

48

Cornish Wafers, a sliced banana and some grapes. She also presents me with a beautiful bangle that she made from her bead kit, and a hand-drawn birthday card depicting me looking pleasingly chic in a camel trench coat and jeans, walking Bobby.

It's raining heavily in her drawing, and the sky is dark and thundery and lacking her signature beaming yellow sun, but at least my eyelashes are lush and my mascara hasn't run, and I am grinning determinedly in it. I decide it isn't intended to represent 'Mum's life being so crappy it's pouring down on her birthday' but, 'Positive Mum, happy whatever the weather'. And if that's the case, my 'everything's fine!' act must be working a treat, which is incredible as I still feel as if I am falling to pieces inside. The only reason I'm still sharing a bed with Andy is because I'm not sure I could get away with moving to Spencer's old room without a barrage of tricky questions from Izzy.

While she rushes off to change from PJs into school clothes – she shuns any assistance from me when it comes to getting ready – Andy presents me with a necklace of milky blue stones on a fine silver chain. 'Thanks,' I say, my eyes welling with tears. *Don't cry, don't cry, don't cry.* There's also a bottle of my favourite figgy perfume and a thoughtful collection of interesting books.

He really has gone to some effort. He is certainly *honouring* the occasion, which, rather than making me happy, is having the effect of triggering such a wave of grief that I can barely hold myself together. 'Happy birthday, darling,' he says, refilling my coffee cup like an eager elf. It's a relief when he sets off to work and it's just Izzy and me, setting off for school.

Although Spencer never gets it together enough to put a card in the post, he calls me at lunchtime, vowing to visit soon. Often, these promises don't come to fruition, and I'm kind of hoping this one doesn't. Whereas Izzy seems to be unaware of the tensions between us, I'm pretty sure our son would detect that something's amiss.

'What are you doing tonight?' he asks.

'Dad's booked dinner,' I reply. 'I'm not sure where we're going. It's a surprise.'

'Aw, that's nice! Somewhere fancy, then?'

'I have a feeling it's not Pizza Hut.' He chuckles, and it occurs to me as we finish the call that it's not the restaurant booking that's significant; it's the fact that Andy sorted out the babysitter too. He had to ask me for her number. But the fact is, he arranged it: *a first for mankind.*

The restaurant turns out to be a wonderful seafood place, which I'd normally love. However, as it stands, I am horribly aware of going through the motions, as if it's a normal birthday and everything's fine; that we are happy and still very much in love. I pretend to enjoy the astronomically priced crustaceans as we fiddle away with all the little tools – the pliers and tweezers and all that pale flesh. I see Andy's face blanch when he glimpses the bill.

Later – after the babysitter's gone, obviously – he's all over me, kissing and touching and madly complimentary about my body, my face, the beautiful embroidered silky slip I'm wearing (my birthday present from Penny). It's hard to believe that, until all this stuff happened, he seemed to regard having sex with me as on a par with the community litter pick-up (which we, being Good Citizens, always take part in). Actually, I used to wonder if he preferred the litter pick-up to doing it with me. He

50

always seemed pleased when Mr Singh, the organiser, handed out the grabber sticks, to the point where I wondered if we should try to incorporate one in our sex life.

But not any more, obviously. We actually do it tonight, for the first time since the Estelle revelations; there's no hint of sciatica/lumbago or any mutterings that he has an early start in the morning. Whilst I feel a little weird and disconnected, it's at least reassuring that we can still make it happen, and that it doesn't feel completely abhorrent, which perhaps hints that there may be a future for us after all.

I still love him, I suppose. It's infuriating, really, how you can't turn off your feelings for someone just because they've been to bed with someone else. It's all still there, bubbling away beneath the surface layer of fury and hurt: my admiration for his commitment at work, and the way he is as a father – as caring and kind as I'd known he would be. I wish I could just hate him, but it's not as simple as that. He's still the man I fell in love with all those years ago, the one I've grown with, and the only person I had ever wanted to have children with. Plus, I suppose I still find him attractive, despite everything. He made a mistake and – God, how grown-up do I sound? – he's contrite, and I *think* we can get over it. While I've been tempted to check his phone numerous times, I've managed not to so far.

I mean, I have to be able to trust him again, don't I? Or what's the point?

Chapter Eight

Three weeks later: Wednesday, March 20

After a full week of rain it has finally stopped. I have a day off work today. Dental appointment, plus I fancied a few hours to myself.

Our house is empty and blissfully quiet, and as I glance out of the kitchen window, I notice how beautiful the garden looks. Our crocuses are blooming, purple and white with orangey centres, and the border at the bottom is filled with daffodils. I love our garden. It's a little wild and untamed but things seem to pop up just where you'd want them to be. Izzy has her own little plot, where she's tending winter pansies in every imaginable colour. After I've picked her up from school we potter about in the late afternoon sunshine, not talking much, just happy working side by side.

My low-level worrying hasn't gone away, and I still wake up in the night from time to time, my heart hammering in panic. However, that had been happening way before I found out about Estelle, and with a start, I realise I am beginning to feel almost normal again. At least, I can safely assume I am no longer on the brink of falling apart.

I used to be of the opinion that, if someone had an affair, that was the marriage over, end of story. And now I'm not sure that's the case. For one thing, it's scary, the idea of being on my own at fifty-three. I don't mean not having someone to drag the wheelie bins out, or to build flatpack. I don't even mean financially (however tricky, I'm sure we would figure things out somehow). It's more the idea of suddenly being single – *alone* – for the first time since I was twenty-seven years old. A tiny part of me thinks that might be thrilling, and that it might have the effect of actually making me twenty-seven again – vibrant, full of life and ambition, smooth of face and pert of arse, with adventures to be had. So, yes, that part seems alluring. But mostly, when I think of starting over as a single woman, I feel deeply sad and frankly terrified. I know it's the life stage when we're supposed to 'give fewer fucks'; to feel emboldened and no longer care what anyone thinks. But is it really? If that's meant to be the natural way of things, then there must have been some kind of malfunction because that hasn't happened to me at all.

That evening, after Andy has gone to bed, I sit outside on the back step, trying to hold on to the calmness I felt earlier when I was out in the garden with Izzy. In a small notebook I write a list titled 'reasons to split':

Because I feel I should.

Not sure I can ever trust him again.

To punish him.

That's all I can dredge up.

As for my 'reasons not to split' list, there are so many

whirling around in my head – such as 'Better for Izzy', 'Avoids upheaval' and 'Should try and rescue marriage rather than giving up'. But I don't jot these down. Instead, I just write:

Because I still love him.

Friday, March 22

During our quiet, unremarkable evening it hits me that something significant has happened. Izzy is asleep, which means we could be going over the whole Estelle thing yet again. But we are not.

Instead, we are just catching up on each other's days over dinner. Whilst Andy never goes into the ins and outs of his dealings with patients, he tells me about a woman who brought her three children along to her appointment today, and they all tucked into an extensive picnic of sandwiches, crisps and Mini Rolls on the waiting room floor. 'No one had the heart to ask them to put it away,' he says.

I realise it's been a long time since he shared anything about his day, being generally 'too tired' to talk to me. As a result, I'd stopped asking. In turn, I tell him about the arrival of my boss's Barbie pink 'stability ball', a kind of giant beach ball that Rose has taken to perching on, rather unstably, as an alternative to sitting on her chair (she hopes to strengthen her core whilst simultaneously dealing with China). Whilst it's hardly scintillating as far as anecdotes go, at least we are communicating relatively normally, and are no longer so on edge with each other. Andy has finally stopped trying to stroke my hair when I'm stacking the dishwasher. I can now stand there folding up laundry without him lurking behind me, trying to kiss my neck. The mad flurry of affection was understandable. But the fact that it has eased off can only be a good thing, surely?

I am starting to think that we really can get over this, and that Andy's affair was one of those 'blips' people talk about. After all, most marriages tend to hit a crisis at some point or other, and I've read many times that it can actually make a couple stronger together, in the long run.

So, this is where we are now; just a normal middle-aged couple hanging out together on a Friday night. It feels kind of right. Never mind Penny's 'tell him to sling his hook' attitude. It's my marriage, and my decision, and I can't bear the thought of throwing it all away.

Sunday, March 24

True to his word – albeit a month on from when it was promised – Spencer has arrived for a visit home. Now the worst of the Estelle crisis seems to be over, it's wonderful to see him. He fills our house with his big, loud laugh and extravagant stories about gigs he's worked on, and I love it. He has brought his girlfriend, Millie, a sassy girl who can unearth a ratty old lime green satin bedspread in a charity shop and make a fabulous skirt out of it.

She has a finely boned face and a mane of crinkly light brown hair. Izzy is transfixed – despite the fact that we've met her several times before – and trots around with her, chatting incessantly. As I look around at the five of us all here together in our sun-filled kitchen, it seems incredible that, barely more than a month ago, I was reading those awful texts in the garden.

As usual, Spencer gave us hardly any notice that he was driving up to Glasgow. He just called from a service station to say he was on his way and would be here in an hour or so – and he didn't even mention that Millie was with him. As we had little food in, I panicked; I like being able to put on a big feast when he's here. 'Just make your omelettes,' he said, and so that's what I'm doing (they're his favourite anyway).

'How's the pellet business, Mum?' he asks cheekily as I bring a huge bowl of home-made fat golden chips to the table, and we all sit down.

'It's completely thrilling,' I reply with a smile.

Spencer fixes me with a look. His blue eyes are bright behind his black-framed spectacles, and now I'm starting to wonder whether he's noticed that *something* has happened since we saw him last.

'You should get back into theatre again,' he says. 'Do something you love, Mum. You're wasted in that place.'

'Oh, you definitely should,' Millie agrees. She is a performance artist who seems to do a bit of everything – dance, spoken word, poetry – and is a regular fixture at the Edinburgh Fringe. It astounds me how together and confident she is at twenty years old.

'Who says I don't love what I do?' I say with a smile, knowing there's no point in explaining that, at my stage of life, manageable working hours are perhaps more valuable than what Spencer would term as 'following your passion'. When does it happen, this decision to veer down the sensible route?

'Can I show Millie my clothes?' Izzy asks, the instant we've finished eating. She adores dressing up.

'Yes, of course,' I say, my heart soaring as the two of them disappear together.

Spencer picks out a few more chips from the bowl. 'That was lovely, Mum. You make the best omelettes in the world.'

'She does,' Andy says. 'I keep telling her that.'

'All this praise!' I remark as we clear the table. 'It's going to go to my head.'

Andy grins at our son. 'She still won't tell me her secret method, even after all these years.'

'If I did, I'd have to kill you,' I remark.

He chuckles and winds an arm around my waist, and I detect a hint of relief passing over Spencer's face, as if he's thinking, *Oh, so they are okay after all.*

Izzy bounces back into the kitchen wearing a flamboyant outfit the girls have put together: yellow top, red trousers, pea green feather boa and more jewellery than I'd have thought it was possible to pile onto a seven-year-old child.

'So you let Millie help you choose what to wear and not your own mother?' I tease her, taking pictures with my phone.

'Yeah, but Millie knows about fashion.' She giggles.

'Penny does too. But you won't let her pick your outfits either.'

Izzy grins slyly. 'Penny said the f-word,' she announces, at which Spencer feigns shock.

'Did she? That's outrageous! What was that all about?'

She looks at me. 'What was it, Mum? She didn't want to put cheese in the soup?'

'My God, Izzy, that was weeks ago . . .' Of course, kids never forget when an adult does something they shouldn't. They file it away for future reference and delight in bringing it up.

'Is cheese in soup a thing?' Spencer muses, when I tell him the story.

'Of course it is,' I exclaim, in mock outrage. 'Tomato soup *needs* cheese.'

'It's kind of retro,' Andy adds, 'but yeah, it really works. You should try it, Spence. But it's got to be cheap Cheddar—'

'Thanks for the tip, Dad.' He grins and turns to me. 'So, how is the lovely Penny?'

'She's doing great.'

'Still seeing that musician guy on the boat?' He means Hamish, with the velvet jackets, cravats and a great bouffe of silvery hair, who has the kind of voice that 'carries' (i.e. he always talks as if he's making a public speech).

'He says he's a *composer*,' I reply with a smile, 'and yes, she is, although I don't know how serious it is . . .'

'He's quite a bit younger than her, isn't he?' Andy remarks. I'm surprised he's even picked up on that. Before the Estelle business he was never interested in my friends.

'Um, yes. He's in his early sixties, I think.'

'That's not young,' Izzy splutters.

'It's all relative,' Spencer says loftily, patting her arm. He turns to me. 'Well, give her my love, won't you?' As Spencer and Millie get ready to leave, I try not to show my disappointment that they're not staying overnight. However, the prospect of a gig in Edinburgh is clearly irresistible, and with a flurry of hugs and kisses, they're off.

'Wasn't that lovely?' I remark.

Andy nods, looking a little deflated now. 'It was.'

'But I wish they'd stayed a bit longer.'

'Me too.' He wipes down the table and looks around the kitchen, as if unsure of what to do next. Izzy has disappeared off to her room.

'It's great that he has his own full life, though,' I add. 'I'm proud of him, aren't you?'

He clears his throat. 'Oh, yeah, of course I am.' There's a slight catch to his voice. He seemed particularly sorry to see Spencer go tonight, and I can't quite work out why. Yes, the visit was brief, but that's hardly unusual. We are used to him bowling up, all singing and dancing, then scooting off before we've had chance to fully appreciate him being home with us again.

While Andy loads the dishwasher I go upstairs to run Izzy's bath and sit chatting to her while she soaks in the bubbles. I read to her in her room – a couple of chapters of *The Twits*, which has her in giggles – then tuck her in and kiss her goodnight.

'Did you enjoy seeing Spence and Millie?' I ask.

'Yeah.' She grins. 'I love Millie.'

I smile and squeeze her hand. 'I do too. She's a great girl.'

'Spence loves her, doesn't he?'

Something seems to clench inside me. 'Yes, I'm pretty sure he does. It's kind of obvious, isn't it?'

She nods. 'Yeah.' A pause. 'Will they get married?'

'Oh, darling, I don't know about that. We'll have to see, won't we? But they're a bit young for that right now.'

I stand up and smooth back the fine hair from her lightly freckled pale face. 'I wish I had a sister,' she adds.

'Like Millie you mean? A big sister?'

She nods.

'Oh, honey, you have Spencer, though, don't you? You're lucky.'

She seems to be considering this, and her expression turns solemn. '*You* don't have anyone.'

I laugh dryly. 'No brothers or sisters, you mean? Yes, you're right there, but it's okay, you know. It's what I'm used to, and I have you guys. You're my family. So I'm very lucky too.'

I turn to her bedroom door as Andy appears, having come up to say goodnight to Izzy too. It's all so ordinary, I muse as he hugs her. Just a dad saying goodnight to his daughter. A month ago, I thought my marriage was over and now here we are, still together, still a family.

It's true, what I said to Izzy just then. I do feel very lucky indeed.

Early hours of Monday, March 25

When terrible things happen you sometimes have the weirdest thoughts. You don't think about big things. You think about trivial details, like: I could have taken the time to explain why my omelettes are so good. If Andy had really wanted to know, I could have gone into the importance of the right kind of frying pan (i.e. a really good non-stick one), the fact that you don't need much butter – a *small knob* will suffice – and that the pan must be smokingly hot before the beaten eggs are tipped in.

I might also have mentioned, had he been genuinely interested, that as soon as it starts to set, the eggy mixture should be dragged to the centre with a spatula, and the pan tipped and swirled, so the omelette cooks as quickly as possible: speed is of the essence. But the truth is, Andy's interest was faked.

He didn't give a stuff about my omelettes, and nor was

he telling the truth when he'd vowed that all communications with Estelle Lang had stopped. They've been in touch the whole time and, he's so sorry, he tells me now, as he hurriedly packs a bag, but they are in love and he needs to be with her.

And that's why he is leaving me.

Part Two

After

Chapter Nine

Four months later: Saturday, July 20

The rice is nearly cooked, my very own four-foot-tall, gap-toothed TV chef says with a flourish of her wooden spoon, *and now we're adding the pine kernels, the salt and the sugar to the frying pan and giving it a big stir . . .* Izzy looks up with a smile. Since her father left another milk tooth has gone. *The sugar*, she adds, as though sensing my note of surprise, *makes it nicer to eat. Now, we're adding some, uh . . .* She picks up a clump of greenery and frowns at it. *Basil?*

'Dill,' I prompt her.

We add the dill and the parsley and cinnamon, uh . . . nearly forgot the raisins!

Who'd have thought that my daughter would acquaint herself with such exotic ingredients? On this bright summer's afternoon she is rustling up the Turkish stuffed tomatoes she first made at Maeve's a few months ago. She has become mad about cooking and taken to demonstrating dishes to me in her one-woman cookery 'show' here in our kitchen. We have ventured far and wide, food-wise, with Thai, Caribbean and even Russian dishes featuring on *Izzy Cooks!* One time she rustled up a spicy Indonesian salad – 'It's called gado-gado!' she announced – which involved covering most of our kitchen with smashed-up peanuts but was, admittedly, so delicious I didn't really mind the mess. These culinary delights have almost made up for the fact that I haven't managed to get it together to book a summer holiday for us this year.

Sunshine is managing to beam in through the grubby window. Izzy's hair is tied back neatly beneath the chef's hat we made from white cardboard, and she's wearing the polka dot apron Penny whizzed up for her on her sewing machine. As there's no production team here, sourcing ingredients has been keeping me busy. Left to my own devices, I'm what might be described as a 'basic cook'. I'd never imagined that Medjool dates and preserved lemons would ever put in an appearance in this house, or that the phrase 'We're out of polenta!' would fall from my seven-year-old's mouth. This new project is ruining me financially and the clearing up afterwards is colossal. But at least Izzy's having fun, making these mad, exotic feasts.

While *Izzy Cooks!* is a fairly new project, lots of things haven't changed since her father moved out. Obviously, Izzy was shocked and upset when we told her ('Mum and I will still be *really* good friends,' Andy explained, twisting his hands together as he sat hunched on the sofa). There were plenty of tears and for a while, she took to coming into my room at night and snuggling into bed with me. But she seems to have accepted how things are. And now, well into the summer holidays – school broke up at the end of June – she is generally back to her sunny, happy self, as if everything is normal.

Which it is, in the ways that matter. Her parents and brother still love her. The tooth fairy hasn't stopped leaving a pound under her pillow. She sees her dad regularly (although he's said he's 'not quite ready' for her to visit his new flat across town, whatever *that* means), and she still loves to sit drawing at the kitchen table. In Izzy's world, there is little in life that can't be made better with a new set of felt tips.

Spencer, too, was initially appalled when news broke, but has come around to a kind of stoical acceptance. Although he insisted that there was no need *at all*, that he was absolutely FINE, Andy and I drove (separately) to Newcastle to talk things over with him. Although we were managing to be reasonably cordial with each other – at least in front of Izzy – I couldn't bear the thought of being trapped in a car with him for the six-hour round trip.

Our son was incredibly sweet and kind about everything. 'As long as you're all right, Mum,' he said, with genuine concern, as I fought back tears over a bowl of noodles I couldn't even eat. A couple of weeks later he arrived in Glasgow to check whether I really was okay, which made my heart soar. It amazes me sometimes that he has grown up into this thoughtful, caring young man despite a cheating bastard of a father being fifty per cent responsible for his genetic make-up.

By then, Spencer had dragged it out of his father that there was another woman involved. And eventually, Izzy asked outright, 'Does Daddy have a new girlfriend?' It all tumbled out that, yes, he has 'a *friend*.' Neither she nor Spencer have met her yet, although I expect they will at some point. All I can hope is that they'll come back to report some unfortunate trait, like horrendous body odour or a screechy voice, the kind that causes babies to start crying spontaneously and have to be hurried out of the room.

Considering Andy's apparent devotion to That Woman, I realise it's pretty unlikely. But we are doing okay, I keep telling myself. We are certainly eating well.

'Shall we keep some of these for Dad?' Izzy asks as we tuck in.

'Yes, we can, love,' I say.

'I'm seeing him tomorrow, aren't I?'

'Yep, he's taking you out for the day.'

'Hurrah!' She grins. 'Where are we going?'

'I'm not sure what he has planned, but I'm sure it'll be something fun.'

We don't have any formal system in place yet, for when he sees her; we are playing it by ear, stepping around each other carefully with brittle politeness. He and Izzy usually see a film, potter around the shops or have a pizza, stuff like that. I know the place he's renting is in the West End. However, although I've managed to narrow it down to a fairly small vicinity, he won't tell me the name of the actual street. He's adamant that this isn't because his new woman is living with him – but I can't think of any other reason why he'd be so cagey about it. What else am I supposed to think?

I look at Izzy across the table as she tucks in. She loves her days with her dad. I can tell she's thinking about him and wondering what treats he has in store.

She glances up at me, mouth full. 'What are you gonna do tomorrow?'

'Oh, I have loads of things to catch up with,' I say,

meaning: *I'll be a whirl of productivity and not roam about the house, feeling abandoned and listless, thinking I really should clean the loo, but not doing it, and I must tackle that box of bath toys as I suspect there's a nasty slime situation developing in there, but not doing that either.*

'Dad said he's going to buy me new trainers,' she says happily, jumping down from her chair.

Sunday, July 21

Izzy is out with Andy and I am alone. With no plans or obligations, the whole day spreads before me. I really must put it to good use.

I could clean the extractor hood or hoover under the beds. I could use the opportunity to take up running to try and shift this menopausal belly of mine – which is starting to look like someone's strapped a cushion to my middle – or see if Jules is around, to make a plan for my life coaching sessions (she's been asking me when I want to get started, and I've been putting her off). There are *so many* things a newly dumped middle-aged woman could do to enhance her life. Instead I find myself frittering away the day by staring at pictures of The Eminent Dr Lang on my laptop – cruelly, there are dozens online – and crying.

'Oh, darling, you need a different hobby,' Penny says, not unkindly, when she shows up to rescue me.

'What, like crochet?' I bleat.

'Crochet is very therapeutic.'

'My fingers are too fat,' I growl. Penny hugs me, turning serious. She looks especially summery today in a shift dress of pink and yellow squares, like Battenberg, accessorised with a chunky necklace of multicoloured stones.

'I just think you should stop staring at these pictures,' she says firmly. 'It's only making you feel worse.'

'I was only having a *little* look,' I fib. 'See, if I do an image search of her, there are tons . . .' Penny leans forward, frowning at the screen as I show her Estelle Lang standing at a podium, make-up immaculate, radiating authority as she delivers a keynote speech at some fucking conference or other. Here she is again, in a more formal headshot this time, wearing a crisp white shirt and navy blazer with a red scarf (possibly silk?) tied nattily at her slender neck. It's a classic, elegant look I have never managed to pull off.

'Why are you doing this to yourself?' Penny asks.

I shrug. 'A kind of self-harm?'

She looks thoughtful for a moment. 'Like you're determined to sink really low, into a cesspit of gloom?'

'Yes, something like that,' I say dully.

'And then,' she adds, brightening, 'when you've hit rock bottom, you can set about building yourself up again!'

I muster a smile, grateful now to her for being here, for marching in when I didn't answer the door. It's a trait of hers that used to drive Andy crazy: 'What makes her think it's okay to just barge in like that? We could be doing anything!'

Like what? I'd shot back at the time. *What, actually, might we be doing?*

'That's not the point, is it? It's bloody invasive, that's all.'

'I hope you're right,' I say now.

'Of course I am. I always am! Now, come on, put that laptop away.'

'In a minute,' I murmur. 'Look, let me just show you something else. If I do another search, just for comparison, *this* comes up—' And here it is: the sole picture of me that's floating about in the ether. There are no glossy headshots, no pictures where I'm exuding glamour and authoritativeness at conferences. Instead, I'm looking fat in a sweat-stained vest, a ripped tutu and mud-speckled bunny ears at the school fun run last year.

'Dear God, what's *that*?' Penny exclaims.

I slam my laptop shut. 'Nothing. No one. Oh, you're right, Pen, I've really got to stop this. Come on, let's go out.'

As we catch the train into town together, the world immediately feels a little brighter. One of the many positive aspects of having Penny as a friend is that she refuses to indulge wallowing. It's precisely what I needed today – to be taken in hand and marched out of my house.

There are other benefits, too, in hanging out with an older woman, in that she can reassure me that the menopause ends eventually, and you come out the other side, and everything is all right. The anxiety abates. The sweats disappear. You stop being a carb-guzzling maniac and emerge as a calm, thoroughly emboldened woman, freed from periods, no longer a slave to your mood swings or worries about how you're perceived.

'You no longer care about anything,' Penny has assured me on more than one occasion. 'You just do whatever you want.' This might explain why, as we arrive at our favourite bookshop café, I choose a small brownie (with all these books around it feels like a fairly low-risk option) while Penny goes for a whopping cream horn (potentially messy, I'd say, if I were performing a risk assessment).

71

'Pen, tell me honestly,' I say, nibbling my brownie primly. 'Did you ever fixate on someone like I've been doing? Like the way I've been googling Estelle Lang, I mean?'

'There was no internet then, thankfully,' she says.

'No, of course not, but did you ever get so mad that you did, I don't know – something crazy and badly behaved? Something ridiculous?' I look at her across the table, willing her to say yes.

She looks thoughtful at this. 'Well,' she starts hesitantly, 'I once got terribly drunk and egged someone's car—'

'You egged someone's car?' I exclaim, delighted. 'Whose was it?'

'Just someone's,' she says airily, waving the horn about, cream bulging dangerously at its fat end. Sitting directly beneath it is an enormous coffee table book (*Through the Lens: Icons of 70s Fashion*). I'm not even sure why she lugged it over to our table. It's not as if she's looking at it.

'What happened?' I ask. 'Were you caught?'

'Of course not,' she says.

'But did it feel satisfying?'

'I suppose so, yes—'

'Maybe that's why Andy's being evasive about where he's living,' I cut in. 'And he won't let Izzy visit, in case she tells me. Perhaps he thinks I'll go round and inflict some kind of damage on his car, or the property . . .'

Penny slips off her turquoise cardigan and drapes it over the shoulders of her pink and yellow dress. I always feel terribly unadventurous in my basic tops and jeans whenever I am in her company. I loved fashion when I was younger and pored over magazines for inspiration. Rather than covering my bedroom walls with pop star posters, I stuck up pages carefully cut out from the women's glossies. Later, as a student, I took to scouring charity shops and pulling together a bright, cheery, mish-mashy sort of look.

When I became a mum, I tried to adhere to a 'lipstick at toddler group' rule and did my best to maintain a reasonable standard of appearance; to take a pride in myself, I suppose. It's only in the past few years that I've opted for the easiest, most sensible choices for work and knocking around at home. Practicality has been my priority, and as a result I have amassed a wardrobe of black, grey and navy basics, with barely a glimmer of brightness anywhere.

Penny wears happy clothes, Izzy observed, soon after we'd got to know her. I hope mine don't scream: *Depressed*.

'Are you sure that woman hasn't moved in?' Penny asks, licking cream from her lips. 'I hate to say it, but I think that's more likely.'

'He says not,' I say with a shrug, 'and I don't see why he'd bother lying to me at this stage.'

'Well, perhaps he's too embarrassed for Izzy to see the place?' she suggests.

'But why would that be?'

She grins at me. 'Maybe it's next to a strip club?'

I almost choke on this. 'I wish it was, but I very much doubt it.'

'Just in a shitty street, then?'

I shake my head. 'He'd never live anywhere too shabby. You know what he's like, such a fuss-pants about things. We once rented an Airbnb in Paris. It was immaculate – really lovely. But Andy got it into his head that there was a lingering cheese smell in the fridge. Honestly, the

73

moaning that went on, the perpetual opening and closing of the door and the endless sniffing. It drove me crazy. I couldn't smell a thing. But he has a thing about odours, a hypersensitive nose—'

Penny smirks. 'Isn't that a bit of hindrance for a doctor?'

'Not really. He's an endocrinologist, remember. It's all about hormonal issues, thyroid disorders, that kind of stuff. He never has to do anything *murky*—'

'What about tests? Doesn't he have to take samples, swabs, that sort of thing?'

'No, he has other people to do that for him.'

'Well, that doesn't seem fair,' she declares, and I smile. Penny is attracted to decidedly un-fussy men; artists or odd-job-types who live in ropey flats with cats constantly meandering in and out or, in the case of Hamish, a composer who lives on a narrowboat on the canal. 'So he never had any gruesome stories to tell you?' she asks.

'No, never. That's the thing about living with a doctor. You imagine you'll hear all kinds of juicy stuff, but all you get are gripes about the fact that the canteen staff aren't allowed to sell buttered scones anymore, so he has to buy an *unbuttered* scone and a tiny foil-wrapped pat of butter that's too hard to spread. Christ, the moaning I had to endure about that—'

'Outrageous,' she snorts, 'a man of Andy's standing, having to spread his own butter . . .'

'And it wasn't just that,' I continue. 'When the new car park system was introduced, staff spaces weren't quite as near to the hospital entrance as they used to be. Honestly, you'd have thought the world had ended.'

'How ridiculous.'

I nod, enjoying offloading to my friend. It sounds trite, but remembering Andy's bad points always makes me

74

feel mildly better about my current situation. 'Then there was the Great Decline in Toilet Paper Quality of 2017, and *then* they made the dramatic switch from plastic cups at the water cooler to cardboard cones . . .'

'He moaned about that?'

'Yes! You'd think he'd have supported the decision to ditch single-use plastic, but no . . .'

'Oh, Viv,' she announces, 'you're well rid of that man—' As if to emphasise her strength of feeling she bites down hard on her pastry, forcing the cream to jet out in a dramatic spurt.

'Penny!' I exclaim, reeling back as a few specks hit me.

'Oh, God, I'm *so* sorry, what a mess.' She snatches my paper napkin and tries to dab at my chest.

'I don't care about my top,' I hiss, indicating the cream-splattered £55 coffee table book sitting between us. 'Look at that!'

Penny glares at it as if it had no business being there and rubs at it with a napkin. Although a delicate wipe would have sufficed, she rubs so hard, she takes the gloss off it. 'Oh, God, I'm just making it worse,' she mutters. 'C'mon, let's go.'

'We can't just leave it!'

She jumps up from her seat and grabs at my arm. 'What else are we going to do? Re-gloss it?'

'Well, maybe we should offer to pay for—'

'Don't be ridiculous,' she splutters. Come *on*.'

I'm not proud of the fact that we leg it from the café. I love this shop, and I'm grateful that it seems to be thriving when so many others are closing down. What if everyone came in here and spurted whipped cream about the place? Was the incident captured on CCTV?

Maybe I'm over-reacting, and no one will actually care

about a ruined book. But it's in my nature to worry and, much as I'd love to be blasé like Penny, I'm not built that way. I worry about upsetting people and causing offence – it's ridiculous really. I worry about Spencer, even though he is a bona fide adult who can drive on the road and runs his own smelly little Skoda, filled with crisps packets, Coke cans and the remains of fast food (I always feel like I need a cover-all suit – like the kind asbestos-removal guys wear – whenever I get into it). And, of course, I fret about his diet and whether he's getting enough nutrients.

I worry about Izzy too, about whether she is really okay about Andy and I splitting up, or is just putting on a brave front. I worry about my future, and whether I'll be a PA at Flaxico until the end of time, and whether we really do have rats in the garden and, if so, will they find their way into the house and bite Izzy during the night?

'Hurry up,' Penny barks, glancing behind as I scuttle after her through the shop like some kind of lady-servant. Seconds later, we reach the exit. She breezes out first, and we speed-walk along the pedestrianised street until we're safely around the corner.

She stops, catching her breath. It's a warm, rather clammy afternoon and my hair is sticking to my forehead. 'Well, that was unfortunate,' she announces.

'God, Penny,' I exclaim. 'You do realise we can never go in there again.'

'Of course we can! No one saw us.'

'Oh, no, we blended *right* in.'

She shakes her head and links her arm through mine as we make our way towards the subway. 'You worry far too much.'

'I know I do.'

'But I'm really sorry about your top.'

'That's okay, it's just an old thing.'

I catch her eye, and she smiles, and I can't help chuckling. Yet again, she's briefly stopped me from obsessing over my husband's new love.

'You know what I think?' she asks.

'What?' I'm anticipating a nugget of sage advice.

'I think,' she announces as we descend into the station, 'they shouldn't sell those kinds of cakes if they don't want customers to eat them.'

Chapter Ten

Wednesday, July 24

Before it happened to me, I'd imagined that being left by one's husband would be traumatic for those first few weeks – and then there'd be a quiet and gradual recovery. The calm after the storm, I suppose. And for much of the time, it *is* like this: reasonably civilised and fairly businesslike. I have done my utmost to remain dignified whenever Andy has come over to pick up Izzy or to take away more of his stuff. I've even gone so far as making him cups of tea (without spitting in them) and helping him to lug bags of books and medical magazines out to his car.

However, on other days, it can feel as if my heart's been broken all over again, and I'm simmering with fury and hurt. I have found myself crying inconsolably in the dairy aisle of the supermarket. I've had to pull over in my car on my way home from work, and sit there mopping at my face, knowing I'm going to look a state when I pick up Izzy from holiday club or a friend's place, but unable to pull myself together. I have ploughed up and down the swimming pool, imagining Andy and her together, *doing it*, my tears mingling with all that chlorinated water. I have called him, intending to shout and rage, but just cried into the phone and then hung up. Such incidents seem to happen in bursts, then a couple of weeks can go by and there's not a single tear shed.

Sometimes, rather than crying, I want to scream and break things and physically hurt him. As it is, I have merely kicked a hole in a wicker waste paper basket, smashed his favourite mug and stabbed a hole in his ratty old gardening sweater with a biro. Thankfully, Izzy hasn't witnessed any of this. The fact that she needs me to keep things rattling along has been something of a saviour.

She's in bed now – it's just gone 9 p.m. – and Andy is here, taking far too long to remove his boxes of paperwork that have been clogging up the cupboard on the landing.

Seemingly, he can't just load them into his car and fuck off out of my hair. No, he needs to carry everything into the living room and sort through it painstakingly slowly without any regard for my feelings at all. I am fidgeting about, tidying up and straightening things unnecessarily, willing him to leave.

'Can't you do that at home?' I ask tersely.

'Yeah, I will,' he mutters. 'Won't be much longer.' He continues to flick through paperwork.

If anything, my Sunday afternoon with Penny has ignited a fresh spark of anger in me. After all, when she was pissed off over some matter of the heart, she didn't sit there feeling sorry for herself. Instead, she got drunk and egged someone's car.

She guzzled a cream horn in a bookshop café because

she wanted one. Although it didn't end well, the fact is, she didn't worry about the possible consequences. *I should be more like Penny*, I decide.

'I really don't want you doing this here,' I bark at him.

'Oh.' Looking startled, he starts to gather up his stuff.

'Can I also ask you,' I add, my heart thudding now, 'if there's some reason why you won't let Izzy visit you at your flat?'

He blinks at me in surprise. 'Er, not really, no.'

'It's just, if there is, I'd rather you said why instead of spouting me a load of old shit.'

'All right. Jesus.' He shakes his head as if I am being entirely unreasonable. 'There isn't much space, that's all.'

'Really?'

'Yes, really!' Clutching a box crammed with papers, he starts to make his way towards the front door.

I can feel one of those hormonal rages building up in me, the ones I have no control over, and I inhale slowly and deeply in an attempt to calm myself. 'I don't mean for her to stay overnight,' I go on. 'I just mean to visit, so she can see what your place is like. I think it'd be really good for her.'

'Why?' He frowns, almost comically.

'To satisfy her curiosity of course. So she knows you're living somewhere nice and that she's welcome there.'

'Well, yeah, but it's really tiny,' he says, raking back his neatly cropped grey-speckled hair.

'She's only four feet tall,' I remark tersely. 'I'm sure she'd manage to fit in—' I break off as Izzy saunters into the room.

'Honey, you're meant to be in bed,' I start, which she ignores.

'We use centimetres at school,' she announces. 'I'm a

hundred and twenty-two centimetres tall, exactly the same as Maeve.'

'Are you? Andy blusters, getting up. 'Wow. I had no idea you were as tall as that . . .'

She plonks a hand on her hip. '*Why* can't I come to your flat, Dad?'

'Ohh . . .' He darts me a thank-you-very-much-for-dragging-our-daughter-into-this look, as if it's my fault. 'I just need to sort things out, love, and make the place nice for you.'

She frowns at him. 'I don't mind what it's like.'

'No. No, I realise that,' he says, cheeks flushed and now seemingly in an almighty hurry to cart his stuff out to his car.

I follow him outside. 'Andy?'

'I'm not really in the mood for this right now,' he huffs, slamming the boot shut.

'Not in the mood for what?'

'For this interrogation . . .'

I look at him, this man who created such a fuss about the unbuttered scone regime when people are starving in the world and would be bloody *delighted* with a plain pastry from a hospital canteen, and who lied to me horribly over months and months. Whatever possessed me to fall in love with him? Was I insane? 'It's only your daughter who wants to visit you,' I snap. 'Not the bloody Duchess of Kent—' I turn on my heel and start to march back towards the house.

'Viv!' he calls after me.

'What?' I stop and glare back at him.

'Please don't storm off like that. Can we talk for a minute?'

'I'm going inside. Izzy should be in bed.'

81

'I really do mean just for a minute.'

I sigh heavily and plod back towards him at his car.

'Look . . .' He pauses. 'I'm sorry about all this. I will ask her over, but just not at the moment, okay?'

'Whatever,' I huff, maturely.

'But, um . . . I did want to ask you something.' He pauses again. 'D'you mind if I take her away for a week—'

'A week?' I exclaim. 'You mean a *whole* week?'

He nods. 'Er . . . yeah. I haven't mentioned it to her yet, obviously. I wanted to check with you first.'

'Oh.' I feel hollow. So this is what we do now, I realise; we take our daughter on separate holidays. Of course we do. What did I expect? 'Well, um, yes. I suppose that's okay. Where are you thinking of going?'

'Just to Lewis and Nina's. They're having a bit of a gathering up there.'

'A gathering for a whole *week*?' Lewis is Andy's youngest brother. He and his wife run an acclaimed restaurant perched on the shores of Loch Fyne. People often imagine that the Highlands are all about fish and chips and pie suppers, basically carbs dowsed with ketchup and vinegar, but The Nest is terribly chi-chi – all samphire and edible flowers served by bearded hipster types. As a family we've had many happy trips there over the years, staying at their pretty white cottage, and messing around with their rowing boat on the loch.

I try not to think about those blissful days as Andy goes on: 'Remember they were building those chalets? Sorry, *eco-lodges*, I should say . . .'

'Er, vaguely.' Although I have to admit, I've had more pressing matters on my mind.

'Well, they're finally finished. The idea is, everyone'll

82

stay for the week and it'll end with a big party in the restaurant.'

'Everyone?' My heart seems to twist.

'Yeah, Mum and Dad and the whole rabble . . .'

With everything that's happened, it hasn't yet sunk in properly that my relationship with his parents will change dramatically. I'm extremely fond of them, and I know they are of me. But what will happen now?

'Seems like Nina's put a lot of effort into fitting them out,' he goes on. 'She's had quilts made – *bespoke* quilts – and there are log-burning stoves and sheepskin rugs . . .'

'It sounds amazing,' I remark flatly.

'Better than camping, anyhow,' he rabbits on. 'You know how bad the midges can be up there—'

'Andy?' I cut in.

'Yes?'

Shit, I think I'm going to lose it now. '*She's* not going with you, is she? To this gathering, I mean?'

'What?'

'You know who I mean. You're not taking her, are you, on your family holiday with Izzy?'

'Christ, no!' he exclaims, looking aghast. 'No, Viv, I promise you . . .'

'If you were, I'd want to know.'

'Of course she's not coming,' he says firmly. 'We've agreed, haven't we, that I'll tell you when – *if* I feel it's okay for them to meet. But that's not happening anytime soon.'

Why not? I want to ask, conscious of my Penny-inspired bravado dwindling rapidly. *Does a tiny part of you wonder if you've made a mistake? What made you want her anyway? Apart from her obvious beauty, intelligence, amazing career and impeccable dress sense, what caused you to choose her over your neurotic, perpetually worrying wife who works at the nerve centre of extruded snack pellets?*

But I don't ask these questions. I don't ask anything at all. I just bark, 'That's fine. About the holiday, I mean.' And I rub at my hot face as, blinking rapidly, I turn and march back to the house.

Chapter Eleven

Thursday, July 25

Well, I handled that well, I decide as I drop Izzy at holiday club and set off on the drive to work. I really held it together brilliantly last night, snapping at Andy in the street while Tim's wife, Chrissie, who happens to be beautifully, serenely pregnant, glanced out from next door, twiddling with their blinds, pretending not to be watching us.

My God though, he's taking Izzy away to have a wonderful time with his parents and siblings! They're scattered all over the country and only get together very occasionally. Will she ever want to come back? They'll have so much fun, she might decide she wants to live with her dad permanently. I know I'm being crazy, and that it's unlikely; for one thing, he would never agree to buy her pomegranate syrup. But even so, it's disconcerting, the thought of him whisking her away for a whole week.

Even before Andy left me, our family felt pretty unbalanced. On his side we have his mum and dad (a sparky and active couple in their late seventies) plus his two brothers and three sisters. At the last count, the Flint siblings have produced fourteen children, including ours. His side of the family is enormous with everyone squabbling constantly but adoring each other really. Perhaps I'm a little envious that there's always so much *going on*.

And on my side? Well, it's a little quieter, to say the least. I am an only child. Both of my parents died thirteen years ago, when Spencer was nine and way before Izzy was born. Dad passed away from complications due to his diabetes, and Mum lost her life to oesophageal cancer a few months later. Both were in their early sixties and I was blindsided by grief.

Although I can hardly bear to think of it now, Andy was fantastic during this time. With no siblings to turn to, I leant on him heavily and he was there at my side, helping with the arrangements, the funerals, the eventual clearing out and sale of their modest terraced house in Glasgow's Southside.

I've relied on him so much, I realise now. Perhaps I took it for granted that he would be strong and always there for me, no matter what.

His parents were marvellous too. 'You still have us,' Cathy, my mother-in-law had said as she hugged me after Mum's funeral, which struck me as remarkably perceptive. She found me in tears in our garden a few days later. 'What is it, Viv?' she'd asked gently.

'I never appreciated them enough,' I replied.

'Everyone feels like that. That's just normal, love.'

'Yes, but I never imagined they'd be gone soon.' As we sat together at our garden table, I told her how my mum had misguidedly booked me in for a make-up session in a long-defunct department store for my sixteenth birthday.

If it had been one of the cool, youthful brands, I'd have been delighted – but, being oblivious to make-up trends, Mum had chosen the counter frequented by demure older ladies. I hadn't wanted to hurt her feelings by saying I didn't want to go.

'You look lovely,' she'd said, with genuine enthusiasm when she'd returned to collect me later. Off we went to meet Dad at an old-fashioned restaurant (as a family we only ate out about twice a year) where the desserts arrived on a trolley and I had to sit there with my caked-on panstick foundation, my frosted blue eye shadow and shimmery pink lips. One of my teachers was sitting at a nearby table, and when she spotted me and waved I wanted to die.

'I was so embarrassed,' I told Cathy that day. 'I hated that my parents wanted to spin out the meal with coffee and petits fours. All I wanted was to rush home and wash off my face.' Cathy had nodded and held my hand. 'I'd give anything to have coffee with them now,' I added. 'I wouldn't mind the shimmery blue eye shadow either. I'd have my whole *face* frosted if I could see Mum again.'

Cathy had seemed to understand. As a mum to three daughters, she knew all about a teenage girl's horror of 'standing out'. We'd even giggled over how she had made her eldest daughter a jumpsuit from curtain material and expected her to wear it, happily, to the school dance ('I found out later that the poor girl had changed outfits in a phone box! What on earth had I been thinking?'). Now, of course, everything is different, and when Izzy talks about 'our family', she really means her father's family – which feels utterly separate from me now. That's just the way it's going to be, I remind myself firmly as I pull into the work car park.

I'm trying to convince myself that it's ridiculous – and selfish – to 'mind' Izzy going away. After all, it'll be good for her to run wild with her cousins in the countryside. She loves them all, and they always have tremendous fun together. And while she's away, I shall put my time to good use by arranging my first life coaching session with Jules. Before Andy left me, I'd wondered whether she might be able to help me to figure out where I was going in life; for instance, how I might move on from being a PA at Flaxico. At this point, leaving my job is the last thing on my mind (I've had quite enough dramatic changes in my life recently). However, Jules insists that coaching could still be 'illuminating', so I should give it a go.

I stop outside the main door of our office building and pull my phone from my bag, poised to text her. But instead, I spot three messages from my boss:

Seen Twitter etc? Major damage limitation work needed this week.

Then: *Now on all news sites. Meeting for all asap, please don't be late!*

Then: *Bloody Kirsty Mitchum's been waiting to land one on us. What a fuck-up this is . . . WHERE ARE YOU?!!*

My heart rate quickens as I step inside. Although I'm *not* late, clearly Rose reckons I should have been here already, and up to speed with whatever drama is going on. As I wait for the lift I flick through the news sites on my phone. First impressions aren't good:

Global food company pushing RABBIT PELLETS on kids . . .

If it's good enough for bunnies . . . here's a tasty treat for your TOT!

Major mix-up means PET PELLETS sold to PEOPLE . . .

Oh, bloody hell. There must be some kind of misinformation out there – fake news – as, understandably, certain journalists are suspicious of the products we make. I mean, *I* am. Obviously, they're perfectly safe to eat – everything's highly regulated – but there's something about witnessing the whole process, the gigantic churning machines and thousands of gallons of beige slurry being pumped around that makes the final puffed corn snack seem . . . kind of less than enticing.

I'm less than happy that Izzy loves some of the snacks that started off in our factory. For the most part, I try not to think about it. The finished products bear little resemblance to what we produce anyway. However, I'm aware that Kirsty Mitchum, a big-shot journalist, thinks about it a lot. As the one who seems to have broken the so-called 'story', she takes a keen interest in food production and, as Rose had stated, she's been waiting to 'land one on us' for ages now.

Maybe she's gained insider info and deduced that the ingredients for rabbit pellets and human-edible snacks are eerily similar. Perhaps there's a *mole* lurking amongst the pellets and we'll all be quizzed at length? Although it seems disloyal to admit it, that might be quite thrilling. More thrilling, anyway, than my usual daily rigmarole of tending to Rose's travel bookings and emails, plus the sourcing of birthday presents for her cleaner's daughter and a man to jet-hose her patio and all the other non-work-related stuff she has me doing for her.

As I ride up in the lift I have already decided that similar-ingredients scenario is what's happened here, suggesting nothing more sinister than, say, if Izzy used her Turkish tomato filling to stuff a courgette. However, when I cross the vast open-plan space and spot Rose in

89

her glass-walled office in the far corner, sipping her coffee glumly, it's clear that the situation is altogether more serious.

'Come in, Viv,' she says, flapping a hand in my direction. 'Shut the door. Sit down.' She indicates the chair opposite and I bob down onto it. Her stability ball has been consigned to a corner with a jacket draped over it.

'I've read the headlines,' I start. 'What on earth's happened? I mean, is it true?'

'Yep, Kytes were supplied with the wrong product from us. That's about the size of it.' She grimaces. 'What can I say? It went right through production all the way to retail and it's out there being sold as a human-edible snack.'

I take a moment to process this. 'Oh, my God. That's terrible.'

'Yes, exactly. Oh-my-bloody-God. Look at this lot.' She delves into the tan leather bag at her side and tosses an array of newspapers across her desk. My gaze drops to a headline:

Watership CLOWNS: Why was bunny food sold to humans?

'Which products are they?' I ask.

'We think it's limited to Crunchy-Bites . . .'

'My daughter has those!'

'It'll be *fine*,' Rose says blithely. 'Nothing to worry about at all.'

I'm aware of a sick sensation in my stomach. 'But what's in them?'

She has the audacity to look irritated. 'D'you really need the ingredients list right now?'

'Yes please,' I say tightly.

Rose sighs and taps at her keyboard: 'Okay. Wheat,

bran, vegetable protein, vegetable oil, vitamin C, mineral premix . . .'

Hmm, not ideal, obviously, but nothing *too* hideous-sounding there.

'Limestone,' she continues.

'Limestone?' I exclaim.

'And, er, mould repellent and that's pretty much it . . .'

'Mould repellent!' I realise it's not helpful, repeating the ingredients back at her, but I'm in a bit of a state. Why do I give in and buy Izzy these disgusting snacks? Jules bakes her own beetroot and sweet potato crisps for Maeve. A hell of a faff, I've always thought, but preferable to feeding your child *limestone and mould repellent*. What kind of mother am I really?

'Will it harm her?' I bark. 'Please be honest with me.'

Rose's expression softens. There's no blow-dry today. Her hair is hanging, deflated, against her sallow face. 'Look, I know it's not great, but honestly, they're completely safe. That's not the issue. The priority now is to find how it happened and what we're going to do next. According to Kytes – and of course they're desperate to assign blame – the batch missed any spot checks of theirs and, well, here we are.' She presses her lips together in a flat line.

'Right.' I pause. 'I assume there's been a product recall?'

'Yes, of course.' She turns back to her laptop and peers at it, attention wavering already. 'As I said in my message, the short-term priority is damage limitation. We need to apologise and reassure customers. I need everyone to be ready for a meeting downstairs at eleven. Could you send a mass email now, marking it urgent, then get yourself down there to help set up the boardroom?'

'Yes, of course,' I say, still thinking *limestone and mould repellent, for crying out loud.* I know I don't make the darn things – I'm just a PA – but still I feel somehow responsible.

'We're being besieged by journalists,' she adds. 'Don't put any calls through to me.'

'No, of course not.'

'And I'll need you to minute the meeting.'

'Yes, no problem.'

'Thank you, Viv.' With another brisk flap of her hand, I am dismissed.

In my five years at Flaxico I'd assumed I'd acquired a decent grasp of what goes on in our company. However, in the hours that follow, the head honchos spout so much waffle, I'd be no more equipped to understand what happens in Andy's consultancy room.

'What we're looking at,' says a short, stocky man with ruddy cheeks, 'is a situation in which Kytes were supplied not with human-edible product but animal feed, and in terms of legislative issues there has clearly been a contractual-something-or-other not to mention a breach of mumble-bumble-rabbit-food-culpability in accordance with essential labelling criteria blah-blah-blah . . .'

Eh, what? I want to shout as, instead of enunciating clearly, he is muttering into his shirt collar, clearly uncomfortable about addressing us at all. I have never seen this man before. Perhaps it's the first time he's been liberated from a secret room. However, the gist seems to be that we're sticking to the 'It's their fault, not ours' line, although I can't see how that holds true. After all, we manufactured and sold Kytes the basic product. In one of the news reports I've read, an angry mother announced: 'If I'd wanted to give my little boy limestone to eat I'd have taken him to a quarry.' Quite right too. I know for sure that Izzy won't be getting any of the snacks made from our products anytime soon.

We've moved on to question-and-answer time now, which seems to fluster the man even further, and as a result his answers expand until, all around me, I catch my colleagues glancing at each other impatiently and stifling yawns. There's a bunch of us who are friendly and usually have lunch together in the bleak canteen. We keep shooting each other 'What-the-hell?' looks, and a few renegade souls are hovering at the back, making goofy rabbit faces at each other. I notice that Bugs Bunny has been drawn on a whiteboard and decide not to minute that.

Clearly, there will be no release for lunch today as one of the other PAs has organised for sandwiches and muffins to be ferried in. Being windowless and lacking even basic ventilation, the lower basement is beginning to feel uncomfortably stuffy, and the last thing anyone wants to do is eat. I have already had one full-on hot flush and can sense further ones brewing. My shirt is clinging to my back. *I think you'll find reptiles are dry-skinned, Viv.*

There's a short break, during which everyone gathers in clusters to admit that they don't have a clue what's going on. Then off we go again, with the same red-faced man *rabbiting* on (ha-ha!) saying 'wherein' and 'therein' a lot, which is causing my last vestiges of oestrogen to dwindle away.

Other things are happening too. By the time he pauses for a sip of water, I fear that any remaining elastin has evaporated from my skin. I can literally sense my face dehydrating and suspect I'll leave this room entirely desiccated. And now, dear God, something else seems to be happening – not to my face but . . . *down there*. While I'm not one of those people who has to double-check everything before they leave the house, I'm pretty sure my vagina was perfectly fine a few hours ago. However, at some point during this man's indecipherable babblings, things seem to have taken a turn for the worse. *Withering* is the only word for it. Of course I can't see it right now, and I wouldn't dream of investigating it in present company – but I can sense it happening, curling up at the edges like those cheese savoury sandwiches nobody seems to want. Apart from the fact that it's not garnished with cress or served on a stainless-steel platter, my vagina is virtually indistinguishable from the unwanted buffet spread.

Naturally, it's now impossible to focus on taking the minutes at all. I'll have to cobble them together later and somehow fill in the gaps; at the moment, I'm focused on trying to reassure myself that it's okay, no need to panic. A few months ago, before I found out about Andy's affair, I was a rampant sex addict on constant heat. Now I never even think about it. So maybe this is just nature's way of streamlining processes; a biological decluttering, if you like. If your vagina doesn't 'spark joy' then it makes sense for it to retreat quietly into a dormant state.

I clear my throat and push my hair away from my hot face. The meeting is finally over. As I gather up my notes and hurriedly make my way towards the exit, Rose calls after me. 'Viv? Just a minute . . .'

'Yes?' I turn and smile as serenely as I can muster.

She nods towards the buffet. 'Those sandwiches have hardly been touched and you seemed too preoccupied to eat anything. Want to take some upstairs for later?'

'Oh, I had something earlier, thanks,' I say with another wide smile, and zoom out of the room.

Friday, July 26

Another mad day at work with me constantly fielding calls to Rose as, naturally, she is being besieged with requests for interviews. We have issued a statement, the gist of which is as follows: *Whoops, something went wrong. Although the rogue batch won't harm anyone, we're still very sorry and will make sure it never happens again.*

If your child had guzzled a packet of rabbit pellets, I don't think you'd find it adequate. Meanwhile, rumours begin to emerge that – *shhhhh!* – this kind of thing happens all the time, and no one ever finds out about it. After all, pet products can be made from lower-grade ingredients than human-edible foods, and aren't subjected to the same stringent tests. And rumour has it that, sometimes, a human-edible product might be, ahem, *blended* with a little of 'something else'.

'But you didn't hear it from me,' whispers Jean, a shrewd woman in her sixties who has handled the payroll since something like 1982 and knows everything that goes on. We are huddled in the ladies, washing our hands. There's been a lot of gossiping in the loos since all this came out. I don't think anyone's got any proper work done.

'It's amazing it hasn't come out before,' I murmur.

'It'll all stop now, of course,' she adds. 'But it's going to mean a massive overhaul with a ton of investment into PR and image and all that.'

'Really? You reckon it'll go that far?'

Jean nods. 'Could be interesting for someone like you, with your background.'

'I was a stage manager, Jean,' I remind her. 'I don't think that'll ever be relevant here.'

'You never know how things'll turn out,' she says, giving me a knowing look. 'I've heard serious talk about the company having to pull out all the stops to seem like a fantastic, modern-day employer.' She pauses. 'So, for people like you, bunnygate might turn out to be a good thing.'

'You really think so?'

'You know Rose,' she says. 'She'll soon stop looking at this as an almighty disaster and turn it round to be some kind of fantastic opportunity instead.'

Christ, I do hope she's right. Whilst I've never loved the place exactly, I hadn't imagined they'd go to such lengths in order to maximise profits. Now, I feel grubby inside; grubbier, even, than when I was rabidly googling images of Estelle Lang. Why can't I have an honourable job, like Andy has? Whatever I think of him, at least he does something worthwhile that helps people. Not me, maybe, but his patients. I can't deny him that.

Back home, Izzy seems a little glum, and I wonder if it's because she's not entirely keen about going away with her dad, her grandparents and all her aunts, uncles and cousins. 'You'll have fun,' I say as I clear the table after dinner. 'You always love it up there, don't you?'

'Yeah, I s'pose,' she says, fiddling with her hair.

Despite my quizzing, I can't figure out what's wrong. Maybe she thinks she shouldn't appear too excited at the prospect of getting away from me? I'd hate her to feel that way, and go all out to enthuse her about it.

Hand-made patchwork quilts! Wood-burning stoves! 'It sounds amazing,' I say in my most positive voice.

Of course, it's her first holiday since her dad and I broke up. It's bound to feel weird for her, with me not going too, and I feel frustrated that I don't know how to make it okay.

Later on, Andy calls to suggest that I might take this opportunity to 'have a holiday too', and that I 'probably need one'. I remind him that I have already taken some leave, and do in fact have a proper job, which might not involve me saving patients from hormonal collapse, but still requires me to give notice before I can have a holiday. Plus – *plus!* – I don't really need him to suggest when I might take time off, *thank-you-very-much!*

On a positive note, it must have been the stress of trying to minute yesterday's meeting that had me imagining all kinds of witherings and/or crumblings happening to my nether regions. I seem to be fine down there, not that I am ever going to do it with anyone ever again, so it doesn't really matter what kind of state it's in.

Chapter Twelve

Penny disagrees strongly. She has a theory that I am 'ready' to meet someone new, that it is 'time'.

'I couldn't be less interested,' I tell her as Izzy and Maeve run ahead with Bobby in the park. Jules and I often help each other out with childcare, for which I've been especially grateful since Andy and I broke up. She and Erol are out on an afternoon date.

'I'm not talking anything serious,' Penny adds. 'I just mean a casual thing to perk you up a bit.'

I splutter. 'I don't need perking up. I'm absolutely fine as I am.'

She rolls her eyes. 'Oh, come on, Viv. We could find you someone nice, just to have fun with.'

'Right, okay.' I chuckle, deciding to indulge her by playing along. 'So who d'you have in mind for me?'

Her brow furrows as she seems to consider my options. Today she is wearing a navy dress patterned with white daisies, which is attracting looks in the park and is immensely cheering. 'When does school go back?' she asks.

'Um, mid-August. Why?'

'Well, I always think that lollipop man at the end of your street's very handsome . . .'

'What?' I splutter.

She grins. 'Well, don't you?'

'Pen, I'm not going to get off with the lollipop man. He must be well into his seventies!'

'Don't be so ageist,' she teases. 'He's in excellent shape, and he's friendly and helpful . . .'

'"Friendly and helpful".' I pretend to consider this. 'Are these the characteristics I should be looking for in a boyfriend?'

She arches a brow. 'Well, he seems obliging—'

'Especially if I need help crossing the road.' I smirk and turn to the girls. 'Are you two ready for ice creams?'

'Yeah!' they yell, charging towards us. We head for the van and, armed with our vanilla cones, we wander a little further towards the lake. It's a warm, hazy summer's afternoon, and the grassy expanse is dotted with families and couples, sprawling groups of teenagers and dog walkers, all drawn to the park by the beautiful day. There are picnics and games of frisbee in progress. The girls crouch at the water's edge, watching the ducks.

'Okay. What about Nick, then?' Penny asks.

'Nick?' I blink at her.

She smiles and licks her ice cream. 'Yep, I think he'd be perfect for you.'

'You mean *your* Nick?' I say, almost choking. 'Oh, sure. Between him and the lollipop man—'

'Actually,' she cuts in, deadpan, 'I'm being serious now. I think you'd like him, and I'm sure he'd like you.'

99

I stare at her for a moment, realising that she really means this as a genuine suggestion. 'But . . . he lives in New Zealand,' I start.

'Yes, but he's coming over on a visit,' she says with a smile.

'Great. Lovely! But that's not really the point. It would just feel too weird—'

'Why?' she asks, seemingly genuinely baffled. 'He's a lovely man, and as far as I know he's single just now . . .'

'Penny, that's an insane suggestion,' I exclaim.

'I don't see the problem—'

'He's your son!'

She actually looks hurt. 'Yes, I'm aware of that. I was thinking you'd view that as a positive, not a reason to discount him straight off.'

'I didn't mean it like that,' I say quickly. 'I'm sure he's wonderful. It's just . . .' I pause, trying to find the right way of putting it. 'It would just feel so *wrong*.'

She looks baffled. 'I don't see why.'

'Because . . . you're my friend. Because you know what an emotional mess I am, and surely you wouldn't want him involving himself with someone like me . . .'

'You're not a mess,' she protests. 'I'd be *delighted*.'

'And because I know all about him eating nothing but butterscotch Angel Delight for a year and running naked around the library.'

She frowns, almost comically. 'He doesn't do that anymore.'

'No, I should hope not. He's, what, forty-eight?'

'Forty-*nine*,' she corrects me, as if that'll swing it.

'Anyway, that's not the point. The point is, well . . .' Actually, there are so many points, I don't know where to start.

100

'Well, look, as I said, he's coming over,' she adds.

'When?' I ask cautiously.

'Towards the end of next month, for a few weeks. He's doing some filming in Yorkshire, some documentary about steam trains or something . . .' She shrugs, clearly nonplussed by his interest in the subject. 'And when that's done,' she continues, brightening, 'he's coming to stay with me. So you'll meet him at last!'

'That'll be lovely,' I say, and in fact I'm curious; I have always been away on holiday, or at my in-laws' for Christmas, on his previous visits. 'You're looking forward to it, aren't you?' I add. 'Having some time with Nick, I mean?'

'Of course I am,' Penny says briskly. 'But, you know, I am very used to pleasing myself and having my own space, and he really does fuss over me . . .'

'You could turn out your lights and hide behind the sofa,' I tease her, 'pretending not to be in.'

She sniggers. 'Or send him round to you, get him out of my hair?'

'Sure! If they still make butterscotch Angel Delight, I'll be sure to stock up—'

'Mum!' Izzy yells as the girls run back towards us. 'Mum, I want to ask you a question.'

'What is it?'

She grins broadly, clearly barely able to contain herself. 'Can I go on holiday to Maeve's caravan?'

There's been no mention of this before, and I'm not sure how to react. I have only just come around to the idea of Andy taking her away, without me. 'Honey, I'm sorry, but you can't just invite yourself on their holiday.'

'I haven't,' she says firmly. 'Maeve's invited me.'

'*Can* she come, please?' Maeve asks. 'Please, Viv. Please!'

101

I exhale. 'We'll have to see, love. I'd need to check with your mum and dad. Maybe sometime . . .'

'She can come *this* time,' Maeve announces happily. 'Mum said it's all right.'

I turn to Izzy. 'I don't think you can. You're going away with Dad, remember?'

As she looks at her friend and frowns, it dawns on me why Izzy has seemed reticent about the Loch Fyne trip. The girls have clearly been hatching an alternative plan.

Jules is apologetic when I drop off Maeve at home. 'I'm sorry if this makes things difficult,' she says. 'The girls were asking me the other day if Izzy could come away with us, and I said it would be fine, of course – but that she'd have to check with you first. I should have mentioned it . . .'

I look at my daughter. 'Why didn't you say earlier, love?'

She shuffles uncomfortably. 'I thought it might upset Dad.'

Well, it will, I reflect. But if forcing her to go away with his family will upset *her*, then I know whose feelings I prioritise.

'When are you planning to go?' I ask Jules.

'On Friday, for about a week.'

I exhale. 'Izzy, are you sure this is what you want to do? You'll miss out on seeing all your cousins. Remember there are those lovely new chalets to stay in.'

She looks up at me, eyes wide. 'I don't want to go there, Mum. I want to go away with Maeve.'

'Okay, okay,' I murmur. 'If you're absolutely sure . . .' I turn to Jules. 'And it's definitely okay with you and Erol?'

'We'd love her to come,' she says, smiling.

'All right, then. I'll just have to tell Dad.' The girls cheer and hug each other, and all the way home, Izzy is full of all the fun they'll have, chattering about the plans they've been making, secretly.

When I call Andy later to break the news, he is clearly put out, but manages to remain stoical. 'I thought she seemed a bit off about it,' he says. 'I was worried she felt weird about, you know . . . coming away without you.'

'Hmm. Well, it's not that,' I say dryly.

'She's not persuadable, is she?'

'I don't think so. She seems to have set her heart on this. I suspect they've been planning it for a while. She was actually worried about hurting your feelings, and how you'd react . . .'

'Oh, God, really?' He sighs. 'Everyone'll be so disappointed if she's not there.'

'There'll be plenty of other times, though,' I add.

'Yes, I guess so. Tell her it's fine, then.'

I already have, I muse, although I don't say it. And we leave it at that, with not a single sharp word between us during the entire eight-minute phone conversation. A little over four months since he left, we are capable of handling a slightly tricky situation in a reasonable manner, which can only be a positive thing, a distinct move forward for both of us.

I still hate the fucker, though.

Monday, July 29

At work, bunnygate is still the full focus, and it's the presence of limestone in the product that the press have

103

latched on to. Never mind that it's only 'trace amounts'. When you consider it's mainly used for concrete and aggregate for road building, *any* amount feels like too much.

However, Rose is keen to move forward with plans to not only rescue our company's sullied reputation but, as she puts it, 'to embrace a bright new future as a modern, customer-friendly brand'. So perhaps Jean, the payroll lady, was right, in that new opportunities may be on the horizon – for all of us.

Startling words like 'nutritious', and even 'fresh', are being bandied about our offices. With impressive speed Rose has gathered together a bunch of top-level food technicians, who have been marching about being loud and jovial as if Flaxico is already one of those fun-filled workplaces you hear of, where everyone seems to spend an awful lot of time playing ping-pong and lolling on beanbags with their dogs. Do such places really exist?

Today we're having a brainstorming session in the lower basement. Everyone is invited to take part – even the tall, gaunt man with the veiny nose whose role I'm pretty sure is to sporadically attend to faulty light fittings and suchlike – because it seems that this is the kind of company we work for now. It is *inclusive*.

Tellingly, there are no menopausal sandwiches this time, no desolate buffet bringing to mind E. coli and early death. Instead, there's a sprightly array of tempting salads, savoury pastries and a gigantic platter of exotic fruits. Perhaps the normal canteen staff were locked in the kitchen while this delicious fare was ferried in.

'Can you believe this is happening?' asks Belinda, one of my lunch buddies who works in HR, as we divide into teams. Rose has asked us to come up with ideas for new products – not just in pellet form, but finished deli-type lines that would be recognisable as food, and which we might actually like to eat.

'You mean *real* food?' someone asked with a splutter.

'Yes,' she said dryly, 'real food. Get to it, people. We're talking blue-sky thinking, no holds barred. This is the start of our bold new future.'

'It does seem like a heck of a leap,' I mutter to Belinda, wondering how our company intends to shift from extruded pellets to the likes of pea and mint patties and feta and olive tarts. I doubt that an olive has ever entered this building before. If it had, it would have been drummed right out again and reported on in the monthly news bulletin. However, Rose keeps insisting that we should 'think without boundaries', and goes on to outline her plan to bring in teams of youngsters – not just those from food technology courses but from the worlds of marketing, media and design.

She is flushed with excitement as she calls us all back together and whizzes through her presentation. 'I imagine that our company might not top many young people's lists of preferred workplaces,' she concedes, 'but I want all that to change. We need to know how young people eat, and what influences a teenager's food choices today. So my plan is to set up platforms for innovation . . .' She pauses to jab at the text on the screen. God knows how she's managed to hammer all of this together so quickly. The slick graphics belie the fact that this apparent new direction is panic-fuelled, in response to the barrage of negative media coverage. She must have been at it all weekend.

'Each platform will be led, not by an old-style manager

but a *mentor*,' Rose explains, beaming around at all of us as we watch attentively from our stackable plastic chairs. 'We're moving into a new culture where every individual will feel empowered, and have ample opportunity for career progression and personal growth.'

'What d'you think this means for us?' I whisper to Belinda, who's sitting next to me.

'Haven't the faintest,' she murmurs back. 'This is all news to me. D'you think you'll still have to sort out her rogue pube emergencies?'

I smirk. 'Maybe one of the new innovation platforms will take care of that?'

We turn back to the front as Rose invites questions. Belinda shoots up her hand. She's an eager, energetic type, whom I imagine was excellent in goal attack position in netball. 'Yes, Belinda?' Rose says.

'Obviously,' she starts, 'there are issues with implementing a policy of recruiting only young people.'

Rose nods curtly. 'Erm, yes, of course.'

'We can't be seen to be discriminatory,' Belinda adds.

'No, obviously not.' Rose beams around the room, clearly trying to mask a flash of *I'd-never-thought-of-that* panic, and eager to wrap things up now.

'Are you planning to launch a graduate recruitment scheme?' Belinda asks.

'Nothing as formal as that,' Rose says breezily. 'I'm just looking to bring in lots of new, young, creative minds to shake things up.'

'Okay. But will HR be involved in the setting up of—'

'It'll be done very carefully,' she says with a note of impatience that clearly means *Oh, do piss off, HR.*

'But what if older people, who are already employed here, want to get involved?' Belinda persists.

106

'As I said,' Rose cuts in, her smile rigid, her tone steely, 'we are looking for a fresh young team, and that can only be a good thing for everybody.' As Belinda throws me a frustrated glance, Rose moves swiftly on to further questions. 'So, what I plan to do next,' she concludes, eyes sparkling, hands clasped before her, 'is to talk to each and every one of you about how you can contribute to our new, exciting future here at Flaxico. Thank you very much for your time, everyone. I hope you've found this useful and illuminating today.'

Belinda gives me another quick look as we leave the boardroom, and there's a distinct buzz of unease as everyone drifts back to their own departments. I'm wondering now if Rose *really* meant: 'And, crucially, I shall decide whether you're going to be part of it or not.' Although she and I seem to rub along pretty well, I have known her to fire people for pretty flimsy reasons, largely ignoring the verbal and written warning procedure that's supposed to be in place. Although I hope she knows I work diligently – and of course she'll still need a PA, whatever happens – I can't help wondering how I'll fit into the new regime. I absolutely cannot afford to be without a job right now.

Early hours of Tuesday, July 30

Although I hate to admit it, Andy was right about one thing: it *is* like waking up in a swamp around here. At 3.27 a.m. I'm lying in bed with my chest soaking and my heart racing, worrying about what's going to happen at work and, more pressingly, how I'm going to get to sleep again now I'm wide awake at this unearthly hour.

I should be used to it by now, the waking up drenched thing. That's what interrupts my sleep – not a car alarm or a dog barking, but my body's overenthusiastic emissions. It's quite a design fault, this perspiring madly: not because I've hauled myself to the gym, but because I've just been *lying there quietly.*

At least, this is how it is for those of us who aren't 'breezing through' the menopause. I know every woman experiences it differently. I'd imagine that Estelle Lang doesn't sweat at all. She probably doesn't even have pores – which seems a little unfair as these days mine are visible from outer space, like vast craters. The last time I braved one of those make-up counter ladies in a department store, she helpfully suggested how I might go about 'filling' them, as if they were holes in the road.

At just before 4 a.m. I get up, change into dry pyjamas and stare at my pallid face in the bathroom mirror. Another hair has poked out of my chin. I'm so used to them now, I almost greet them like friends, and at least I've spotted this one in its infancy. The ones I worry about are the audacious buggers that have been swaying about in the breeze for God knows how long and no one's had the decency to point them out.

Back in bed, I try to settle back to sleep, sprawling over the dry area where I haven't been lying. I guess that's one positive thing about being dumped in favour of another woman.

At least there's plenty of room in the bed.

Chapter Thirteen

Wednesday, July 31

After being in meetings for most of the morning Rose reappears on our floor and beetles over towards me, heels clacking. 'I can't say anything just yet,' she hisses, 'but I'd like to talk to you at some point about a new opportunity that might be coming your way . . .'

'Really?' I ask, spirits lifting immediately. 'What kind of opportunity?'

'I need to finalise things before we can discuss it.' She smiles conspiratorially. 'Sorry I've hardly been around this week. So much going on, as you've probably gathered . . .'

'Yes, of course. I understand that.'

'So what d'you think of all the changes we're proposing? I know things have happened very quickly.'

'It all sounds pretty positive,' I reply.

She beams at me, looking as excited as a child at a birthday party. 'I'm so glad to hear that, because I really think you could play a crucial part. I have a proposal that I think has *you* written all over it.'

It seems a little unfair of her to land this on me without a hint of what it might be. But what can I do? I just need to get on with my work and see what happens. I also probably ought to stop smiling hopefully – with a 'Tell me! Tell me!' expression – every time Rose saunters by.

Back at home, there's no chance to mull things over as Izzy is intent on doing her TV chef thing tonight. I agree, rather wearily, that she can make us an extensive Mexican feast. There are so many components that it's gone 8.40 p.m. by the time we can sit down to eat, by which time I fall, ravenously, upon the array of dishes. I have to say, these *Izzy Cooks!* episodes might not be doing much for my waistline, but by God, sour cream and refried beans sure taste good.

Friday, August 2

Although no further information has been given, the thought of something happening, something new and positive to shake me out of my work rut, is pretty thrilling. I've missed having a job I genuinely love, that I can throw myself into and feel that I'm good at. I miss making a difference in a more meaningful way than organising taxis to pick up Rose from various airports around the world. I know I'm lucky to have a steady job that's not too arduous. It just feels kind of . . . *empty* sometimes. However, the promise of some kind of change keeps me buoyed up all day, which helps to make up for the fact that Izzy sauntered off with Jules, Erol and Maeve first thing this morning. I know she'll have a brilliant holiday. I experienced only the *tiniest* snag at my heart as she leapt, delightedly, into their car.

110

Home to an empty house now, I soak in the bath, making a mental note to spruce up my CV over the weekend, in case Rose asks me to attend a formal interview. As I used to remind Spencer before his exams, 'You can never be too prepared.'

'Really, Mum?' he'd say, with an infuriating smirk. 'I thought I'd not bother and just go in and, like, wing it?'

Saturday, August 3

So, a whole week, all by myself. It's going to be *great*, I decide, sipping my coffee and trying to shove away feelings of bleakness. Of course I'll miss Izzy, but I'll make the most of the time. There are so many things I can do.

First, I deep-clean the kitchen, stopping to marvel at all the swanky ingredients we have now: the chilli oil and porcini mushrooms, the smoked paprika and black cardamom pods bought in for future episodes of *Izzy Cooks!* I rearrange our food cupboards several times before putting everything back in their original positions.

Next, I work my way through all the laundry, including the teeny socks that have been lurking in the basket since Izzy was about three, and would barely fit a dolly (not that Izzy has ever shown the slightest interest in dollies). Disconcertingly, I also find some boxers of Andy's festering at the bottom. If I had his address I'd be tempted to stuff them in a jiffy bag and post them to him, addressed to *her*. Would Estelle feel the same about her hot doctor lover if she ripped open a package to be confronted by his unsavoury pants? Sadly, as he's still being weirdly cagey about where he's living, I am to be denied the chance of doing this. Hacking them to bits with the kitchen scissors would seem a little pointless and only serve to contaminate a kitchen utensil. Picking them up gingerly by their waistbands, I settle for slinging them in the kitchen bin.

For the first time this century the laundry basket is empty. Having allowed myself the luxury of gazing into it for a few moments, I make myself another strong coffee and sit at the kitchen window as I drink it, wondering what to do next. I'd sit outside in the sunshine but Tim-the-rat-worrier from next door is in his back garden, along with Chrissie and their young son, Ludo. Being the same age as Izzy, he should probably be a friend of hers, but most definitely isn't.

Tim is beavering away, pruning and hoeing and dragging enormous sacks of clippings about. Heavily pregnant now, Chrissie is barking commands from the patio. But only directed at Tim, it seems; apparently no one minds that Ludo appears to be intent on destroying their brick shed with a hammer. Even from here, I can see bits pinging off it, yet neither his mother nor father seem to be telling him to stop. This is how they 'parent': by letting the pint-sized vandal do whatever he wants.

They must reckon it's a 'learning experience' for him, battering a shed.

A few weeks before all the Estelle Lang stuff came out, when life seemed to be reasonably normal, Andy and I were in pottering about in our own garden when we saw him throwing stones at a cat on the wall. 'Don't do that, Ludo!' my husband called out in a perfectly pleasant tone.

Chrissie must have overheard as she zoomed out of their house. 'We don't *say* no,' she admonished us.

And now, even though it's not my shed, I find myself growing more and more agitated watching the kid

112

attacking it, to the point at which I have to move away from the window and try to find something else to do instead.

I could call a friend. However, I remember now that Penny was planning a trip on her boyfriend Hamish's narrowboat (Izzy finds it hilarious that I refer to him as her boyfriend, but it's Penny's favoured term, so what else should I call him?). I could try my oldest friends, Shelley and Isla – the three of us go way back to primary school – but it would feel kind of invasive, pinging into their weekends with no notice.

I know that by the end of the working week, Shelley is always pretty shredded, and that she and her partner Laurence cherish their low-key weekends with their dogs. Isla, a single mum whose three teenagers still live with her, is Curator of Natural History at a rather dusty, somewhat forgotten museum, and seems to spend every spare moment ferrying her offspring about and basically looking after everyone. Whilst I love seeing my friends, I'm aware that any message sent now would have that distinct 'Help, I don't know what to do with myself!' tone to it. And I'm determined *not* to be that person, the woman who can't survive alone for more than a few hours. But I could call Spencer, I decide. Surely he'll be delighted to hear from me on a Saturday afternoon?

'Hi, darling,' I chirp. 'Just wondered how you are.'

'Hey, Mum!' He sounds surprised, and no wonder, as we normally text unless there's something specific to discuss. 'Everything okay?'

'Yes, great, thanks.' I launch into a preamble about asking how he is, how work's been lately, which bands he's been working with and how his flatmates are – aware that I am building up to the thrilling suggestion that I

113

jump into my car and drive down to Newcastle to visit him right now. He'd love that, wouldn't he, his mother arriving with hardly any notice, looking a bit deranged?

'Are you out at the moment?' I ask, suddenly aware of the jovial background chatter and faint music playing. But it's only lunchtime. I know he usually works late on Friday nights and had assumed he'd just be getting up.

'Yeah, there's a few of us out,' he says. 'We're in this lovely beer garden, just having a few drinks.' A few drinks, in the daytime, while I've been mopping the floor?

'That sounds nice,' I remark.

'It is, yeah.' *And I need to go now*, is what he's trying to convey. 'It's Millie's birthday,' he adds.

'Oh, is it? Wish her happy birthday from me, love. I was only wondering how you are. I miss you.'

'Miss you too, Mum. And thanks, I'll tell her. See you soon, yeah?'

Hang on a minute! How about I nip down right now and take you both out to dinner; i.e. bribe you to spend time with me? 'Yes, see you soon then, darling,' I mutter. 'Bye.'

We finish the call and I wonder what the heck to do next, aware that this is pretty dysfunctional, this not knowing how to occupy myself. It's just that, since Andy and I broke up, I realise I've hardly been alone like this. I've been at work or with friends or, more likely, with Izzy. If she's been out with her dad, it's only been for a few hours.

And now she's on holiday without me, and Spencer is out celebrating his girlfriend's birthday and Andy is doing God knows what with that woman. I'm sort of used to it now, the fact that our marriage is over – or, at least, I don't wake up in shock anymore. There's no opening my eyes expecting to see Andy gazing adoringly at me from his pillow (that hasn't actually happened since about 1916, but still). Yet the fury can still boil up in me, and occasionally I'm seized by an urge to stop being so mature and reasonable and just call him and yell that it's not fair, and what kind of penis-driven idiot would have exchanged our lives together – our *family* – for the chance to jump into some other woman's pants?

I manage not to call him, and to firmly shove such urges to the dirty recesses of my mind. The rest of my eerily people-less Saturday is spent on deep-cleaning the bathroom, specifically digging away at the tile grout with Andy's special folding toothbrush that he liked to take on holiday, in the hope that it will create an aura of contentment over a job well done (it doesn't).

I also use to it clean underneath the rim of the loo. And when I've done that, I rearrange the potatoes in the vegetable rack.

Sunday, August 4

I know what to do. Some gardening! Our borders could certainly do with attention, and I love being out there normally, poking about. It's one of the many reasons why I hope to hang on to this house once Andy and I get around to dividing up our lives (the main one being that it's the only home Izzy has ever known). While it pains me to give him credit for anything, I have to admit that Andy has never been mean where our kids are concerned. He has also made it clear that he will continue to contribute to our household without any hassle. God knows what'll happen further down the line, though. It's a concept I seem to have difficulty even coming to terms with: the idea that at some point, we might sell this house and divide the money and I'll buy a flat, which would be *fine* of course, but all the more reason to cherish our garden now.

As I start to pull out weeds, my mood eases. *This* feels better. Repetitive, soothing work is good for the soul; I'm sure Jules would say that. An hour or so passes, and the drab morning has unfolded into a glorious afternoon. The sky is searing blue, smudged with white clouds. Look at me, I reflect: a single woman alone for a whole week, having finally found a way of being content with her own company. Maybe this is how I'll be as I grow older; not a wildcat like Penny, who remarked recently that 'doing it on a boat doesn't half make it rock about' – but a serene lady who enjoys gardening in a straw hat.

I must get a straw hat, I decide, straightening up and stretching my arms high above my head, the way Jules does when she's limbering up for a yoga session. And then I think, sod it, I might as well do a few sun salutations too. After all, it *is* sunny, and no one's watching, and she's shown me the basic moves.

And so I begin, trying to ignore the audible creaks that seem to be coming from my various joints and sockets as I work my way through the sequence. Reach up to the sky, fold down forwards, arms dangling heavily. Slide a foot back, then the other; lower to the floor into upward dog. Now downward dog, no doubt alarming anyone who might happen to be glancing out of a window, but what the hell? I am a yogi now with my arse in the air, worshipping the golden orb in the sky.

'You should never feel pain,' Jules advised me, and actually, this *is* pretty painful, so maybe I'm not doing it right – but it's better than the kind of pain I've experienced whilst gawping frenziedly at pictures of my husband's new lover. That sort of pain is just mental anguish. This is the *good* kind that invigorates the mind. It's – ow!

I collapse onto the lawn as something hits my backside. Scrambling back up, I look around indignantly. Did a bird just hurl itself at my bottom? As I bend to brush grass from my knees, something whooshes through the air, narrowly missing my cheek.

High-pitched giggles are coming from next door's garden. 'Oh, hello, Ludo.' I bare my teeth at him.

'Hello Viv.' He grins malevolently.

'Did you throw something just then?' Mindful of Chrissie's 'We don't say no' school of parenting I'm doing my utmost to address him in a cheerful, non-threatening manner.

'No?' he says with an infuriating grin, although the small clod of earth I've spotted lying close by would suggest otherwise. Then: 'Where's Izzy?'

'She's away,' I reply.

'Where's she gone?'

'She's in the Lake District with Maeve's family.'

His face clouds and he pushes back his shock of wavy blond hair. 'I don't like Maeve.'

'Don't you? She's really nice, Ludo.' *Unlike you, you cat-stoning little brat.*

'She never lets me play.'

'Oh, that *is* a shame.'

He fixes me with a cold stare. 'Where's Andy?'

It feels like a short, sharp punch. I mean, he's been gone for nearly five months, and it's not as if the two of them enjoyed any kind of special rapport. Quite the

117

contrary. 'Irritating little psycho' was Andy's favourite private name for this child.

'He doesn't live here anymore,' I say cheerfully.

'Why not?'

I stare at this small human, aware that *because he had sex with someone else* would not be the appropriate response. 'That just happens sometimes,' I say, hoping he'll leave it at that. Any normal child would; i.e. one brought up to be aware of quaint concepts such as manners and politeness.

'Where does he live now?' Ludo wants to know.

Search me, mate! 'In a flat of his own.'

'Why—'

'So, bet you're looking forward to having a new brother or sister!' I cut in to swerve him off the subject.

That's taken the wind out of his sails. Ludo digs at the ground with the toe of his trainer and declines to answer.

'It'll be lovely, won't it,' I chirp, 'having a new baby around?' *Crying in the night, getting all the attention, making Mummy and Daddy tired?*

'S'pose so,' he growls.

'What names d'you like?'

He mumbles something unintelligible.

'Pardon?'

'Attic,' he barks.

'Attic?' *Why, is that where you'd like to put it, when it's been born?* 'D'you mean Atticus?'

Ludo nods glumly as he retreats from me, far less eager to chat now he's no longer probing me about my marital disaster. I turn and make my way back towards the house, feeling for my phone in my pocket. It's not there. Maybe it fell out when I was downward dogging.

I go back and scan the lawn for it. I really must drag

the mower out soon. That was always Andy's job and from now on, obviously, it'll be mine. Everything is my job now.

'Are you getting *divorced*?' Ludo yells from the back step.

Jesus Christ, where the hell are his parents? Miraculously, a tinkling sound starts up on the lawn, alerting me to my phone's location.

I snatch it and take the call. 'So how's the weekend of freedom?' Penny asks. I can tell immediately that she's a little sparkly with drink.

'Oh, fine,' I reply. 'Just out in the garden, chatting to Ludo.'

She chuckles. 'That twisted little miscreant. Is he being as unpleasant as usual?'

He is studying me intensely from his back door, hands thrust into his shorts pockets. 'Yes, pretty much business as usual here.'

'Hmm. He thought I didn't notice him pulling Bobby's tail that time. You know he's never been a biter, but sometimes I think that's a shame. Let's hope the new baby turns out nicer. Anyway,' she goes on, 'you're probably loving your time alone, and I don't want to disturb you—'

'You're not disturbing me,' I say quickly as Chrissie comes out, beams indulgently at the devil's spawn and starts to peg out washing. Great. Now he can lob clods of earth at Tim's zingy white Calvins. 'But I thought you were away with Hamish?' I add.

'Oh, that hasn't happened,' Penny explains. 'Engine trouble, apparently, and Hamish is up to his elbows in grease. And I thought, it's a beautiful day. Far too lovely to waste sitting on a stinky old boat that isn't going anywhere . . .'

'You're right about that,' I agree, making my way into the house now.

'It's the perfect day for a chilled glass of white, in fact.'

I smile. At just gone 2 p.m., the idea isn't completely abhorrent. 'That sounds excellent.'

'Well, come and join us!'

'Us? Who are you with?'

'Friends of yours.' I catch laughter in the background. 'I ran into Shelley and Isla in Kelvingrove and we're waiting for you now. But hurry up, darling – you certainly have some catching up to do.'

Chapter Fourteen

Forty-five minutes later

It's not that I'm desperate for company. However, I manage to shower, dress, do my make-up and be out of the door in record time, and by the time I arrive at the pub, my friends are all chatting away like old buddies, at an outside table in the dappled sunshine.

Despite only having met them a couple of times, apparently Penny zoomed right over and persuaded Isla and Shelley to join her for wine. A bottle juts from an ice bucket on the table and Bobby is lying contentedly at Penny's feet. It turns out that, while I've been lonesome at home, Shelley has also been at a loose end as Laurence, her partner, is away visiting his parents, and Shelley couldn't face going; apparently her mother-in-law can talk for about seventeen hours without drawing breath. Meanwhile Isla 'had to get out' as living with three teenagers is proving testing. So why didn't anyone call *me*?

'We thought you'd be loving having time on your own,' Shelley admits.

'We didn't want to interrupt your reverie,' Isla teases.

'I wasn't in a reverie,' I retort. 'I was being pelted with clods of earth by the kid next door while I was downward dogging.'

'The one whose parents let him play with matches and cooking oil?' Shelley asks.

'That's the one. His mum believes everything is a "learning experience".'

Penny splutters. 'That'll be educational for him, when the fire brigade have to drag them all out of the house.'

Isla leans forward with interest. 'What d'you think about these pampered children, Penny? We indulge our kids so much these days. You must think we've all lost our minds.'

Penny smiles and flicks her bouncy highlighted hair, clearly pleased to be quizzed about such matters. 'I suppose some children were always spoilt. But the big difference was, parenting wasn't even a thing back then. Not one's entire life's work, I mean. "Parenting"—' she waggles her fingers around the word '—basically meant trying to ensure they didn't eat anything poisonous and went to bed at a reasonable hour so you had some time to yourself.'

'I wish I'd been like that,' declares Isla, who has remained on remarkably good terms with her ex. 'My oldest expects me to write his English essays for him. There are few enough benefits to being fifty-two. Surely not having to sweat over the symbolism in *Macbeth* should be one of them.'

'You're a total marvel,' I say, meaning it. 'They have this belief that you can fix everything, *do* everything, so they all lean on you a lot.'

'But why do I always agree to help?' She pushes back

her no-nonsense blonde cropped hair. 'I still try to trick them into eating vegetables too. It's ridiculous. My oldest is eighteen.' She turns to Penny. 'Did you ever do that? Did you liquidise mange tout for pasta sauces?'

'No,' Penny retorts, laughing, 'because I wasn't insane.' And then, of course, I have to persuade her to tell them about the Angel Delight, and the strip-off in the library, which they find hysterical.

'You're so refreshing,' Isla says, wiping her eyes. 'People take parenting so bloody seriously these days. We don't just bring up our kids and hope for the best. We raise them with such care and attention to detail, as if the future of the human race depends on us getting it right.'

'What does Nick do now?' Shelley asks.

'He makes documentaries,' Penny replies.

'Oh, what about?'

'Anything he really cares about. He's based in Auckland – he married a New Zealander, but that didn't last for very long. He's coming over soon . . .' She gives me a quick sideways look, which I choose to ignore.

'How did he get into that?' Isla asks.

'By teaching himself how to make films,' she says with a rare trace of pride, 'with equipment he'd borrowed from friends, in the early days. He's very determined and excellent at what he does.'

'Did he go to university?' Shelley asks.

'I think he might have,' she says with a shrug.

'*Penny*!' I exclaim, realising she's teasing as she laughs and tops up our glasses. She knows how outraged I can be by her approach to mothering ('benign neglect', she calls it).

'Girls, we should eat, shouldn't we?' she says. 'I really

do need to move on to solids or things are going to get messy. What do they have here?'

Obviously, at our age, crisps/nuts won't suffice. We are relieved to find that they do tapas, and soon an array of tempting plates crowd our table.

'Doesn't Andy live around here?' Shelley asks as we all dive in.

'Yep, allegedly. I still don't have his address, though. He's incredibly cagey about it.'

'Why *is* that?' Isla asks, frowning.

'Honestly, I have no idea.'

Penny turns to me. 'You should find out. Why don't you call him, make some excuse? We could pop round to see him en masse.' She grins mischievously.

'I imagine he'll be on his way to Loch Fyne right now, or maybe he's there already. And the signal's terrible up there.'

'Give it a try,' Penny adds. 'Say you need his address for something while he's away.'

I laugh and sip my wine. It dawns on me how lucky I am really, having the freedom to be out on a glorious day with my friends, without having to rush home or be answerable to anyone. I know Izzy is having a wonderful time, as we have chatted and Jules has already sent me pictures of the girls playing at the lakeside. Although things feel uncertain at work – Rose still hasn't even hinted at what she has in mind for me – I really don't have too much to worry about. I make a mental note to appreciate what I have, instead of allowing dark thoughts about Andy and his new woman to infiltrate my brain.

'*I* know,' Shelley announces suddenly. 'Tell him you want to forward some letters that look important. Say you want them out of your way, in case you lose them in the house.'

I frown, considering this. 'That doesn't sound feasible.'

'Just give it a go,' she cajoles me. 'He can only say no, can't he?' And so I text him a rambling request, which obviously baffles him as he replies, almost immediately: *Can this wait? Just arrived. Everyone says hi.*

'How long does it take to type an address?' Shelley remarks.

'He's just palming you off,' Penny adds. She snatches my phone from the table and jabs at it.

'Penny! What are you doing?'

Beaming, she hands it back to me. To give her credit, her method turns out to be more effective than mine as, in response to her *GIVE ME YOUR ADDRESS!* command, he has replied, obediently: *Flat 1/2 19 Kinnerton St.*

'So?' Penny smirks as we divvy up our bill. 'We're so close, it seems silly not to check it out. Let's go.'

I can only surmise that the wine and the sunshine have messed with our heads as, minutes later, we arrive in a straggly group, giddy and sniggering at the end of Andy's road. As it's not a part of town I visit often, I hadn't realised that this street in particular is as charming as it is. Tucked away from the main thoroughfare, it's a mixture of well-kept red sandstone tenement flats, a couple of traditional pubs and a row of cheerily painted shops. There's a baker's, an upmarket off-licence advertising gin tastings, a grocer's and a quaint tea room, plus a specialist cheese shop, which is emitting a pungent aroma across the street.

'That's very . . . ripe, isn't it?' Isla remarks. 'I mean, I love cheese but that's seriously strong. Imagine working in there.' As we cross the road towards it, I check the numbering system of the flats.

'Andy's flat's directly above it!' I announce.

Penny turns to me. 'He lives above the cheese shop?'

'Yes! Look – that's number nineteen.' I grin at her and her grey-blue eyes crinkle with delight.

'Didn't you once tell me he was obsessed with an imaginary cheese smell in the fridge, when you were in Paris?'

'I did, yes.'

'I remember that,' Isla exclaims. 'You were demented by the time you came back. Are you sure this is his address?'

'It definitely is, absolutely.'

'But why would he choose to live here,' Penny adds, frowning, 'if he's hypersensitive to strong smells?'

'God knows,' I say as we make our way into the shop. It's a beautiful store, with mirrored walls and hand-painted tiles, like an old-fashioned dairy, and the array of cheeses on display is literally breathtaking.

The young sales assistant smiles from behind the counter. 'Can I help you with anything?' she asks.

'We were just, um, *drawn in*,' I say, taking a big inhalation. 'It smells amazing in here.'

'If you love cheese, it does,' the young woman concedes. 'And it's particularly pungent at the moment.'

'Because of the weather?' Shelley asks, managing to keep a straight face.

'It's more down to the varieties we have in just now,' she explains. 'There's a few that vie for the word's smelliest award and I'm proud to say we have them all.'

'Ooh, which are they?' Penny asks eagerly.

The shop assistant indicates the varieties all beautifully

arranged on the counter before her. 'That's Brie de Meaux and this one's a Vieux Boulogne, which is probably the strongest of all. Stinking Bishop is pretty pongy too. Would you like to try some samples?'

'Yes please,' I reply eagerly.

As she cuts tiny slivers for us, asking if we'd like wine, too – 'Oh, go on then,' Shelley says, as if she's taken some persuading – I start to feel quite hysterical that the man with whom I shared my life for a quarter of a century now lives directly above a giant reeking Stilton wheel. If it weren't for that – or my tipsiness – it might have felt awful to be confronted by the undeniable evidence that Andy really does have a home away from Izzy and me, and isn't merely floating about in the ether like a kind of philandering spectre. But as it is, my seemingly bleak Sunday has turned out to be far cheerier than I could have imagined.

'You know the flats upstairs from here?' I venture as the young woman pours our wine.

'Yes?'

'Does the smell from the shop carry up there, d'you think?'

She chuckles and hands around the cheeses and wine. 'I'd imagine it must do. Maybe not so much to the top floor, but definitely to the one above. It was empty for years, actually. Someone only moved in a few months ago.' She grins and passes around more samples. 'They must *love* cheese, is all I can say.'

'Yes, they must,' I agree. We finish our samples and wine, and naturally, the chunk of Brie de Meaux I feel obliged to buy sets me back a few quid. But I shall relish every morsel, I reflect, as Penny and I share a taxi home.

'Fancy coming in?' she asks as we pull up at her block.

127

'We could round things off with a G&T. I even have lemons. And ice!'

Normally I'd have enjoyed ending the evening in her cluttered flat with the beaded curtains and twinkling chandelier, the shelves teetering with artefacts and hand-crocheted blankets strewn about. But our afternoon boozing has knocked me for six, so I thank Penny for her offer, deciding instead to take myself home and soak in a deep bath.

There I wallow, inhaling the mandarin scent of my favourite bath oil and wondering if Estelle Lang enjoys her sojourns to the stinking love nest. Perhaps it adds a certain piquancy to their sex life? He swears they're still not living together, so maybe she has a flat of her own in town somewhere, or is still living in Edinburgh. He hasn't divulged, and I wouldn't dream of asking i.e. giving any indication that I give a stuff about their domestic arrangements. But now I'm wondering: does he take the cheese smell with him when he visits her, stuck to his clothes and hair?

These thoughts are immensely pleasing as I towel myself dry, pull on soft cotton pyjamas and climb into bed. Picturing Andy choking on Camembert fumes, I slide into a blissful, booze-induced sleep.

Chapter Fifteen

Wednesday, August 7

Halfway through the week already, and *still* no hint from Rose as to what kind of new role she has in mind for me. Although, in her defence, she's been crazily busy and hardly in the office due to all her meetings and press interviews and whatnot.

Now, I'm starting to wonder if she has me earmarked for working with these new teams of youngsters in some capacity. Not as their *mentor*, not running these 'platforms for innovation', as she keeps calling them, but perhaps as an older, wiser (ha!) participant to help to keep things on track? There must be some benefits of not being young anymore, e.g. *the accumulation of life experience. Being (fairly) unflappable when things go wrong.* Maybe Rose sees me as the wide old sage who'll inspire the youngsters to come up with innovative new product lines without tumbling into bickering and disarray.

I like to think I'm pretty good with young people. After all, it's not so long since Spencer was living here and I was having to deal with his teenagery behaviour. We rubbed along pretty well, apart from the brief period from when he was around thirteen to eighteen, which I realise now is *not* such a brief period. He was capable of being a royal pain in the arse, burning his French jotters in the garden and patronising me by patiently explaining the situation in Palestine, as if I had the mental capacity of a sea sponge. But we staggered through it eventually, and apart from that, I worked with numerous youth groups in theatres over the years. And if I learnt one thing, it's that young people are generally fine – and can actually be lovely to be around – if you're not their mum.

Anyway, at least my prospects are looking hopeful, whereas Isla has just been given the startling news that the museum, where she has worked for fifteen years, looks set to close early next year, if visitor numbers don't improve. She sounds terribly stressed, so I persuade her to leave her kids to their own devices for a few hours, and to come over to mine for the evening.

She looks tired and drawn as I make us pasta and pour her a glass of wine.

'I'm not sure management have it in them to change the way we do things,' she says, swirling tagliatelle around her fork at the kitchen table. 'They're so set in their ways, and we all know we can't compete with the big, exciting temporary exhibitions – the crowd pullers like Coco Chanel, Frida Kahlo or a Tyrannosaurus Rex. And so we end up just pottering along, the way we always have done. I can't imagine that changing.'

'Yeah, I can see that. God, Isla. It's so sad, though.' I picture the natural history department, which she oversees, and which consists mainly of stuffed animals from Victorian times. It's dated, yes, but charming; like stepping into a bygone era with its reverential atmosphere and smartly uniformed staff. Spencer used to love it whenever I took him there, and Izzy does too, although she used to find the stuffed animals a little scary when she was very young.

'I do realise taxidermy isn't sexy,' Isla adds. 'It can actually make people angry these days. We try to explain that the animals all died of natural causes and have historical value but there's no appeasing them sometimes.'

My kind, gentle friend seems pretty worked up, and I feel powerless to help.

'What about some kind of fashion event?' I suggest. 'Could the costume department pull something together, get the place talked about again?'

'Actually, I suggested that,' Isla says. 'The trouble is, the really popular stuff tends to be mid-Fifties onwards and we don't have much from that era. The collection's mostly Edwardian and Victorian, and I know plenty of people love that too. But it just doesn't have that mass appeal.'

'Well, maybe Penny could help?' I add. 'She probably has a few original pieces stashed away, and she definitely has the knowledge and the expertise. And I'm sure she'd be happy to at least come in for a chat . . .'

'I'll talk to management,' Isla says, perking up a little now. 'Fashion would be great. We really need some kind of event to bring in younger visitors.' She smiles. 'Let's face it, taxidermy probably has a bit of an image problem. No one's excited by an ancient beaver with moth-eaten ears, clinging to a tree stump.'

'Is Tinder really that bad?' I ask.

She laughs. 'It's just not what people are looking for on a day out. If they're into natural history they expect biospheres and simulated volcanic eruptions. And if it's history they love, they want to be transported through reconstructed Pictish villages with authentic smells of early latrines.' She takes a big swig from her glass.

'*That* sounds fascinating. Even Spencer would come home to see that. Remember when I took him to that museum in Edinburgh and he saw a pickled human penis in a jar?'

'God, yes!'

'He talked about that for about three years afterwards. For a while it felt like part of the family. I suggested we should start sending it a Christmas card.'

'That's it,' Isla sniggers. 'That's *exactly* what we need. A severed member to bring in the crowds . . .' She grins at me, and we do that telepathy thing that only close friends are capable of.

'I wonder where we could get one?' I muse, getting up as my phone starts ringing. I show Isla the name displayed: *Andy.* She splutters as I accept the call.

'Hi,' he says, 'is this a good time?'

'Actually, Isla's here at the moment.'

'Oh. I won't keep you a minute—'

'We were just talking about severed penises. Peen-*eye*. What *is* the plural, anyway?'

'Huh?' A sharp exhalation. 'I was hoping to talk to Izzy, but I'm guessing she's still away?'

'She's back on Saturday,' I say, thinking: I'm sure I told him this.

He sighs. 'So, how she's getting on? Have you heard from her?'

'Yes, of course I have. She's having a great time.'

'That's good.' Andy pauses. 'So, she's having lots of fun?'

As I've just stated, yes. 'Sounds like it. She's loving being in the caravan.'

'Ah, that's good. I've missed her, though.'

'Yeah, I'm missing her too,' I say briskly, eager to finish this call. It always puts me on edge when Andy slips into this 'can we be mates?' kind of tone, which I've noticed creeping in recently.

'I'm hoping to nip down to see Spence soon,' he adds, 'but he's always so busy . . .'

'Yes, I know he is.' *Stop trying to elicit sympathy, idiot.* 'So,' I add, 'how are things up there at the loch? Are your parents okay?' I know he loves it up there normally; bracing waterside walks are very much his thing.

'Yeah, everyone's fine.' He pauses. 'But the set-up hasn't been quite what I expected.'

'In what way?' Now my interest is piqued.

'Well, you know there are these new lodges, and me and Izzy had been allocated one?'

'Yep.' The bespoke quilts, the log-burning stoves and all that.

'Somehow, there'd been a mix-up with numbers and when it turned out to be just me, without Izzy, I was put in a tent in the garden and you know what the midges are like up here.'

'Oh.' A smile tweaks my lips. 'So, you've been bitten, then?'

'Eaten alive,' he bemoans. 'Scratching all night. Can you believe I only brought shorts with me? Stupid, I know. I've tried all the lotions but you know what I'm like, how I react so badly. Once I'm bitten I get the wheals and the blisters . . .' What a pity, I muse, that Estelle isn't up there to witness her lover, clawing at himself in a tent.

'Couldn't you just come home early, if it's that bad?'

'The party's tomorrow. It's a huge deal to them and I've promised to help with the barbecue.'

Ah, of course. He does enjoy showing off at the coals, grappling sausages in his manly way. 'Ah, I see. Well, like I said, Isla's here so I'd really better go.'

'Okay but, um, I wondered if we could talk for a moment—'

'What about?'

'It's just, I'm feeling pretty bad, you know. And I just thought maybe—'

'I'm sorry, but I'm not about to drive up to Loch Fyne with calamine lotion,' I cut in. 'Borrow some trousers or wrap yourself tightly in cling film. Can midges bite through that?'

'I'm not sure,' he mutters. 'But, Viv, I just wanted to tell you—'

'Bye, Andy,' I say quickly. 'Goodbye.'

Friday, August 9

Home and shattered after a full-on working week. It's so tempting to fall on my laptop, tip wine down my neck and spend the evening googling Estelle Lang. But I shall resist. Instead, I make a pot of virtuous mint tea and google: *Can midges bite through material?*

Happily, the answer appears to be, 'Yes, unless it is extremely thick.'

Monday, August 12

Izzy is back from the Lake District, brown as a biscuit and full of the joys of the World's Most Disgusting Caravan (™) which, by all accounts, is a little piece of

134

Paradise in the Lakes. Sadly for me, she has also gone back to school today, so I haven't had much chance to hang out with her, apart from to supervise a brief episode of *Izzy Cooks!* last night, as she was keen to demonstrate Jules's home-made sourdough pizza method. As I swept up scatterings of flour she told me all about the friends she and Maeve had made at the caravan park, and how they were appalled to discover that Scottish kids return to school a month earlier than their new (English) mates. Of course, we started the holidays a month earlier than they did, but that did nothing to assuage the huff she was in this morning.

'It's not fair,' she muttered as we strode along to school. Despite Penny's insistence that I should look at the lollipop man 'in a different way', I could only look at him in an awkward way today, which I suppose *was* different to how I used to look at him – only not in the way she'd meant. I wonder if I'll ever be able to look at him neutrally again?

And so to work. As Rose is perennially involved in back-to-back meetings I still don't know what she has in store for me. Maybe she's forgotten that she sort of promised me something? Or has she changed her mind? 'You mentioned we should have a chat, a little while back?' I venture, taking her a coffee when she reappears briefly at her desk.

'Yes,' she says, nodding, 'and I promise I'll clear some time at some point.'

Which hardly sounds like it's going to happen anytime soon. So, after my initial excitement, it's a bit of a come-down really.

I try to stay perky, I really do. But the sky is a flat wash of gloomy grey, the summer holidays are over, Izzy and I haven't been away together and it doesn't look as if anything thrilling is about to happen at work. On top of all that, I seem to be having one of those perpetually-on-the-brink-of-blubbing days. They still happen to me, sometimes with no obvious trigger – although today I'm all too aware that it's my mother-in-law Cathy's birthday (being a wife, such dates have been indelibly inked into my brain). And although I have sent a card from Izzy, Spencer and me – conscious of it virtually pulsing with the omission of Andy's name – I'd usually call her too.

Right from the start, from when Andy first took me to Inverness to meet them, his parents were always welcoming and kind. Cathy fussed over me, unable to rest until I had sampled both her lemon drizzle cake *and* her cinnamon buns, and his dad, Will, used to jokingly call me 'Vivacious' ('That's what Viv's short for, right?').

Our visits to their place were always fun, with wine flowing, and everyone talking over each other in that effusive way the Flint family has. *They're quite loud, aren't they?* my mum murmured, looking startled, after the first time our parents had all met.

To give her credit, Cathy has phoned me from time to time since Andy left, and I've done my best to stay in touch. It's all very delicately handled ('We do hope you're okay, Viv. We're very sorry . . .'), with both of us clearly doing our utmost to pretend that there's no awkwardness. Whilst Cathy has said that she doesn't understand why Andy 'did what he did' (she can't even bring herself to specify what that was), she adores all six of her children and, naturally, that's where her loyalties lie. These days, I always detect her relief when I pass the phone on to Izzy so she can have a nice, relaxed chat with her granddaughter.

In the work canteen, I pick at a soggy apple turnover

and scroll to Cathy's mobile number. Ridiculously, I am wondering whether Andy remembered her birthday, and managed to navigate Marks & Spencer to choose a blouse for her. Christ, does he even know her size? Does he know she shuns pastels and short sleeves? Would he be able to name her favourite fragrance (J'Adore by Dior) if someone pointed a gun at his head? Probably not, as I took care of roughly ninety-eight per cent of all gift buying for his family during our years together. The one time I rebelled, when I was up to my eyes with a Christmas production, he manfully took the reins and genuinely thought it would be okay to give his parents a sole *joint* present – of a tin of biscuits with a picture of Father Christmas on the lid. 'I thought they'd like them,' he'd said, looking hurt.

'If you ever give me biscuits, it's over,' I'd warned him, to which he quipped, cheekily: 'What, even dark chocolate digestives?'

Pushing such unwelcome thoughts from my mind, I make the call. Cathy answers, sounding pleased, but a little taken aback, to hear from me. 'Hello, Viv. How are you?'

'I'm good, thanks, Cathy. Just wanted to wish you a happy birthday.'

'That's very kind of you to remember.' *Of course I remembered. I've remembered for twenty-odd years!*

I clear my throat. 'Are you enjoying your day?'

'Yes, very much, thanks. We're just about to go out for lunch, actually.'

'Oh, I won't keep you . . .'

'No, it's fine,' Cathy says quickly. It feels like a punch, the realisation this awkwardness between us isn't just a temporary thing in the wake of the break-up. Of course, everything has changed, and it would be naive of me to expect us to be able to chat away, like in the old days, when she'd almost seemed like a surrogate mum. ('The old days.' Is that what they are already? If I'd known I'd have appreciated them more!) I can hardly believe I cried in her arms after my own mum died thirteen years ago. It strikes me, too, that this is a new and undoubtedly difficult situation for her; out of the six siblings Andy is the only one whose marriage has failed. By all accounts, everyone else's is blissfully happy.

'Did you have fun up at Loch Fyne?' I ask, in order to fill the lull.

'It was lovely,' Cathy says. 'We did miss Izzy, though. Everyone did. Such a shame she couldn't come . . .' She seems to catch herself then and tails off. I nudge the pastry crumbs together with my finger on the plate.

'I know, and I'm sorry. But she'd set her heart on going to her friend's caravan.'

'I understand that,' she says, and another pause settles over us. *Did you miss me too?* I want to ask, like a needy kid.

'Is she there now?' Cathy asks brightly. 'I'd love to say hi—'

'Who, Izzy? Um, no, she's at school—'

'Oh, of course she is. How silly of me. The holidays whiz by so quickly, don't they?'

'Yes, they really do!' It's clear now that this is how we have managed our conversations, since the split: muddling through the preliminaries before I've passed the phone to Izzy and everyone can relax. Whatever possessed me to call her from my work canteen?

'Thanks for the beautiful bracelet,' Cathy adds, which feels like another thud to the gut.

'The bracelet?'

'Oh.' I can sense her frowning. 'It's just, the turquoise colours are so you, I assumed you chose it.' What, like five months ago, when Andy and I were still together? Or does she think he keeps me on a retainer to take care of the choosing of gifts?

'No, I'm sorry, Andy must have picked it.'

'Right, well, it was lovely anyway,' Cathy blusters, sounding relieved when I explain that I'm at work, and I really must go now.

Andy must have got it together to visit a jewellery counter, I decide, as I head back to my own floor. Or maybe Estelle buys Cathy's presents now, and visits his parents to be festooned with cinnamon buns?

Chapter Sixteen

Tuesday, August 13

'When are we starting your life coaching?' Jules asks, as we meet while picking up our girls from after-school club.

I look at my friend, always perky and fresh, brimming with energy. I'm still feeling pretty crap after talking to my mum-in-law yesterday, and can't seem to be able to shake it off. 'Are you sure you want to take me on?' I ask.

'Yes, of course I do!' She glances at me as we leave school together. 'It's normal to feel a bit apprehensive before your first session but I promise you, it'll be great . . .' She smiles encouragingly. 'There's *so* much you can do, Viv. How about we get started this Saturday? Just be open-minded and ready to chat. Is eleven any good for you?'

I pause and consider this. Izzy will probably be out with Andy, I figure. And if he has alternative plans, he can change them and fit around me for once. 'Okay,' I say hesitantly. 'Do I need to prepare, or do anything—'

'You just need to be *there*,' she says, flashing another

wide smile, and by the time Izzy and I arrive home I've begun to feel grateful to Jules for being so insistent. Although I've certainly been coping better generally, I'm still prone to bouts of self-pity and emotional outbursts over the most ridiculous things.

By rights, I should have no tears left in me – but as the evening progresses I find myself blubbing at a video clip of a seagull being detangled by experts from a wire on a building, and thus saved; plus another of a bride and groom – whom I don't even know – having their photos taken outside a church (Q: How do you know if you're menopausal? A: When you start crying at unknown people getting married).

I'm not sure whether tonight's teary episodes are linked to Cathy's birthday yesterday, and having my present-sourcing duties torn away from me, or are just part of the general hormonal shitstorm that seems to be going on. If it's the former, I should be *pleased* that parental gifts are being taken care of. I'd hate to think of my mother-in-law's birthday being forgotten, or for her to be palmed off with biscuits, even in a fancy tin. However, it has also occurred to me that, if Andy is such a whizz at shopping these days, then why did I spend twenty odd years haring about town, sweating like a horse as I sourced presents for his entire family and their billions of children, not to mention wrapping them with fancy bows?

'Mum?' Izzy cuts into my thoughts. She has just had her bath, and is pulling on her pyjamas as I gather up her dirty laundry.

'Yes, love?'

She frowns at me across her room. 'Why are there tears in your eyes?'

141

'It's just sweat, love. I'm hot . . .'

'You're sweating out of your *eyes*?'

I force a laugh. 'I know. Weird, isn't it?' I rub at them, and quickly tuck her in and kiss her, relieved when no more quizzing comes. And it occurs to me, as I head downstairs, that I lost so much in all those years I spent with Andy: my spirit and, latterly, my dignity, plus all that time I spent running around, being the dutiful wife. Even if I'd fancied having a ruddy affair of my own, I'd never have had the opportunity. I was too busy choosing sheepskin slippers for his dad and a Winnie the Pooh mobile for his niece.

Wednesday, August 14

As Izzy has been invited to a friend's house for tea, I have a little extra time on my hands after work. With a rough plan to spend too much money on unnecessary items, I detour to the vast shopping mall on my way home.

Not being a huge shopper generally, I rarely venture into its enclaves. However, occasionally I am seized by an urge to be somewhere dazzlingly artificial, with bland music playing, where you only have to set foot in a store for young women to hurtle towards you with fragrances to try.

The cosmetics hall here has a very different vibe to that wood-panelled department store where I was fussed over by pansticked ladies on my sixteenth birthday. Here, the atmosphere is more 'skincare lab' than 'we cake stuff onto your face'. While I'm not expecting to *shop* my way out of my current malaise, everything is so shiny and beautiful and heavenly-scented that my spirits begin to lift immediately.

At an upmarket skincare counter I give the sales adviser – thankfully a properly grown woman, and not a mere child – carte blanche to start dabbing her wares onto me. She has one of those cheery faces you warm to immediately, and her rosy complexion is certainly a good advert for a decent moisturiser.

'You have lovely skin,' she assures me. I wait for her to add, 'For your age', or even, 'For someone whose appearance is clearly not a priority', but nothing else comes. Instead she sets to work, demonstrating the youth-giving properties of serums, eye creams, moisturisers, masques and something called a highlighter which, apparently, is making me glow like a halogen bulb.

'What d'you think?' she asks, smiling brightly as she hands me a mirror. I blink at my reflection, taking in my revitalised skin before noticing – Christ! – a ruddy black whisker sticking out of my left cheek. Instinctively, I go to yank it out.

'Ooh, hang on a sec.' The woman produces a tiny pair of scissors and hands them to me.

'Thank you.' I snip it off. 'How embarrassing,' I add.

'Not at all,' she says with a dismissive wave of her hand.

'Honestly, I didn't know it was there.'

'It's these lights in here,' she says, as if they are to blame for accelerating its growth, like the Glo-faster lamp my dad bought, in the hope that it would boost his tomatoes in our greenhouse.

'I think it's more my time of life,' I say with a smile.

'God, tell me about it,' she says.

I turn and study her seemingly flawless face. 'Do you get them?'

'All the time,' she says with a chuckle. 'Have to give

myself a good going-over with the tweezers every time I leave the house.' She pauses. 'But it's not all bad, is it, this mid-life business? I love it that I can blame any bonkers behaviour on my hormones being out of whack.'

So cheered am I by this woman's positivity, I find myself slipping into dream customer mode as she recommends the products I might like to buy. 'The super-charged Vitamin C capsules make a visible difference . . .'

'Hmm, yes, I'll take those . . .'

'And the hyaluronic microspheres help with plumping . . .'

Plumping: not so great arse-wise but facially, yes.

'Maybe a gentle exfoliant to refine the surface texture? I call it a holiday in a pot.'

Well, I haven't had a holiday this year, have I? Sold!

'Have you thought about hands?' she asks now.

'Hands?' I repeat, holding up mine for inspection. Whilst not quite the claws of a crone, they could certainly do with attention.

'Deep-nourishing serum is big news right now,' the woman explains. And so it goes on, with the goodies stacking up rapidly – the toners and sheet masks and ampoules of joy, giving me an almost sexual frisson as I picture Andy's face. Not because I'd ever want to do it with him again – I wouldn't, even if he were the last man on earth, begging me with a million quid stuffed in a pillowcase. No, the source of my pleasure is in imagining how aghast he would be, if he could see me now – spending something akin to the monthly grocery budget on my addled face.

As I glide out of the store, clutching my crisp white paper carrier bag, it occurs to me that perhaps the woman's rosy glow was in fact induced by the commission

144

she was racking up rather than any personal skincare regime. But what the hell, she earned it, and I'm boosted – to the point at which I have already decided to arrange a little get-together tomorrow night.

So what if I'm now bankrupt? If I had to justify my spending – which I don't, and never will have to ever again – I'd just say my hormones were thoroughly to blame.

Thursday, August 15

Isla is here for dinner on this warm summer's evening, along with Penny and Hamish, her boat-dwelling boyfriend. My thinking was that we could sound out Penny about whether she'd be willing to offer her fashion expertise, and possibly even help come up with potential events to put on at the museum. Apparently, things are so dire, there needs to be some kind of urgent action plan.

Izzy was chuffed to be allowed to chop the vegetables for a huge goat's cheese lasagne, and we have eaten at the garden table. Thankfully, there's been no sighting of the Lesser Spotted Ludo tonight – and Izzy feels terribly grown-up to be allowed to stay up a little later than usual, on a school night too.

My plan, of course, is for Penny to be persuaded to go in for a meeting with the museum's management team. 'They're really excited,' Isla is telling her, when I reappear after taking a reluctant Izzy up to bed. 'Obviously, you were a huge player in Seventies high street fashion – but there's the Glasgow connection too. They're thinking a fashion event could really work for us, and maybe Girl

Friday could be a part of that. D'you have any original clothes from your shops?'

'Oh, they're all long gone,' Penny says.

I look at her. 'Really? Didn't you keep any original pieces at all?'

She shakes her head. 'It was a very long time ago, you know. We're talking forty years, remember?'

I nod, a little taken aback. I'd have thought she'd have kept a few key pieces; after all, the business was a huge part of her life. 'So what?' Hamish booms. 'This could really rev up some interest in you, Pen. Don't you think it could be a real opportunity?'

'An opportunity to do what?' she asks.

'To get involved, of course,' he says with a barely perceptible eye-roll.

'I don't need to *get involved* with anything,' she says tartly. 'I have quite enough going on in my life as it is.'

'But we're only talking about a meeting,' I say quickly, sensing things veering in the wrong direction. 'You could really help out here. You're a mine of information—'

'Oh, I don't know about that.' She purses her lips, and I decide to let the matter drop as Isla and I clear the table and we all make our way indoors.

'Why are you so against this, Penny?' Isla asks lightly. 'Maybe we were being presumptuous, but Viv and I thought you'd love to be involved.'

She throws me a quick look and laughs dryly. 'I very much doubt if I could help to turn around the fortunes of your museum, darling. That's all.'

Disappointment settles over me as I fix drinks for everyone in the living room. In her red top and shimmery gold, knife-pleated skirt, Penny cuts an extremely glamorous figure tonight. I'm utterly baffled by her reaction.

146

Perhaps she's just content with pottering around with Bobby, and can't see the point of involving herself with a faded institution?

Hamish beams around at us, flicking on the charm, the old let's-face-it-I'm-still-terribly-attractive demeanour with the glinting brown eyes and manly jawline that brings to mind 1970s aftershave adverts. In truth, though, I'm not entirely sure about him – although he clearly adores Penny. Over the year or so that she's been seeing him, I've heard all about his days as a highly successful composer of TV theme tunes. Anecdotes from his world travels and endless name-dropping pepper his tales.

It's not the fact that he lives on a boat that makes me wonder whether he was as successful as he claims. It's the fact that his boat appears to be held together by sticky tape and hope, and that I've been able to find nothing about him by googling. And if he was so renowned back in the day, why isn't he still composing now? I haven't mentioned any of this to Penny; it's none of my business, and she seems to accept him as he is (and, as has recently come to light, maybe I'm not the best judge of character anyway).

'Are you sure you wouldn't just come in for a chat, Penny?' Isla persists. 'They're really keen on a Seventies fashion angle. It's recent enough to bring back memories, and retro enough to be properly vintage. People our age – and older – will remember the styles, and fashion students will love it—'

'Sure,' she cuts in, 'I think it's a great idea. I just don't see what I could bring to it . . .'

'Oh, Penny,' Hamish exclaims. 'You were a Seventies icon. A pioneer! You'd be a fantastic resource—'

'I'm not a resource,' she says, her patience clearly fraying now, 'and I'm not just about the Seventies either.'

'Ah, here we go,' Hamish teases her. 'Don't get her started on the Rolling Stones thing.'

'What Rolling Stones thing?' Isla looks at him quizzically.

'You know.' He grins. 'You go and see them in concert and they insist on playing the new stuff – the entire latest album – when really all anyone wants are the old hits that everyone knows.'

Penny looks aghast at this, and we all fall silent for a moment. He has a point, of course; after Girl Friday's demise, apparently she tried to kick-start numerous other ventures. But her various stints at working as a fashion illustrator, print maker and interior designer seemed to fizzle out. Girl Friday was her golden era, which strikes me as incredible when she was a single mother to a young son at the time. *We don't know how she does it*, read a headline of a magazine interview with her back then, accompanied by a photograph of her in a fabulous white floppy hat.

Well, I don't know either. But she won't be persuaded, and, as everyone gets ready to leave, I realise there's no point in trying to cajole her. Once Penny's mind is made up, that's that.

Later, as I pull on my pyjamas, it occurs to me that perhaps her reluctance to be involved might simply be due to her age. Lines and wrinkles – the bugbears of ageing, which I spent an obscene amount on trying to eradicate yesterday – Penny never seems to give the time of day to. But perhaps she *does* care, deep down, and it's a sensitive issue? After all, she was a teenage model, then a fashion designer – and both careers are obviously appearance-focused. And maybe the idea of being called upon as an expert on Seventies fashion would make her feel, well . . . *old*?

Although it's entirely feasible, it's a possibility I'd prefer not to dwell upon. Because if Penny is insecure about ageing, what hope is there for the rest of us?

I apply an extra layer of my new night cream before going to bed.

Chapter Seventeen

Saturday, August 17

'So,' Jules says, 'let's start by talking about where you are now.' We are installed on my sofa, with a coffee each, having just started my first life coaching session. Of course, she doesn't mean where I am physically. She means mentally, emotionally – all the inner stuff.

With Izzy out with her dad for the day, I'd hoped that Jules would march right in and give me an extensive list of instructions for how I might fix my life. Now I realise it doesn't work like that. She has explained that a coach's role is to help you to identify where you are now, what's going on around you and where you would like to be. I guess it's a little like finding yourself in an unfamiliar city and stopping to ask a passer-by, 'Excuse me, d'you know the way to the railway station?' And they look thoughtful and say, 'Well, it might be that way. Or it could be down there. Which way do *you* think it is?' Which is sod all use, when you think about it. You'd miss your train.

'I don't really know where to start,' I admit.

'Well, we could talk about how you're feeling generally,' she explains, looking relaxed and about twenty-five in indigo dungarees and a fresh white T-shirt. 'And then we can take things from there.'

I clear my dry throat and adjust my position in an attempt to appear more at ease. 'Well, you know a lot's happened over the past few months,' I begin. 'Andy's gone. Izzy seems to be coping fine, which I'm grateful for and pretty amazed by, to be honest.' I hesitate, and Jules nods encouragingly. 'Shall I talk about work too?'

'Yes, if you'd like to. Feel free to mention anything that comes to mind.'

'Erm, well, there are huge changes going on. Since the rabbit food scandal the whole company is being given a major overhaul. It's a way of rescuing our reputation, I suppose. And Rose has promised that she has something in mind for me, something new and exciting, but she hasn't told me what that is yet.' I pause and sip my coffee. Even though we're friends, or possibly because of that, it feels odd, talking to her like this.

'How do you feel about that?' she asks.

'Oh, really happy,' I say. 'I'm so ready to move on with work, Jules. I feel like I'm treading water, to be honest, but I don't know what to do about it.'

'I'm not surprised, with everything that's happened in your personal life these last few months. Would you say that's taken priority lately?'

'Yes, definitely,' I reply.

'Okay,' she says. 'So, without thinking too hard, can you describe, in just a couple of words, how you would *like* to be, right at this moment, in an ideal world?'

I consider this for a moment. 'Less fat,' I reply.

A small smile plays on Jules's lips.

151

'Is that the right kind of thing?' I ask, feeling my cheeks reddening. It's ridiculous, to feel embarrassed in front of her. I'm sure she's heard people spouting all kinds of crazy stuff.

'There's no right or wrong thing,' Jules says kindly. 'Whatever you want to express is valid. So, can you expand on that a little bit?'

'Well . . .' I start, noticing the empty family-sized crisp bag lying on the armchair, which I must have delved into last night after Izzy had gone to bed. That's how meaningfully I guzzled those crisps; I have no recollection of stuffing them into my face. 'I suppose,' I add, lapsing into a silly jokey tone, 'I don't exactly feel like my best self right now.'

'Hmm. Well, that's understandable.'

'I feel like shit a lot of the time, actually,' I add, and Jules nods. Mercifully, she isn't taking notes or – horrors – recording me. 'On Thursday,' I continue, 'I went out and spent over two hundred quid on stuff for my face.'

She blinks at me. I know for a fact that Jules uses one product, which costs something like £3.99, from a supermarket. 'There's nothing wrong with treating yourself,' she says.

'Yes, I know – but it helps if you can afford it, which I couldn't, and anyway, I don't think it's terribly healthy to think, okay, if I slathered this stuff on, if I looked a bit better, then maybe my life would improve. Don't you think that's a bit . . . *desperate*?'

'Viv, I have to say, I think you're being pretty hard on yourself,' Jules cuts in. She looks at me for a moment. 'How about focusing on the aspects of your life that you feel you're handling well?'

I clear my throat and try to think. 'Well, I suppose I'm

getting along day to day. I mean, all the basic things happen. Izzy's well looked after; at least she hasn't been torn away from me by social services. I don't seem to have messed anything up too badly, so far . . .'

'You've handled being a mum, and your work life, amazingly well throughout the break-up,' she remarks.

'I'm not sure about amazingly well,' I say with a shrug, 'but from the outside I suppose we are functioning.' I'm starting to relax a little now. If nothing else, Jules has a wonderfully sympathetic manner, and one of those soothing voices that would be perfect for narrating audiobooks for bedtime.

'I'm glad you're giving yourself recognition for that,' Jules says. 'Can you think of any specific recent achievements you're proud of?'

'Proud of?' I frown. 'That might be overstating things a bit.'

'How about things you've enjoyed lately? Positive changes you've made in your life?'

I ponder this. 'Oh, I know – Izzy's become fanatical about cooking. This is all your fault!'

Jules laughs. 'She's a natural, isn't she?'

'She is. She loves playing TV chef in our kitchen. It's a regular thing with us now, her *Izzy Cooks!* shows. So that's been fun. I mean, it used to be virtually impossible to wrangle her away from pasta, noodles, rice – all the plain carbs. And now she's demanding manuka honey and Himalayan pink salt. Obviously, her mission is to ruin us financially . . .' I break off. Is that the best I can do? That I'm encouraging my daughter to vary her diet? I think of Penny, and her son Nick, and the Angel Delight ('He turned out just fine! What's the problem?').

Jules smiles. 'And you've been encouraging her and

facilitating all of that.' She'd never use that word normally: *facilitating*. For some reason, I want to laugh.

'Yes, I suppose I have.'

'How about we go back to achievements?' she suggests. 'Any more you can think of?'

'I don't think so,' I say.

'They don't have to be huge things. Small ones are important too. But it's important to recognise them because, so often, we don't even notice what we're managing in life. We just think it's part of being a woman, a mum, all that. We don't give ourselves the credit we deserve.'

I exhale, trying to dredge up something else.

'Take your time,' she says.

So that, in my sun-filled living room, is what I start to do, simply because Jules has asked me to. Never a natural rebel, I have always been happier to follow instructions. And I haven't achieved *heaps*; I don't save lives or speak at conferences. There are no pictures of me looking polished with a microphone, beaming confidently from behind a podium. When I was a child, I didn't do brilliantly at academic subjects; I passed my exams through sheer hard graft, wanting to please my parents and teachers and feel that I'd done well.

Maths baffled me. Biology was manageable, but physics and chemistry scrambled my brain. This frustrated my mum a little, as she was a science teacher herself. Dad, who ran his own wedding photography business, was more relaxed over school-related matters. I loved drama, mainly: writing and helping to stage school plays, rather than performing. I enjoyed college, opting for theatre studies, and had a wonderful career, or so I thought; but like so many women I allowed it to falter, and then fizzle

154

out completely. Perhaps I should have cast the net further when looking to get back into theatre after I'd had Izzy. Temping at Flaxico had seemed like an easier option at the time. I could kick myself now for lacking the determination to find a job I loved.

But then, Jules is encouraging me to think of achievements, and on a positive note, I am *managing*. Although I've had plenty of wobbly moments, I haven't entirely lost the plot since my marriage fell apart. Nor have I gone round and brained Andy in that cheesy flat. I haven't descended into a state of shabby personal hygiene, or got hideously drunk (at least, not too often). Meanwhile, what I *have* done is played with Izzy, helped with her homework and read her bedtime stories. I have weeded the borders, de-mossed the patio (no high pressure hose man for me!), cooked endless dinners and managed to shield Rose from countless journalists on the phone.

As far as achievements go, these are starting to feel distinctly barrel-scrapey. But Jules insists they are all significant, and listing them – whilst feeling slightly silly – at least proves that I haven't just been flailing around these past few months.

I've been surviving, all these little things seem to say. *I might have shelled out £49 on a tiny pot of 'microspheres', but I have also taken care of the important stuff and been getting on with my life.*

Before she goes, Jules seems to break her own rule by offering one small suggestion. 'Perhaps,' she ventures, 'you could talk to Rose on Monday and find out what sort of plans she has in mind for you?'

'I do keep asking,' I say, 'but she's always too busy to talk.'

'Could you ask her to schedule some time for you, then?' she asks with a wry smile.

I nod. 'Yes, of course.' Now, why didn't I think of that?

'And next time we get together,' Jules adds, 'we can talk about how that went. Because I think she's very lucky to have you.'

'Really?' I exclaim, blinking at her.

'Yes, really,' she says, hugging me as she leaves. It's even more effective than the rescued seagull video at making me burst into tears.

Chapter Eighteen

Monday, August 19

As it turns out, I don't have to ask Rose about her plans for me, because as soon as I sit down at my desk, she appears and asks if I can clear some time to chat today.

Today, just like that!

'Yes, of course.'

'Can you do lunch?' she asks.

'Sounds great,' I reply, trying to mask my surprise. 'Shall we go up together or shall I meet you there?'

'Oh, let's not eat in the canteen,' she says quickly. 'Let's go somewhere proper, away from this madhouse. I'll book.'

A proper lunch, out of the building, where normal people go! And Rose isn't even asking me to make the reservation! Already I'm picturing myself telling Jules about this at our next session: how we went somewhere fabulous where Rose laid out her plans for my glittering future.

In terms of achievements, it's a step up from 'managing to not brain Andy'.

Her choice of venue is surprising, but I take it as a good sign. It's a 'chef's theatre' place, where the tables are either in booths, or arranged in a semi-circle around the cooking area where the chef is chopping vegetables with aplomb. Actually, I'd say it was more like 'showing off'. A carrot flies above his head, to be grabbed mid-air and slammed down onto the chopping surface with a sharp thwack. Rose probably thought it would be 'fun', which suggests that she's in a positive mood. We are seated in front of the chef in the vast, under-populated restaurant, which he seems to take as a sign to rev things up a notch.

Immediately he starts to juggle in the style of a flame-thrower, not with torches, but leeks. In between giving him the odd polite smile, we try to peruse the menu, which is proving tricky as the chef has moved on to tossing sliced sautéed potatoes directly from the sizzling hotplate towards our heads. 'What are you doing?' Rose exclaims, ducking as one whizzes past her ear.

'It's fun,' replies the grinning chef, clearly misjudging our keenness to be pelted with scorching Maris Pipers as several more oily discs are pinged at us.

'What the fuck?' Rose mutters under her breath.

'I think we're supposed to catch them in our mouths,' I say, trying not to laugh.

'Fine, but can he stop now?' She gives me a wide-eyed stare, clearly expecting me to sort it. If this is meant to be some kind of test – i.e. to find out how I act under pressure – surely she knows me by now? Or perhaps it's a simple mistake, and she's so unused to booking restaurants that she genuinely had no idea where to go?

'Let's move tables,' I say, masterfully, summoning a waiter who ushers us to the safer environment of a booth.

We order, and Rose looks across the table at me, grimacing. 'I didn't realise it was this kind of place. Look at that.' She indicates a greasy mark on the front of her azure silk shirt from one of the flying potatoes. 'I'll send them the dry-cleaning bill. Who enjoys that kind of thing, really?'

'Teenagers on a date night?' I suggest. 'Honestly, I have no idea.'

'Maybe this shirt should go in as soon as we get back?' She frowns. 'I have a spare one in the office I can change into. Would you mind?'

Would I mind sorting it for her, she means. 'No, of course not.'

She smiles stoically. 'Anyway, sorry it's taken so long for us to get together . . .'

'I know it's been crazy busy lately,' I say.

'Just a bit.' She smiles ruefully. Despite her tendency to use me as an all-round fixer, I like and admire Rose. I know she's at least a decade younger than I am – barely forty, I'd say, although she keeps her age under wraps – but there's something oddly ageless about her. I can imagine her organising her playmates with formidable determination when she was nine years old. 'So, lots of things are happening,' she start as bowls of uninspiring noodles are set before us. I suspect all the effort goes into the performance aspect here, rather than the actual cooking. 'I'm especially excited about the platforms for innovation,' she adds.

I nod and spear a slithery noodle. 'I think it's a great idea to bring new life into the company. I know we do our own consumer research, but there's nothing like having young people involved right from the ideas stage all the way through to design, packaging, the whole lot.' I pause, actually quite impressed with myself. I believe it, though, about the benefits of bringing young people in. Flaxico has been a creaky old organisation, as huge and unwieldy as a shabby ocean liner, for far too long.

'I agree, absolutely,' Rose enthuses. 'But they'll need careful management to bring out the best of them. We can't just shove a bunch of youngsters into a room and hope for the best.'

'No, I can imagine that could spiral out of control,' I say, remembering the time I let the sixteen-year-old Spencer and his mates 'take charge' of a barbecue in our garden and foolishly took my eye off the ball. They had somehow got hold of about fifteen types of meat and fish – I suspected they had plundered the freezers of everyone they knew – which was served in states varying from barely defrosted to burnt black. The boys tanked into a load of beers (illicitly) and one of them threw up all over the patio. I overheard one of Andy's doctor pals muttering, 'Isn't anyone in control of this thing?'

All valuable experience, I'm thinking now as I wonder if my hunch was correct: that Rose is working up to suggesting that I might step into one of the mentoring roles. Otherwise why would we be here, talking about the new young teams she's planning to take on?

'Didn't you used to work in theatre before you came to us?' she asks.

'Yes, that's right.'

'And what did you do exactly?' It's the first time she's ever thought to ask. I was never formally interviewed for the PA job; Rose just gave it to me after a perfunctory chat when the vacancy came up.

'Stage management,' I reply, 'which meant everything really, apart from performing, as most places had pretty small teams.'

'So you're used to supporting people, assessing their needs?'

What does she think I've been doing for her, these past five years? 'Yes, definitely,' I reply. She chats on a little more about the new product lines she's hoping to launch, assuring me that the bunnygate fallout seems to be fading. And now I'm thinking: there are definitely gaps in my knowledge, if I were to head up a group of young employees. I'd need to learn about food technology, budgeting, every stage of production. It would be a huge learning curve for me, but doable. *She's lucky to have you*, Jules said. And I decide that, as Rose clearly hasn't brought me here for the food, this is my chance to sell myself.

'I think I'm the ideal person for this kind of thing,' I say, as our greasy bowls are whisked away.

'Really?' She looks pleased, but surprised.

'Yes, I do. You know, people are always moaning about youngsters today, how unmotivated they are – all these pampered snowflakes a mere unripe avocado away from mental collapse . . .'

Rose smiles in recognition. Although she doesn't have children, occasionally she mentions her nieces as if they are a species of exotic bird that she admires, but doesn't fully understand. 'I have to say, I've met a few who fit that description.'

'But most kids aren't like that really,' I add. 'My son and his friends are all working hard. They care about their futures and the wider world, and they're out there, getting their lives together.' I pause for breath. 'They're just a little different to us.'

161

'In what way?' She seems genuinely interested.

'Well, they expect a lot, you know? I don't mean in an entitled way. I mean in terms of things being just right. For instance, my son's girlfriend makes jewellery and sells it on Etsy. She knows her customers are just like her – that they don't just want a bracelet stuffed in a Jiffy bag. They expect a beautiful hand-written note with their purchase, written with a quill . . .' Rose chuckles. 'They care about ethics,' I add, 'and sustainability . . .'

'Do they?' she asks, looking amazed.

'Yes! They're passionate about environmental issues and they boycott big, tax-avoiding conglomerates. Imagine that, that they think about tax, at twenty years old!'

'That *is* impressive,' she says thoughtfully.

'So, if you're suggesting I work with these young people, I'd like you to know I'd be delighted—'

'Oh, I wasn't thinking of that.' She smiles tightly and blinks at me.

'Weren't you?' Hotness whooshes up my neck.

'Um, no, not *exactly* . . .' Her jaw seems to tighten as she looks around the restaurant. The only customers who appear to be appreciating the potato-throwing routine are two almost identically dressed girls with silken black hair, who are sitting directly in the chef's firing line. 'I was thinking I'd like to see you in a more . . . visible role, though,' she adds.

'Right,' I say, nodding. 'Well, that would be great. I do feel I'm ready for a new challenge.'

'Yes, I can see that. But it wouldn't be working with young people.' She sips her water.

'Oh, really?' I'm trying to appear positive and open to all kinds of possibilities.

'No, the way I see it, you'd be working more with . . .'

What, for crying out loud? 'Older people,' she says. 'I mean people – women – more of . . . *your* sort of age.'

I stare at her over the plastic tray bearing smeary bottles of soy and chilli sauce and a bunch of paper-wrapped chopsticks in a lacquered pot.

'My age?'

'Yes,' she says, brightening now. 'The way I see it, inclusivity will be all-important from now on. We'll have our young, vibrant teams, the ones pushing us forward with exciting ideas, fizzing with energy.' I nod, aware of a tightening in my gut. 'But, as a company, we also have to . . .' It's almost imperceptible, the wince that flickers across her face, but I definitely see it. 'Well, we can't be seen to be discriminatory,' she adds.

'No, of course not.'

'So, we might as well face the fact that we'll always have older people working for us too.'

'Erm, yes, I suppose we will.' Dear God. Is the lower basement going to be converted into a euthanasia clinic?

'So, what I'm thinking,' she goes on, 'is that we should appoint someone to address the issues that these women are facing every day of their lives.'

I must look baffled, because Rose seems to realise that she's being less than clear. 'What I'm saying is that I'd like to appoint a Menopause Ambassador.'

At first, I assume I misheard. 'A Menopause Ambassador?'

'Yes, to have one-to-one chats with anyone who's at that life stage, and then assess their needs, so we can fully support them.'

'Erm, how would we do that?'

'Well, we'd find out whether they're comfortable at work, temperature wise . . . you *do* look quite hot, Viv, if you don't mind me saying. Are you feeling okay?'

163

'Yes, I'm fine,' I say, trying to radiate how comfortable I am, how effective my body is at regulating its own temperature.

'And they'd talk to everyone individually about what they might need, such as, um, a fan on their desk, or to sit near an open window.' She beams at me. 'They might want to talk about issues like, erm, aches, pains and, uh, any intimate problems they're facing. Problems *at home*.' Problems in their pants, does she mean? Is that the kind of 'home' she's referring to? 'Talking always helps, doesn't it?' she adds. 'Knowing you're not alone?'

'Oh, yes . . .' But not at work. Not with an 'ambassador'.

'We could have lunchtime talks, question and answer sessions, experts brought in,' she continues, really getting into her stride now.

Hmmm, like an endocrinologist-type expert? I could ask the ever-sympathetic Dr Andy Flint to pop in!

'So,' she adds, 'that's the kind of role I have in mind. What do you think?'

I pause and drain my water glass. So this is my future. At night I lie there, wet as a trout. And by day she wants me to be the Hot Flush Lady, so whenever any woman 'at that life stage' sees me approaching, they'll think, *Shit, here's Viv. Quick, talk to me, make it look like I'm busy so she doesn't ask me if I'm experiencing vaginal atrophy and finding intercourse difficult.*

It might be well-meaning. Hell, maybe some women would relish that sort of role in the workplace. But I don't want it to be me.

'I'm really not sure,' I murmur. 'I need time to think—'

'I should make it clear,' Rose cuts in, 'with this being

164

a new idea, a pilot scheme if you like – I'm afraid there wouldn't be a change of grade, or a salary increase.'

'Oh, really?'

'Yes, because it's not actually a new job. Everything else would stay the same.'

'So . . . I'd still be your PA?' I ask, trying not to sound appalled.

'Oh, yes, absolutely. This would just add an extra layer of responsibility and an enhancement of status.'

I stare at her, not knowing how to respond. She smiles briefly and checks her tiny gold watch, then summons the waiter to bring our bill. 'Think it over, will you?' she says, whipping out her company credit card. 'Because I'm very much hoping that person could be you.'

Chapter Nineteen

Later that evening

Well, bloody hell, that serves me right for getting ideas above my station. A mentor indeed! What the hell was I thinking? I'm a PA and that's that. I might as well get used to the idea that no one's going to offer me a fantastic job on a plate.

Anyway, there's plenty going on in my life without a new, complicated position to get to grips with. I told Jules I was 'stuck' and 'ready for change'. But my life *has* changed; it's always changing, more than I want it to sometimes. For instance, in terms of the inhabitants of this house, first we had:

Me, Andy, Spencer.

Then: Me, Andy, Spencer, Izzy.

Then: Me, Andy, Izzy.

Then: Me, Izzy.

And now: Me, Izzy . . . and *Ludo*.

It's just temporary, mercifully, but the minute Izzy and I arrived home this evening, Tim appeared at the door, gripping his surly son firmly by the hand and saying, 'Viv, I'm so sorry but we think – I mean, we're pretty sure Chrissie's in labour . . .'

'Is she okay?' I asked, alarmed. 'It's early, isn't it?' We often chat in our back gardens and she's been keeping me up to date. I've felt sorry for her, actually. From being voluntarily laissez faire regarding Ludo's antics (read: rampant destruction), lately she's just seemed steamrollered by it all.

'She's thirty-seven weeks,' Tim said. 'I'm going to take her to hospital now. The problem is, my parents had planned to come and take care of Ludo but they're still on holiday, not due back till Wednesday night. There really is no one else I can ask.'

'Of course he can stay with us,' I said, reaching for his hand. 'It's no problem.' Ludo looked decidedly unimpressed, and Izzy was studying him with interest as if he might suddenly launch into an exotic dance. 'Come on in, Ludo. Have you had dinner yet?' He shook his head.

'Sorry,' Tim muttered. 'We haven't managed to get anything together . . .'

'Don't worry, I'll fix something. Just get off to hospital, okay?'

He smiled bravely and gave me a quick, awkward hug. 'Thank you so much. I'll call when we have news.'

'Can't I come, Dad?' Ludo whined.

'You can't go to hospital,' Izzy retorted, 'when your mum's having a baby. Come in with us.'

So here he is, still clutching his small tartan rucksack, peering around our kitchen in the manner of a health and safety officer who is finding the premises sorely lacking. Admittedly, standards are lower here than at his place. Potatoes are creating their own little sprouty jungle in the vegetable rack, a load of non-perishable groceries has been sitting on the worktop for two days, waiting to be put away, and a box heaped with bottles is parked by the back door, awaiting recycling. I pour the kids glasses of orange juice, prattling on about how school is, and what does he think of their new teacher (Izzy and Ludo are in the same class, although you'd never know it by all the interaction that's going on). Really, I'm just jabbering away, filling space, leaving no gaps for him to start quizzing me about divorces again.

After my lunch with Rose, what I'd dearly love is to flop onto the sofa with a cool flannel placed on my forehead, before adjourning to bed. I want to lie there, alone – ideally for two weeks, with drinks and snacks brought to me by a dashing waiter, as if I'm on one of those all-inclusive holidays that Andy never let us go on ('They're for people with no imagination,' he reckoned. Copious food and unlimited cocktails to tip down my neck? I've always thought they sound heavenly). However, the kids must be fed and, aware that Ludo is out of sorts – understandably, as his position of Lord of the Manor is about to be usurped by a hollering baby – I must rise to the challenge of bashing a meal together for them.

'What d'you like to eat, Ludo?' I ask as I start to put the groceries away.

It seems ridiculous that I know so little about this child who is the same age as my daughter and has lived next door for the past three years. However, despite Chrissie's suggestions that they should play together (why? Because they are small humans of roughly the same size?), it has always been apparent that that would never be a happy situation for anyone.

'Dunno,' Ludo says.

I try again. 'If there's something you really like, we might have it in and I can make it for you.'

Silence descends. Izzy glances at me, a small smile playing on her lips.

'What d'you like, Ludo?' she prompts him.

'Cola bottles and fried eggs,' he replies.

'Oh. You mean a drink of cola with your fried eggs?' I ask. Brilliant. That's easy. We always have eggs – my whole family has always been mad about them, in all forms – and although we don't have cola, I'm sure I can palm him off with the rather flat lemonade in the fridge.

I open it and reach for the big plastic bottle. 'I mean cola *bottles* and fried *eggs*,' Ludo barks.

'Yes, I'm just getting the eggs out too.' I place them, along with the lemonade, on the worktop. Izzy is sitting on a wooden chair, swinging her bare legs, observing the proceedings with fascination.

'Not those kinds of eggs,' Ludo retorts.

I look at him, uncomprehending. 'What d'you mean, love?' *Duck eggs? Quails' eggs? A Fabergé egg?*

'D'you mean those fried egg sweets?' Izzy asks levelly.

'Yeah.'

'And cola bottle sweets?' He nods, and Izzy turns to me: 'That's what he means, Mum. The *sweets*.'

'Ah, I'm sorry,' I say, feigning regret, 'but we don't have those in, Ludo. And I was actually thinking more, um, dinner-type food . . .'

'I could make something?' Izzy suggests.

Somehow, I'm not sure that Turkish tomatoes or even her sourdough pizza would be greeted with enthusiasm by our young guest. 'It's okay, Iz. Thanks, but I think we'll just have something simple—'

'I like . . . pancakes,' he announces.

169

'Pancakes?' I beam at him. 'I can do that. D'you mean the small, thick kind, or big and thin?'

'Big and thin.'

'Right! Pancakes it is then,' I announce, much to Izzy's surprise and delight. Normally, we only have them on weekends. 'Honey,' I add, 'could you go through and put on cartoons for you and Ludo while I make them?' I am aware of the children eyeing each other, thrown together by circumstance. Neither of them seems to want to go anywhere.

'I'll help you,' she says.

'I will too,' adds Ludo. I'm about to say *no thank you* but, hell, his mum has just been rushed off to hospital, and he's probably staying with us overnight – I'm not sure if he ever goes on sleepovers, I suspect no one ever invites him – so, to that end, I make a firm decision to be as kind and amenable as is humanly possible.

Gratifyingly, Izzy is happy for Ludo to do the mixing, and I turn a blind eye to the fact that batter is splashing everywhere. I do draw the line at letting him *fry* the pancakes, even though his mother regularly allows him to play with hot oil, by all accounts ('We don't say no!') – but that's not happening on my watch. However, I do let him choose his pancake toppings, catching Izzy's look of amazement as he rejects my suggestions of grated cheese and ham, opting instead to smear on Nutella *and* jam, plus a liberal sprinkling of granulated sugar.

On and on I fry, sweating like a short order cook, totalling what feels like about 200 pancakes (because he keeps asking for more) until the kitchen – and I – reek of burnt butter.

Ludo doesn't want a bath, and I'm not about to push him on the matter. Nor does he want a story or to clean his teeth, although I do insist on the latter. When his mother comes home, he might complain that our house is scruffy and we don't have his favourite gummy sweets. But by God, he will still be in possession of his teeth.

Tuesday, August 20

Chrissie has had an emergency caesarean, which was pretty shocking for both of them as apparently Ludo was born at home, with scented oils burning and Tim reading the poems she had selected beforehand. There was no poetry this time. However, mother and baby daughter (name yet to be announced) are doing fine, and I've communicated that Ludo is fine too, a delight to have around.

Chrissie wants me to stay here, Tim has texted, *prob overnight. She's just a bit shellshocked. So sorry. Is that okay with you?*

Of course it is, I assure him.

I drop off the children at school, both of whom barely spoke on the way, and hoping that Ludo is so far untraumatised by his stay with us. He shouldn't be. For breakfast he requested toast and Nutella, giving me a challenging stare when I caught him dipping a knife into the jar and licking it. Still, he didn't sever his tongue, so no harm done. And now, my spirits lift further as I drive to work, remembering that Rose flies to Beijing this morning for the start of an extensive tour of our Chinese customers, which will keep her out of my hair for two weeks. So, any further ambassadorial conversations will have to wait.

Later, as I collect Izzy and Ludo from after-school club,

Tim texts again to say that Chrissie still doesn't feel ready to be left at the hospital without him. So he'll be staying with her for a second night, parked in a chair at her bedside, and Ludo will remain with us.

Absolutely no problem at all, I assure him when he pops home, briefly, to see his son, and tries to show him photos of the baby (I try to compensate for Ludo's lack of interest by gushing madly over the blurry shots). And it really isn't a bother. After all, Ludo's grandparents are back from holiday tomorrow night, and surely Tim will be released by then anyway.

We have spaghetti for dinner, one of the few savoury meals that Ludo appears to regard as acceptable. While I'm knocking it together, he hoists himself up onto the kitchen table and is now sitting there, cross-legged, scratching at his white-blond hair and surveying Izzy and me like a little emperor.

'Would you mind taking your shoes off, please?' I ask.

'Why?' Ludo frowns.

Because this is my house and my rules. 'Well, your shoes have been on the ground, and we eat off this table.' I smile pleasantly. Surely that's a reasonable request?

He stares at me, radiating defiance. Maybe he's allowed to sit on the table with his shoes on at home. If he wanted to do a crap on it, would that be allowed too?

'Please take your shoes off,' Izzy says, like a prim teacher. I'm trying to act casual, stirring the tomato sauce as he *slooooowly* peels off one shoe, during which several new stress lines have etched into my forehead. He tosses it onto the floor with a thwack, and I scald myself as I'm draining their pasta.

'*Ow!*'

172

'Are you all right, Mum?' Izzy asks, alarmed.

'Yes, I'm fine love,' I say, teeth gritted as I hold my wrist under the cold tap and Ludo's second shoe slams to the floor.

Only twenty-four hours till Tim's parents get back, I remind myself later as I turn out their bedroom lights.

Wednesday, August 21

Day three of Ludo. I have taken to closing my eyes at certain points at work, willing Chrissie to feel amazingly well today, so she and the baby can come home, or at the very least, Tim can be released and scoop up their firstborn and return him to the homestead. Several colleagues have asked if I'm okay, as I look a little stressed. Belinda even appears with a present for me: a tiny portable fan for my desk.

Back home, Tim pops in again briefly, and it's all I can do not to throw myself at him and gather up Ludo's things, stuff them into his rucksack and shimmy them out of the door. But alas, Tim's presence is still required at the hospital and, in a flurry of sincere apologies, he zooms off again.

Still, his parents are back tonight, right? So they can take over the care of their grandson tomorrow.

Meanwhile, Izzy has become obsessed with Ludo's toothpaste. Apparently, Tim and Chrissie 'don't believe in' fluoride, as if it's God, or Father Christmas, and not merely a tooth-strengthening substance highly recommended by the NHS. So sugar-guzzling Ludo never has tap water (in case 'they', whoever 'they' may be, have put

173

fluoride in it) and his toothpaste is some vile-looking gunk made from sage.

No wonder the kid is reluctant to clean his teeth. What's wrong with mouth-freshening mint, for God's sake? The sage toothpaste's rich, herbal stench has permeated our entire upper floor.

Thursday, August 22

Our fourth Ludo day. As Tim's parents came back from holiday last night, the plan was for me to pick up Izzy and Ludo from after-school club and bring them home, as normal, and then the grandparents would appear as my saviours and whisk him away. However, Tim's father is apparently unwell with food poisoning, or possibly dysentery, so they are 'not up to' looking after Ludo right now.

Neither am I, actually. As we walk back from school, with him demanding to stop off for sweets, and complaining loudly that our favoured shop – rather than the one they usually go to – doesn't stock his required cola bottles/fried eggs, I pause to post a letter and inadvertently post my house keys as well.

'Call the postman,' Ludo commands, 'and get him to open it up.'

'He won't do that, Ludo. That's not how it works, I'm afraid.'

His dark eyes beam annoyance. 'Why not?'

'Because he only comes at certain times,' I mutter, panic juddering up my chest. Ludo squints at the notice on the postbox that reads: 'Next collection 10 a.m.'

'We could sit here and wait?' he suggests.

174

'No, we can't do that.'

He frowns. 'It's not that long. Look – it says he comes at ten o'clock.'

'Yes, but it means ten o'clock in the morning,' I explain, trying to sound in control of the situation and not at all frazzled.

'We can't wait here all night!' Izzy exclaims, looking up at me in alarm.

'Why not?' Ludo wants to know.

Oh, sure, we could nip home and fetch three sleeping bags and come back and lie here on the pavement all night, lined up, the way people used to sleep in tube stations when there was an air raid on, only without a tube station, or a war.

'Because we can't,' I say firmly, grabbing both of them by the hands and marching onwards, ignoring his witterings and stopping only to google and then call a local locksmith along the way. Back home, the three of us sit, mournfully, waiting for him to appear and let us in. If it were just Izzy and me, I'd call Penny or Jules and see if we could go round to either of their places, and wait there – but I'm not prepared to inflict our houseguest on either of them.

Ninety minutes later, when we all stomp into the house, Ludo marches across the kitchen to the glass recycling box and announces, 'You drink an *awful* lot of wine.'

Friday, August 23

Day ninety-seven of Ludo. At least, it feels like it. I'm starting to wonder if Chrissie, Tim and the baby are really still at the hospital, or have snuck off for a little holiday

175

– a 'babymoon' – without Ludo wrecking their fun. Who could blame them, really? Maybe they're planning to never come back? I'd probably do that, if I were them. I can't imagine Ludo taking well to Chrissie trying to establish breastfeeding (although apparently he himself was a keen boob-guzzler until the age of four, and would only be persuaded to stop when Chrissie fibbed that there was 'no milk left', that it was 'all gone'. Although she never says no, she's clearly not above lying through her teeth when desperation strikes).

I'm also a little suspicious of Tim's father's illness. Do people really contract dysentery on the Costa del Sol? My energies are flagging, and Ludo has already mooted the possibility of pancakes again. To ward him off, I decide to throw together whatever I can find in the fridge and present it to the kids as a picnic. As the days have gone on, they have at least tolerated each other, playing the odd muted game, watching cartoons together, inhabiting the same room without incident. On the rare occasions that Izzy has grumbled about him being here, I've explained that it's hard for Ludo, his parents disappearing like that, and this monumental change about to happen in his life.

'I want to have it outside,' he announces.

'Yes, that's what I mean,' I say. 'A picnic in the garden. It's a lovely evening for it.'

'Can we have crisps?'

'Yes, of course.'

'Orange squash?'

'Coming right up,' I say, smiling.

'D'you have straws?'

'I think so.'

'Curly ones?'

'We might have one lying about somewhere, I'll have a look—'

'And I want to eat on the grass,' he snaps, 'not at the table.'

'No problem.' *You can have your picnic on the grass, and then you can invade Poland, will you be happy with that?*

Perhaps, I decide a little later, as the three of us sit there eating together, it's just as well that Rose didn't view me as being suitable for leading teams of youngsters to greatness. What chance of success would I have if I can't keep a sole visiting seven-year-old under control? As it is, Ludo got hold of Izzy's knitted sandwich – which she wanted to be part of the picnic – and has now dowsed it in orange juice and thrown it over the fence, into his own back garden. As she yells in fury I scramble over the fence to retrieve it.

That's it, I decide as I clamber back. I've had enough. He needs to know what's acceptable and it's just not on, this rudeness, this behaving like—

'Hi,' Tim calls out, appearing at his back door and waving. 'We're back!'

About sodding time! 'Hi, Tim,' I exclaim, grinning. I'd never have imagined that the sight of a short, bald quantity surveyor would fill me with such joy.

He comes closer and beams over the fence. 'Hey, guys. Hi, Ludo! So, how is everyone?'

'Hi, Dad,' Ludo mutters.

'We're good, Tim,' I reply. 'We're great. How are Chrissie and the baby—'

Before he can answer she appears at the door, looking pale and drawn but blissfully happy, with their new, pink-faced daughter wrapped in a yellow blanket in her arms.

'Ludo, darling,' she cries, spotting him. 'Look, it's your new baby sister. Isn't she lovely?'

He eyes her across the fence as if she's showing him a new kettle.

'Hey, Ludo,' Tim blusters, sliding a hand over his shiny head, 'we'll come round so you can meet her properly. She's *so* looking forward to meeting you.'

It's lovely to see how thrilled Tim and Chrissie are and, naturally, my eyes brim with tears as I have a little hold of the baby. In fact I almost feel sorry for Ludo as we all coo and fuss over her. Her name is Lara. Tim and Chrissie gush thanks to Izzy and me for taking care of Ludo.

'So,' Tim announces, 'we'd better get you home, Ludes, and leave these guys in peace.'

He glances round at the scattered remains of our picnic. 'Don't want to come home yet.'

'C'mon, love,' Chrissie says, 'you've been here all week. Don't you want our family all to be together?'

'No.' Ludo shakes his head. 'No, I don't.'

Chrissie sighs and ruffles his hair. 'I guess you've had too good a time here, huh?'

'Yeah, I have.'

She smiles wearily. 'Well, look. Maybe Viv would let you stay one more night?'

Oh, no, no. I don't think Viv would like that.

'Maybe,' she adds, 'we could ask Viv if that would be okay, and you could come home tomorrow morning instead?'

Maybe Viv wouldn't think that was okay? I look at Tim with a tight smile, teeth gritted, as I transmit the message – *please take your son home* – which, thankfully, he seems to receive loud and clear.

178

'Nope, sorry,' he says, grabbing Ludo's hand, 'Viv's done more than enough for us this week.'

'Aw, Dad!' Ludo exclaims, but for once, a parent takes charge as his possessions are gathered, and as they leave I hear Tim asking, 'So, what did you like best at Viv and Izzy's?'

'When Viv put her keys in the postbox,' Ludo replies.

Chapter Twenty

Saturday, August 24

Viv and Izzy's, it is these days, which feels normal, I guess, to the point at which Andy seems like an awkward visitor whenever he comes to pick up our daughter. While Izzy's up in her room, getting ready for her day out with Dad, he and I are obliged to make chitchat.

Thank God there is always information to be exchanged about Izzy. 'Has she managed to shake off that cold?' 'Has that wobbly tooth fallen out?' He pings questions at me and I answer with curt politeness. 'How's she getting on with that natural history project?' he asks, sipping his coffee and leaning against the kitchen table.

'It's coming along really well,' I reply.

'Wetland habitats, is it?' Ah, so he's trying to impress with his knowledge of what's going on in her life (when he was here he never seemed to have a clue about school-related stuff).

'That's right,' I say, tempted to add, *She could start right here, by examining my bed after a sweaty night.*

But I'm not sure Andy and I will ever reach the stage where we can laugh about that.

A small silence descends. 'You're looking well,' he remarks.

I beg your pardon? 'Am I? Thanks.'

'Yeah, really well,' he confirms. Christ, is he my hairdresser now? Is he going to ask if I've been away? He, on the other hand, is not looking his 'best self' on this fine summer's morning. His hair is mussed up and outgrown, which is unusual for him, and clearly he hasn't got it together to shave for a couple of days (also unusual). Dark shadows lurk beneath his eyes, and his lids are heavy. I'd surmise that he's been up all night, shagging the foxy doctor, but there's a distinct lack of joie de vivre about him. But then, he'd hardly bound in, announcing that they had a magnificent session last night.

Maybe they've had their first tiff? They've been together for around ten months, by my reckoning. Long enough for cracks to have appeared in his best behaviour facade. By this point, he might have slipped into a habit of 'forgetting' to flush the loo (i.e. it's too arduous a task). There might even have been a flurry of careless farting. I'm still not sure whether she's living with him, or what their situation is, and I don't ask. The truth is, I still can't bear the thought of them together, and the less I know about their situation, the better it is for me. On a happier note, I have managed to not look at any of those Estelle Lang pictures for ages now, which I'm proud of. Maybe I should mention it to Jules as an 'achievement', when she arrives for my next life coaching session in an hour's time?

'Izzy, are you ready?' I call out. 'Dad's waiting for you, love.'

'Coming,' she replies, and I can hear her clattering

about overhead. They're only going to the cinema and for a curry. But a day out with her dad has to involve the packing of numerous items in her backpack, plus the careful selection of accessories, specifically hair-related, and she continues to refuse my offers of help.

Andy has finished his coffee, and our talk has turned to Spencer and his travels. Our son has spent much of the summer working at festivals, seemingly having a ball. Spain, France, Bulgaria: what it is to be young, and to be paid to do something you love. I should take a leaf out of his book. At least I have made a firm decision to turn down the Menopause Ambassador role, as soon as Rose is back from China. The idea of at best being seen to be patronising my colleagues, and at worst, attracting derision and hostility? No thank you.

Conversation is waning now. We have discussed our offspring at length and now I'm more than ready for him to leave; specifically to stop contaminating our kitchen table by resting his Levi's-clad arse on it. Funny how I use to lust after that butt, appreciating its cheeky curves, especially when clad in snug-fitting stretchy white boxers. Whereas now, if I think about it at all, I just imagine my booted foot colliding with it at speed.

'Hi, Dad!' Mercifully, Izzy has appeared and is ready to go.

'Hi, angel,' he says.

'Guess what. Chrissie had a baby!' she announces.

'Really?' he says, feigning interest. If it wouldn't delay him further, I'd be tempted to foist all the details – the emergency caesarean, Chrissie's cracked nipples, the early, mustard-coloured poos – onto him. For a medical man, he has always been oddly iffy about bodies (apart from Estelle's, obviously).

'Yeah,' Izzy says. 'She's *so* cute. Ludo stayed with us.'

'Did he? Wow.'

'For a *week*,' she adds.

'A week? How was that?' He glances, wide-eyed, at me.

'It was fine,' I reply. Is he planning to take his daughter out, or are we going to stand here yabbering away all day? My eyes flick to the wall clock. I'd prefer him to be well out of the way by the time Jules shows up. Occasionally, he has shown up when either she or Penny has been here, and the stilted politeness has been excruciating.

'The baby's called Lara,' Izzy adds, at which Andy smirks.

'Lara?' he says with a snigger, 'Not Cluedo, or Snakes and Ladders?'

I am dying of mirth here. Now please leave my house.
'What d'you mean?' Izzy asks, looking confused.

'You know,' Andy says. 'Ludo's a game, right?'

'Is it?' She frowns.

'Yes, it is,' I say quickly, fixing Izzy's small spotty backpack on her back as a signal to Andy that I've had quite enough of his company today. To make doubly sure he gets the message, I indicate the door with my eyes, in a similar way to how I communicated telepathically with Tim yesterday.

'Right, Iz,' Andy announces. 'We'd better be off.' I must be getting better at transmitting my thoughts in this way. Perhaps I'll arrive at a point where I don't have to say anything to Andy at all?

As soon as they've left, I flit about tidying the living room, grabbing at sweet wrappers that Ludo apparently managed to scatter about the place – why bother with bins when the floor will do? – then try to smooth down my rumpled hair and assume a calm, reflective manner.

The day is sunny and breezy, and I make a pot of fresh coffee and open the kitchen window, as if to blow away the invisible traces of Andy's visit. Chrissie is out there in their garden, sitting on their bench, feeding Lara. It's 11 a.m. She catches my eye and gives me a little wave, and I smile and wave back, then go through to answer the front door to Jules.

'Hey,' she says, smiling, 'you're looking well.' Coming from her, it feels like a genuine compliment.

'Thanks. I feel good, actually. Shall we go through?' I bring through our coffees and we settle on the sofa.

'So, how have things been since last week?' she asks.

'It's been kind of hectic,' I reply, filling her in on the Ludo visit, the posted keys, the endless negotiations required in order to get him to do anything, and how I've had little chance to put my mind to anything else.

'I'm impressed,' she says. 'That was some undertaking, but you coped, without any notice. You managed the whole thing brilliantly, it seems to me.'

'Thanks,' I say, a little overcome by her praise.

'It might be helpful to take a moment to really acknowledge what you've achieved,' she adds.

'Right.' I smile. 'Um, well, yes, I suppose I *am* pleased.'

Jules shifts on the sofa and pushes back her cropped hair. 'This might seem a little odd, but there's a technique I suggest to clients sometimes that can really help to create a sense of positivity.'

'What's that?' I ask.

'Can we go through to the kitchen?'

'Sure,' I say, intrigued as she follows me through.

184

She smiles encouragingly. 'Could you stand there, in the middle of the room, and say, "I'm brilliant"?'

I laugh involuntarily. 'Oh, Jules. Do I really need to do this?'

'You don't *need* to,' she says, 'and I know it goes against human instinct to praise yourself out loud like that. But go on – give it a try.'

I hesitate, sighing like a petulant child, before positioning myself in the middle of the floor. 'I'm brilliant,' I say in a resigned voice.

'A little louder, perhaps?' Jules suggests. 'With a bit more conviction?'

'I'm brilliant,' I say in a firmer tone. 'I'm *brilliant*.'

'Again, but louder.'

'I'm brilliant,' I announce, my cheeks burning now. It feels ridiculous, but why not do as she asks? What's the point of refusing when I'm supposed to be on this life coaching 'journey' with Jules, as she puts it? Some people – e.g. Andy – might scoff, but any port in a storm, I reckon. And no one forced me to do it. I asked for her help, and maybe it'll enable me to become stronger and better at speaking my mind – so I'll no longer endure Andy hanging about, drinking my coffee and saying I 'look well' when I can hardly stomach the sight of him.

'Say it again,' Jules commands.

'I'm brilliant!' I yell.

'That's better. Now, hop up on that chair and say it again, but louder. Really yell it this time.'

'You want me to get up on the chair?'

'Yes.'

'I might fall off!'

'I doubt it. Take the risk.'

Grinning, I clamber up and look down at her. She looks

185

so neat and pretty in her little blue shift dress with bare legs and flats. Like a woman whose life is together, I decide. Like someone who somehow manages to be lovely and widely liked, yet doesn't take any crap from anyone.

'Now really shout it,' she barks at me.

'I'm brilliant!'

'Up onto the table now.'

'*What?*'

'Get up on the table and shout it as loud as you possibly can.'

'The neighbours might hear.'

'Sod the neighbours.'

I glance to the window. 'Chrissie's sitting out there. I might scare the baby.'

Jules chuckles. 'Or she might be subconsciously infused with a message of female empowerment . . .'

'Or traumatised by a demented woman screaming . . .'

'Which'll stand her in very good stead growing up in a household with a big brother like that.'

What the hell, she's probably right. I kick off my shoes – outdoor footwear on the table is a bridge too far, even if I'm about to make a spectacle of myself – and climb up. 'I'm brilliant!' I roar.

'Shout it out,' Jules enthuses, gazing up at me. 'Think of how far you've come these past few months. Think of all the praise you dish out every day, to Izzy and Spencer and all your friends, and how that's helped to make them the people they are. And now celebrate yourself. Yell it as loud as you can from the top of your lungs. Yell, "I'm fucking brilliant."'

I laugh into my hands.

'Do, it, Viv—'

'I'M BRILLIANT!' I bellow. 'I'M FUCKING BRILLIA—'

186

I stop abruptly, staggering slightly as the kitchen door swings open. Penny is standing there in a bright pink dress, her mouth open in a delighted grin as she stares up at me. Beside her stands an unfamiliar man; a tall, dark-haired, clean-shaven and terribly handsome man, who looks *astounded*.

'Oh God, I'm so sorry,' I exclaim, scrambling down to the floor. 'It was only, I was just—'

'Don't apologise for anything,' Penny exclaims with a gravelly laugh. 'It's absolutely true, you know. And it's me who should apologise for marching in like that . . .'

'It's fine, honestly,' I bluster, face burning.

She beams at me, then turns to the bemused-looking man at her side. 'Viv, darling, here's someone I'd like you to meet. This is Nick, my son.'

Part Three

Moving On

Chapter Twenty-One

Twelve days later: Thursday, September 5

Rose isn't best pleased when I explain that the role of Menopause Ambassador isn't for me. I'd like to kid myself that it's due to a reluctance to 'be defined by my menopausal status' (a phrase I played around with when I was planning what to say). However, what it comes down to really is that, even if I did want to take it on – which I strongly don't – I'm not convinced that the women I work with would regard it as A Good Thing.

'I'm just worried it could come across as patronising,' I explain in her office.

Rose frowns across her desk. 'Why d'you think that?'

'Because . . .' I start hesitantly. 'I'm not convinced that women want to be approached about that kind of stuff at work, you know?'

'Why not?'

'Well, there'd be no getting away from the fact that the basic message would be, "Hello, you're a middle-aged woman, possibly menopausal, judging by the way you snapped at Belinda by the printer, and I saw you sitting there crying in your car in the car park the other day. And, actually, have you put on a little bit of weight lately? Around your middle? Maybe you'd like to talk about that?"'

'Oh.' Rose looks crestfallen. 'Do *you* cry in the car park?

Only occasionally. 'No, never,' I fib.

She smiles briefly. 'That's good to hear. And I do understand your reservations, but I'd imagined it would be more of a positive thing.'

'How would that work, though?' I ask, genuinely baffled.

'I just thought they'd like to feel supported.' *They*, as if we over-forty-fives are a different species.

'I'm not sure how we'd do that without making women feel singled out,' I say, trying to think of another way of putting it. 'You know all these school and college leavers who've been coming in for interviews?'

She nods.

'Imagine if we had an equivalent for them, like an Ambassador for Youth, who went around asking them how they're feeling generally, whether they're experiencing any difficulties in their personal relationships or body issues or whatever . . .'

She brightens. 'D'you think they'd value that? We could have one of those too!'

'No, Rose, I don't think they would. I think they'd find it weird and intrusive. And if they have issues concerning their job, or anything that's affecting their performance here . . .' I pause. 'That would be the mentor's job, wouldn't it? To support them with that?'

'Right, I see your point,' she says thoughtfully. While

Rose is undoubtedly highly talented when it comes to business negotiations, her people skills can be lacking somewhat.

'I'm delighted that you thought of me for the role, though,' I add. 'I mean, I'm flattered.'

'Well, you were my obvious choice.'

'Really?' Perhaps this is a good thing, I reflect; an indication that she views me as a decent communicator, and approachable – or least that I have a reasonably un-scary face.

'Yes,' Rose says, repositioning the phone on her desk unnecessarily. 'I know you don't talk about it much, Viv. You just work on and on without making a fuss. But I do often see you looking a bit hot.'

The whole drive home, it's playing in my mind: so that's how I'm viewed. Not as someone who's been doing her best at work, and who has managed the last few months pretty admirably, if I say so myself (despite having married an unfaithful clod), and who deserves to stand on the kitchen table shouting 'I'm brilliant!' She hasn't picked up on any of that. She just sees an unremarkable grafter who *works on and on without making a fuss*.

I'm still huffing internally over this, over-reacting perhaps, while I make pleasantries with the after-school club ladies as I pick up Izzy. It's still buzzing in my brain as we walk home, and Izzy is chattering happily about the model castle ('with lights in!') that they've been making from old boxes and junk at after-school club, and her eighth birthday, which is still many weeks away ('Can I have a party?').

All the while, I'm thinking, *So I don't make a fuss*. Would anyone actually enjoy being described in that way?

193

Not Jules, who has carved out an entirely new, successful career for herself and is clearly loving her life. And not Shelley, who I know makes a fuss on a daily basis – otherwise the numerous families that comprise her caseload wouldn't have anything like the support she ensures they receive. She deals with child protection issues, alcoholic parents, violent partners, neglect, poverty, mental health issues, drug addiction; she is a *walking fuss*. Isla, too, makes a fuss in her own persistent, focused way; I know she's refusing to sit back and accept that the museum may have 'had its day', as one of her colleagues suggested recently. As for Penny – her entire life seems to have been fuelled by fuss, from the days when she started selling her clothes on a Portobello market stall to being at the helm of a nationwide fashion chain.

Fuss is good, I decide as I make dinner. It gets people noticed and makes things happen. 'Not making a fuss' seems to equate to remaining under the radar, being insignificant, trying to please and do the right thing, and receiving no recognition for it.

I'm aware that Rose's previous PA – my predecessor – was known as a 'bit of a character', and a 'powerhouse'. Although our paths rarely crossed while I was temping, it was clear that she wasn't the kind of woman Rose would ask to deal with pubic hairs on loo seats, or her patio-hosing man, or to research 'the best kind of eardrops, the really strong kind – so when you put them in, you can hear the wax crackling. That's the kind I need. Could you get on to that for me, Viv, and have them delivered tomorrow?' *Sure. Would you like me to drop them into your lugholes while I'm at it?*

I glance across the kitchen at Izzy, who's doing her homework diligently at the table as I stir our pot of unremarkable, workaday Bolognese. Christ, even my cooking is without fuss. I can remember this being one of my mother's staples, circa 1983. Nothing wrong with that; she worked full-time in a secondary school, and back then few people knew about preserved lemons and or how to 'toast' pine kernels in a pan. If my mum had been presented with a Yotam Ottolenghi cookbook she would have laughed bewilderedly and maybe used it to prop up a wobbly bed.

So it's fine, this life of ours. But is 'fine' actually enough anymore? Have I slumped, unwittingly, into a dreary *working-on-and-on* kind of rut, and is that the real reason why my husband stumbled into the knickers of a swishy blonde doctor with perfect teeth?

Meanwhile Izzy has been given the task of making a poster about wetland habitats in Britain, and the issues and threats they are facing. Yes, she's the kind of child who works on and on – she actively enjoys homework – but she gives it her all, she goes the extra mile, not to gain praise but because it excites her to do her best.

When *she* cooks, it's a fuss. No one grinds up garlic and rock salt with a pestle and mortar if they want a quick, easy supper. And now, as well as the poster, Izzy has taken upon it herself to make her very own nature magazine: *The Wetland Wanderer*. I found her some paper and stapled several sheets together, and now she's filling the pages with facts and drawings, a cartoon strip of a duck family, environment-themed quizzes, a short story about an otter, and a hand-painted poster in the centre featuring a barnacle goose. She's been using my phone to send photos of her pages to Spencer, who's responded with, 'Great work sis!' And 'Looking forward to issue two. And a forthcoming media empire!'

195

Later, while she has her bath, I try to beat back her chaotic bedroom into some kind of order. And later still, when she's in bed, I settle downstairs on the sofa with my laptop. I'm intending to browse career advice from those websites aimed at mid-life women; the ones filled with inspiring stories of women who have changed direction and achieved wonderful things.

I don't even consider googling Estelle Lang. The last thing I need this evening is to be confronted by her challenging gaze. However, I do find myself veering off track, first as I try again to find out any information about Penny's boyfriend, Hamish Knowles, the supposedly celebrated composer. Nothing new to unearth there, as far as I can make out.

Moving on to Penny herself, I sip my lukewarm tea as I flick through interviews with her from back in her heyday (would she take exception to that? That I regard the Seventies as her 'golden years?'). Although they hark back to a pre-internet era, there's tons about her online. Some of those early interviews have been reformatted for slick, modern fashion blogs, or scanned in from the original magazine pages.

When we first became friends, I looked her up and read some of these features out of sheer nosiness. After all, it's not often you stumble upon someone like Penny Barnett in the park. Izzy and I pored over them together, marvelling over pictures of her as a stunning, vibrant woman in her twenties, not so different to how she is now (she is blessed with one of 'those' faces, with big, bright eyes, full lips and incredible cheekbones, that ages beautifully). However, now I'm discovering many more interviews with her – and gorgeous photos – that I'd never seen before. The sight of her smiling face, so open

196

and joyous, plus her glamorous floppy hats and red lipsticked smile, lifts my spirits.

Since Nick has arrived from New Zealand, I haven't seen much of her. Despite her grumblings that he'll 'only be checking I'm coping', I have backed off a little, having assumed that they'll want to spend as much time as possible together. I also worry that his first impression of me is of a raving madwoman (this seems to be bothering me more than it should). Penny has assured me that of course it wasn't, that he'd been 'surprised, yes, but impressed by your performance', and that it was one of the highlights of her year so far. 'I might start doing it myself,' she chuckled.

Curling up on the sofa now, I finish my tea and settle on an article about her from a newspaper's Sunday supplement in 1978.

My friends and I loved fashion, it reads, *but we had very little money and we couldn't find clothes we liked. We were paid a pittance in a typing pool in West London. I'd modelled a little, but I wasn't a big-name model and I didn't do catwalk or glossy magazines – my look was classed as 'young and fun' and I was mainly booked by teenage magazines, or the odd advert for shampoo or lip gloss. And even that was starting to fizzle out.*

By then I had a young son and his father's architectural practice had gone bust. We'd split up anyway, so there was barely any money, and I had the idea of making clothes to sell at affordable prices to my friends, many of whom were in the same boat as me. So I bought fabric cheaply and started to make outfits late at night to wear at the weekend.

I was like my own advertisement, running around London in my home-made clothes. Friends would ask me to make similar pieces for them: little A-line minis, shift dresses and simple tops. All very basic but in fun, bright colours: pinks, oranges, yellows. I'd go to Portobello Market on Friday lunchtimes, as it was close to my office, and I got to know one of the fabric stall owners there, a man called Saul Jackson, who was quite a bit older than me. He started calling me Girl Friday and we became friends.

'Hey, Girl Friday!' he'd say. 'What are you going to make this weekend?' And I'd laugh and say, 'Mischief!'

Saul helped me get my own stall on Saturdays, so I could sell my clothes there. Week after week, I kept selling out. I made kids' clothes too – my son would be with me, helping, and wearing them. But it was still tough, money-wise, surviving in London. My boy and I were living in a disgusting flat, and the landlord was a monster who was constantly harassing me. There were barking Alsatians below us and a brothel upstairs . . .

I pause as this new information sinks in. I had no idea it had been so tough for her when she'd started out. From what she's told me – the Angel Delight period, Nick running naked around the library – I'd imagined it had all been rather bohemian, full of capers and fun. She hadn't seemed to need the mother and baby groups that I'd clung to like life rafts when I first became a mum. When I'd happened to mention Izzy's school's PTA, Penny had had no idea what I was talking about.

'PTA?' she'd repeated. 'Is that something to do with time of arrival?'

'That's ETA. PTA is the parent-teachers association. It's a bit of Mafia actually . . .'

'God,' she'd shuddered. 'Why on earth would anyone want to be involved with that?'

I read on: . . . *So I made the decision to move back to Glasgow, where I was born and brought up. My son and I lived with my parents at first. I found a tiny shop in a part of Glasgow that literally no one ever went to. The place stank. We scrubbed it and fitted it out ourselves, and people liked it. So they kept coming back.*

How did I arrive at the Girl Friday style? [Pauses, considers this]. I knew the clothes I wanted to wear myself. I could picture the outfits right down to the braid, the buttons, the finish on a hem. So I made them just like that – not from anyone else's patterns or designs, but from the pictures in my own head.

I close my laptop, feeling a little overwhelmed, like when you emerge from the cinema having watched a film that's totally entranced you. Then you step outside the cinema, into the bright sunshine, and it takes a few moments to readjust to the real world.

'I made them just like that,' Penny had said, as if she'd been talking about constructing a hedgehog pincushion in needlework class (a project that took me an entire term to mess up; not even my mum could find anything positive to say about it). And I replay Rose's words from this morning, the gist being: if I don't want a Menopause Ambassador role, then there's nothing else she can offer me. At least, nothing new. No promotion, no opportunity in the whole 'let's invigorate Flaxico' mission.

But I don't need Rose, I decide now, as I go through to the kitchen and unload the washing machine. I don't have to sit there, year after year, running her errands 'without fuss'. Penny, Shelley, Isla and Jules are all strong, confident women seemingly unhampered by fear. I might not possess anything like their courage and drive, but I can stand on my own kitchen table, bellowing my lungs out.

I think again about Isla; my quieter friend, who is passionate about the museum where she has worked diligently for so long. Her attention to detail is astounding, her knowledge vast. I know she'll be heartbroken if the place closes.

She agrees that a fashion event is a brilliant idea, and now I'm convinced that Penny should be involved – not merely as an adviser for a Seventies theme, but as the sole focus of a show. Okay, the museum might not have the resources to stage a major Dior or Frida Kahlo exhibition – but the thrilling thing is, a Girl Friday fashion show has never been done before. It would be unique, focusing solely on the Glasgow girl who sat up half the night, her sewing machine whirring, and was, for a few years in the 1970s, one of the shining lights in British fashion.

As I start to wash up, I remember that evening when Penny, Hamish and Isla were here, drinking wine in the garden; how reluctant she seemed to have her work celebrated. And her prickliness over Hamish's Rolling Stones remark: 'All anyone wants are the old hits that everyone knows.' But she doesn't *have* to know; at least, not in the early planning stages. We could keep it under wraps. We could go all out to gather in as many original Girl Friday pieces as possible, then set them all out to show her, and tell her what we've been up to – in secret.

She'll be thrilled! In fact, I suspect she'll be overwhelmed. I know Penny is rightly proud of what she achieved, even though she tends to underplay it. It's understandable, I guess. She admits that it had a 'shelf life', and ultimately Girl Friday went the way of the poncho at the start of the Eighties, possibly in a messy and unpleasant way. Although she's never divulged who her

200

backers and business partners were, she couldn't have established and grown her fashion empire from her market stall takings.

So, yes, Girl Friday died a possibly painful and ugly death. Perhaps that's why Penny seems unwilling to recognise the impact she had, and why she shrugged off the suggestion of getting involved with the museum at all. Maybe – and I still find the possibility hard to believe – she views herself as a failure.

It strikes me now that, whenever we talk about those days, it's usually me who's brought it up. Izzy, who adores dressing up, isn't shy of quizzing her either. However, Penny's designs were fabulous; high fashion with instant appeal, yet apparently extremely well made, due to her attention to detail. So the chances are, there are plenty of pieces still in circulation. Surely vintage stores must have the odd item; collectors too. There might even be some stashed in wardrobes, possibly still worn.

It's entirely feasible, I decide. I'd imagine the museum has virtually no budget, but that's okay; pieces could be borrowed, then returned to their owners after the event. When I worked in theatre I often pulled together productions with hardly any cash. I'm used to operating on a shoestring; in fact, I love the challenge.

My heart is racing now as I make a vow to myself to put together a proposal for a fashion show and exhibition, with all the details worked out. I'll take it to the management team at Isla's museum – not for money (I'm aware that there isn't any), but because it will be a brilliant project, in the way that *The Wetland Wanderer* is brilliant.

Sometimes you take on a thing just for the love of it. You hurl yourself at it, despite the fact that your confidence has been battered and your boss takes you for granted and has you running around, researching the pillow quality at hotels all over the globe. You do it simply because you know it'll be amazing – and because, if anyone can make it happen, it's you.

Chapter Twenty-Two

Friday, September 6

Rose remarks that I am looking 'jolly' today. First hot, now jolly; I sound like an overworked clown.

'Just feeling good,' I say with a smile. Meanwhile, our workplace is a hive of activity. The air buzzes with drills and sanders and whiffs of fresh paint. The low boardroom is being transformed into an open-plan 'space' (not an office) where the Platforms for Innovation (now 'PFIs') will be based. It's going to be beautifully designed, ultramodern, with special fake 'windows', according to Jean, who seems to have her ear to the ground.

'What d'you mean, fake windows?' I ask over lunch.

'They're designed to look like windows,' she replies, 'with glass and a frame and everything, but there's a special kind of daylight-type light behind them.'

'As a way of *un-basementing* the basement? That's clever!'

She nods. 'The design guy who was here, he reckons young people regard natural light as pretty important.'

'They're so demanding,' I chuckle, 'with their avocado on toast and their fondness for being able to look out and see the sky.' I finish my tuna salad. As part of the modernisation of Flaxico, the canteen now offers fresh greenery, the appearance of rocket causing almost as much of a stir around here as the rabbit food scandal.

It's all positive, of course. I'm cracking on with my work and scheduling interviews, as Rose is focused on a rapid recruitment drive. Meanwhile my head is buzzing with the Girl Friday project, and the list of vintage stores I've started to compile, with a view to a mass mail-out to try and gauge how many original pieces are still out there in circulation. I started researching last night: the brand history, the key pieces, any associations with big-name models and celebs of the day. It was fascinating, and I ended up beavering away up until 2.45 a.m., boosted by Isla's enthusiastic response to my text and her promise to show my proposal to the person who makes the decisions about temporary exhibitions. If that goes well – and I'm pretty certain it will – then the next step will be a face-to-face meeting.

So I'm sleep-deprived, yes, but also 'jolly'. Perhaps all this excitement is even having the effect of magically balancing out my hormones. This morning, I didn't even have to wring out my pyjamas.

Sunday, September 8

I have never owned a dog. My parents were cat people, and I was brought up to regard any hound as potentially dangerous and, as Mum put it, 'likely to turn'. But I know Bobby well. Turning is not in his nature. He is a delight, pottering around our house in his schnoodly way, and whining at the bathroom door when I go to the loo to the point where it's easier to let him come in and watch me. While it's a little bizarre, it's also heartening to be needed so much that someone wants to gaze at you while you're doing your business.

Penny and Hamish have gone for a jaunt on his boat, and Nick is apparently out of town filming, hence her asking if we could step in and help out. Naturally, Izzy and I were delighted. Unlike Ludo, Bobby didn't bring foul-smelling toothpaste and hasn't demanded that I sweat over the pancake pan for fifteen hours. As Nick intends to be back late tonight, the plan is for him to come round in the morning to pick up our canine guest. Before I left work on Friday, I managed to arrange to take a day's holiday tomorrow, ostensibly to let a tradesman in but really to knock my proposal into shape.

I am still a little mortified about Nick witnessing me shouting about my brilliance on the kitchen table, but what the heck; he makes 'human interest' documentaries, and I was certainly being very 'human' and possibly even 'interesting'. And I'm sure he's seen worse.

It has also occurred to me several times that he is *extremely* attractive; i.e. fanciably attractive, which is a bit of a shocker to me. Not because I expected him *not* to be, with a good-looking woman like Penny as his mother. But from the sole picture she'd shown me, all I'd glimpsed was an indistinct lean, tall and beardy figure, taken from some distance across a beach. I hadn't been prepared for the loveliness of his clean-shaven face.

Since Andy left, I had assumed I'd never register a man's attractiveness again. And the idea of involving myself with anyone, of letting down my guard and allowing someone into my life – at least, as anything more than a platonic friend – is too bizarre for me to even contemplate. I mean, practically, how could I ever think of introducing 'someone new' (argh!) into Izzy's life? *Hey, darling, this is my friend Stephen!* The very concept of throwing an adult male into the mix seems as bizarre and unnecessary as having a hot tub installed on our patio. I'm sure it's enjoyable to have one, and fun to start off with, but the novelty would wear off and pretty soon its maintenance would outweigh the positives.

However, my ability to register a man's attractiveness clearly hasn't died. Perhaps it's the novelty aspect; there hadn't been a handsome newcomer in my house since the cute tiler redid our bathroom six years ago, and Jules kept making her 'How's the grouting going?' jokes. So, with the prospect of Nick's visit tomorrow being a little nerve-racking, I have already decided that the Bobby handover will be conducted in a brisk and businesslike fashion.

'Is that Bobby?' Ludo calls over the fence when Izzy and I are playing with him in the garden.

'Yes, it is,' I reply.

'Why's he at your house?'

'He's just here for a little holiday,' I say. 'Penny's away overnight.'

He comes right up to the fence and peers over, blond hair falling shaggily into his face, and something like blackcurrant jam smeared around his mouth. 'Hi, Izzy.' He grins at her.

'Hi, Ludo,' she says, throwing Bobby's tennis ball, which he scampers after gleefully.

'Is it nice, having him to stay?' he asks.

'It's lovely, yes,' I reply.

'What does he eat?' Ludo wants to know.

'Erm, he likes fresh meat.'

'What kind of meat?'

'It's a kind of steak for dogs.' In fact, being Penny's dog, and adored to the point of distraction, Bobby consumes only the finest minced beef, which comes in plastic trays; no dry pellets or even canned dog meat for this little prince. It is virtually on a par with human food. I describe this in detail to Ludo, before moving on to questioning him about the baby ('What does she do?' 'Poos and pees!'). Although he won't divulge much more than that, it's preferable to any further grillings about the whereabouts of my errant, soon-to-be-ex-husband.

'Can I come round and play?' he asks hopefully.

I hesitate, but decide to allow it, for the sole reason that I can't think of a reason to say no, and don't want to seem mean. And, surprisingly, the afternoon passes pleasantly, with me being on high alert, watching Ludo's every move in the manner of a store detective shadowing a potential shoplifter. Chrissie seems overwhelmed with gratitude when I return her son, happy and tired, several hours later.

'Say thank you to Viv and Izzy for having you,' she says.

'Thank you,' he mutters to his chest. Then, as I turn back to our house: 'Will Bobby sleep in your bed?'

'No, Ludo. He has his own luxury basket,' I say with a smile. 'I wouldn't let a dog sleep on my bed.'

'Does he have a duvet as well?'

'Er, no. It's a fleecy blanket.'

I take in Ludo's eager, attentive expression. Something has happened since the arrival of his baby sister. He's less shouty, less aggressive; less likely, perhaps, to try and

207

stone the local cat population or smash down a shed. I'd like to think that being around a small, pink baby girl has softened him, but suspect he's just shattered from all the crying during the night.

Hours later, at around midnight, I'm aware of Bobby's soft breathing close by, in-and-out, in-and-out, as I drift towards sleep. So much for him kipping in his basket. He made it clear he wasn't having that, and who was I to argue when he sat there whining at my bedroom door? Now his head is on the pillow beside me, with one ear sticking up. Like a small, furry husband who doesn't steal all the duvet, he emits the odd muted snore.

As a bed companion he's perfect. And, as a bonus, it occurs to me how disgusted Andy would be to see him here.

Monday, September 9

Nor does he wake up complaining about a swamp-like bed. He just gazes at me, eyes bright and adoring, tongue lolling as he pants in readiness for the day ahead. I can't remember a morning when anyone has looked so happy to see me.

Maybe this is my future, I reflect as I get dressed. Not with another man, taking up wardrobe space and commandeering too many hangers, but with a small affectionate animal with slightly stinky breath.

Meanwhile, I have the prospect of Nick coming around later this morning, whom Penny seemed to have marked as a possible love interest for me. Never mind that he's her own flesh and blood, who happens to live in New Zealand, and that the idea is as ridiculous as me trying

208

to set up Spencer with someone. Even if he were single, he'd laugh in my face. He won't even let me choose a T-shirt for him. My hooking up with our friendly lollipop man (whom I have since found out is seventy-eight years old – although admittedly well preserved!) is more likely. I thank him warmly as Izzy, Bobby and I cross the road on our way to school.

Back home, I catch sight of myself in the hall mirror, unwashed and unkempt in my baggy grey sweater and jeans, hair stuffed into a scraggy ponytail; my default day-off-work look. Thirty minutes later I am showered and blow-dried (only for speed, not because I'm making a special effort), and wearing a blue cotton dress (first thing I put my hand on), *and* eye shadow, mascara, lipstick and a touch of blusher (only because the dress demands make-up) as I flit about the house.

The doorbell goes. I stride towards it, with Bobby charging ahead of me, trying to settle my expression into bright/perky/not mad-looking in preparation for greeting my gentleman caller.

'Hey, you're all dressed up,' says the postman with a grin, handing me a parcel. 'Going somewhere nice today?' He stoops to pat Bobby.

'No, just hanging around really.' I smile. *I always wear a dress and full make-up for cleaning the kitchen.* He leaves, having added that I have 'brightened up' his morning, and I check my face in the hall mirror again; those rogue facial hairs are only visible in certain lights. Not that I am concerned with impressing Nick. But I don't want him to think his mother hangs out with a ragbag who could do with a shave.

To keep myself occupied I let Bobby out into the back garden, regretting it immediately as Chrissie is out there,

209

pegging out nappies (naturally a sage-toothpaste family opt for terry nappies). 'Ooh, your hair looks nice today,' she calls over with a smile.

'Does it? Thanks!' I feign surprise, as if no hairdryer has been utilised in the creation of this flouncy style.

'You put me to shame, Viv,' she adds. 'You're so glam!'

'Not at all,' I bluster, sensing myself flushing. 'And you look great. No one would ever guess you've just had a baby.'

She grunts and grimaces, muttering something unintelligible.

'How are things going?' I ask, strolling closer. 'I've seen Tim out and about with Lara a few times. She's absolutely beautiful. She's so like you!'

Chrissie smiles wearily. 'We're doing okay, I suppose, and Lara's wonderful, of course. But it's exhausting, and sometimes I don't feel up to it – all the stuff you have to do. I guess I'd forgotten what it's like.'

'It's all-consuming, isn't it?' I say, remembering it now: that weird, milk-and-nappy-scented bubble, the drifting around in a whiffy dressing gown, barely able to distinguish night from day. 'The feeding and changing, I mean,' I add. 'I hope you're managing to get some rest.'

She rubs at her eyes. 'Hmm. Chance'd be a fine thing with all the singing, the facial exercises and all that . . .'

'Facial exercises?'

'Oh, *you* know – the routine with the big smile, the sticky-out tongue, the whole range of movements . . .'

'Really?' I ask, genuinely intrigued, and remembering Penny mentioning her 'benign neglect' approach to mothering with Nick. 'What's all that for?'

She gives me a startled look. '*You* know. So the baby can copy your expressions. It aids development.'

Christ, is that what's expected these days? Maybe – apart from the fact that I have no one to do it with – it's just as well that I'm way past my reproductive prime. 'I must admit, I never did any of that.'

'Yes, well, you're a relaxed mum and I admire you for that.' Ah, we know what *that* means.

'I'm not really,' I start.

'But you are,' she insists, her eyes filling with sudden tears. 'Ludo told me what it was like at your place. How you cooked whatever the kids wanted and let them have pancakes instead of a proper meal. And if they wanted to flop into bed, all dirty without having a bath, you were fine with that too . . .' For Christ's sake – did he file a full report on me? And, actually, Izzy did have her nightly baths!

'That's only because Ludo didn't *want*—'

'And you don't mind mess,' she goes on. 'You're not like me, always running around, picking things up, wanting the house to look decent . . .'

'Chrissie . . . are you okay?' Any defensiveness fades immediately as her tears spill over. She nods mutely. 'You're just exhausted,' I add. 'D'you want to come round and have a cup of tea with me, leave Lara with Tim for a little while?'

'He's at work,' she says, sniffing.

'Bring her over, then,' I say, figuring that Nick is due any minute and, actually, having Chrissie and the baby here might help to defuse any awkwardness.

'Thanks, but Lara's napping and I don't want to disturb her.'

'Okay, if you're sure. But any time you want to chat—'

She rubs at her eyes again and smiles shakily. 'Thanks,

Viv. It's so stressful, you know, trying to do everything right?'

'Please don't be hard on yourself. I'm sure you're doing a great job.'

She pushes back her dishevelled blonde hair. 'Tim says so. The health visitor says so. But I never feel as if I am, you know?'

'It's natural to feel like that. Lara's only three weeks old. Your body's just been through a huge thing, and your hormones are probably all over the shop.' Get me, the hormone expert all of a sudden.

She nods. 'I just feel . . . useless half the time. Ludo won't listen to anything I say. I'm not giving him enough attention.'

'I'm sure Ludo's fine. He's great!'

'I guess my self-esteem isn't too hot right now,' Chrissie adds, turning back to her clothes pegging. 'I should take a leaf out of your book, Viv, all blow-dried and wearing a lovely dress, not afraid to shout about how brilliant you are . . .'

I blink at her. 'Sorry?'

She smiles another watery smile. 'The day after we came home from hospital. I heard you shouting in your kitchen—'

'Oh, I'm sorry about that,' I say quickly. 'It was, um, a kind of exercise. A sort of self-empowerment thing. Jules made me do it . . .'

'No need to apologise,' she says, brightening a little now, clearly enjoying the memory. 'But I won't forget it. In fact I'm thinking of trying it too.'

'You should! It's good for the—'

'Confidence?'

'Yes, and for making a complete fool of yourself,' I

212

add, breaking off as my phone rings in my pocket. I pull it out: an unknown number. 'Sorry, Chrissie, I'd better take this . . .'

She nods. 'Thanks for the pep talk. It's helped, actually.' I give her what I hope is an encouraging smile as I accept the call, and she heads back into her house.

'Hi, Viv? It's Nick here. Penny's son.' Penny must have passed on my number without my permission. That shouldn't surprise me. She never knocks or rings my doorbell either – she just barges right in – but of course it makes sense, with the Bobby handover being imminent.

'Hi, Nick, how are you?' I say, stepping into the kitchen with Bobby close at my heels.

'Good,' he says, 'but yesterday's filming ran over and I ended up staying here in a B&B last night. I've just stopped at services. I'm so sorry. I should be with you in a couple of hours.'

'No problem,' I say. 'I'm here all day so there's no rush.'

Keep it speedy and businesslike, I remind myself as I pace about with Bobby following me. I try to kid myself that I am merely 'exercising' him, and not marching around, unable to settle to anything due to Nick's impending arrival. There'll be no need for a big chat, I remind myself, quickly checking my reflection again and wondering if my hair is in fact overly bouffed up, and might startle him. He's probably busy anyway and will just want to grab Bobby and go.

At one o'clock precisely, Nick is sitting at my kitchen table, and I am serving us lunch.

Chapter Twenty-Three

Lunchtime

Well, it would have been rude not to, considering he arrived just as I was starting to feel peckish. I had already decided that I didn't want him to witness my usual home lunch of hummus, cherry tomatoes and crackers, and maybe a pear or a tangerine if I'm feeling really fancy. Not that I remotely cared what he'd think – but I'd happened to spy some parmesan, bacon and cream in the fridge, and we always have plenty of garlic for *Izzy Cooks!* Anything savoury has garlic in; it's the law.

'Would you like something to eat?' I asked after our slightly awkward hellos, how are yous, and gosh, that was embarrassing when you arrived here with your mum ('Your mum'! As if he's nine years old). He'd said no thank you at first, but I soon wheedled it out of him that he had just driven up from Keighley, in Yorkshire, where he'd been filming his documentary about steam locomotives. And he'd had nothing apart from a dismal croissant about three hours ago.

'That does smell really good,' he conceded as I made a sauce, which happened to be enough for two people.

'Oh, it's nothing really.'

With a jolt, I realised what I was trying to do: give the impression that this is how I roll, like blinking Nigella, throwing together a sort of carbonara when I'm home alone on an ordinary grey-skied Monday.

And now here we are, tucking into my pasta, while he asks, 'So, have you and Mum been friends for long?'

'About five years,' I reply, going on to fill him in on our initial chats in the park, our meet-ups, and how fond my daughter is of her too. 'She's a wonderful person,' I add.

'Yeah, she really is,' Nick says. 'She's a bit of a one-off. I wish I could see more of her, obviously.'

'How long have you been in New Zealand?'

'Coming up for ten years,' he replies.

'Did you move there for work, or—'

'Um, not really.' He smiles. He has her cheekbones, I realise, and those soft grey-blue eyes. His short dark hair is flecked with a touch of grey, his build slender, verging on rangy; he looks young for his years in a black T-shirt and jeans. There's a touch of shyness about him, and it's clear that he is unaware of how attractive he is. 'I was on holiday in San Francisco,' he goes on, 'and I met someone there. It was a bit of a whirlwind thing. She's from Auckland, and we moved there and got married, but it didn't work out.' He does a sort of shrug thing as he lays his fork in his bowl.

'But you decided to stay there?' I prompt him.

'Yeah, work had sort of taken off for me there. I hadn't had much luck over here.' He smiles self-deprecatingly. 'I don't know what it was – maybe a bigger fish in a smaller

215

pond, kind of situation? Anyway, I got lucky, and this latest thing – the steam railway project – was ideal. It meant I could combine work with spending some proper time with Mum.'

I nod, now picturing the two of them way back; the depressing flat with the barking dogs below, and the brothel above. Penny moving them back to Glasgow, and finding that first shop and, when that took off, somehow persuading a backer to fund the opening of further stores. And while I'd love to ask Nick more about his childhood – and his mother – I manage to hold back. I'm sure he's been quizzed about his mum all his life.

'How about you?' Nick asks as I clear away our bowls.

'Oh, I just have a bring-in-the-money sort of job at the moment.'

'Right. What kind of work d'you do?'

And so I tell him about Flaxico, just the bare bones, with bunnygate dropped in as an attempt to raise my account of my working life from the humdrum.

'That's pretty major,' he exclaims. 'How d'you think it happened?'

I smile as I make coffee. 'You won't make a documentary about this?'

Nick laughs, and it occurs to me how easy he is to talk to, and how ridiculous it was to feel even remotely agitated about him dropping by. 'I promise.'

'Well, it kind of looks like it wasn't an accident.'

'Wow, really?'

I nod and pour our coffees. 'Yeah. They've been up to this kind of stuff for years, apparently. It might have been careless, but the rumour is they were short on fulfilling an urgent order, so they sent the wrong product.' I grimace. 'It's scary, actually, how similar our human and pet products are, ingredients-wise. But now it's all been glossed over, and they're kind of reinventing the company as this purveyor of fresh, modern, health-giving foods – so it's probably turned out to be a good thing.'

He smiles, and we move on to chatting about Izzy and Spencer – Nick doesn't have kids – and before I know it, the afternoon has flown by. 'I'm sorry,' I say, 'but I need to pick up Izzy from school.'

'God, I'm so sorry. I've taken up your whole afternoon.'

'No, not at all. It's been great to meet you properly.'

He looks around for Bobby who's been lying at my feet the whole time. 'Thank you so much for lunch. It was lovely.'

'It was nothing, really!'

'And for looking after Bobby.'

'A total pleasure,' I say.

There's a bit of a kerfuffle while we gather together Bobby's things: the luxury basket with its fur-lined interior; his 'daytime cushion' and fleecy blanket, plus tennis balls, food and water bowls and the 'spare' meat in its plastic tray, which Penny had given me to keep in the freezer 'in case something happens'. Nick is laden with all of this stuff – as Penny had been when she'd brought him yesterday. If I'd known Bobby would come with so much equipment I'd have helped her to lug it all around. So, despite Nick's protests, and to save him from going back to Penny's to fetch his hire car, I help him to carry it all to her flat. On the ten-minute walk I find myself telling him about the struggling museum and my plan to propose a fashion show in her honour there.

'Really? That'd be incredible!'

'But I'm not so sure how she'd feel about it,' I add.

'Why's that?'

I tell him about the night the museum's future was discussed, with Isla and Hamish, and how Penny had shunned the idea of involving herself even in an advisory role.

'Well, that's just Mum,' he says. 'She can be surprisingly modest and I'm not sure whether she thinks of herself as being any kind of expert on anything.'

'I can't understand why not,' I say.

'Yeah, me neither. So, d'you mean the whole event would be about her and the Girl Friday boutiques?'

'Yes. At least, that's what I'm thinking, if they decide to go for it. You don't think that's a crazy idea, do you?'

We're at Penny's flat now, a smart 1960s block with a neat communal garden at the front, where Nick lets us into the hallway. He unclips Bobby's lead and he scampers upstairs ahead of us. 'No, I really don't.' I hesitate in the doorway as he unlocks the door to his mother's first-floor flat.

'She wouldn't be overwhelmed by all the fuss and attention, if we managed to make it happen?'

Nick smiles as Bobby runs into the flat. 'The thing is with Mum, as I'm sure you know, you can never quite predict how she'll react to anything. She might be shocked, or think she's not worthy of something like that, or . . .' He pauses. 'She might be thrilled and hugely flattered. And I think that's more likely. I've been saying for years that she should do something to try and revive the Girl Friday name. We know how much people love retro stuff these days – that whole Seventies thing. And it'd be great for her, to be finally recognised at this stage in her life.'

'That's so good to hear,' I say, almost wanting to hug him. 'It's exactly what I'd hoped you'd say.'

'But I also think,' Nick adds, 'maybe keep it to yourself,

just for now? In the early planning stages, I mean? Just in case she kicks up a fuss or gets cold feet. You know how prickly she can be, how downright stubborn—'

'Oh, yes, I'm aware of that. That's what I was thinking too. I hate the thought of her dismissing the whole thing before we've even had a chance to start pulling it all together.' I hesitate. 'Has no one ever approached her before, about something like this?'

'I'm sure they must have,' Nick says, 'but nothing has ever come off.' He smiles warmly. 'Look, I do know Mum can be a bit sensitive about living in the past, as she puts it. But maybe now's the right time, with you being a friend, someone she knows and trusts, and this being in her home city, *and* possibly saving a failing museum . . .' He pauses as Bobby runs back to him, and picks the dog up in his arms. 'I'd say go for it – and let me know if there's anything I can do to help.'

Later, with midnight oil burning

Woolliness of brain is a lesser known menopausal symptom that I have no time for tonight. Fired up from my chat with Nick, I force my way through it as I start on the bare bones of a proposal, to include:

- The reasons why it's precisely the right kind of event for our city.

- The wide appeal it would have to fashion students, fans of Seventies style, people who remember the boutiques and shopped there for their weekend outfits (the nostalgia aspect).

219

- How we would go about amassing a Girl Friday collection (I'm deliberately not focusing too closely on this aspect right now, as I don't want fear to dent my sudden burst of confidence. I just keeping trying to picture myself standing on my kitchen table, and shouting, with Jules looking on encouragingly).

- The key pieces from the shops' heyday. This part has been particularly fun to research. I'd assumed Girl Friday was mainly about dresses and separates, but now I've discovered that accessories were a big thing too: the 'Jinty' handbag, the 'Carly' floppy hat, the 'Rita' belt in rust-coloured suede. And the knitwear; by God, it was gorgeous! Along with the cute sweaters and tank tops there were woolly dresses and crocheted tops – and, best of all, the apparently iconic 'Pippa' Poncho, an explosion of red, orange and yellow with an extravagant fringe edging and pompoms on strings at the neck. Featured in all the magazines, and worn by models and celebrities, it summed up the whole Girl Friday spirit: fun, bright, joyful. We must have a 'Pippa'. That's the piece that'll appear on the posters and all the advertising. Even if it means driving to Cornwall to fetch one, I'll do it somehow.

- How we would stage the actual show (with models from local agencies? And perhaps older women who wore the outfits back in the day?).

- Costings: tricky to figure but, as I work away steadily into the night, I'm aware of something happening, something building in me: a tight ball of excitement that I haven't felt for a very long time.

Whatever it takes, I have to make this happen. In the way that Penny 'just' created the outfits from the pictures in her head, so I 'just' need to convince the museum bigwigs that this would be the most amazing event, and that they would be utterly mad not to say yes.

Chapter Twenty-Four

Thursday, September 12

My proposal is finished, having been polished way into the night, to the occasional sound of Lara crying next door. I think I'm happy with it. It certainly seems to convey my enthusiasm and passion. It was quite a beast by the end, having grown from my brief points into a splurge about how great Penny is, such an asset to our city who has never been properly recognised – at least, not in recent years.

I fire it off to Isla at lunchtime at work. She has agreed to give it a once-over, and tart it up if necessary (being more au fait than I am with museum-type speak). The plan is, she'll then pass it over to her colleague who has the power to make decisions about temporary exhibitions and events.

I am beside myself with anxiety as I wait for Isla's response. The mental woolliness is back – the affliction that caused me to post my house keys – and Rose is in meetings all afternoon, requiring the ferrying in of numerous trays of coffees and teas. In and out I flit, barely acknowledged until she finally glances round and suggests that biscuits would be welcome: 'Any of those shortbread fingers kicking around, Viv?'

At just gone 4.30 there's a text from Isla: *No need for any tarting up. It's perfect as it is. I'm printing it off now, will let you know the response asap. It's brilliant!*

Rose catches me later, buoyed up as I finish up for the day. 'Everything okay today?' she asks, pausing by my desk.

'Yes, all good thanks.'

She studies me as if I have done something different, either to my face or my hair, and she can't quite figure out what it is. 'Thanks for doing all that running around for me today. Fetching all the teas and coffees, I mean.'

'No problem,' I say.

'And thanks for fixing that thing with the PowerPoint.'

'That's no bother at all.' I smile at her and she wanders away, then looks back.

'I just wanted you to know you're appreciated,' she says, holding my gaze for a moment before slinging her camel leather bag over her shoulder and striding out to the lift.

Friday, September 13

I know it's only been twenty-four hours. People are busy – of course they're not going to respond right away. But by the end of the day I have still heard precisely nothing yet from Isla. I'm reminded of my dad, catching me glancing accusingly at the phone when some boy or other hadn't called.

'A watched phone never rings,' he remarked with a smile.

'Leave her be,' Mum chastised him. 'You're only making it worse by going on about it.'

He looked at me and grinned. 'Is it all right if I make a phone call, or d'you want to keep the line free?' That was Dad all over; gently teasing, making me smile amidst the angst. Anyway, today is Friday the 13th – not that I am remotely superstitious – so maybe it's best that I don't hear anything?

At the office, so I can't endlessly check for messages. I resort to hiding my phone in a drawer.

Saturday, September 14

Still no news from the museum. I doubt if the people who make the decisions are even there today. Anyone on duty will probably be tending to one of the five visitors who are pottering about, admiring the ceramics. I know what it's like in there. The staff are lovely, all over you, pointing out things, telling you the history of a bejewelled corset or a set of tiny dolls' combs, carved from bone; it's all well intended, although sometimes you just want to browse uninterrupted. Reminding myself that there's no point in constantly checking for messages, I do some more research on vintage shops to add to my list and, thrillingly, spot a couple of Girl Friday pieces on eBay – a banana-coloured blouse and a tangerine tank top – which I bid for.

Andy arrives to take Izzy out, still looking rather out of sorts. I will not ask him why he chose a flat above a cheese shop. I will not.

And I will not pester Isla about the proposal. *I will not.*

It's a cool, bright, cloudless afternoon, and as Izzy is restless, I suggest picking up Maeve and heading over to the park. As we cross the wide expanse of grass, en route to the swings, I notice the two of them pointing at something. Izzy swings round to face me. 'Mum, look!'

'What is it?' I can't see anything out of the ordinary.

'It's Bobby! But he's not with Penny.'

I'm about to say it can't be Bobby then; as far as I've gathered we are pretty much the only people who are permitted to walk him. 'It's a man,' Izzy announces. 'Why's Bobby with him? Who *is* he?'

I follow her gaze and spot Nick in the distance. I wave, and he waves back. 'That's Penny's son, Nick,' I explain, surprised by how happy I am to see him again. We make our way over, and I introduce the girls.

'Nick lives in New Zealand,' I explain, 'but he's working here at the moment and spending some time with his mum.'

Izzy looks up at him with interest. 'Penny's your mum?'

'That's right,' he smiles.

'How far away's New Zealand?' Maeve asks.

'About 11,000 miles,' Nick replies.

'You live that far from your mum?' Izzy exclaims.

'I do, yeah, unfortunately.' Nick smiles.

She looks astounded. 'Why?'

He chuckles and catches my eye. 'It's just the way things turned out. But it's great to be back here for a couple of months. I was hoping a job would come up, and it did.'

'Nick makes documentaries,' I explain.

'About penguins and stuff?' Izzy asks hopefully.

He smiles. 'Not yet, but you never know what might come up in the future. The one I've just been working on is about steam trains.'

'Aw,' Maeve says, looking unimpressed.

'But basically,' he adds, 'I'm interested in anything that people would like to see a film about.'

'Maybe Nick could film *Izzy Cooks!*,' I say as a joke.

'What's that?' he asks, and Izzy blurts out a hurried explanation, before running ahead with Maeve and Bobby. Nick and I stroll after them towards the lake.

'Thanks again for lunch the other day,' he says.

'You're very welcome.' He's wearing a pale grey T-shirt and jeans, and he's lightly tanned, and a little stubbly. It suits him, I decide. I'd still never have recognised him from the blurry photo Penny showed me, and now I'm getting to know him a little, it seems hard to believe that he 'fusses over' her, in the way she described; that he regards her as anything less than entirely capable of looking after herself.

'So, how are things, now you're staying with your mum?' I ask.

'It's great,' he says with a smile, 'now I've acclimatised myself to her again.'

I glance at him. Izzy and Maeve are on the swings now, competing as to who can swing highest. 'Acclimatised?'

Nick chuckles. 'Well, she's brilliant, as you know . . .'

'Yes, course.'

'And it's all my doing really,' he adds, hands in pockets as we stroll along.

226

'*What's* your doing?'

He pauses as if trying to figure out the best way to put it. 'Mum and me – well, we were such a tight little unit, you know. When I was growing up, I mean . . .'

I nod. 'I've always got the impression she was quite . . . relaxed as a mother.' I glance at him, keen to hear about his childhood from his perspective. Angel Delight, and the library-streaking incident, spring to mind.

'Oh, she was,' Nick says, 'in the best possible way. She treated me like her little mate. Mum never believed in being any different with children to how she was with adults, you know?'

'So you were super-close, the two of you?'

'Yep, all through when I was growing up, and then I had the audacity to start travelling – for fun at first, and later for work – and, I have to say, that was a bit difficult.'

'In what way?' I ask.

He sighs. 'It was a wrench for both of us, but I was up for adventure. So it was probably a lot harder for her. I mean, she didn't try to stop me, or cause a fuss, but I knew it hurt her when I moved away permanently.' He pauses.

'I'm sure it did,' I murmur.

'So, whenever I come over on a visit, Mum's very . . . attentive, is probably the best way of putting it.'

'Really?' I'm tempted to mention that I hear he checks for dust and out-of-date food, but I'm not sure whether it would go down too well. 'You mean she wants to do everything for you?'

'Oh God, yes. And I'm sorry, and it *is* very kindly meant, but I can't have someone running my bath for me at forty-nine years old.' We both laugh.

'She thinks you're incapable of operating the taps?'

'Clearly.' He grins at me.

'It's a short step from having her take the top off your boiled egg.'

Nick chuckles. 'I've seen her hovering with a teaspoon.'

We walk in easy silence for a few moments while I picture her fussing around him, so different to how Penny painted it. 'She probably just misses you terribly,' I suggest, 'and has stored up all this caring, this yearning to mother you. And now you're here, even though you're a bona fide adult, she can't stop herself.'

'I suspect that's it.' He smiles.

'And mothers can't help it,' I add. 'We worry, you know. We're still the parent, no matter how old our kids are. Like, I know how slapdash my son Spencer is with cooking. He's twenty-two, and he's been living away from home for four years – but when he told me they'd started doing Sunday roasts in the flat, I couldn't settle until I'd sent him a meat thermometer.'

'Which was very thoughtful and caring of you,' Nick says.

'It's probably pointless,' I say with a smirk. 'I can't imagine he uses it.'

'But you feel better, knowing it's there,' he adds, at which I laugh. I'm actually impressed, how he seems to 'get' it.

'Slightly, yes.'

'Did you buy him a cycle helmet too?'

'I did,' I exclaim, 'last Christmas!'

'I thought you might have. Was he thrilled?'

'Of course he was,' I snigger. 'So much so that he nearly forgot it when he went back to Newcastle. At a guess, I'd say it's been worn precisely zero times.'

228

Nick chuckles. 'Well, you did what you could.' He pauses. 'I'm not *complaining* about Mum, you know . . .'

'No, I realise that. You're just saying.' He smiles and murmurs in agreement. 'We both know how wonderful Penny is,' I add.

'Of course we do,' Nick says.

'She's been a great friend to me,' I continue, 'right from the start, but especially since, well . . .' I pause for a moment. 'Since it all came out about my husband, I mean. I found out he was seeing someone else when we were still together,' I say quickly, immediately regretting divulging such personal information. 'What I mean is, she was really supportive and always there for me if I wanted to talk.' I clear my throat. 'She's been lovely, you know?'

'Yeah.' He nods, and I can sense him digesting this new information; that is, if Penny hadn't filled him in on it all already, which I now suspect may be the case. 'That must've been a really tough time for you.'

'Yes, well, he's gone now,' I add. 'At least he's not really in my life. No more than necessary anyway, and these things happen, don't they?'

'Er, yes, they certainly do.'

'And everyone gets on with their lives,' I add, conscious of adopting a brisker tone. 'Oh, I meant to tell you,' I add quickly, 'I wrote the Girl Friday proposal and sent it off.'

'Brilliant,' he says. 'Any news yet?'

'No, nothing so far.' I glance at him. 'It's driving me mad, this waiting. I know it's only been three days, and I need to stop being such a child about it . . .' I pause. 'If they decide to go ahead, could we get together and have a chat about your mum, and your memories of that time?' I break off, remembering the interview I read, about how hard it was when Penny was starting out. 'If it wouldn't be an imposition,' I add, at which Nick chuckles.

'An imposition? Not at all. I told you I'd be delighted to help. And even when I'm back home in New Zealand, I'm only a message or a call away if you need anything.'

'That would be great, thank you.'

'I've always wanted to make a film about Mum you know,' he adds. 'It's the obvious subject for me – the whole Penny Barnett story from the sewing machine on a desk in her bedroom to the height of her success, and why it all ended, if she'd be prepared to talk about that. But it's unlikely to ever happen. I've tried to broach it, but she's always seemed terribly unkeen.'

'D'you know why?' I ask, intrigued.

Nick shrugs as the girls run towards us with Bobby tearing ahead. 'I suspect it's a mother-and-son thing, that I'm too close to her, and maybe she worries she'd reveal too much.' He shrugs. 'But I'm only guessing. Maybe she thinks it'd be too much hassle, and she can't see the point.'

'That could be it. What a shame, though. A film about her would be fascinating.'

'Yeah, but this event you're proposing, with a show and an exhibition – I was going to say it's the next best thing, but in some ways, it could be even better.'

'Really? Why's that?'

'It'd seem more real, somehow,' he replies, 'seeing the actual clothes being modelled, right here in her home city, like Girl Friday coming back to life. And who knows what it could lead to for her?'

230

I look at him and smile. 'That is, if she's happy about having her life put on display like that.'

'Yeah. But honestly,' Nick says, as we all head towards the park gate, 'I think she'd love it really. I mean, how could she not?'

Chapter Twenty-Five

Monday, September 16

Lunchtime at work. Spinach, roasted cauliflower and pomegranate salad is on the menu, packed with fresh herbs and scattered with petals. Petals! Previously, the only plant life around here was a beleaguered yucca in reception. These days, the canteen's offerings look as if they've tumbled from a food magazine; it's one of the more positive aspects of the recent changes. Already, the Platforms for Innovation are being formed, and teams being recruited. The average age seems to have plummeted from around fifty to twenty-five. Everywhere I look there are young people in jeans, skinny T-shirts and little sundresses – even shorts and playsuits. And we have music playing now. It's definitely more Urban Outfitters than Nerve Centre for Extruded Pellet Snacks.

As I tuck into my lunch, sitting at a favourite corner table with Belinda and Jean, I make a silent vow to forget about my proposal, and to be patient and just wait it out. I did succumb to calling Isla last night, ostensibly for a catch-up, and heard about how Megan, her daughter, had nagged for hair extensions (apparently they look natural these days, merely giving the impression of thicker hair, rather than the blatantly acrylic tresses I once begged my mum for, to no avail). Finally, Isla offered to pay for the things – more than she paid for her first car, apparently – but they turned out to be the wrong kind, and they've matted.

I made sympathetic noises, and of course I *cared* about the matting, but really, I wanted to blurt out, *But what about the proposal? D'you think anyone's read it yet?*

Isla then went on to tell me about how she is teaching her son Danny to drive, and that for the whole time he's at the wheel, sweat is pouring out of her. 'And honestly, I didn't think it would be possible. With the nights I'm having, how can there be any left in me to come out?'

Then she had to rush off because Rohan, her youngest, was heading out and needed money. We hadn't even got around to talking about the proposal.

I finish my lunch and work as diligently as I can all afternoon. It's when I'm driving home through steady, fine rain that my phone rings, and as soon as I pull up at school, I check the missed call.

Isla! I ring back immediately. 'Hey, everything okay?'

She clears her throat. 'D'you have a minute? I mean, is now a good time to talk?'

I literally have *one* minute; parents are supposed to collect children by five. I am parked in a side street and spot the odd familiar parent and child, hurrying along in the rain. A man in a yellow hi-vis jacket is picking up litter with one of those grabber sticks that Andy was always so keen to get his mitts on. 'It's fine,' I say. 'So, um, did the extensions de-matt?' I'm aware that I'm

233

putting off hearing bad news. We've been friends since we were seven years old, and I can sense her discomfort by the first sound that comes out of her mouth.

'No, they'll need redoing. It's like having a second mortgage, the maintenance of Meg's hair.'

I chuckle dutifully. *Okay, now tell me what happened, and why they think it's a bad idea.*

'Anyway,' she goes on, 'I gave Hannah your proposal, first chance I had . . .'

'Right . . .' I'm trying to sound positive.

'She's the Senior Exhibitions Manager,' Isla explains. 'She was off last week. I was told it'd be better to wait until she was back, that no one else could take it forward . . .' She pauses.

'But it's not good news, is it?'

Isla sighs. 'I'm so sorry, Viv. I know you put tons of work into it. It was her first day back today and, I don't know, maybe if I'd waited . . .' My heart seems to have crashed. 'But I was so impatient,' she goes on, 'and I just couldn't wait to share it with her.'

'She's said no, then?'

'Not exactly. I mean, it wasn't as if she thought it was a terrible idea. She could see its potential. She said maybe we could have arranged a chat, if it wasn't chaos around here, after what happened this morning . . .'

'Wait . . . *what* happened?'

'Oh, there was some vandalism. It's been pretty bad, actually. Someone went straight down to natural history with a hammer or something – I don't know what it was exactly. I was in the café when it happened. It was some man, a crazy person. He started smashing the display cases, threatening staff, shouting that he was going to liberate them . . .'

'Liberate the *staff*?'

'No – the collection. The snow fox and red squirrel. The wildcat and elk.'

'The stuffed animals? That's terrible!'

'It is. The whole floor's a wreck. God knows how long it'll be closed for. That is, if it even reopens at all.'

'What was he on about, liberating them?'

'I know,' she exclaims. 'It's taxidermy, for God's sake. Most have been dead for over 150 years. What did he think they'd do, scamper off to the wilderness?'

'There's no wilderness nearby.'

'No, just a Lidl over the road.' She snorts. 'So that's what's been going on here today. Hannah liked the idea, for another museum, maybe – or even for us, if this hadn't happened, and we had the time and resources to put on something like that. But we don't. It'll be all hands on deck with assessing the damage and costing up repairs.'

I glance at the time on the digital display in my car. 'Okay, well, look – thanks for showing it to her anyway.'

'Oh, Viv. I thought it was a brilliant idea. I'm so sorry. I'm gutted.'

'Me too, but never mind. We tried, didn't we? And it *was* a great idea. But I'm at school now, and I really have to go.'

Tuesday, September 17

I can hardly fall apart over a rejected proposal when such a terrible thing has happened to the museum. Inflicting damage on it – when it's threatened with closure anyway – seems as low and disgusting as attacking a frail elderly person and stealing their purse.

235

And what a mad thing to do anyway! Freeing battery chickens and laboratory animals, I can understand; i.e. *living* creatures. But not a faded stoat that's been gazing out of its glass dome since something like 1867. So I decide to try and put it out of my mind, and focus on things that really matter.

For instance, Izzy, who is thrilled by the news that, finally, a place has come up for her at Brownies (like the most coveted handbags, the local pack has a waiting list), which means she can start next week.

We while away the evening researching Brownie Badges online, and deciding which ones she might go for first:

Painting

Baking

Inventing

Mindfulness (yes, really . . .)

Grow Your Own

And for me? All I can think of is all the time and energy and hope I poured into that proposal, and how it's ended up being pointless. Unfortunately, there doesn't seem to be a 'Well, at least she gave it a shot' badge.

Chapter Twenty-Six

Thursday, September 19

A crappy day all round. Work was a drudge, and now we're home Izzy seems to have a cold. She is listless and runny-nosed. I try to cheer her up by chatting about the upcoming Brownie camp, hoping she'll be well enough to go. She was so enthusiastic last night when I picked her up from her first meeting. As lots of her friends (including Maeve) are in the pack, it felt both familiar and thrillingly new.

However, tonight she just lies on the sofa, wrapped up in a blanket, sipping hot blackcurrant squash and seemingly feeling even sorrier for herself than I do.

Friday, September 20

As Izzy's cold has worsened, I've taken the day off work. To give Rose her due, she's always been fine whenever I have needed to do this. Izzy spends most of the day dozing, or blearily watching cartoons. I catch up on housework, trying not to think about my proposal, and focus on the positive aspects of my life instead.

For instance: my bedroom is much improved since Andy took that dowdy old standard lamp with the olive-green tasselled shade that he was so fond of, and which I hated. The worrying fan heater has gone too. Small joys, I realise – in fact, they could be construed as straw-clutchy – but I am trying to derive glimmers of pleasure wherever I can.

Saturday, September 21

Penny drops by with Nick, plus Bobby, which cheers up the still cold-ridden Izzy. I've noticed that Penny has started a new thing, where she prompts me to tell Nick one of my supposedly 'hilarious' anecdotes. 'Tell Nick about that thing when you . . .' she keeps saying. I'm not quite sure why she's doing this, as if I'm incapable of interacting with other adults without her help. I just hope to God she's not trying to show me off in my 'best light' – i.e. pimping me out – in the hope that some kind of romantic spark might develop between Nick and me (admittedly, he's lovely, handsome, clever, all the right things – *for someone who might be looking for That Kind of Thing*).

As I pour their coffees in my kitchen, she starts asking about Andy, and whether I've found out why he took the flat above the cheese shop yet; she seems to be trying to signal: 'My Friend Viv Is Single, Nick. Pay Heed.'

'I'm trying to keep communications with him to a minimum,' I say with a smile.

238

She tries again. 'The things that man moaned about. Like the scones in the hospital canteen! Tell Nick about the scone thing,' she prompts me.

'What scone thing?' I ask, genuinely confused.

'You know – the thing with the hard pat of butter.' Oh, God. This is worryingly reminiscent of when Spence was learning guitar. Whenever Andy's parents visited, Andy would say, 'Go get your guitar, Spence! Play "Whisky in the Jar" for Grandma and Grandpa.' And he'd skulk off to fetch it and play it dutifully, emitting gusts of resentment, until he reached thirteen and point-blank refused.

'You mean at the hospital?' I ask, and Penny nods. So I launch into the background info, about Andy's perpetual moans about the hospital car park, the low-grade loo roll and the hard pats of butter, and how he was driven one day to *sitting* on one (still in its foil wrapper) in the canteen, in order to soften it for spreading, and it oozed out and made an oily stain on his trousers.

Nick laughs, but not in the natural, spontaneous way as he has on the other times I've seen him. Perhaps my delivery could have been better. I hate being pressurised to recount anecdotes like that.

Wednesday, September 25

Izzy was finally well enough to go back to school today. Happily, it means she'll be able to go to Brownies tonight, and to the camp in Perthshire this coming weekend. I must make the most of this time, when I'll be alone – but not lonely, most definitely *not*. I plan to treat it as a weekend of relaxation and culture, visiting museums – no, not museums! I might give those places a miss for a while.

The cinema, then. And perhaps some exercise: a little light jogging, or a swim, ploughing up and down the pool by myself, trying to beat back the cushiony wodge that appears to be growing by the day around my stomach. I might even go for a spin on my bike. That's it, I decide; it'll be a practical, purposeful, health-giving weekend, beneficial to body and mind. I can't wait.

Saturday, September 28

Annoyingly, I've had to resort to asking Andy to pop round to access the loft. I hate asking him to do anything. I can't bear his bouncy, 'Sure, happy to help!' attitude, all muscles flexed and penis swinging, perhaps because it brings to mind his Eager Elf, lightbulb-changing period, when he was still secretly shagging Estelle Lang but trying to seem like the good guy around the house.

Anyway, never mind that now. The attic is where our lesser spotted camping equipment is stashed (with all his lumbago/sciatica moanings, Andy never took to the under-canvas life). And as I've neglected to buy Izzy a new sleeping bag for the camping trip – which would have avoided this scenario – I now need him to shift the awkward hatch and manoeuvre himself up into the gloomy space, which only he has ever been able to do successfully.

He was handy for some things, I guess. He certainly always seemed keener to forage about in the attic than in my underwear.

He's up there now, biffing around and humming cheerfully. A few minutes later the hero reappears, clambering

240

down our flimsy stepladder and presenting the sleeping bag to me like a prize pike. '*There* you go.'

'Thanks. You know I really can't manage to lift that hatch. Or, if I do, I always think it's going to smash down on my head.'

Andy pulls a concerned face. 'You don't need to do it. Just phone me.' We head downstairs where he sips the coffee I made him. 'You can always ask me to do anything, you know,' he adds.

'I don't think I'll need anything else,' I say quickly.

'Okay.'

'And if I did, I'd just get someone in.'

He gives me a resigned look. 'Yeah, well, I just thought I'd say, that's all.'

Izzy appears, clutching the 'things to pack' list she was given at the last Brownie meeting. She has insisted on doing it herself, although obviously I'll check everything before she heads off this afternoon (I'm aware that we are cutting it fine, and that the other Brownies were probably all packed and ready a week ago). 'It says don't forget to pack a toy,' she announces. 'Shall I take Woolly?' Her knitted sandwich, she means.

'I think you should,' I say.

'Will anyone laugh?'

'Of course not,' I exclaim. 'Why on earth would they?'

She grins. 'I think Woolly will like camping more than Dad did.'

'Hey, I loved it!' Andy protests.

'You said you got no sleep, Dad,' she reminds him. 'You hurt your back. You got that . . . thing, the thing that made you shout at Mum.'

'Sciatica,' I say, helpfully.

'Yeah, but I enjoyed the *experience*,' he says, pulling

241

on his jacket now, 'and I'm sure I didn't shout. I loved the nature aspect, being outdoors, cooking on the little stove . . .' He was a little less keen on washing up at the communal sink block – being chronically injured from having slept on a blow-up bed – but I decide not to remind him of that.

'I wish we could go camping again,' Izzy adds, giving her father and me a wistful look.

'You are,' I say quickly, deliberately misunderstanding. 'You're going today.'

'I mean with you and Dad.'

Andy catches my gaze. 'You'll have great fun with the Brownies, honey,' he says quickly. 'You don't want your parents wrecking your fun.'

'You never wrecked my fun, Dad.' She knows he's joking, but is pretending not to.

'Hey, Dad's about to go,' I say. 'You'd better finish your packing, darling.' She hugs her father goodbye and tramps back upstairs.

I exhale slowly as I see Andy to the front door. 'Thanks for coming over and helping with that.'

He shrugs. 'Like I said, it's no problem.'

'Well, it's appreciated.'

He nods and looks at me. 'Are you okay?'

'Yeah, I'm good. It just felt a bit weird there, Izzy mentioning our camping trips . . .'

'Yes, it did a bit.' His voice catches. 'Our last one was, what, about three years ago?'

'That's probably right. I'm surprised she remembers.' I pause. 'D'you think she's doing okay?'

'I hope so,' he says. 'She seems happy, and we always have a nice time together. And she's pretty excited about this trip.'

'Yeah.' I sense a tightness in my throat. *Why did you do this to us?* I want to blurt out. *What was so dreadful about our situation that you had to have a drunken fling and then carry it on for months on end, behind my back, and fall in love with her?* If it had been a one-night stand, and he'd been genuinely remorseful, it might not have finished us off. I'd have been hurt and furious – but quite possibly, we might have got over it. I know lots of people do.

I'm aware of Andy studying me. 'You seem a bit down,' he adds.

'Honestly, I'm fine,' I say as we stand there at the doorway, with him still looking concerned, and me wanting to talk to him, to someone, to anyone really – but not about us, or his new woman. Instead, I find myself telling him about the museum being in dire straits, and Isla and I coming up with the initial idea for the fashion show. I pour it all out: about my proposal, the crazy vandalism, the attempted freeing of the taxidermy – and now nothing. No money, no resources, no interest in Girl Friday; it's just not the right time. Hannah Jeffers from the museum has since emailed me:

We really appreciate all the thought and effort you've put into this. I think it's a wonderful idea and perhaps it might have wide appeal across our city. But sadly, we are not in a position at present to take this any further.

Andy sighs. 'Sounds like you put an awful lot of work into it.'

'I did,' I say, 'but that's not the point. I don't really mind about that. What I do mind is that I know it'd be great for the museum, and for Penny. I mean, her son thought it was a fantastic idea.'

'Yes, but he would, wouldn't he?' Andy remarks.

I frown. 'What d'you mean?'

'Well, she's his mum, isn't she? And he's obviously proud of her.'

'Andy,' I start, 'she was a renowned designer. She was incredibly successful and influential. You're making it sound as if she won first prize in the Victoria Sponge section of a village show.'

He laughs, with a hint of exasperation. 'I don't mean it like that. I'm aware of what she did, Viv.' He isn't really, but never mind. 'Of course her *son* would love to see her designs on a catwalk, and a whole exhibition dedicated to her . . .'

'Not just her son, Andy. It could be huge!'

He peers at me as if I have taken leave of my senses. 'D'you really think so? I mean, isn't it a bit niche?'

'Of course not,' I retort. 'Every woman of a certain age remembers the boutiques, especially from round here. This is where it all started.'

'Yeah, but . . .' He winces, infuriatingly. 'Seventies fashion, Viv. Think about it. The flares, the massive collars, the horrible synthetic fabrics, the *ponchos* . . .' A maddening chuckle. So he's quite the fashion guru now? 'It's not everyone's cup of tea, is it?' he adds.

I blink at him, fury bubbling up in me now. 'Well, I think it is.'

He shrugs. 'Yeah, well, I guess you know best.'

'I obviously don't,' I say hotly, 'because it was turned down, wasn't it?'

'Okay, Viv,' he says, giving me one of those *here she goes, going off on one* looks. 'If you say so.'

If I say so! *I think you'll find it wouldn't be to everyone's taste . . .*

244

We exchange rather stiff goodbyes, and off he goes. It takes an almighty effort to appear normal, and to seem as thrilled about the Brownie camping trip as Izzy is, as I turn back into the house.

Chapter Twenty-Seven

Late afternoon, with Izzy gone

Maybe it's the hormones again. Maybe I've swerved back down into 'irrational alley', as Shelley calls it – yet another symptom of being fifty-three with bugger all oestrogen remaining; a 'trace element', like limestone in rabbit food. Grab it now while stocks last!

Or maybe I am just pissed off.

How dare Andy imply that I was wasting my time with the proposal? *Did* he suggest that, or am I over-reacting? Perhaps I need to start recording my every conversation, so it can be analysed later, because now I have no idea. The fact that my anger is mixed up with gratitude (for Andy having accessed the attic), and possibly a little shame (for being such a grumpy, ungrateful arse; *and* for not buying Izzy a new sleeping bag) is only confusing things further. What I do know, however, is that swimming/jogging/cycling won't be happening today, and nor will 'culture'. I'd half-heartedly considered going to see an arty Italian film that Jules had been raving about, but fuck that. The only Italian I'll be reading tonight is the label on a bottle of cheap Pinot Grigio. I have already stomped out to buy some, and I fully intend to neck it alone like the sad, dumped wife that I am. And now, at 5.38 p.m., far too early to start drinking, I am ceremoniously pouring my first glass.

It's insufficiently chilled, and has a hint of bubble gum and a lingering note of having been manufactured at a vast plant in Warrington – but what the hell. I take a big swig. Spotting my laptop sitting on the worktop, I consider googling Estelle Lang, but no, that would be a step back and I'm past that stage now. I sit drumming my fingers on the table, waiting for the urge to go away.

I seem to have finished my glass of wine very quickly. What kind of mother sits there intending to get pissed the minute her daughter's gone away on a wholesome camping trip? This one, obviously. I pour another glass, remembering that I haven't eaten tonight, and check the fridge to see what I could throw together for my solo supper. Hummus, eggs, cherry tomatoes and half a tub of cottage cheese, with milky liquid pooling in it. Some out-of-date ham and a bendy courgette, which I bin. I decide to just have wine.

By the end of the second glass, I'd have hoped to have felt more relaxed, and possibly pleasantly *naughty*, sipping away at my corner shop plonk that Andy would scoff at ('You'd barely class that as wine,' he's observed on many occasions). However, I am not relaxed. I'm far from it. The booze seems to have triggered a powerful hot flush, and now, because I'm sitting here alone in my kitchen, fanning my face with a magazine, and with my laptop within arm's reach on the worktop, it starts happening again: a small niggle, like a craving for a cigarette. *Just the one, then I'll stop and that'll be the end of it.*

Just one little peek at those photos of Estelle Lang.

But no – I *definitely* don't do that anymore. I know it's bad for my mental health, and I have better things to do, like getting sloshed on my own. I get up and bring my laptop to the table and sit there wondering what I could look at instead, to take my mind off staring at pictures of her.

I pour more wine – a huge glass, well over half the bottle gone already. How did that happen? *Mid-life women are self-medicating with wine*, I read the other day. I've never liked smoking a joint – it makes me agitated and paranoid – and I'm not about to start on the 'party drugs' at my advanced age. Even if I fancied a go, I wouldn't know where to get them, and my mental capabilities feel impaired enough at the moment without being chemically altered. So what else, other than wine, am I meant to self-medicate with?

I open my laptop and stare at the screen, sipping more wine and willing myself not to do anything stupid, not to torture myself in my empty house by peering at those pictures again. I need a substitute activity, that's it; Penny has suggested several times that I could do with a 'hobby'. She even brought me over a bag of wool and some needles a few weeks ago, to 'get you started with crochet', as she put it. 'I'd teach you, but you seem more like someone who wants to learn at your own pace.' (I'd told her about the hedgehog pincushion debacle at school.) 'You might be better learning from YouTube tutorials,' she added, 'rather than from me.'

I'm definitely too tipsy to try to learn to crochet now. But I decide to have a browse on YouTube anyway, and soon I'm swigging yet more wine, tucking into the hummus, some crisps and the baggy-skinned cherry tomatoes, as I watch all kinds of daft stuff: a sped-up film of someone making a pizza (not a patch on *Izzy Cooks!*, in my opinion), and then a traybake incorporating Maltesers and bashed pretzels (interesting!). Stuck for what to watch next, I sit through a few news clips of Flaxico's bunnygate fiasco. There's a chilly-looking young female reporter standing in front of our headquarters, and interviews with mums who are using words like 'disgusting' and 'horrified' and vowing to never buy anything connected to Flaxico again. In one segment, a child of eight is crying because she is afraid of the snack's effects on her health. This is neither fun nor soothing, which is surely what a hobby is supposed to be. Perhaps I should give macramé a go? Or, alternatively, what would happen if I put 'Estelle Lang' in the search bar?

Nothing, I tell myself. Why would Estelle Lang be on YouTube?

I type in her name – and, bloody hell, she *is* on there. In fact it looks like there are several videos of her, being a 'leading endocrinologist with a wealth of insight and advice for any woman at this rewarding, yet challenging, stage of life.' That's what it ruddy says. She even appears to have her own channel. I can't imagine how she finds the time, what with being a medical superstar and shagging other women's husbands – but she's obviously highly efficient on top of everything else.

I cram more crisps into my mouth and wash them down with more wine, ready to watch.

This isn't the same as looking at pictures of her, I reassure myself. It's an entirely different thing. I'll have a tiny peek, just to see what she's like when she's moving and talking. It doesn't mean I'll get addicted.

I click 'play' and sense my lifeblood dwindling a little. It's just a static image to start with, and some ripply harp music. She's sitting on a pale grey sofa, poised and chic in a crisp white shirt. Then the video starts.

'Hi, I'm Dr Estelle Lang,' she says, leaning forward and beaming. 'Thanks for joining me today. I'd like to talk to you a little about menopausal symptoms . . .' I watch, disgusted, munching away on my cheese and onion crisps. 'Not the obvious ones like hot flushes,' she continues. 'We covered that last time. Today, I'm focusing on the general sense of low-level irritation, and those bursts of anger that can overwhelm you when you least expect them. There are ways of handling these,' she goes on in her soothing tones, 'and the good news is, there are plenty of alternatives to medication . . .'

I should be irritated now, watching her looking all polished in her shirt, which is probably from somewhere like Jigsaw, her cheekbones thieved from Meryl Streep and her shiny blonde hair hanging neatly at her chin. I should be seething with rage that, despite the fact that she and my husband were meeting secretly over several months, she still sees fit to sit there and tell other women how to manage their lives.

And yet . . . I actually want to know what she's going to say. I'm genuinely interested in how to be like her (calm, attractive) rather than me (dishevelled, drunk). So I sit there, alternatively munching and sipping as she talks about 'owning the menopause' and 'acknowledging that these feelings and symptoms are quite normal, and incredibly common, rather than something to be ashamed of, or even to think of as a problem at all.'

Quite right, Dr Lang! Who would ever regard the menopause as a problem when they're as glossy and unsweaty as you appear to be? I bet she's never even had a hot flush. Is she menopause-proof, like some kind of android? Is she on HRT, or those bio-identical hormones I've often wondered about going on, which Andy wouldn't even discuss with me?

'A big factor,' she continues, 'is having supportive people around you, who understand, and who take the time to listen sympathetically . . .'

Ah, right! Like starting the day with a cob on and blurting out, 'Christ, it's like waking up in a swamp around here'? 'Fuck off,' I say out loud. 'Just fuck off and leave me alone.' I shut my laptop abruptly, tip the last of the wine into my glass and down it in one, before opening a second bottle and pouring some more.

Sod her and Andy, the perfect ruddy doctor couple who have upended my life. I think I'm coping, and manage to convince myself that life is so much better without that ugly lampshade/temperamental fan heater – but it's not really, is it? He lied to me for months. He patronised me by feigning interest in how to make omelettes. Bloody omelettes! I leap up from my chair, open the fridge so forcefully it makes the bottles wobble on their shelf on the door, and stare at the eggs.

Instantly, I have an idea of how to make myself feel better, and how to salvage this dismal night. I know it's a mad one, and I'm also aware that I wouldn't be even considering it if I wasn't drunk. But what the hell – Izzy is away on her camp, and no one's going to figure out that it's me. It seemed to work for Penny; she admitted it was neither big nor clever but that egging some mystery person's car made her feel a whole lot better about whatever it was she was angry about.

My heart is pounding excitedly now. Intending to put

my own personal twist on it, I hope it'll do the same thing for me.

Around midnight, drunk

Taking a taxi diminishes the drama somewhat, but there was no way I could drive, and I decided not to risk cycling either; I wasn't ready to die for my cause. So a cab it was, with the driver asking, perkily, 'Off on a night out?'

'Sort of,' I replied, conscious of my boozy breath.

'Anywhere nice?'

'Just seeing who's around,' I said, which probably made it sound as if I were some lone woman, without friends or plans, who had decided to head out just before midnight in the quest for company or possibly even love.

'Have fun, then,' he said with a smirk as I paid him.

Now here I am, standing outside Andy's flat, the cheesy whiff teasing my nostrils. A sign in the window, printed in elegant script, explains to customers that the shop has been specially fitted out with slate tiling and a foot-deep concrete floor, to mimic cave-like conditions and offer the perfect storage conditions for the 52 varieties on offer.

Although I love cheese normally, after too much vinegary wine and a sackload of crisps, the smell is making my stomach shift uneasily. I glance up at Andy's flat; a light is on in what I presume is the living room. Is he home, I wonder? And is *she* there? Are they doing it now, or engaged in something altogether more humdrum, like washing up? Unlikely, I know, at midnight – but who knows how he rolls these days.

Anyway, whether she is there or not is of no consequence to me right now. She might be the big-shot doctor with her own YouTube channel, but hey, there's that photo of me in the net tutu and bunny ears floating about in the ether, and at least that showed courage, and a willingness to have a go when the mums' race probably ranks as the low point in my 'sporting calendar'. And I'd like to see *her* haring across the field, amidst the pack of ferociously competitive women, some of whom take the event so seriously that training commences six months in advance.

That's my epitaph, I decide, as I move away from the cheese shop and wander unsteadily down the street: *She had a bloody go. She worked on and on without making a fuss.* What a thrilling specimen I've become in my fifties: unexpectedly single, with a job that bores me rigid – and was only meant to be a stopgap until I found a theatre company that could utilise my talents. Here I am, five years later, tottering drunkenly with a carrier bag with the thing in it; the thing I have transported across Glasgow in a taxi for the purpose of . . . what exactly? To do something mad. To show him I'm still angry about his reaction to my Girl Friday rejection, and that it'll take more than him scrabbling about in the attic for us to become 'friends' (or whatever arrangement he hopes to arrive at, coming round with his hangdog face).

That is, if he even realises it was me who did this tonight. He might not. He might think it's just a random nut-job, which, actually, would be preferable: to put the fear of God into him that he has a crazy, omelette-depositing stalker! Because that's what's in my carrier bag: a four-egg omelette devoid of cheese, seasoning or any flavour at all; I wasn't prepared to waste a speck of black pepper on that fuckwit. But I didn't begrudge the eggs. If my omelettes are so bloody great – and he was at pains to praise them – then see how he likes this one, slapped on his precious car!

I scan the street for it. It hadn't occurred to me that it might not be parked conveniently outside his flat. It takes a few minutes' strolling to find the black BMW, which Andy adores, and keeps as clean and shiny as a snooker ball (pigeon shit is regarded as a personal affront, as if the bird had specifically targeted his bonnet out of spite). Maybe that's the real reason why I'm doing this – to violate his precious motor – or maybe it's the cheap Pinot Grigio's fault.

Whatever the reason, I'm pulling the cold, flabby omelette from the carrier bag now, lifting a windscreen wiper carefully and sliding my eggy offering under it, then rubbing my greasy hands on the front of my jeans and running away. As I ride home in a taxi, I try to picture his face when he sees it, but I can't quite bring it into focus.

'Good night out, love?' the driver asks, his gaze meeting mine in the rear-view mirror.

'Brilliant, thanks,' I reply, thinking: it was, in a way. At least, no one can say I didn't make the most of my child-free night.

Chapter Twenty-Eight

Sunday, September 29

Like the mature, sorted woman I am, I wake up fully dressed on the sofa, shoes still on, cringing as the memory of last night's mission starts to filter into my hungover brain. My phone rings, and I scramble off the sofa and retrieve it from my bag.

Andy! In panic, I run through what to do if accused: deny, obviously. *Are you mad? D'you think I have time to go around putting omelettes under windscreen wipers?* Act outraged. Suggest that it was probably just some random drunk person wandering by. (Ahem). Who happened to have an omelette about their person. Maybe they stole it from a hotel breakfast buffet? A fried egg would seem more feasible. Christ.

The ringing stops, and by the time he calls again (which I knew he would) I'm primed to sound purposeful and together, as if have been up for hours, tackling jobs around the house, making the most of the day.

'Hi,' he says, 'how's things?' He sounds oddly normal.

'I'm fine,' I say.

'Just wondered when Izzy's back? I thought maybe she and I could spend the afternoon together?'

Perhaps he hasn't needed his car today, and therefore hasn't seen the omelette yet? Or maybe a fox took it in the night?

'She's not back till tomorrow teatime,' I reply. 'It's a school in-service day.'

'Ah, shame. Just missing her quite a bit at the moment, that's all. Heard from Spence lately? He's hopeless at replying to texts . . .'

'Yeah, I know. I think he's still in Italy.'

'Yep, you're probably right. Catch you soon, then.'

'Okay.'

'Oh, Viv?'

'Yeah?' My heart quickens.

A pause. 'You didn't . . .'

'I didn't what?'

'No, it's nothing. Forget I even said anything. See you soon, okay?'

Monday, September 30

Off work for the school in-service day. Before the Brownie camp was announced I'd assumed Izzy would be home, but instead I have a free day stretching out ahead of me. Determined to make use of it this time, I go for a swim and a sauna, the latter of which helps me to literally sweat out the last residues of shame. Back home, I spruce up the house before setting off to pick up Izzy from the Brownie hut. By now, I have managed to convince myself that the omelette mission was nothing more than an amusing jape.

That's why I've allowed a little extra time to pop in on Penny. As predicted, she is quite hysterical with laughter when I tell her about my Saturday night. 'This,' she says, 'is possibly the most brilliant thing I've ever heard.'

'You don't think I'm unhinged?'

'Of course you are!' she hoots. 'But there's no real harm done. It was only a soft, harmless omelette.'

I nod. 'It's not as if I pelted his windscreen with tins of baked beans.'

'Not that I'd blame you if you had.' She smiles. 'So, you're still angry with him, aren't you?'

I exhale. 'I probably shouldn't be. I mean, it's been six months since he left. I should be used to it and pretty cool about everything . . .'

'What's all this "should"?' she asks. 'You feel how you feel, Viv. No need to make excuses or apologise for it.'

'Yeah.' I nod, grateful that Nick isn't here. I wouldn't want him to think I'm some kind of maniac. 'Sometimes,' I add, 'the anger just wells up in me and I can't help it.'

She touches my arm. 'That's understandable.'

'But what if I never get over it, Penny?' I ask. 'What if I spend the rest of my life feeling furious, hating him, wanting to leave cold fried foods on his beloved car? I can't bear to go on feeling like this. He's Izzy's dad, so he'll always be around, whether I like it or not . . .'

'Look,' she says, 'you're not always like this, are you? Most of the time, you're amazingly calm and sensible about everything.'

I look down at the floor. 'I wouldn't say that.'

'And the omelette thing? It just came to you, and you ran with it. There's no harm done.'

'I guess so,' I say, wishing I could tell her what the main trigger had been; i.e. being upset over the proposal for the museum, and Andy failing to understand why it had mattered so much. 'Please don't tell Nick about this,' I add as I'm leaving.

'Why not?' she asks.

'Because he might not approve. He'll think I'm crazy.'

'Ah, I'm sure he won't, but okay.' She grins and taps her nose. 'Your secret's safe with me.'

I set off, trying to forget all about it now, and relieved that Izzy will be home soon, which will prevent me from losing the plot anytime soon. The coach hasn't arrived by the time I reach the Brownie hut. My phone rings, and I flinch, hoping it's not Andy again; but it's an unknown number.

'Hello, is that Viv?' It's a woman's voice; not Scottish but from the north of England. She sounds warm, friendly and efficient.

'Yes, speaking?'

'Hi, it's Hannah Jeffers from the museum. I emailed you about your Girl Friday proposal?'

'Oh, yes.'

'I'm sorry,' she adds. 'I probably dashed it off in a bit of a hurry.'

'That's okay,' I say.

'We've had a bit of a time of it lately – a pretty bad case of vandalism, which is really not what we need right now. Or at any time really.' She pauses.

'Yes, Isla told me about that. It's terrible. I'm so sorry it happened.'

'Yes, well . . . I've now had time to look over it again.

258

Your proposal, I mean. I wondered if you might have time to come in and talk it over?'

My heart quickens. 'Oh! Erm, yes, that would be fine,' I say, trying to remain calm.

'Isla said you work full time?'

'Yes, but I can easily make some time—'

'I don't want to put you out. I'm sure you're very busy—'

'Not at all. I could take a holiday or pull a sickie . . .' What made me say that? 'Not that I ever do that kind of thing,' I add, 'but if it would help—'

'There's no need to do that,' Hannah says, a trace of amusement in her voice now. 'We're open later on Thursday evenings. If that suited you, I could stay behind and we could have a chat then?'

I take a moment, trying to regain my composure and give the impression that I am mentally running through my packed schedule. 'This Thursday evening, you mean?'

'If that suits you. How about six-thirty?'

'Yes,' I say, all brisk and businesslike now, 'that works for me.'

Tuesday, October 1

'Viv?' Andy says. 'D'you have a minute?'

'Just about to grab lunch,' I reply. 'Is something wrong?'

'Erm, well . . . this is a bit awkward.'

My heart starts to thud. I decide to take the stairs rather than the lift to the canteen so we can talk. 'What's the matter?'

'Erm . . . I wasn't going to say anything. I thought it might be better to just leave it. But I suppose, well . . .

259

it's been playing on my mind, and I need to talk to you.'

I stop and look out onto the flat, unremarkable landscape. 'Well, what is it?'

He sighs. 'I'm worried about you.'

'What? Why are you worried?' Surely it can't be the omelette; that was three days ago. He'd have mentioned it before now if he'd suspected I did it. Maybe I should never have shared all that stuff about the museum? Serves me right for letting down my guard and confiding in him.

'I'm just wondering if something's wrong,' he murmurs.

'Nothing's wrong, Andy. And if it's not important, I'm going to go and have lunch now . . .'

'Viv, look . . . I'm sorry if this embarrasses you, okay?'

I feel sick now. That must rank as the top phrase from the 'things you never want to hear' list.

'But you were seen,' he adds. The second-top phrase. 'On Saturday night, at around midnight.'

'What are you talking about?' *It can't have been me. I was tucked up in bed, reading and drinking chamomile tea!*

Andy exhales. 'You were seen wandering about pissed in the street by my flat, and then fishing about in a carrier bag and stuffing some kind of egg thing under the windscreen wiper of my car.'

I open my mouth to speak. I could say, 'How dare you suggest I'd stoop to such ridiculous behaviour?' But I can't bring myself to do it. Standing here, with colleagues passing me on the stairs, smiling briefly while I try to look normal, I am incapable of feigning outrage. 'Some kind of . . . egg thing?' I ask.

'Yes, that's what it looked like, she said. Like a tortilla.'

'A tortilla?' *Don't we call them omelettes anymore?*

260

'Viv, look,' Andy blusters, 'I don't want to make big thing of it. There was no harm done, it's not about that. It's more about . . . you.'

'What *are* you talking about?' I ask faintly.

'I'm worried about you,' he exclaims, adopting a head-masterly tone now. 'Getting drunk – okay, we've all done that . . .'

'Please don't start crowing at me.'

'We've all been pissed, we've all done stupid things . . .'

'Can you stop this phoney concern please?' I cut in, anger rising in me now. 'Okay, so I did it. I'll admit it now, and it was a bit mad, a bit stupid, not exactly how I'd planned to fill my time when our daughter was away at Brownie camp.' I focus hard on the uninspiring view of car parks, garages, shabby low-rise buildings and scrubby ground. It's mainly light industrial units around here. When Flaxico's sweet potato falafels are released into the wild, the cutely illustrated packaging will suggest they've come from a country kitchen with its own vege-table plot. But they'll have been churned out in the factory like everything else we make.

'It was dangerous,' he adds gravely.

'It wasn't dangerous. It was just . . . ill advised.'

'Anything could've happened to you, tottering about on your own like that.'

'I was just a little bit tipsy,' I mutter, teeth gritted, wishing this wasn't being discussed on the main stairwell of my workplace. 'I was hardly lying comatose on the pavement with my knickers on display.'

'I think you'll find you were more than just a little—'

'Don't *I-think-you'll-find* me!'

'What?'

'It's a thing you say. It's so patronising. "I think you'll

261

find the fan heater's fine." "I think you'll find reptiles are dry-skinned, Viv".'

'What are you on about? Jesus, I really am worried about you. Should you see a doctor?'

'For anti-depressants, you mean?' I snap.

'Well, for something anyway. I don't know . . .'

'Don't try and come over all concerned about my mental health now. It's a little late for that, isn't it?'

'I'm only saying,' he cuts in.

'Who saw me, anyway? Who saw me doing that thing?'

'Erm, Estelle did,' he says quietly.

I let this new information sink in for a moment as Jean approaches on the stairs. Seeing me, she raises a brow and makes a knife and fork motion with her hand. I nod and will her to move on. More people are coming now; it seems to be a craze right now, this taking the stairs rather than the lift. At least, amongst us older ones it is. The youngsters seem to ride up and down in the lift all day, slurping their calorie-laden lattes, without worrying about it.

I wait until no one seems to be around. 'She saw me?'

'Yes, she did, I'm afraid, just after she'd left my flat, on the way to her own car.'

'But . . .' I push my hair back from my clammy forehead. 'How did she know who I was?'

Andy sighs heavily. 'She, erm . . . recognised you from seeing pictures on my computer and stuff.' So he's shown her our family photos? 'And she took a picture of you with her phone, and I said yes – it was definitely you.'

'She photographed me? Isn't that a bit creepy?' It's a little hard, at this stage, to maintain any sense of indignation.

'I think it was kind of justified,' Andy says wearily.

'Oh, do you? And you confirmed my identity?'

262

He sighs. 'Yes, of course I did. She was just concerned, that's all, seeing a woman out on her own, staggering about—'

'I wasn't staggering!'

'And she knew it was my car, so she thought she'd better take a photo as evidence.'

'Why didn't she just come over and say something?'

'Because you looked, I don't know . . . kind of scary, I guess.'

'She was *scared* of me?'

'Yes! I would've been scared, seeing someone running rampage with a tortilla.'

'Can you stop saying "tortilla"?' I say sharply as I start to head up the stairs. 'This is Glasgow, not Madrid. It's a ridiculous affectation.'

'Omelette, then,' he mumbles.

'So,' I say, my embarrassment starting to morph into impatience as I reach the top floor, 'she somehow managed to be both concerned about my welfare *and* frightened of me, and then she came back to your flat and showed you the photo? And I suppose the two of you had a good laugh about it?'

'Of course not,' he says, sounding exasperated now. 'We didn't have a good laugh, and she didn't come back to show it to me. Quite the opposite, in fact. She sent it to me with a curt message saying, "I think this is your wife?"'

I frown and stand there for a moment, at the door to the canteen. 'And that was that?'

'Yep, that's the last communication we've had,' he says dryly. 'I might as well tell you, we've broken up.'

Afternoon, in the aftermath of Andy's news

I've fantasised about this so many times. I've pictured myself laughing in his face, then 'turning on my heel', as women do in the movies, leaving him standing there, forlorn and loveless, cursing himself for being such a fool. I have even imagined him turning up late at night, banging on my door and dropping to his knees as he begs forgiveness, and trying to lick my shoes – or more likely my slippers if it's at some ungodly hour. But the funny thing is that sometimes, when you've yearned for something and it finally happens, the last thing you feel like doing is punching the air and revelling in smugness and delight.

The truth is, I am neither delighted nor smug right now. I just go for lunch as normal, sitting with Jean and Belinda by the window, proud of myself for not reacting to his news, other than uttering, 'Oh, really.' I have no idea why they broke up, and I certainly wasn't going to let him think I cared by quizzing him about it.

My afternoon is spent mainly on setting up Rose's next trip. Now and again, when Andy pops into my mind, I reflect on how unremarkable this news is to me, considering it's his affair with her that ended our marriage. Perhaps I've moved on more than I'd realised? It's a cheering thought, and one that carries me through the rest of the working day with a spring in my step.

I pick up Izzy from after-school club, along with Maeve and Esme, another friend from their class, both of whom we'd arranged to have over for tea. As I'm tending to a chicken stir-fry on the stove, Chrissie knocks at the door, clutching a colicky baby, with Ludo hovering beside her, looking morose.

'Is everything okay?' I ask, beckoning her in, as supper is still sizzling in the wok.

'I'm sorry to just bowl up like this,' she says over Lara's fretful crying. 'Tim's out this evening at a work thing, and I'm at the end of my tether, frankly. It's okay for him, going out whenever he wants to.' Her voice rises shrilly. In fact, I've never known a man to be more 'present' on the home front than Tim is, with a tea towel almost permanently welded to his hand. 'I'd have called you first,' Chrissie adds, 'but I can't find my phone, I think it might be in the pocket of my jeans that are on a forty-degree cycle right now.'

'Oh, no. You could try rice—'

'That's what Tim said, last time it happened: "Try rice!" As if that sorts out all the world's ills. Anyway,' she goes on, 'Ludo was asking – begging, actually – to come over to yours.' She pulls a pained expression as she rubs Lara's back.

'Really?' I look down at him. He smiles hopefully. 'Of course. That's absolutely fine.'

'Thank you so much. He loves it here, don't you, sweetheart?' He glances at me, nodding mutely. 'And no wonder,' she adds, 'when Viv's so kind and welcoming to you, and so *relaxed*.'

So Ludo stays for dinner, and is actually pleasant, saying 'please' and 'thank you' and carrying his plate to the sink, which is as startling as if he had lapsed into Japanese.

The kids all play together – even Maeve seems to have realised that Ludo's okay really – and he behaves extremely well. Perhaps he is conscious of making a good impression, in the hope that this may become a regular thing. I don't think he and Izzy will ever be best friends, but there has definitely been a marked improvement in how they get along.

'Ludo seems to like our house doesn't he?' I remark later, when it's just Izzy and me, curled up on the sofa together with hot chocolates.

'Yeah, it's 'cause there's no baby,' she says.

'Actually, I think he likes it here anyway. I don't think he just wants to escape from his little sister, do you?'

Izzy shrugs. 'I'd love it if we had a baby here. If *you* had a baby,' she adds.

'Um, well, I'm afraid that won't be happening, love.'

She nods gravely. 'Because you're not with Dad any-more?'

'Er, well, yes, but actually, I'm a bit too old now.' *Please don't ask about baby-making now*, I will her. I'm not against her knowing, of course I'm not. They've started on the basics at school, just the body parts, stuff like that, and I'm not planning to promote any 'special kisses' nonsense. It's just . . . I'm not up to it at this precise moment.

So, hoping she'll forget about babies, I usher her upstairs for her bath; and later still, I chatter on, looking through her books for something she might like me to read to her. I keep pulling out stories to show her, but she doesn't seem interested.

'Are you really too old to have another baby?' she asks from her bed.

I look around, taken aback momentarily. 'I kind of am, love. But that's okay, you know? I'm very lucky to have you and Spence.'

'When do women get too old?' she wants to know.

I smile; what a question. 'For babies?' She nods. 'Um, it just gets more difficult to make a baby as you get older.

In your forties, I mean, although it depends on the person. Everyone's bodies are different.'

'Were you old when you had me?'

'Not really, sweetheart. Older than some mums, yes – but not ancient.'

She nods and seems to be mulling this over as I pull out another book and sit down on her bed.

'Mum?'

'Yes, love?' I am primed for more baby-related questioning.

'D'you mind if I read by myself now?'

I look at her, confused for a moment. 'D'you mean just tonight? Or would you prefer that from now on?'

'I'd prefer it. I'm nearly eight.' She smiles.

Something seems to twist inside me as I kiss her forehead and get up from her bed. 'I know you are, honey. And I also know you're a good reader.'

I say goodnight and leave her to read by herself, still feeling a little strange as I make my way downstairs. So much so that I can't settle to anything; so I step out to the garden and sit at our wrought-iron table on the patio for a while, just being quiet. Only a couple of stars are visible tonight, and without the app I can't identify them.

So, Izzy doesn't need me to read her stories anymore. I suspect that she hasn't for a while, but wasn't sure how to break it to me.

No need to be sad, I decide as I wander back into the house. I've loved reading those bedtime stories, first to Spencer and then to Izzy; all the dragons and witches and elves. I've loved the feeling of a warm, sleepy child snuggling next to me, transfixed by the tale. But moving on from that stage is just the natural way of things, and it hardly amounts to rejection. My daughter is just growing up.

Chapter Twenty-Nine

Thursday, October 3

'Viv, hi . . . is it Viv? Or d'you prefer Vivienne?'

'Everyone calls me Viv,' I reply, jumping up from the chair in the foyer as Hannah greets me. We shake hands, and she beckons me into the office. While the public parts of the museum are all polished wood and ornate chandeliers, the staff areas appear to have a more beleaguered air. The grey carpet in the cavernous space is grubby, and desks are cluttered with paperwork, the odd tired-looking plant, and wire trays bearing messily stacked folders.

There's tons of stuff on the walls: calendars depicting wildlife and city scenes, and posters of various exhibitions held here – Jewels From The Tombs, Pictish Village Life, Curios Under Glass: The Art of Taxidermy. All look slightly yellowed and are curling at the edges. There's a smell of dust and a hint of disinfectant. Various whiteboards and charts have apparently been scribbled on in haste – unless everyone has terrible handwriting around here – with marker pens. I follow Hannah through to a smaller room, right at the back of the main space, presumably so we have privacy, although the only other staff I have seen this evening were the front desk personnel.

'Please, take a seat,' she says. This is far cosier, more like a snug than an office. There are two squashy armchairs upholstered in burgundy velvet, with a small low table in between.

I spot my proposal sitting there.

Hannah picks it up. For a moment, she doesn't say anything. I'd guess her at late thirties; her face is make-up free, apart from a neutral lipstick, and she is wearing a khaki linen button-through dress and tan flats.

'Thanks for taking the time to see me,' she says with a bright smile. 'I really appreciate it, especially after all the work you've done on this already.'

'That's okay,' I say. 'I was happy to come in.'

'I won't keep you too long, I hope.'

'It's fine, I'm not in a great hurry.' I give silent thanks to Jules for having Izzy after school today.

'Can I start by asking how well you know Penny?'

So, here I go.

I breeze through how our friendship began, with her walking her little dog, and how my daughter and I started meeting her regularly. And then how we heard all about Girl Friday; and before I know it I'm launching into a spiel about how I've known Isla since we were in primary school, and how the idea came about, and how brilliant it would be for the museum, and our city: 'Because Penny is just a normal woman,' I explain. 'She didn't come from a privileged background. She wasn't trained in fashion, she never even went to college – she just did a bit of modelling and worked as a typist, yet she went on to become huge, in that world, for those few years. Not in

269

a Studio 54 kind of way, not like a Christian Dior or a Coco Chanel, but a real, normal woman who was entirely self-taught, and got off her arse and made it happen—'

I stop abruptly. I am sitting here with Hannah, a top person at this venerable institution, and I have just said 'arse'.

She looks me right in the eye and smiles. 'And that's exactly what I love about this idea.'

I frown, confused.

'I mean your absolute passion for it,' she adds. 'It shines out of your proposal – your enthusiasm and absolute belief in the project.'

'Oh.' I smile. 'Well, thank you. I just feel—'

'But when it dropped on my desk I was up to my eyes,' she cuts in, 'trying to convince the people who decide these things that the attack in the natural history department doesn't mean we have to close permanently.' Incredibly, her eyes well up. 'I was up all night figuring out plans, doing budgets, trying to work out how we might recover from this, and it occurred to me . . .' She looks down and flicks, seemingly randomly, through the pages of my proposal. 'It occurred to me that, okay, we can repair the exhibits, we can sort that out. It's not the end of the world really.'

'I'm sure it can all be fixed,' I say, as if I know anything about antique taxidermy displays.

'Yes,' Hannah says, 'but then, when the dust had settled, so to speak, I started to think, the reason it happened – that crazy man barging in with the hammer – is because we *are* traditional, and that has its place, of course. But maybe an incident like that might be, well, not exactly *good* for the museum, it's a colossal expense – but it might make us think about our future in a different way.'

270

'In what way?' I ask, not sure what she's getting at here.

'In a way that might make us more . . . broad-thinking,' Hannah says, 'and more appealing to a wider audience than we've ever attracted before.'

She is still clutching my proposal. For a moment, I try to rein in the excitement that's welling up in me. However, it's occurred to me now that bunnygate caused Rose to think differently, too – radically, really, considering that the word 'fresh' had been unheard of at Flaxico. And suddenly we were propelled into the world of deli-type lines, recruiting young people, transforming the low boardroom into some kind of playroom, with huge TV screens, enormous L-shaped sofas and even a fish tank.

'Unfortunately, we're under severe budget restraints,' Hannah adds, almost apologetically.

'Yes, but it wouldn't cost a lot,' I say quickly. 'I've worked out how we can pull together a Girl Friday collection, from vintage shops and collectors—'

'Yes, I've read all that, you've gone into incredible detail—'

'And the staging needn't be expensive either. I used to work in theatre. I've managed productions where, honestly, you wouldn't believe how little money we had. And a fashion show can be very simple. We're just talking a basic runway, and seating of course. And I'm sure we can find plenty of models.'

Hannah nods. 'Once we have the clothes, we can start to do the graphics and the displays. That could all be done in-house . . .' She pauses. 'Would Penny be on board with all of this?'

'Erm, I haven't been through it all with her yet,' I bluster, 'as I wasn't sure whether it would actually happen.'

'You didn't want to build up her hopes?' she suggests.

'Kind of.' I smile to disguise a flicker of panic. What the hell am I getting myself into here? 'Her son is on board though,' I add. 'He's completely behind it. He was there, of course, when she started out, and he'll be a huge help when it comes to pulling the whole Girl Friday story together.'

'Well, that's great,' she says warmly, 'and I'm sure Penny will be delighted once we get things in motion. How could she not be, really? So . . .'

'So, what you're saying,' I interrupt, barely able to contain myself now, 'is that you want to go ahead?'

'Absolutely,' Hannah replies with a wide smile, clutching the proposal to her chest. 'We all think your plan is brilliant, Viv. So it's a definite yes.'

Part Four

The Show

Chapter Thirty

A month later: Saturday, November 2

Izzy wanted a camping party for her birthday. She was determined to recreate the Brownie experience in our garden, but as I was unwilling to risk any of our young guests suffering from hypothermia, I have transformed our living room into a sort of indoor camp site, complete with two new, cheap festival tents, plus strings of fake flowers, bunting and balloons.

Silvery fairy lights are strewn across the ceiling, to create a starlit sky effect later tonight. Jules is here, ferrying food and drinks back and forth from the kitchen, ably assisted by Nick, who showed up with Penny. I was pleasantly surprised to see him, as I wouldn't have imagined that a children's party would be quite his thing. But as it is, he seems to be perfectly relaxed and happy to be here, gathering up wrapping paper and helping to rescue a collapsing tent, and in no hurry to rush away. Meanwhile Penny is observing the proceedings from a comfy chair, sipping her drink and nibbling on sausage rolls. Izzy was thrilled with Penny's present of a set of four knitted doughnuts.

And now Andy has appeared, laden with gifts from both himself and his parents (as today is Izzy's actual birthday). I beckon him through to the living room where the main party action is happening and introduce him, briefly, to Nick: 'This is Andy, Izzy's dad.' Once that's out of the way, I catch Andy flinching at the sight of so many kids piling in and out of the tents. He checks his watch as if calculating how soon he can remove himself without seeing rude.

Right now is the correct answer, which I try to transmit by giving him a 'Thanks for popping round, now off you go' kind of look – but my telepathic powers seem to be lacking today as he has taken it upon himself to try and make conversation with Penny, which must be a first.

Andy: 'How are you, Penny?' He glances down at her glass. *Is that a G&T at five-thirty in the afternoon?*

Penny: *Indeed it is, and what of it?* 'I'm good, thanks, Andy. How are you?'

Andy: 'Oh, you know. Busy. The usual.'

Penny: 'No rest for the wicked, eh?'

Andy, laughing awkwardly: 'Ha-ha, yeah.'

Penny, dryly: 'Still at the hospital?', which makes it sound as if it's just a holiday job.

Andy, disconcerted: 'Er, yes. Yep, still hanging on in there.'

Penny, patronisingly: 'Good for you!' She turns away from him and catches my eye, grinning playfully as I glide by – regally, I hope – with a tray of chipolatas. I smile back. Despite his presence, the party is going well. I'm proud of my ability to remain polite and cordial as Andy gets ready to leave.

'Great sausages,' he says. 'Did you marinate them?'

'I did,' I reply, 'with honey and soy.' I blink at him. 'Would you like me to stuff some under your windscreen wiper?'

His mouth twitches and he laughs. 'Oh, Viv.'

'Don't "Oh, Viv" me.'

He inhales and fixes me with a look when we reach the front door. 'That was some stunt you pulled, crazy girl.'

Crazy girl? That's a tad familiar, I feel. 'It was a minor aberration,' I correct him, 'which I've apologised for and regret.'

'Of course,' he says quickly, hands shoved in pockets, 'and you were entitled to be pissed off. Of course you were. Christ, I wouldn't have blamed you if you'd done worse, if you'd, um—'

'There's no need to list all the things I could've done.' On the doorstep now, I glance back into the house. There are shrieks of laughter, and I'm aware that I have left Jules and Nick in charge of proceedings. I imagine Penny is just sitting there serenely in the corner, sipping her gin.

'Okay,' Andy says. 'But, look . . .' He rubs at his forehead. 'You do know it really is over, don't you? That, uh, thing I did, I mean?'

That thing he did? That minor matter of him shagging Estelle Lang for months on end, and finally leaving me for her? That 'thing'?

I study his face for a moment, wondering how he expects me to respond. By commiserating on his newly single status? By digging him out a hot water bottle in case he gets chilly at night? 'You did mention it,' I remark.

'Well, erm . . . I thought, maybe we could get together and talk sometime,' he adds, 'when things are less hectic.'

'Talk about what?' I ask, genuinely confused.

He shrugs. 'About, well . . . *you* know. Stuff. How we're going to go forward with things—'

Impatience is rising in me now. What is this, a board meeting on my doorstep? 'D'you mean legally,' I start, 'or money-wise, or—'

'Viv, when can we have some birthday cake?' Ludo shouts from the hallway.

'In a minute, love,' I call back, silently thanking him for the interruption. Andy and I look at each other until Ludo has rejoined the other children in the living room.

'That kid,' he mutters with an eye-roll.

'He's much better now, actually. And, look, I really can't discuss anything right now . . .'

'No, of course not,' Andy blusters, reddening. 'I realise that. I didn't expect to—'

'I need to go back in,' I say firmly. 'I can't stand here chatting. I'm sure you've noticed that I have a party going on.'

Izzy and her friends are supposed to be settling down to sleep in the tents. But of course, they're not. They are giggling madly with torches flickering on and off. Every so often, someone appears in the kitchen, claiming to be 'starving' and loads up a paper plate with supplies before disappearing again.

At one point, Ludo sneaks out to the garden and trips, and I rush out to tend to his grazed knee (incredibly, Izzy invited him of her own accord and is clearly concerned about his minor injury). Jules left at around seven, and Penny followed soon afterwards to let Bobby out 'to do his necessaries', as she put it, leaving Nick and me together, alone. At least, alone with thirteen children.

It's not quite how I imagined tonight would pan out. As I thought I'd be left alone here, trying to maintain control, it's been a delightful surprise, and Nick is lovely company. I realise I'm wrong to assume that the child-free – particularly child-free men – are keen to avoid large numbers of excitable children. At least, Nick has shown no signs of wanting to dash away.

'Don't keep him up *too* late,' Penny chuckled as she left; her implication being that we might be up to something. But it *is* late now – it's half past eleven – and, yes, we are up to something, although not what she might be implying. The thought of how she'll react when she finally finds out about the museum project is enough to trigger a swill of nerves. But I've tried to push that aside as Nick and I have sipped mug after mug of tea, whilst discussing the project: specifically, how the fashion show might be staged and the exhibition presented in the space Hannah has allocated. We've come up with a decent publicity plan, combining both my theatre experience – often, I had a hand in promoting the productions – and Nick's preferred tactics for publicising his own films.

Finally, the children's excitable chatter dampens down. I go through from the kitchen to say goodnight, and when I return, Nick looks round from the table. 'That's the party finally over?'

'I can only hope,' I reply, feigning an exhausted swoon.

He laughs. 'Seemed like it was pretty successful.'

'It was, yes.' I smile. 'I even managed to be pleasant to Andy.'

Nick raises a brow. 'It seems very civilised between you two, from an outsider's point of view.'

'I suppose it is,' I say with a nod. 'At least, now things have settled. In fact . . .' I pause. 'He seems to want to be friends, as if the events of seven months ago were just a blip, and perhaps we can make everything better again if he's charming to my friends, and praises my sausages.'

Nick chuckles. 'They *were* very good, Viv.'

'Thank you,' I say grandly, grinning as I sit back down opposite him. 'He's also keen to stress that he and Estelle are no longer in contact, that it's definitely over with her.' I smirk. 'But, considering his past record as an accomplished liar and fraud, they might well be planning their wedding.'

Nick smiles. 'You really do seem amazingly fine about it all.'

'Oh, I wasn't at first,' I say quickly. 'For months, I was in quite a state, and I still have my moments sometimes. But there's definitely been, well . . . a power shift, I suppose. I mean, I don't feel particularly angry or sad anymore. I look at him and feel . . . well, nothing very much, really. Apart from noting that his hair could do with a better cut and his jeans are a bit saggy.'

'That sounds like a pretty healthy way to be,' Nick remarks.

'Yes, I guess it is. It suggests I'm recovering, at least. And, you know, it feels like my life is opening up again. The museum project's helping.'

'I'm surprised you've had time for anything else,' he jokes, and it's true that it's been all-encompassing, having gathered momentum faster than I could have imagined. Upstairs, away from Penny's gaze, I have already amassed quite a collection of pieces, and each day seems to bring a new lead to assist with my search, or even the arrival of a Girl Friday piece. I am no longer simply surviving day to day. I am actually *living* again. And even although Andy showed up today, skulking about and bothering

280

my friends, Izzy's party was a huge success, and it was all down to me, with a little help from Nick and Jules. I'm proud of Izzy – and myself – for managing this new situation.

'I'm really glad you were here to help,' I tell Nick, getting up to fetch slices of birthday cake, which we both pick at.

He smiles warmly and meets my gaze. 'I enjoyed it, especially the marshmallow toasting.'

'You're clearly an expert,' I tease him.

'Hey, there's a lot of skill involved!' He laughs. 'It took me back to being a Scout.'

I peel a strip of icing off the cake. 'Did you love all that outdoorsy stuff?'

'Oh, yeah. I didn't get to do a huge amount of it – Mum pretty much had her hands full with everyday life – so the camps were brilliant. It was great to get out of the city, up in the Highlands and have the chance to run wild. And, as an only child, all I wanted was to be with a big pile of mates really.'

'Yes, I can imagine.' I smile, trying to picture him as a mussed-haired kid. 'My parents were pretty set in their ways when it came to holidays – year after year it was a week at Mrs Wilkie's B&B on Arran. Dad was a keen fisherman so we'd borrow a boat and end up with an all-you-can-eat mackerel sizzle on the beach.'

'Now *that* sounds idyllic,' Nick says with a smile.

'Now I realise it was. At the time, I was probably a bit eye-rolly about it, especially when I reached my teens and all my friends seemed to be jetting off to Spain or Greece, and then school would start again and it'd be all, "What did you do on your holidays, Viv?" And I'd be like, "Gutted a load of fish!"' Nick laughs. 'Of course,' I add, 'after Mum and Dad had both gone, I'd have given anything to be sitting on Lamlash beach with them, in the drizzle, covered in scales and bit of fishy insides.'

Nick nods. 'Mum mentioned that they both passed away fairly young. That must've been hard.'

I look at him, surprised but pleased that she's shared some details about me with him. 'It did seem terribly unfair,' I concede. 'They hadn't even retired. Mum worked as a science teacher and Dad had a wedding photography business. They'd talked endlessly about leaving Glasgow and buying a little cottage at North Berwick, and enjoying their later years by the coast. Mum was going to start painting and they'd planned to get a dog. Dad wanted to buy a little sailing dinghy . . .'

'So they were full of plans,' he says gently.

'Yes, they were.' I drain my mug. 'What about your dad?' I ask adding quickly, 'I hope you don't mind me asking—'

'Not at all,' he assures me, 'although there's not an awful lot to tell. You know he moved to Canada?'

'Yes, Penny mentioned that.'

'So I saw very little of him when I was growing up.' He smiles wryly. 'He wasn't exactly a family man, by all accounts, although Mum tried to protect me from all of that . . . I mean, the details of what he'd got up to when they were still together. But let's put it this way, I don't quite know how many half-brothers and sisters I have—' He breaks off as Izzy appears, in her new birthday pyjamas, and stares at him.

'You don't know how many brothers and sisters you have?'

Nick looks at me, then back at her, and laughs. 'It's a bit complicated, Izzy.'

'Why?' she asks.

He pauses, clearly wondering how best to put it. 'My dad, erm, had other girlfriends, after he and Mum split up . . .'

She frowns and looks at me. 'But why don't you ask him—'

'We only speak occasionally,' he says quickly, 'at Christmas, his birthday, occasions like that. And it never quite seems the right time to ask, "Hey, Dad, how many kids d'you have?"'

I chuckle and turn to Izzy. '*I'd* ask,' she says.

'I know you would, darling,' I say, 'but c'mon now – stop grilling Nick. Bed, please. It's *very* late.'

I usher her back to camp, and when I return, Nick explains – as I'd suspected – that not even his father is entirely sure of the precise number of offspring, 'although there were already two more when he took me over to Vancouver with him . . .'

'*You* went to Canada?' I exclaim.

'Yes, just the once, when I was four years old. He seemed to have a sudden burst of wanting to be a great dad, or at least to give that impression to his new partner. It was short-lived, thankfully. Just a rush of blood to the head.' He smiles, and as those grey-blue eyes seem to fix on mine, something seems to happen to, I don't know – my heart perhaps? It kind of . . . *turns*, making me aware of its presence, reminding me that it is still a fully functioning thing.

Oh, but he is extremely attractive. Even I – a woman who'll never be concerned with such matters ever again – can't dispute the fact that his eyes radiate kindness, and are quite lovely. I'm regretting the fact that my face is undoubtedly shiny and pink, and my hair a state from running around after the kids for hours on end. I haven't looked in a mirror since around 8 a.m. and, although I am wearing a decent dress, neatly fitted with a tiny black and red check, I've now noticed a smear of creamy cake icing on the front.

I wonder what happened in Canada, and why Penny has never mentioned Nick's trip to visit his dad. However, after Izzy's quizzing I decide to leave asking for now. Instead, I say, 'I know it's late, but would you like to come upstairs?' I catch myself immediately and silently curse my sizzling face. 'To see the Girl Friday collection,' I add quickly. 'I'm storing it all in Spencer's room.'

Nick grins and gets up. Did he catch my blustering just then? 'Yes, of course,' he says, cool as anything. 'I'd love to see it.'

Chapter Thirty-One

Early hours of Sunday, November 3

Over an hour, we've been up here, examining his mother's designs which, bizarrely, have colonised my son's bedroom. I have hung up as many of the garments as possible: bright, block-coloured trouser suits, jaunty jackets and print dresses emblazoned with oversized flowers and graphic prints. Despite my rather workaday approach to dressing these past few years, as these pieces have arrived I've remembered how much I used to love to dress up for a special night out, and how uplifting and unashamedly *fun* fashion can be.

A cluster of patent leather shoulder bags hangs from a hook on the door like a bouquet of cartoon flowers. There are embroidered corduroy flares, brightly patched denim hot pants and rainbow-striped skinny-ribbed sweaters. A flurry of hippie dresses arrived a few days ago, with prints varying from swirling Paisley patterns to oversized daisies. On Spencer's bed lies an array of accessories: stripy knee-high socks, suede belts, patterned headbands and all manner of headwear from a pink peaked cap to a lime green floppy hat with fake poppies attached.

On the floor, the footwear is neatly paired up in rows: boots, sandals and platform shoes, the latter of which fascinated Izzy when they arrived by courier. I let her try them on and have a clomp about, but playing with the rest of the pieces is not allowed, which she accepted with only a minor sulk. I can't face trying to keep track of it all, on top of everything else. I know from past experience that a simple dressing-up session in Izzy's bedroom can quickly morph into feather boas and capes being discovered, weeks later, rain-sodden and smeared by slugs at the bottom of the garden.

'How have you managed to get so much stuff?' Nick marvels, studying each item in turn.

'With an enormous amount of phoning and emailing,' I explain. 'Isla helped with that. We worked our way through my list of vintage shops, starting with Glasgow, then radiating out until we'd covered pretty much the whole of Scotland. Then, gradually, we worked our way across the north of England.'

'Amazing,' he murmurs.

'We still have a long way to go,' I add. 'I have the Midlands to cover next, then Wales, London, the South-East, the South-West . . .'

'I can help too. I'm around for a good while yet, so please give me lists and instructions. Tell me what to do.'

I chuckle. 'I definitely will. The more help the better, really.'

He shakes his head in wonderment as he examines a

fringed red suede waistcoat. 'I still can't imagine how you've managed to do all of this. It's incredible.'

'It sort of gathered momentum,' I explain. 'Maybe it's because it's been so long since I've been able to really throw myself into something creative, you know?' He nods. 'I mean, it's been years really, since my theatre days. Although I am a little sleep-deprived,' I add with a grin, indicating an eye bag. 'Can you tell?'

'No, I can't,' he says, laughing. 'Not at all. So, when you tracked down the clothes, were the shop owners cooperative? About sending them to you, I mean?'

'Mostly, yes. I managed to blag a small budget from Hannah at the museum, so we've been able to cover postage and courier costs. Some pieces, I've collected in person if they've just been across town.'

'So they're all on loan?' Nick asks.

'Yep. Returning them after the show will be the really fun part.' I smile. 'But we can hang on to some long-term, because the plan is to keep a small collection on display, once the show's over.'

'It's amazing,' Nick says, looking at me. 'It really is. I wish we could show Mum now, don't you?'

'I'm nervous, Nick,' I murmur. 'What if she's really not happy about all of this? If she's annoyed because we kept it from her—'

'Come on,' he says firmly. 'She'll be overwhelmed and incredibly touched. Seeing it all now, I'm sure she will . . .'

'Yes, but what if—' I break off at the sound of raucous laughter coming from the camp. 'They're still awake!' We head downstairs, and from the living room doorway I insist that they go to sleep.

'We *are* asleep.' That's Ludo, giggling.

287

'I don't think you are, Ludo.' I suppress a smile.

'He is, Mum!' Izzy insists, and there's more laughter, and torches strobing inside the tents.

'Can you handle this lot alone?' Nick asks, jokingly, as he pulls on his jacket in the hallway, getting ready to leave.

'I think so. But I'll send up a flare if I need help.'

He smiles, and his eyes meet mine again. 'I think you're an amazing person,' he says suddenly.

I look at him, not quite knowing how to respond. 'Thanks,' is all I can think of to say.

And then I realise he isn't just referring to the Girl Friday project. He hasn't stayed on after Izzy's party because he had nothing better to do, or even to help with the publicity plans. He just wanted to be here, I decide, and I wanted him to be here too.

'I mean it,' he adds. I smile, catching a look in his kind eyes, and sense something stirring inside me; my heartbeat seems to quicken. It strikes me that I view Nick as a friend already, but perhaps there is more to it than that. Unless I am completely wrong, and have lost any ability to gauge these things, it feels like there is a spark of something between us.

Of course, the very thought of it is ridiculous. He doesn't even live here – or even in the same hemisphere. He'll be heading back to New Zealand in a few weeks' time, to carry on with his life there, and I might never see him again. It's not as if he comes over very often. It seems to be once a year, if that. But he seems happy to be here right now, and maybe that's why he kisses me, quickly and lightly, on the cheek. Because he's glad to be home.

Or maybe he just wanted to, I reflect, unable to dampen

my ridiculous smile as I say goodnight. I watch him for a moment, tall and gangly, as he strides away down the street. Then, despite the fact that I am currently sharing it with thirteen children – who'll expect pancakes first thing – I sort of *float* back into my house.

Chapter Thirty-Two

Saturday, November 9

Chrissie and I appear to be competing on the sleep-deprivation front: her with baby Lara, and me on my quest to amass more Girl Friday pieces, which involves more emailing late into the night. Because normal life must go on, and I can't get away with working on the project at the office, beyond cramming in as many phone calls as possible at lunchtime.

Meanwhile, Nick has now joined in with the hunt, and a week since Izzy's party a new clutch of goodies has arrived. We've now acquired a beautiful baby-blue jacket, a pair of outrageous silver boots, a crocheted waistcoat and a bunch of brightly beaded necklaces, chokers and belts. Still no poncho, though, and my hope of finding one is starting to wane.

'Does that matter?' Chrissie asks as I show her the growing collection in Spencer's room. She's wearing her blonde hair in a wilted topknot, and Lara is asleep in a papoose against her chest.

'It does to me,' I say. 'I'll just keep looking. The show's happening on the first of December so there's still time.' I look around as Izzy wanders in to see what we're up to.

'What'll the show be like?' she asks, gazing around in wonder.

'Well, there'll be models dressed up in all these clothes, with spotlights and music and loads of people watching. At least, I hope people will come.' I take her hand in mine. 'You do remember all this is a secret, don't you?' I add.

'Yeah, 'course I do.' She looks up and smiles. 'Don't worry, Mum. I won't tell.'

I turn to Chrissie. 'You too,' I tease her. 'Penny still knows nothing about this.'

'Of course,' she says firmly. 'Oh, I wish I could come and see the show, Viv. It's going to be amazing!'

I look at her, momentarily confused. 'I was hoping you'd be there. Can't you come?'

'I doubt it,' she says briskly, following Izzy and me back downstairs. 'There's the baby, you know. It's kind of difficult.'

'But . . . it's only a few hours on a Sunday evening. Tim would be fine with the kids, wouldn't he?'

'Yes, well, *he* says so . . .' Hmmm. Being their father, and generally responsible and capable and all that. 'But it just feels too soon to leave her,' she adds.

'You wouldn't be *leaving* her,' I chastise her gently. 'She'd be with her dad, and the show's almost a month away. Please come, Chrissie. I'd really like you to be there.'

She shakes her head, and I recognise it now: that befuddled look, when day and night blur into one; I guess she's edging ahead on the sleep-deprivation stakes. 'I tell you what,' I add, as she's leaving, 'never mind the show. I mean, I'd love you to come but I think, actually, a night out would be even better. Why don't we go out?'

'Me and you?' She seems to brighten at the possibility, then her face falls again. 'But I'm not drinking. Well, only the occasional small glass of wine.' She pats Lara's head gently. 'Feeding this little one.'

'Of course, yes, but we could still have a lovely evening. I mean,' I add, smiling, 'the drink part doesn't matter. I don't have to get trolleyed whenever I go out.'

Chrissie looks aghast. 'Oh, I wasn't suggesting—'

'No, I know you weren't. So, how about tonight?'

'Tonight?' she gasps. 'That's too soon.'

'Come on, be spontaneous—'

'I haven't been spontaneous since 1996!' My God, Chrissie can actually laugh at herself. 'Sorry to be a wet blanket,' she adds. 'It's just . . . it'd need some planning. I'd have to rev myself up for it, make arrangements, dig out something decent to wear . . .'

'I'm not asking you to be my plus one at a wedding,' I tease her. 'I'm only talking a bite to eat at the Pig and Pint.'

She laughs again, and I realise I can't remember the last time I saw her all giggly like this. 'Well, that sounds—'

'Look, there's Tim,' I say quickly, spotting him unloading shopping from the boot of their car, with Ludo loitering at his side. I stride towards them, and a few quick words are exchanged, with Chrissie still dredging up numerous reasons why she cannot possibly leave the house after dark, without an infant strapped to her person.

'No, Chrissie,' Tim says firmly, glancing at me, 'that's it settled. *I'm* looking after Ludo, Lara and Izzy tonight. And you're going out with Viv.'

'But how will you manage all three of them?' She turns to me. 'Isn't Izzy with Andy right now? Could she stay with him overnight?'

The cheesy flat shimmers into my mind. 'Not really. In fact, she's due back any minute . . .'

'Of course I can manage,' Tim says, blowing out air as he smirks at me. 'Izzy can stay over so you don't need to worry about rushing back for her.'

'But Tim—' Chrissie breaks off as Ludo announces that Izzy *must* come over – 'No one ever comes to play with me!' – and together, we carry the shopping bags into their house.

'I'm impressed, Viv,' Tim murmurs with a smile. 'You're obviously more persuasive than I've ever managed to be.'

So here we are, Chrissie and I, a few hours later, in the lively local pub where we managed to bag the last vacant table. We have already eaten elsewhere, at a nearby Italian. It was Chrissie who decided on stopping off here on the short walk home, which surprised me. Even more surprisingly, it would appear that the two men sitting nearby are attempting to chat us up. It feels bizarre and unintentionally hilarious – as retro as a Girl Friday tank top.

'Off the leash tonight then?' the sandy-haired one remarks.

'Yes, we're allowed out very occasionally,' I reply.

'Two young ladies like you?' asks his friend (shaven head, tiny spectacles, full sleeve tattoo).

'Looks like it.' Chrissie laughs. 'Will we be safe?' She has already had a glass of red wine in the restaurant – a large one! – and giddily announced that it had whooshed to her head. And now, in her rather slinky black dress, heels and red lipstick, she is eagerly quaffing her second. I nearly fell over when she appeared on my doorstep, all dressed up and ready to go.

'Well, if the two of you are forcing me out,' she'd retorted, 'I thought I might as well go for it.'

There's more joviality from the men, who have introduced themselves as Tony (sandy-haired) and Gus (shaven). While they're bantering between themselves I lean forward to Chrissie: 'So which one d'you fancy?'

She snorts. 'Oh, I'm not fussy. Either will do. Shall we have another wine?'

I look at her. 'Are you sure?' Whilst I'm not averse myself, I don't want to be held responsible for corrupting her. 'I expressed some milk for later tonight, just in case,' she says conspiratorially.

'Good work,' I say, grinning. And so we have another drink, and are flirted with so ineptly – it's all clumsy compliments – that I become aware of observing the process as if we are all in a nature documentary: *So, here's what happens when two males in the wild are looking to mate.*

'Are you two sisters?' Tony wants to know.

I splutter at this. I'm dark-haired and curvy, Chrissie's blonde and slim; plus, there's the minor issue of me being fifteen years older. 'No, we're just friends,' I reply.

'*We're* brothers,' he announces, 'from other mothers.'

'So you're friends, then,' Chrissie remarks dryly.

'Yeah, but if we were brothers,' Gus adds, 'we'd be twins 'cause we were born on the same day.'

'Really! That's amazing.' She is showing herself to be quite at ease in licensed premises.

'Guess how old we are,' Tony urges us.

I blink at him. The amusement factor is waning now,

and I'm starting to think: perhaps we should head home and check if Tim is 'coping'?

'I don't really enjoy the guess-my-age game,' I reply.

'Why not?'

'Because,' Chrissie starts, before I can answer, 'no one ever wants to play it unless they think they look remarkably young for their age.'

I turn to her, pleasantly surprised by her attitude tonight. The 'we don't say no' approach to parenting, plus the sage toothpaste, had coloured my view of her, but she's far sassier than I'd ever imagined. 'You're absolutely right,' I say. 'I've always hated it too, and I could never figure out why.'

'It's a vanity thing,' she observes.

'Yes, it absolutely is!'

'He's fishing for compliments,' she adds with a wink.

'Aw, just have a guess,' Tony says, frowning.

'Fifty-five?' Chrissie deadpans.

'Hey,' he exclaims. 'We're forty-two!'

'Oh, I'm sorry,' she says. 'I really am rubbish at this game.'

I'd have hoped that that would put a lid on it, but the men seem to be stuck on the topic of age, and now they are loudly telling us how 'natural' we look. 'It's great that you're not the types to have stuff done. I mean, the whole ageing thing is so much easier for men,' Gus observes.

'Is it really?' I ask. 'Why's that, then?'

'We don't have to worry, really. It just happens. It's no big deal.'

I catch Chrissie's eye, and she understands immediately and starts to pull on her jacket. 'So, how d'you think it is for women?' she asks.

'A bloody battle,' he chuckles. 'My ex-wife was always

having things done to her face – Botox, massage, awful skin-peeling treatments that stripped off the top layer . . .'

'The top layer of what?' Tony asks, looking alarmed now.

'Of her face,' Gus exclaims shuddering, taking a fortifying sip of his beer. 'I can see it's not a big thing for you, Viv,' he adds. 'Having treatments, I mean.'

'Can you?' What possessed me to tell him my name? If I'm going to be out roaming in public I need to become more adept at this.

'Yeah. That's what's so refreshing about you. You look great, just as you are . . .'

'Thank you,' I say graciously.

'. . . for your age,' he concludes.

I bestow him with further thanks as Chrissie and I leave the pub, because naturally, a woman should be grateful for any raggedy scrap of a compliment that might flutter her way.

Once outside, I grab her arm as we start laughing. 'So that's what it's like,' she announces, '*out there.*'

We start to speed-walk home. 'Clearly. I'm so glad I'm single and able to start dating again,' I remark with a smile.

'Really? Are you sure you're ready for that?'

'I'll *never* be ready for that,' I exclaim. 'Lovely night, though—'

'It really was. Let's do it again . . .'

'But maybe somewhere else?' I suggest, and she laughs.

'Sure. And it's true you know,' she adds with a cheeky grin as we make our way down the street. 'You do look good – *for your age.*'

Chapter Thirty-Three

Wednesday, November 13

As arranged, Nick comes over while Izzy is at Brownies, and we run through our publicity plan in more detail. I have already drafted a press release and sent it over to Hannah for approval. Last night, Spencer's joiner friends and I dropped into the museum where the boys measured up in order to put together a plan for a basic runway. As it's in aid of the museum – and word has travelled about the trashing of the taxidermy – suppliers are apparently willing to offer materials at knock-down prices. For an institution that no one seems to visit very much, it certainly seems to hold a place in people's hearts. In some ways, in creating a bit of storm in the local press, the stoat-liberating maniac did the place a favour.

So it feels as if things are starting to come together, although I suspect it's something of a miracle that anything is happening at all. Isla and Hannah aside, the museum staff seem to be a particularly ponderous bunch, gliding around in a haze; they appear to operate on 'museum time'. While I'm hardly the fastest-moving individual on earth, I found myself gritting my teeth and digging my nails in my palms while the kindly white-bearded man explained, so *slooowly* I could feel the final traces of collagen draining from my face, that the rear south wing will be the site of the exhibition. Forty-five minutes, it took, to explain something that could have been explained in fewer than thirty words.

Maybe it's me who's out of kilter, and I've just become too accustomed to the self-consciously dynamic, rather shouty atmosphere that pervades Flaxico's headquarters these days. I fill Nick in on all of this, and find myself enjoying myself immensely, sharing all the details with him. His is an attentive listener, chuckling and smiling and chipping in.

'It'll be announced online soon,' I remind him. 'We'll have to tell Penny before that happens.' I've stopped all that 'your mum' nonsense; it felt ridiculous, and he is a bona fide adult after all.

'Yep, we just need to pick the right time,' he says, 'and I think you should be the one to do it, don't you?'

'Yes, I guess so.' I muster a smile. 'She is going to be okay about this, isn't she?'

'I'm sure she will be. She'll be more than fine . . .'

'As long as she feels consulted,' I finish. 'The way I see it, there'll still be time for her to get involved. I need to find models, and that's proving a lot trickier than I'd expected – the agencies are just too expensive. There's hair and make-up too. I really want it to look professional—'

'Of course you do.'

'I'd hate it to be shabby and to let Penny down,' I add, 'so I think I'm going to have to pull in a *lot* of favours.

298

Once that's all sorted out, the outfits still need to be chosen and put together and styled. And I'm hoping that's where Penny will come in.'

'Yeah,' Nick says. 'That's her forte, after all.'

I nod. 'It's essential, really. I mean, it's her look. She created it. So she'll be our . . .' I pause, trying to think of the correct title. 'Creative Director.'

'Creative Director in Chief,' he suggests, and we smile. It feels so right that Nick's here, checking in and supporting me. But I can tell that he's conscious of not overstepping things. When Andy and I were still together, I found myself often deferring to him, which seems ridiculous now. In all our years together, if there was a debate over the tiles we'd pick for the bathroom, or whose parents we'd spend Christmas with, he would generally get his way. Film choices, meals out, holiday destinations; I'd have my opinions but Andy had a way of turning things around so *his* choice would seem like the one to go for. I lost my backbone, it seems, and I'm almost ashamed of it now. Was it a gender thing, or the fact that he enjoyed more status, career-wise? I suppose I'd never been the most confident young woman. Anxiety had always niggled away at me, to some degree; my parents, although loving, were never the 'You can achieve anything!' types. Perhaps I felt flattered and lucky to have met and married someone like Andy. But everything's different now, and for the first time I am acutely aware of being in charge of my own life, and it's quite exhilarating.

I am definitely recovering, I realise; I was being truthful when I told Nick that I'm no longer angry with Andy. I used to compile mental lists of reasons why I was glad we'd split up, in an attempt to haul myself through the heartbreak. For instance: the 'I think you'll find' thing.

And the way he sometimes referred to his stomach as 'my tummy', as in: 'My tummy really hurts' (said in a whimpery voice whilst rubbing it with a pained expression). The way he'd ask: 'Do we have any Rennies?' That was another thing that drove me mad: this constant asking if we 'had' things, as if I were Monitor of Household Medicines (wasn't *he* supposed to be the doctor in the house?) and could see into cupboards without opening them. And now it's just me, with no adult male moaning about his acid reflux, or complaining that Shelley, Isla and I were 'pretty raucous' when we had an evening together around our kitchen table.

Somehow, since Andy left me, I've kick-started this project that seems to be well on its way to becoming a real event – and I'm the one driving it, ably assisted by the terribly handsome man who is sitting in my kitchen.

'So, what else needs to be done?' Nick asks now, finishing his mug of tea.

'We still need more clothes,' I reply. 'There are certain key pieces that I haven't been able to source yet.'

'Really? What are you looking for?'

'The Pippa poncho, for one thing.'

'Oh, I remember that.' He beams at me. 'Featured on the cover of *Honey* magazine, I think it was. For years, we had the image blown up to poster size and framed on our living room wall. Mum wore hers constantly throughout a whole winter, until there was some disaster with it getting trapped in a car door and dragging along in the road.'

'A hazard of the poncho, I'd imagine,' I snigger.

Nick smiles. If he wasn't my friend's son, and we didn't have *business* to attend to, I might . . . well, I might allow myself to have proper crush on him (a crush, at my age! Who'd have thought I was even capable?). I might even flirt a bit, like I did with the handsome tiler who came to do our bathroom, according to Andy, who kept teasing me: 'Oh, look – we've got Bourbons all of a sudden. Are they his favourites?' Yes, I would definitely flirt, if Penny hadn't been giving me the occasional bemused look, and bringing him round to my house, *parading* him, as if anything is likely to happen.

'I'm happy to do lots of phoning around,' he says now, 'but wish I could do more to help. What about the practical stuff? Is there more to do there?'

'We're okay with the runway,' I say, 'and Spencer and his mates are taking care of the music and lighting—'

'How about I film it?' Nick cuts in suddenly.

'The actual show, you mean? Well, that would be great—'

'Well, yes, I'd cover that. But I'm thinking more of the whole story, the preparations, the build-up to the main event. What d'you think?'

'Yes, sure,' I say. 'But who'd be in it?'

'Everyone who's been involved,' he says. 'At least, as many people as possible . . . Mum, when she knows all about it. The models, make-up artist, hairdresser . . . maybe women who bought the clothes in the Seventies and loved wearing them out on a Friday night. And people who worked in the shops, if I can track them down . . .'

'What about the museum staff?' I ask.

'Yes, of course. There's Isla, Hannah – and you, of course.' His gaze meets mine and he smiles.

'Me?' I exclaim. 'But I'm not staff—'

'No, but you're making this thing happen!'

I look at him, stuck for words for a moment. 'I can't

301

be in your film, Nick,' I mutter, shaking my head. 'Sorry, but that's *so* not my thing . . .'

'But you'd have to be,' he protests. 'It's only happening because of you. Think of all the hours you've put in, all that effort and energy. How could I possibly make a film without you in it—'

'But I'm not an actor or a presenter,' I say firmly. 'I'm a behind-the-scenes person. I always was. That's why I became a stage manager, and it's probably why I'm a PA now. I'm a doer, a fixer . . .'

'Hey,' he cuts in, briefly touching my hand across the table. 'You're all of those things, but you're so much more. Please, Viv. I'll make sure it's as painless as possible. It might even be fun. Please say you'll be in my film.'

This has to count as *the* most unexpected thing anyone has ever said to me. And of course, because it's him, I regain my composure and smile graciously and say, 'All right, I'll do it, if you insist. As long as you get my best side.'

Chapter Thirty-Four

Friday, November 15

Disconcertingly, Andy has taken to dropping in more regularly when it's not even one of his Izzy days. It happened a couple of days ago – apparently, there were some crucial books he needed, which I didn't even have – and now here he is again, ostensibly to 'look at' my car, which I happened to have mentioned has died on me.

He had the good manners to call before showing up, but only with fifteen minutes' notice. He seems a little lost, and is looking thin around the cheeks. There's a definite lack of sparkle in his eyes these days, and I'm starting to understand that life didn't turn out quite how he thought it would, when he left me. But that's not my concern. I'm still not even sure what he wants from me; surely he's not nurturing some hope that we might get back together? Whatever's on his mind, he seems disappointed when I tell him my car is being taken to the garage first thing tomorrow, and that his assistance won't be required.

'Are you sure I can't have a quick look?' he asks.

'The garage guy knows this car,' I say, trying to remain patient, 'and he reckons it's something serious with the water-cooling system. I don't think you poking about under the bonnet would have much effect.'

Now that's been confirmed, I wait for him to leave. But he hangs out with Izzy for a while, quizzing her about school and even – irritatingly – watching a cartoon with her, despite having never shown any interest in doing so before.

It is, I realise with a gnawing sense of unease, as if he doesn't want to go home. I could ask him to go, but don't really want to in front of Izzy; by God, I've done my utmost to make it seem as if everything is friendly and cordial between us, and I'm not going to crack now. Perhaps that's something I should focus on, during my next life coaching session: my previously undiscovered ability to *pretend*?

'Izzy was saying the fashion show's going ahead,' he says casually, having wandered through to bother me in the kitchen.

'Um, yes, it is.' I continue with putting away cutlery. 'Penny doesn't know about it, by the way, in case you happen to run into her. Not that that's likely, I know.'

'Really? She has no idea?'

I toss in the last fork and turn to look at him.

'No.'

He frowns. 'Are you sure that's wise?'

Sometimes, I swear he can't possibly realise how irritating he is. I must have become desensitised to it – immune, really – during all our years together, otherwise I'm sure I would have lynched him.

'Nick and I think it's best.'

Andy looks at me, steadily, as if trying to bring me into sharper focus. 'Nick and I?'

'Yes,' I say firmly, determined not to rise to the bait. 'I didn't want to tell her at first, in case she dismissed it before we'd even had a chance to get things started. And now it's definitely going ahead, and has gained momentum, but it's never seemed like quite the right time. So Nick and I think . . .'

'Nick and I?' he says again, looking at me quizzically from the doorway.

'Why d'you keep saying that?' I glare at him.

'Oh, nothing,' he blusters. 'I just wondered.'

'You wondered what? Who Nick is? He's Penny's son. You met briefly at Izzy's party, remember?'

'Oh, *that* Nick,' he says, infuriatingly.

I study his face, wondering what he's getting at here, then stride past him on my way to take Izzy a drink of juice in the living room.

He trails after me as if I am an estate agent, showing him around the house. 'So, are you seeing quite bit of him, then? This Nick, I mean?'

Izzy's not there. I hear her pottering about upstairs. I switch off the TV and start to gather up her pens and colouring books from where she's left them scattered on the floor. 'Why are you asking me this?'

'Oh, I just wondered, that's all.'

I frown. 'He's actually been helping me a lot with the show. And he's going to make a film – a documentary – about it—'

'A film? Wow!'

'That's what he does,' I say impatiently. 'It's his job. So yes, he has been around here a fair bit, and he'll continue to be, I'd imagine.'

A small pause. 'He's from New Zealand, isn't he?'

'Yeah.' I nod. 'That's where he lives anyway.'

'And when's he going back?' he asks, affecting an almost comically casual air.

I give him a look before marching back through to the kitchen. 'I'm not sure exactly. Sometime in December, I think. Why are you so interested?'

'I'm not,' he protests, still hot on my heels, just like Bobby was, but without the endearing quality. If I went to the loo, would he try to follow me there too? 'I'm sorry,' he mutters, as if it's dawned on him how bizarrely he's behaving. 'Of course, it's none of my business if you're, um, getting close to someone . . .'

'If I'm *getting close* to someone?' I almost laugh. 'I'm not sure what you're implying, but if you're wondering whether there's anything going on . . .' I lower my voice to a murmur. 'I can assure you there's not.'

'Okay, okay.' He steps back, looking shamefaced now. 'I'm sorry. I really am. God, Viv, I can't seem to be able to say anything right at the moment. The last thing I want to do is fall out or upset you.'

I exhale. 'I'd just like to get on with things now, if you don't mind.' Preparations for the show is what I mean – and my life. *I want you to leave me alone to get on with my life.*

'Yes, of course. Sorry,' he says again, then he calls up to Izzy to say he's off now, and he'll see her tomorrow. She says bye and waves from the top of the stairs – I don't insist that she comes down to hug him – and just as he's leaving he adds, 'If there's anything I can do to help – with the show, I mean, or your car, anything – just let me know.'

'I think I'm okay, thanks,' I say firmly as I see him out.

306

He nods and turns away, making his way to his car. 'Unless you can source a Pippa poncho?' I call after him.

He looks back, and his face brightens. For a moment, he looks like a child who's been told he can 'help' to water the garden with the hose. 'What's a Pippa poncho?' he asks.

'Nothing,' I say with a small smile. 'At least, it's nothing you can help with—'

'Are you sure? Because, honestly, it seems like you have so much on your plate, and I only want to—'

'It's fine, Andy,' I say firmly. 'Thanks for your offer, I really appreciate your help and everything – but I'm fine, really. So *goodnight*.'

Chapter Thirty-Five

Saturday, November 16

Occasionally, at college, I'd be roped into 'performing' in a play – although I use the term loosely. I'd be the third cheerleader in *Grease*, a prostitute in *A Streetcar Named Desire* or simply 'Girl' in *The Crucible*, and only because I could move and speak, and was *there*, rather than due to any particular talent on the acting front. The truth is, an old kitchen cabinet dragged onto stage would have been more engaging to watch. And that's what I'm reminded of now, as Nick sets up his camera in Spencer's room. This is going to be terrible. I won't know what to do with my hands or my face, and I'll speak in a weird, posh voice – and now, inevitably, here it comes: a raging hot flush.

'Are you okay?' Nick asks, with a look of concern.

'I'm just . . .' I flap at my face with a Girl Friday sun visor (why didn't Penny do fans?). 'It's a hot flush,' I add. 'It happens sometimes. It's because of—'

'Yes, I know what they are,' he says, unflinchingly. 'Can I help at all?'

'Not really, unless you can do something about my hormonal fluctuations.' I muster a smile.

'That might be a bit beyond my capabilities.' He pauses. 'Look, I don't want to put you under pressure,' he adds. 'Are you sure you're okay to do this now?'

I exhale. Izzy is out with her dad, so it's an ideal opportunity to get this done; I'm feeling self-conscious enough without her insisting on watching, as I know she would. 'Remember, I'll shoot loads,' he says, 'and edit it down. So just chat naturally, like you usually do. It'll be a conversation between us. Try to forget there's a camera here at all.'

I laugh. 'I'm sorry, my brain won't let me do that.' But we start anyway, and as Nick prompts me with questions it starts to feel . . . well, not wholly natural, but not *quite* torturous either.

'What about that trouser suit?' he asks, indicating it hanging on Spencer's wardrobe door. I explain its significance – the fact that it was the first outfit that the young magazines really picked up on, being so bold and beautifully cut, and it was featured widely. Soon, an actress in a soap opera wore it as her going-away outfit at her wedding, and that was it. 'She was like an influencer of her day,' I say. 'Suddenly, this boutique stocked with affordable clothes that pretty much any girl could buy, became something everyone wanted a piece of.'

He knows this, of course. But he nods encouragingly, and so I continue by explaining how, as each new piece has arrived, the Girl Friday ethos – fun, fashionable and full of life – began to come into focus for me.

'I started to really get it,' I tell him, holding up a banana-yellow cheesecloth tunic to illustrate my point. 'I remembered how thrilling it was to go shopping with the money from my Saturday job, when I was young. I didn't have Girl Friday, of course. That was gone by then. But it was a similar thing that Penny had set into motion the decade before. It was all about dressing up, feeling good, going out with my mates on the weekend.'

I pause; I could almost be in my own teenage bedroom now – not my son's – which Mum had allowed me to decorate, although my choice of purple cork-patterned wallpaper had baffled her. *I wish she'd gone for something more classic, Dennis!* she'd said to my dad. When I'd left home she'd redone it in magnolia.

'When you grow up,' I continue, 'you accumulate all these responsibilities. You might enjoy yourself still – of course you do – but it's a different kind of enjoyment. It's not that feeling of pure, unadulterated fun and freedom that you have when you're young. And that's what *this* makes me feel.'

I break off and look around the room, which is exactly how Spencer left it when he moved out. However, the band posters and haphazardly Blu-Tacked photos of him and his mates have been entirely obscured by the clothes I've strewn about everywhere. Even the window is mainly covered by a fringed suede jacket hanging there. Multicoloured patchwork dungarees hang from the back of the door, and there's barely an inch of floor space visible for all the boots and shoes. 'It's like being young again,' I add, grinning now, not caring how crazy that sounds. I have *almost* forgotten that the camera is there. 'That's what this whole project has been like for me, right from the start. It's about joy.'

I look at Nick, and he meets my gaze and he smiles. My heart does that thing again; that *flip* that catches me by surprise, as I'd never imagined I might have those kinds of feelings again, for anyone.

310

He stops filming and rakes a hand through his hair. 'That was brilliant,' he says. 'I knew you would be. That was just what we need.'

'Are you sure I wasn't just babbling on?' I grab a straw hat and fan at my face again.

'Not at all,' he says firmly, and I'm wondering now where it came from, that burst of confidence and ability to feel completely at ease? I might have thought it was something to do with Nick; he's the professional, after all. He's used to interviewing people, helping them to relax in front of a camera. It's his *job* to coax the best out of people. But actually, I don't think it was really his doing at all. Somehow, it just came from me.

'Nick,' I say as he's leaving, 'I'm thinking . . . maybe I should tell Penny tonight. We're getting so close to the show now, and Hannah is keen to go full on with publicity, which makes sense of course. I don't think I can hold her off for much longer.'

He nods. Although it's to be a free event, to attract as large an audience as possible – it's about bringing people into the museum, not making money – it'll still be ticketed and word is bound to get around. 'I dread her finding out before I've told her,' I add.

'Yes, I think you're right,' he says. 'Shall I ask her to drop in when she's taking Bobby out tonight?' Even though Nick's staying with her, she still insists on doing the evening walk herself. *My breath of air*, as she puts it.

'Good idea,' I say. 'I just want her to know now.' And I smile, trying to summon the confidence that somehow filled me when he was filming tonight.

'It'll be okay,' he says, squeezing my hand. 'Honestly, I'm sure she'll be completely bowled over by everything you've done.'

Later, 5 p.m.

My mobile rings when I'm in the supermarket's bakery aisle. 'Hello, Viv? My name's Tricia Spalding, from Love Vintage in Grange-over-Sands. You emailed me about a project you're working on? A Girl Friday fashion show?'

'Oh, yes,' I say. After Nick left, and Andy brought Izzy home, she pleaded to cook dinner so we've nipped out to buy a few necessary ingredients. Somewhat unwillingly, I've left Andy at the house, mowing the grass like the eager-beaver helper he is now. Admittedly, it's become wild out there, neglected due to my attentions being focused on the project. Even Tim had asked if I'd like him to cut it for me. What is it with all of these men, clamouring to assist me all of a sudden?

'Thanks for calling,' I continue. 'I thought your shop looked great, from your website . . .' I'm bluffing here. I have contacted literally dozens of shops, and it's impossible to keep track, beyond noting who has already sent pieces, or has promised to.

'Well, we only have one Girl Friday piece at the moment,' she says, as Izzy takes charge of the trolley, 'but I'd be happy to loan it to you. It's pretty special so I'm not keen on posting it. Could you come over to pick it up?'

'Where did you say you are again?' I ask, giving Izzy a quick nod as she indicates the crumpets, not that they were on our list. She grabs a packet and drops it in our trolley.

'Grange-over-Sands. The thing is, I'm closing the shop for a couple of weeks from Monday. I'm off to the States to source more stock for the shop. So, if you could maybe pop by tomorrow?'

312

Pop by? I'm not sure quite how far it is, but I know it's hardly 'poppable'.

'Would it have to be tomorrow?' I ask. 'Could you leave it with someone, and I can arrange to have it picked up?'

'I'm sorry, I have way too much on at the moment,' Tricia says, adopting a brisker tone.

'Could you post it recorded delivery? Or courier it to me? I'd cover the cost, of course.'

'No, things are always getting lost,' she says, 'and I want to make sure it gets to you. You see, this poncho—'

'A poncho?' I gasp. 'You mean, an actual Girl Friday poncho? The *Pippa* poncho?'

'Yes,' she says, as if to say, what else would it be?

'Is it orange, brown and yellow, with pompoms at the neck?'

'Yes, that's it.'

'And is it in good condition?' I ask, my heart racing. I am in a state of heightened excitement over an item of knitwear, I realise. What has happened to me?

'Everything we have is in excellent condition,' she says, in a clipped tone. 'So, look, if you'd like to borrow it, it'll need to be picked up tomorrow, I'm afraid. I'd love to be more helpful but that's the best I can do for you.' It occurs to me now that perhaps she is testing me, to see how much I really want to borrow this thing. 'D'you have my shop's address?' she asks.

'Yes, I do. And I'm sure I can sort something . . .' But I have no car, I realise. Could I do it by train and take Izzy with me? It really is the last thing I need to fit into my Sunday, and I can't see how it's doable. Plus, I'm supposed to be meeting four actors for coffee in the afternoon; all striking, confident women whom I know from way back when we worked together, and who seemed amused but intrigued by the idea of a little catwalk modelling. With only two weeks to go now, I decided I'd have to pull out all the stops, or we'd have a mountain of clothes and no one to model them. A headache starts to niggle at my temples. Izzy has deposited a packet of iced doughnuts in our trolley and is marching off in search of Parmesan.

'I'll leave that with you then,' Tricia says briskly. 'If you could let me know when it's being picked up, I'll be sure to open up the shop.'

Later still, 8.20 p.m.

Nick has texted, saying that Penny is 'staying over on the love boat tonight', meaning Hamish's narrowboat. So telling her will have to wait. Perhaps it's just as well, as Andy is here again, having asked if he could drop off a couple of books he'd bought for Izzy to help with her wetland habitats projects.

I seem to be seeing more of him than when we were together. Although his reasons for visits are valid, I'm not sure that we can continue in this way. But, for the moment, I'm putting on a cordial front for Izzy's sake.

'So, how's it all going?' he asks now, as we clear the table after Izzy's baked courgettes. It twisted my heart a little to see how happy she was, all three of us eating together. Delighted with the books, she insisted he stayed to watch *Izzy Cooks!* and, naturally, to enjoy the resulting dish. 'With the fashion show, I mean,' he adds.

'Pretty good,' I reply. 'I'm meeting the women who I hope will be our models tomorrow. At least, some of them. We need a span of all ages and it's the older ones who seem to be trickier to find.'

'Could *you* do it?' he remarks, at which I laugh.

'I don't think so, do you?'

'Why not?'

I study his face, wondering if he's having me on. Izzy is pottering about in her room, and Andy seems to be in no hurry to rush back to his flat. 'I'm more of a behind-the-scenes person,' I say. 'You know that. And anyway, I'll kind of have my hands full on the day.'

'Have all the clothes arrived now?' He really is taking quite a keen interest.

'Nearly, but there are still a few things I need. I was really hoping to find a poncho, d'you remember me saying?'

'Erm, I think so,' he says noncommittally.

'Well, I've found one, but it's in Grange-over-Sands and the owner refuses to post it. I have to collect it, she says. Tomorrow.'

'Really? Christ, I bet you don't need that.'

I sigh. 'I've decided I can't do it. Rearranging meeting the models is too complicated, and we're kind of running out of time now. The posters have been designed, and Spencer's friends, remember Callum and Mark—'

'Er, yeah . . .' he says vaguely.

'Well, they've come up with a design for the runway. So, you know, we're getting there.'

'It's so impressive,' he says, perching on the kitchen table.

'I'll just have to forget about the poncho,' I add. 'Without a car it'd be a nightmare to get there.'

'Where is Grange-over-Sands?' he asks.

'Well, it's on the coast . . .'

315

'Obviously . . .'

My jaw tightens. 'It's in Cumbria, about a hundred and sixty miles away.'

'I could do it,' he says, affecting a casual tone.

I look at him, wanting to laugh. 'That would be crazy, Andy. Don't be silly.'

'No, it wouldn't,' he says, sounding hurt.

'You mean you'd do a five-hour round trip just to pick up a poncho?'

'If it's important to you, then yes, of course I would.'

I stare at him, not entirely sure if he's serious. And I can't help but think of the time when we were having a birthday party for Izzy, and I'd promised to make mocktails with crushed ice, and realised I'd forgotten to make ice. Would he nip out to buy some? 'Couldn't you make some?' he suggested. There wasn't time, I exclaimed. Did he think I could freeze water instantly, perhaps by staring at it? I ended up rushing out and buying ice cubes myself, and he commented that I seemed 'a bit agitated' as I battered them into shards with a rolling pin.

'What's the address?' he asks now.

'This is mad, Andy. Just forget it. We can do without it, okay?'

'But you said it's iconic,' he insists. 'It's the piece used in the famous adverts, you told me.' My God, he's started referring to a garment as a 'piece'. Does that mean he's actually been listening to me? 'And if this shop has one,' he adds, 'and it's the only one you've been offered, then surely it's important to go and get it?'

'Honestly, it doesn't matter. We can do without it. If I'd been desperate I'd have asked Nick, but I decided it was far too big a trip—'

'Just give me the address,' he cuts in.

316

'No!'

'Why not?' He frowns at me, clearly exasperated.

'Because . . .' I exhale. 'Look, I know what you're doing here.'

'I'm not trying to do anything,' he protests. 'I mean, I'm just trying to help.'

I look at him, holding back from what I really want to say, and what we both know; that he is trying to make it up to me. He wants – well, I don't know *what* he wants exactly. Perhaps he just wants to make things right between us. We're still Spencer and Izzy's parents, after all; still a team, of sorts. But maybe it's more than that, and he really thinks we could mend our marriage, and somehow get over everything that's happened since he went to that conference, over a year ago now.

Could we do that? I might have forgiven him a few months ago. I might have accepted that he'd made a mistake, that he'd lost control of his mind, and his trousers, and that maybe I'd been at fault too; it's never solely down to one person, after all. But I'm a different person now. Or maybe, like with the lawn mowing, the scrabbling about in the loft for a sleeping bag and now the proposed poncho mission, he just wants to help.

Perhaps he's not quite so despicable after all.

'I want to do it,' he says firmly. 'I want to go to Grange-over-Sands and fetch your poncho.'

I can't help smiling. 'I bet that's a sentence you never thought you'd say.'

He laughs dryly and shrugs.

'You're just trying to be nice,' I add. 'You want to please me like . . . like a dog, running to fetch a stick . . .'

'That's charming,' he exclaims.

'You know what I mean,' I say, reddening now. For

317

the first time since we broke up, I almost feel bad about being mean to him.

'Are you getting me back,' he says with a slight smile, 'for calling you an amphibian?'

'What?'

He looks at me levelly. 'You're not, by the way. Not remotely.' He turns and fills the kettle, as if he still lives here. Not that he needs permission to turn on a tap, or make tea – but still. I sense him trying to edge his way back to me, subtly, as if he's hoping I won't even notice it happening.

He clears his throat, and an awkward silence hovers between us, which seems ridiculous. Nine months ago we were living under the same roof, and wandering about naked, scratching our bums, picking at our toenails and spitting into the washbasin after flossing, all that unseemly bodily stuff.

We even did our loo business in front of each other. Okay, not poos – but wees, certainly. When you fall in love, you promise yourself that'll never happen; you won't become one of those couples where you pee merrily whilst remarking that the bin men seem to have changed to a Friday, and do we have much in for dinner tonight?

'Viv?' His voice jolts me back to the present.

'Yes?'

'Give me the address of that woman's shop.'

'No, Andy. I appreciate your offer but this is ridiculous.'

'Remember when you badgered me for *my* address?'

'Er . . . yes?'

'I knew you didn't really want to forward some mail to me,' he retorts. 'What could've been so important that it couldn't have waited until I got back from Loch Fyne?'

I shrug. '*Something* could've . . .'

'You sent me some junk mail from credit card companies,' he remarks, 'and a leaflet advertising conservatories. Like, really urgent. You just wanted to check out where I lived so you could do that omelette thing.'

'No, I didn't. I hadn't even thought of—'

'Just give me the address, Viv.'

He stands there, waiting. 'Okay,' I say reluctantly. 'If you're sure.'

He leaves, finally, and later, once I've said goodnight to Izzy, I text Tricia from Love Vintage to let her know the poncho will be picked up by 'Andy' (no further details supplied) at noon tomorrow.

Perfect, she replies. *It'll be waiting for him.*

And now, in this still, quiet house, I wonder whether I've done the right thing, to allow myself to not be angry with him anymore. In the early days of this mess – and the not so early ones actually – I truly thought I would never get over the hurt. That I would hate him for ever and never involve myself with another man. That he'd *ruined* the part of me that could love someone. I was certain that he, coupled with the sweaty, hormonal mess I was in, had put paid to me ever being able to be close to anyone ever again. And it would just be me, alone in my clammy pyjamas, in my swampy bed, for ever.

I'm no longer so sure of that. I think of Nick, filming today, and how at ease I felt, how passionate about the project – *our* project. How I try not to think about him returning to New Zealand because, well, I am kind of liking him being around.

My phone pings, and I grab it, half expecting it to be Nick with some further suggestion or comment about the film he's making, or the show. But in fact – mild disappointment – it's Andy, suggesting that perhaps he should buy us a new lawnmower: *It really is on its last legs, Viv.*

I don't need him to assess its condition, I decide. I can buy a new mower as and when I need one, and I can mow my own lawn. I can mow it just as well as he did and he'll see, next time I do it. But, actually, I can't help feeling touched by his thoughtfulness. And as I text, *Okay, thanks*, it occurs to me, shockingly, that the man who once called me amphibious, and refused to buy ice cubes for his daughter's party, is actually capable of being kind.

Chapter Thirty-Six

Sunday, November 17

I called Nick mid-morning to see if Penny was home yet but no, she had yet to reappear. It felt like checking up on a teenager, and I reminded myself that she's a grown woman who, naturally, wants to spend time with her boyfriend without being hassled by her friends. Never mind that I am now burning to tell her about our project. Specifically, I'd hoped she would agree to come along today and meet our prospective models for the show. But, for now, being in possession of a mobile phone that she refuses to ever turn on, she is uncontactable. So I set out to the museum alone.

When I meet the four women in the small, cramped café, I am overwhelmed by their welcome, and how much they remember about our time together; we all worked together on *The Glass Menagerie* back in the day. There was the huge drama when two of the cast, both of whom had partners, were discovered to be having an illicit affair, which exploded in a public row, leaving us without our male lead. There was the panic over the flamboyant dress, which had fitted perfectly, but which was then deemed to be 'excruciating' by the prima donna star, and a replacement had to be found with four hours' notice. Then, more happily, a dress rehearsal had ended in a spontaneous birthday celebration when I'd brought in cakes and champagne and we'd partied until 4 a.m. But then, why wouldn't these women remember those times? I certainly do – I'd adored my job then, despite the perpetual panics – and it was only a decade ago. It just feels like a whole other life, and I feel like a different person now, although perhaps I'm not really, underneath.

'I'd love to do the show,' announces Charlotte, who's in her late thirties, with a shock of curly red hair that springs around her pale cheeks.

'Me too,' says her friend Sammia. 'Can I bag a trouser suit, though, and not a mini?'

'The skirts aren't terribly mini,' I say, smiling. 'Remember, this was the Seventies, not the Sixties . . .'

'But what about hot pants?' she asks, cringing.

'Oh, yes.' I smile. 'There are a couple of pairs of those, but we'll see what everyone feels comfortable wearing. We'll have dress rehearsals. It's crucial that everyone feels totally comfortable in their outfits.'

'Oh, I can't wait,' Sammia says, grinning. 'My mum used to shop at Girl Friday. Can she come?'

'Of course she can,' I exclaim. 'You can all bring guests. It's the least we can do to thank you.'

There are four actors here, ranging from Erin, who's the youngest at twenty-nine, to Grace, who's in her late forties. I still haven't found my older model, and we really are cutting it fine now. The posters and programme have been designed, and Hannah is keen to get them finished.

However, once they're out there, Penny is sure to find out. 'Can we hold off,' I had asked Hannah, 'until we've got our poncho? I really think we need one, worn by one of our models, for the poster. Let's just wait a few more days.'

There is still so much to do, and some nights I've been waking up, not with the sweats but with a tight sensation in my chest, and my heart racing. Panic, I think it's called. The old anxieties are still there, rumbling along beneath the surface, although mainly I am being propelled along by excitement and a dogged belief that it will actually happen, just as I've planned it.

By the end of our meeting I have four enthusiastic models all signed up for the show. They want to be part of it, not for money (there still isn't any) but because they love the museum and, just like Izzy, they love to dress up. Which makes me believe that perhaps everything will be okay, after all.

'Of course it will,' Andy says, when he shows up just after 10 p.m., presenting the poncho to me like a prize. It's a thing of wonder: wild, playful and utterly impractical really. But all the lovelier for it.

'Thank you so much for this,' I say, meaning it. 'Erm, I'm so sorry about this, but Nick wondered if he could nip round and film you, arriving with it?'

'What, now?' Andy looks appalled.

'Yes. He's only round the corner at—'

'Yeah, I know where Penny lives,' he says distractedly. 'Does it have to be tonight, though? I mean, I already have arrived, haven't I? So, he's missed that part, the dramatic moment.' A smile plays on his lips.

'We can just pretend.'

323

He sighs. 'Could we possibly pretend another time?'

I check his face; of course, he's tired from the drive, and I relent, deciding he has done enough for me today. Instead, I make us mugs of tea, which we take through to the living room, where we sit side by side on the sofa.

We settle into silence. It's not awkward exactly, although I get the feeling he wants to talk. So far, I've avoided it as much as possible; proper talking, that is. But now, curiosity is starting to niggle at me.

Was it the omelette thing? Did he and his new woman row over that? I glance at him, at this man I loved crazily and who now shows up, wanting to help out as if he is still part of the family. It seems almost unbelievable that we were a couple who managed to conceive twice, with fifteen years between our children. Some family planning – although I wouldn't have it any other way.

'So,' I start, as Andy blows gently across his mug of tea, 'd'you want to tell me what happened with you and Estelle?'

12.27 a.m., a new day

He's still here. We didn't plan for that to happen. I certainly never imagined we'd ever sit up again, talking into the night.

He wouldn't tell me much at first, refused to divulge many details. Then a couple of hours ago, Izzy came down in her nightie, looking a bit bleary but pleased. 'Dad's still here,' she said with a smile.

'I'm going soon,' Andy said, giving me a quick look. A hopeful look, as if willing me to say, *Oh, you don't have to. You can stay the night.*

But I didn't. I coaxed her back to bed, and now he is finally telling me what happened with him and the Celestial One.

'I think I went a bit mad,' he says. 'It was never right. I wasn't thinking straight.'

I frown at him, knowing he's being as honest as he can be. 'You thought you were in love with her?'

He nods. 'I did. I am so sorry.' His eyes fill with tears. 'I kept trying to stop it, you know, before I left you. It was always, "I'll just see her one more time, to be a fair and decent person and to end it properly. We'll have coffee and that'll be that."'

But it was never just coffee. 'Estelle would get so upset,' he says now, 'and swear that she was just about to leave her husband. But she never did. She couldn't bring herself to do it.'

So, despite the promises, Andy hung on waiting, and finally it was him who ended it – on omelette night. 'No, of course it was nothing to do with that,' he says, frowning. 'But it *had* just happened when she saw you. She'd just left the flat for the last time.'

If only I'd known when I'd been tottering about drunkenly with my eggy mess. But then, what would I have done – gone up there and gloated? Or coaxed him back home?

He reaches for my hand. 'I realised I'd made a mistake,' he says as I pull mine away. His touch feels so odd now.

'So, you finished it because she wouldn't leave her husband and commit to you?'

Andy hesitates. 'I didn't want to be with her anymore, Viv. I only wanted you.' He squirms uncomfortably, and I'm feeling oddly dispassionate as the real story unfolds. All I can think is: *Well, that wasn't the best decision to make: leaving your wife and daughter and upsetting your son, to wait dutifully for your new girlfriend to leave her husband . . . Only to find she never would.*

As a punchline, I'm sure he'd agree it was disappointing.

'And . . . there's something else I have to ask you,' I add.

He nods. 'You can ask me anything you want. Anything at all.'

'Okay, so your flat . . .'

A *here-we-go* kind of look crosses his face. 'Yep. That flat.'

'Well . . . I'm just a bit surprised, that's all. Why you chose it. I mean, I know you've been contributing here; you've been decent about that – about money and everything. But you're hardly broke, Andy. Couldn't you have found somewhere less . . .'

'Less cheesy?' He raises a brow.

'Well, yes. You can't stand the smell, can you? Remember the fuss you made about that fridge in Paris?'

'I didn't make a *fuss*—'

'Come on. How come you moved in there? There are thousands of other places you could have rented—'

'The thing is,' he says quickly, 'it wasn't supposed to be a long-term thing. It was literally a stopgap, just until we, um . . .'

'Ah, right. Until Estelle left her husband and you could be open about things, and get a place together?'

'Well, yes, I thought that was the plan,' he murmurs, reddening.

I study his face. It still doesn't make sense. 'You still could've found somewhere a bit nicer, couldn't you?'

A resigned look settles onto his face. 'I'm really touched that you're so concerned about my accommodation, Viv.'

'Not concerned. More . . . curious, I suppose. Like I said, I remember how you were with that imaginary smell in Paris—'

'It wasn't imaginary!'

'Andy, there was nothing there.'

He shakes his head. 'If you say so.' Then: 'Okay, so I moved into the flat because it was vacant and I honestly thought I'd be there a month or so, no more than that.' He looks at me. 'It's Estelle's flat but it had lain empty for years.'

I blink at him. 'Is the shop hers too?'

'Yes, it is.' He nods and rubs at his face. 'She's not actively involved – but it was her dad's business. She inherited it and put a manager in.'

'She's not interested in it at all?'

'It's not really her thing,' he says. *And neither were you*, I reflect, glancing at him as I sip my tea. At least, not enough for her to upend her comfortable life. I don't feel sorry for him exactly. It just seems so foolish, so deranged, and so unlike the man I thought I knew. He always gave the impression that his decisions were the right ones: where to spend Christmas, or go on holiday; where we'd eat out, which wine we'd have. Cool, confident, successful Dr Flint, a man at the top of his game, always. The one who commandeered the barbecue and was the star of the monthly litter pick-ups, with the other women all fluttering around him. *What a catch!* was the general impression around here. But he'd got this one all wrong. She simply didn't love him enough; at least, not as much as he'd thought she did.

We take our mugs through to the kitchen, and I thank him again for the poncho. 'Why have you never let Izzy visit you?' I ask as he's leaving. 'At the flat, I mean?'

327

He exhales forcefully. 'Oh, I know it's stupid. But obviously, she'd have made a big thing about it and told you. And, quite rightly, you'd have found it hilarious.'

'I'm not sure I would have,' I say, deciding to never mention my trip there with Penny and the others. How we'd gone into the shop and quizzed the woman who worked there.

'Why did you care what I thought?' I ask.

'I've always cared what you thought. I always will.'

I am stumped for how to respond to that. 'It's been good to talk tonight,' he adds.

'It has,' I say truthfully as, in a peculiar way, I know Andy better now than I ever did when we were together. I feel equal to him, at *least* equal; not that I am interested in power games. Right now, I'm dog-tired and interested only in sleep. 'So, you'll be moving out of the flat, I guess?'

Andy nods as he steps outside. 'I'm not sure where I'm going to go.' I'm sure I catch it then; his quick glance towards our home. A hopeful look. Or maybe I imagined it?

'So,' I say, 'the cheese thing doesn't interest her at all? Even though it was the family business?'

Andy shakes his head, and a tiny smile forms. 'She's dairy intolerant,' he says.

Chapter Thirty-Seven

Monday, November 18

Penny has gone AWOL. At least, she and Hamish seem to have gone off on a jaunt on his boat, and there's no way of reaching her. It seems crazy, that a person is uncontactable in this day and age. 'Last thing I heard, they were having an impromptu holiday,' Nick says, with a trace of exasperation when I call him at lunchtime from work. 'I think it's because I'm here, and Bobby hates the boat, apparently. He gets anxious and sick and he won't wear his little life jacket.'

'Can't they just . . . put it on him?'

Nick chuckles. I push aside my haloumi salad and make an apologetic face at Belinda, who's sitting opposite. 'I think Mum finds it aesthetically unpleasing.'

I splutter with laughter, despite the anxiety that's rising in me now; we really must tell her soon. I inhale deeply and sip my glass of water. 'What can we do, then?' I ask.

'Hamish is bound to drive her mad,' Nick assures me. 'She'll be back soon, and as soon as she appears, I'll call you. Please don't worry. There's no way she'll object to it, now we're almost ready to go.'

Tuesday, November 19

Still no sign of Penny. It's a little baffling, as she's not even keen on Hamish's boat: 'It's what you'd call basic,' she's told me, pulling a face. 'That chemical loo is not something you'd want to acquaint yourself with, if you could possibly avoid it.' However, these late autumn days have been blue-skied and crisp, so perhaps they're making the most of it. Well, good for them. How lovely to be chugging along on our inland waterways! But I hope to God she comes back soon.

Wednesday, November 20

Still no word from Penny. Is Hamish holding her hostage? Has she fallen overboard? Even Nick is growing agitated now, although he pretends he's not when he drops by briefly, whilst out walking Bobby. 'Maybe they've run off to get married,' I remark. As a joke, it falls flat.

'They're probably just having a lovely time,' Nick says, and I have to concede he's probably right. But I'm *dying*.

Thursday, November 21

Sammia has been photographed in the poncho, and the posters and programme are all ready to go. Miraculously,

I've managed to stall Hannah from making it all public by explaining that we need Penny's approval first.

'It all looks amazing!' she says, when she calls me just after I've arrived home from work. 'I can't wait to hear what she says.'

'Me too,' I say, trying to radiate positivity. We finish the call, and I gave Izzy a drink and a biscuit in the living room. She's chattering away about school, and how they're going to start cross-country running, which she's a little perturbed about, and her class teacher's picking a quiz team, which is more her thing. Whilst I'm trying to listen, and reassure her that they won't be required to run for hours and *hours*, as rumour suggests, and yes, I'm sure she has a good chance of being picked for the team, I'm still distracted and tense, which seems to have become my near-permanent state over the past few days.

Where the heck is Penny? Of course, she's entitled to a holiday, I try to reason with myself as I go through to the kitchen and start knocking together a pasta sauce. Her life isn't bound by any work-related timetable, and maybe she's decided Hamish's chemical loo isn't so bad after all. Or perhaps she's forced him to abandon the boat and adjourn to a hotel? As for her unwillingness to engage with social media, or even switch on her mobile (what's the point in having one if it's always off? 'Saving the battery!' is her stock response). Well, I guess that's fine too. At least fine-*ish*, until someone needs to ruddy well get hold of her, like me who's getting pretty desperate—

'Penny, hi!' I drop the wooden spoon onto the worktop as she strides into my kitchen. Her expression is bizarrely flat, possibly even angry. She didn't knock, but then, she never does; it's the trait of hers that drove Andy most crazy. *I mean, what if we were in the middle of doing something?* Bizarrely, Chrissie – who *is* a polite door-knocker – seems to have followed her in, and is looking pale and quite upset.

'Hi, Viv,' Penny says sharply.

I push back my hair and turn off the hob. As the two of them are no more than acquaintances, I have no idea what's going on.

'What . . . what's happening? Is something up?' I look at them both in turn.

'Viv, I'm so sorry,' Chrissie starts. There's no bold red lipstick today, and her hair is stuffed back into its topknot. 'He didn't mean it,' she adds, her eyes wide with alarm. 'He really didn't. It just . . . happened.'

'Who didn't mean what?'

'Ludo,' she exclaims. 'You know how sweet he is, how he'd never want to upset anyone. And he didn't realise, and it's all my fault . . .'

The cat-stoning incident springs into mind. 'Has he hurt Bobby?' I gasp.

'No, of course not!' Chrissie cries. 'He'd never hurt an animal—'

'Look, I know about this thing at the museum,' Penny cuts in, her gaze meeting mine. 'I know that you and Nick have been in cahoots, planning it, this thing that's going to be *huge*, apparently, and neither of you thought to say a word about it to me.'

I stare at her, my mouth open, feeling as if I've been punched in the gut. 'Viv, I'm so sorry,' Chrissie goes on, although my gaze still is fixed upon Penny's face. I have never seen her looking angry before. Disgruntled, yes, and irritated, when she's had a spat with Hamish, but never properly furious like this. Oh, shit. I have misread things so badly and made a terrible mistake.

'We ran into Penny in the park after school,' Chrissie adds, biting at a fingernail. 'She was out with Bobby and of course, Ludo ran straight over to play with him. You know how he loves animals . . .'

'Never mind, Chrissie,' I say distractedly. 'It's done now, and it can't be helped.' I turn back to Penny. 'Pen, look . . . we were planning to tell you. Of course we were.'

'So, why didn't you?' She plonks her hands on her hips.

'You've been away,' I say faintly. 'I've been wanting to talk to you, but—'

'That was only for a few days,' she cuts in. 'You've been planning this for weeks—'

'Where's Nick? Have you spoken to him at all?' Christ, now it sounds as if I am trying to shift the blame, which isn't my intention at all.

'He's in town somewhere,' she says briskly. 'I haven't seen him yet. To be fair, I realise it's not just you. I'm just as annoyed with him, plotting and scheming—'

'But it's not like that,' I exclaim, sensing my cheeks flaming. 'Honestly, we just thought it was for the best. At first there was no guarantee that it would happen at all. In fact, the museum initially turned the idea down. And then it *was* happening, but it seemed such a monumental undertaking that I really wasn't sure if I could pull it off. Then the clothes started to arrive – Isla and I, then Nick too, between us we'd contacted literally hundreds of vintage shops. It was slow to begin with, then things seemed to gain momentum and all these pieces were arriving, sent by shop owners because they trusted us, they believed in the project and they wanted to help . . .'

My voice cracks. I fix my gaze on Penny's blue-grey

eyes. Chrissie is staring down at the floor, and Izzy is still watching TV in the living room, apparently oblivious. 'They wanted to be involved,' I continue, 'and I decided, once we had everything pretty sorted, then *that* would be the best time to tell you. I knew you might be unsure about it, after your reaction when we first talked about a fashion event. So I wanted you to see how brilliant it would be, and how excited everyone's been to play a part in it—'

'So it would be a fait accompli?' she asks coolly.

'Erm, well, yes. But in a *good* way, a way that would make you so proud and thrilled. I mean . . .' I pause, aware of the desperation in my voice, 'if you're planning a surprise party, you only want the person to find out when everything's perfect and ready and—'

'But I hate surprise parties,' Penny snaps. 'Who likes them really? A party they've had no hand in planning and no chance to prepare for, no outfit picked out, no chance to get to the hairdresser's . . .'

'Yes, but—'

'Do *you* like them?' She turns to Chrissie who looks up, startled.

'Um, I'm not a massive fan of them, to be honest,' she mutters, throwing me an apologetic look.

'And the two of you seem to have forgotten that this is *my* thing,' Penny goes on. 'Girl Friday is mine, Viv. It was *my* name, and *my* brand. And why on earth would I want the whole thing to be raked up again when I explained, quite clearly, that night with Hamish and Isla and you, that I didn't want to be roped in as some kind of consultant?'

'But you wouldn't be a consultant!' I cry, stepping towards her.

She shrinks back. 'No, clearly not. No one's consulted me at all!'

I nod distractedly. 'Penny, please,' I say. 'I know I should have told you. I've really screwed up, and I'm sorry. But can you just tell me why you're so against the idea? It would celebrate you and your success! You deserve that, don't you? And everyone thinks it'll be amazing.'

'Yes, but who'd want to come?' she barks, her voice rising now. Izzy has appeared in the doorway and is staring, wide-eyed, at us all. 'In the end it was a failure,' Penny adds, 'so why have an event to supposedly celebrate something that went tits up?'

Izzy gasps audibly. 'Iz, please go through to the living room,' I say quickly.

'But, Mum—'

'Please, love. Just for a few minutes.' Reluctantly, she slinks away.

Penny glowers at me. 'Why would you want to put on an event that no one will care about, or come to see, and it'll be humiliating all over again?'

'It won't be *humiliating*,' I say firmly. 'Why d'you say that?'

'It doesn't matter,' she snaps, and I notice that Chrissie's eyes are brimming with tears.

'Ludo didn't mean any harm,' she says. 'He just said, "Penny, Viv's doing a show all about you!" Because he'd heard me and Tim talking about it. It hadn't occurred to me that he'd say anything . . .' She tails off, crying properly now. 'I feel so responsible, Viv . . .'

'Chrissie, it's okay,' I murmur, putting my arms around her as the tears start to roll down her cheeks.

'It's not. I've ruined everything.'

335

'No, you haven't,' I say firmly. 'You haven't at all. You're not responsible for this. Ludo isn't either.'

'He's so upset,' she adds. 'You know how fond of you he is, how he loves coming here, and now he's all worried that he's done the wrong thing, and you won't let him come over again. He loved staying with you that week when Lara was born, and the camp-out in your living room – my God, he's still talking about that now, about the marshmallows and sausages and being allowed to stay up all night. It's so much more fun at your place, that's what he says—'

'Chrissie, please,' I cut in. 'I'm not mad at him. He's welcome here anytime. If I'm mad at anyone it's myself, for pushing on with this without telling Penny.' I turn to her. 'I'm so sorry, Pen. I got carried away – obsessed, I suppose. The whole project's been all-consuming and maybe I lost perspective along the way. But, look, when it comes down to it, it's only fashion, it's just clothes, and what I really care about is that you're okay, and you too, Chrissie – and Ludo.'

Chrissie extracts a crumpled tissue from her jeans pocket and blows her nose into it. 'I'm okay,' she murmurs.

'Penny?' I look at her, wanting to hug her but aware that her mouth is still set in a terse line. 'If you don't want it to happen, then it won't happen,' I say firmly. 'I'll call the museum, the joiners, Spencer, the models – everyone who's involved. Without your blessing, it can't possibly go ahead.'

I see her swallow hard and look down at the floor, and hear a whining sound from the hallway. Bobby has been there the whole time. He must have sensed the tension in here and decided, wisely, to stay away. Izzy is out there now, murmuring comfortingly to him.

336

'Okay,' is all Penny says.

I sigh. 'Would you like to come up to Spencer's room and see the clothes? The Girl Friday collection, I mean? It really is amazing, what we've managed to gather together.' She shakes her head. '*Please* come and see. You might change your mind, if you just have a look. Your old designs are there, all the key pieces that everyone loved . . .' I stop, because I feel that I, too, could cry.

Penny's face seems to soften, and she looks at me as if considering it for a moment. Then she turns and says, 'I need to get Bobby home. He'll be ravenous and I think I forgot to defrost his beef.' And then they're gone.

Chapter Thirty-Eight

Friday, November 22

I consider calling in sick at work. However, guilt gnaws at me so I end up phoning Rose and telling her the whole story, the entire sorry mess, and when I've finished there's silence.

'Rose?' I prompt her. 'I'm sorry – I know I've been consumed by this these past few weeks, and maybe my mind hasn't seemed completely on my job. I know I've been distracted. I've tried to keep everything going but—'

'I had no idea you were doing this,' she says, sounding genuinely shocked. 'No idea at all.'

Christ, I don't think this is going down well, and no wonder. Secret side projects imply not being fully committed to work, and if there's one thing Rose insists on, it's one hundred per cent commitment. 'No, well, of course you wouldn't,' I murmur.

'I mean, I had no idea you had this huge, other thing going on,' she adds. 'And you haven't seemed distracted. Quite the opposite, in fact. You've seemed so . . . oh, I

don't know how to put it without sounding patronising.'
She pauses. 'Look, I know I got it all wrong, with the
Menopause Ambassador thing, so I'm trying to be careful
here – but you've seemed so dynamic lately, so revved up
and full of energy. Not that you aren't always, of course!
You really are. But this has been like . . . an extra layer,
so to speak. And I wondered if you were, you know . . .
over those symptoms.' The hot flushes and all that, I
assume she means. Despite everything, I smile.

'They're waning a little,' I say.

'Well, *that's* good to hear. I wondered if it was this
place,' she adds with a chuckle, 'with all the new, young
people about, the general shaking up. Because it's been
better, hasn't it?' There's a note of hope in her voice.

'Er, yes, it has.'

'But, actually . . . it was this all along.'

I inhale deeply. 'It's been really important to me.'

'Yes, I can imagine. I also understand how disappointed
you must be, so please, don't even think about coming
in today. Just take the day off and rest, relax, whatever
it is you want to do.'

'Thank you,' I say, awash with gratitude.

Rose sighs. 'Are you sure your friend's not persuadable?'

'Erm, I don't think so, no.'

'That is a great shame, Viv. For you, and for everyone
really. But you tried your best, and you gave it your all,
it sounds like. And that's the best you could do.'

'Thank you,' I say again, feeling almost guilty about
how shocking that conversation was to me. After all, it's
not as if Rose isn't a decent person underneath the bluster
and insensitivity. And I'm wondering now if, despite
having me ordering her eardrops and dealing with pubes,
a part of her actually *cares*.

Minutes later, she texts me: *If you do get a min, could you ask that new maintenance guy to put that exercise ball somewhere else? It's cluttering up my office and is useless as a shelf.*

'Have you called Hannah yet?' Nick asks, when he phones.

'Not yet,' I reply. 'I'm just trying to figure out the best way of putting it. She'll be far from pleased, I do know that. They've designed the posters and programme and planned the exhibition space. Then there's all the time they've spent on our meetings – it's been a complete waste of time for everyone, and they're stretched and under-staffed as it is. And the worst thing is, Hannah assumed that Penny was on board by now, that she knew all about it and was fully supportive. And I didn't put her right on that. I just let her *think* it, Nick. She'll be livid . . .'

'I'm sure she won't—'

'It was only Isla who knew we hadn't told her yet. I haven't even called *her*, either, and she's one of my closest friends. I feel such an idiot.'

He clears his throat. I didn't mean to blurt out all of that, but I couldn't help myself. 'Is there anything I can do? I mean . . . could I call anyone?'

'No, don't do that!' I bark at him. 'Please don't call anyone. I'll do it—'

'Well, look . . .' He pauses, and I hear him exhale. 'I don't think you should phone anyone just yet.'

I pace across the kitchen, kicking one of my discarded trainers out of the way. 'Well, I'll have to soon. I can't keep them hanging on. The sooner they know, the better, really. Press releases have gone out already so that's going to be embarrassing for them – publicising something that's not even going to be happening. And we were due to roll

340

out all the online publicity this weekend. So I really do need to call Hannah today . . .'

'Viv, please,' Nick says firmly. 'Just hang on for a little while—'

'Stop telling me what to do,' I snap, regretting it immediately.

'I'm not,' he says levelly. 'I didn't mean it like that. I just meant . . . maybe it's best not to do anything yet, okay?'

I open the back door and step out into the garden, inhaling lungfuls of cool, crisp air. The sky is pale blue, the air sharp and wintry. It's the kind of morning I love, usually: the sort that makes you feel alive. But it doesn't today. Instead, I shiver in my thin sweater and skirt, and head straight back inside.

'Can I come over?' Nick asks. 'Please, Viv. I'd just like to see you so we can talk about stuff.'

'There's not much to talk about really,' I mutter.

'Come on, I won't keep you long. I can be over in a few minutes . . .'

'All right then,' I say huffily, knowing I'm coming across like a grumpy child. 'But I'm sorry, I don't think I'm going to be exactly sparkling company today.'

So he comes round, looking a little hesitant as I open the door to him. Bizarrely, Penny is standing rather stiffly at his side. 'Oh!' I exclaim. 'Erm, come in . . .' It must be the first time she hasn't marched right into my house. My chest tightens, and I'm primed for another dose of her wrath. But she isn't angry, it seems. She is rather subdued and, bizarrely, she is clutching a bottle of champagne. 'As a peace offering,' she says, barely audible. 'I'm sorry,' she adds, as the two of us settle onto the sofa, and Nick perches on a chair.

'Oh, Penny. There's nothing to apologise for,' I say flatly. 'It's me who should be sorry. But thanks for the champagne, although I'm not sure I've done anything to deserve it.'

'No,' she says, more firmly now, 'you most definitely do deserve it, and I think I should explain.' She looks at Nick, and he smiles encouragingly. The bond between them is so clear to see. I still don't understand why she affected such a brusque attitude about him coming to stay, and implied that he's a difficult houseguest, bordering on critical. I simply can't see it at all.

'Girl Friday ended pretty horribly,' she begins, pushing her dishevelled hair from her face, 'and although I blamed competitors copying me, that's not really true. I've learned to accept it was all my fault.'

'So . . . what happened?' I ask, still wary.

She sighs heavily. 'Do you remember I mentioned a man called Saul, who helped me to set up my stall at Portobello Market?'

'I do, yes. The one who called you Girl Friday right at the beginning?'

Penny nods, and a wistful look crosses her face. 'Well, he was my backer too. He became a very good friend, and he tried to advise me, but I was so headstrong in those days, such a wilful girl who thought she knew it all. I made so many bad decisions, Viv – expanding too quickly, taking on premises I couldn't afford. Rolling out too many new pieces, too quickly, as if I was in some kind of race, and being unable to pay my suppliers. It all blew up in my face, and Saul kept telling me where I was going wrong, to slow down and be more considered, and to have an actual plan.' She grimaces. 'You know, like any sensible adult would. But I didn't want to hear it.'

I nod, waiting for her to go on. She takes my hand and squeezes it.

'Oh, I behaved terribly,' she continues. 'When things were getting really bad, and I couldn't pay bills, I went down from Glasgow to London for an emergency meeting with him. I couldn't even afford the train. Nick and I travelled on a rickety bus. And the meeting went badly because I simply couldn't admit that I was wrong, that I'd made any mistakes at all. I shouted at Saul for trying to tell me how to manage *my* business, that I'd created, and I stormed out. And I did the most terrible thing.'

'What was that?' Nick asks.

'Oh, it was so silly and juvenile.' She looks around at both of us. 'I egged his car.'

'It was his car that you egged?' I exclaim. 'Not a woman's?'

Nick's eyes widen, and he catches my gaze briefly. 'Yes, it was Saul's,' Penny murmurs, her cheeks reddening. 'I did that to the man who'd shown nothing but kindness to me when I first started out, and was the only person who'd ever had faith in me really, because my own parents certainly thought I was mad—'

'I never knew that, Mum.' Nick comes over, sits beside her and wraps an arm tenderly around her shoulders.

'It's not something I'm proud of,' she murmurs. 'I've tried to forget about it and move on. All the other projects, the new lines I tried to get off the ground . . . Can't you see how much I wanted to prove that I wasn't incapable?'

'I know, Mum,' Nick says carefully. 'But Girl Friday was still a wonderful thing. You won't believe how positive people have been, how excited and nostalgic, when we've contacted them . . .'

'And the fact that it ended eventually doesn't mean the

343

show can't go ahead,' I add. 'I know things went wrong and the business collapsed. But when you see the actual clothes, you'll remember how much they meant to young women back then.' I look at her, imploring her to give us her blessing. 'Can we go ahead, Penny? We can do anything you like. You can invite anyone – all your friends, and Hamish, of course; it'll be a real celebration, just a fun night with people who love you.'

'Oh, he's preoccupied right now,' she mutters.

'What with?'

'Something to do with his glow plugs.'

'Is he ill?' I ask, concerned.

'They're part of the engine on his boat,' she says impatiently. 'Honestly, that thing of his – it's a bloody embarrassment. And he won't admit it. He won't let it go.'

Nick's mouth twitches into a smile. 'He loves it, though.'

'Yes, because he's an idiot.'

'And he loves you too,' he adds, gently teasing her, 'doesn't he?'

Penny scowls. 'I suppose so,' she says tersely, 'in his own way. But I still haven't forgiven him for the Rolling Stones thing.' I look at her, wanting to ask, *Yes, but do you love him, despite that terrible faux pas?*

'Mum, I hope you don't mind me asking,' Nick remarks, 'but whenever you talk about Hamish it's usually to run him down or complain about him . . .'

She blinks at him and shrugs.

'He's right,' I add, catching Nick's eye and quickly suppressing a smile. 'But, you know, you have been together quite a while now.'

'Well, he is good fun,' she says briskly.

'And you have just been away on the boat,' I remind her, at which her expression softens.

'Um, yes, well, that was lovely actually. I mean, he knows I'm not a natural boater but it was touching, the effort he'd gone to, to make it more comfortable for me. There's a new bed, and bunting strung up, and cushions . . .'

'He's trying to woo you with bunting and cushions,' Nick says, chuckling now.

'Hmm, yes. The silly man.' She smiles now, and fiddles with the ankle strap of her red patent shoe. Hamish, and even Nick, her own son; it's as if she can't resist being snarky about people who love her. 'So, tell me this,' she goes on, looking at me now. 'How did I get involved with a boat man who's invented this entire personal history based on one, silly little ice cream advert jingle that he composed about fifty years ago?'

I laugh. 'Is that true? I mean, is that all he's done?'

'Pretty much,' she retorts, 'although he's loath to admit it. You know what a terrible bragger he is.'

'Well,' I venture, 'maybe he's told those stories so often, he actually believes them.'

'And the jingle was pretty good,' Nick adds, grinning. 'Catchy. You have to give him that, Mum.'

'It was actually.' She smirks, and the sparkle seems to come back to her wide, expressive eyes as she gathers herself up, smooths her honey-blonde hair and looks at Nick, then at me. 'Anyway, at least he knows how to have a good time, and better that, I suppose, than being saddled with some boring old duffer.' She shrugs, waving a hand, as if to signal that the topic is finished. 'Anyway, about this show. I suppose I'd better get involved, hadn't I? If we're going to tell *this* story right.'

345

Chapter Thirty-Nine

Sixteen days later: Sunday, December 8

The enormous Christmas tree glitters magnificently in the dimmed lights. Smaller pockets of light illuminate tantalising corners of the main exhibition space of the museum. Spencer catches my eye and raises a brow, and there's a quick smile before he turns back to the matter in hand.

The music starts. The hubbub of chatter dies down and the faces of the audience seem to light up. From my position at the doorway to the side room, I have an uninterrupted view of the runway, and I'm poised to signal to each model when it's time to come out.

Charlotte is first, sashaying out in a gauzy floral dress accessorised with bright wooden beads and a white floppy hat. My gaze skims the display panels covered with photographs, magazine cuttings, posters and original advertising paraphernalia from the Girl Friday shops. It looks wonderful.

With an impressively proficient catwalk turn, Charlotte

strides back, and I check the rapt expressions of the key members of staff: Isla, Hannah, and the others who worked on the graphics, displays and publicity. Everyone pulled out the stops, when it counted. 'Museum time' certainly sped up.

Andy is on the front row with Izzy sitting beside him. Millie, Spencer's girlfriend, is on Izzy's other side. Both girls look entranced, and even Andy appears to be watching intently, turning away only to murmur occasionally to our daughter. Jules is here, with Maeve, plus Shelley, Chrissie and the baby, Tim and Ludo, Spencer's friends who built the runway, and a whole bunch of my mum mates from school. There's a significant number of younger audience members: the fashion and art students, and the girls and boys who have come out of curiosity, perhaps. And there are older women too, some of whom I know Nick tracked down and interviewed for his film. They are the original fans of Girl Friday: the customers, sales assistants and die-hard devotees. Some, I noticed with delight when they arrived, are wearing original Girl Friday outfits. A dapper woman whom I'd guess at late sixties is wearing a purple peaked cap.

The vintage shop owners, who lent the pieces, have come out in force, some from as far as Cornwall and London – and Tricia Spalding from Grange-over-Sands is watching with keen attention. Every press contact we emailed has turned up for the show; there are editors, journalists and bloggers, many of whom I know for a fact attend all the *real* shows in Paris, London, Milan and New York (hang on, ours is a real show too!). A couple of fashion editors are even sketching as Sammia strides past in the red trouser suit (as promised, I didn't try to coax her into a mini), shortly followed by Grace in multicoloured patchwork dungarees. Erin appears, her blonde hair flowing as if in a shampoo ad, wearing a folk-art-inspired crocheted top and butter-yellow corduroy flares. As each model walks, Spencer follows her expertly with a spotlight while the music captures the spirit perfectly. In the side room, outfits are changed with impressive speed, with the hair and make-up artists fixing ponytails, reapplying lip gloss and powdering shiny noses and cheeks. The air is thick with hairspray.

Although it's a tense operation, and my old anxieties are still there, fluttering like moths around a flame, I sense myself relaxing a little as the models come and go, striding past me with wide smiles and breezy confidence. There is one wobbly moment when Sammia teeters on her platform boots, but she rights herself, and there's an audible gasp of relief. Ludo giggles and kicks at his chair legs, and I catch Chrissie shushing him. *No, Ludo*, she mouths. *Be quiet.*

Ludo hearing the word no? This must be a first. I turn to Nick, who's sitting beside me – he knows all about my neighbours – and he smiles almost imperceptibly.

Back and forth, the women stride, in a dazzling array of colours. And then we are nearing the end, and the music cranks up as the last model appears, the indubitable star of the show: Penny, with her blonde hair bouncing in tumbling waves and her lips painted glossy red, as she sashays out in elegant black trousers and strappy espadrilles, topped off with the most fabulous piece of all.

There is applause, and everyone is standing now and cheering, as Penny beams with delight, twirling in her Pippa poncho, before taking a bow.

We have drunk Penny's champagne, Nick, Penny, Spencer and me. Others came back too – Chrissie (minus the baby), and Isla, Shelley and Jules – but now it's just the four of us, celebrating. Izzy and Maeve are asleep upstairs – or, at least, they're supposed to be. More champagne was fetched from the shop down the road, and G&Ts mixed for Penny. And after a fair few, and her thanking me so much I've had to deftly change the subject, I have started to understand why Penny does this 'brush-off' thing, this trying to distance herself from her own son, as if her own life is far too busy to accommodate him comfortably.

Because she misses him dreadfully, I have come to realise. But she can't bring herself to admit it. She goes so far as to imply that he's a nuisance – perpetually checking for dust – when in truth her heart is breaking at the thought of him going back to New Zealand. She tries to coax him to stay by running his baths and fussing over him, getting in his favourite foods as if he's a little boy. She even managed to track down butterscotch Angel Delight. But he has to go back, he explained, when she became a little gin-teary earlier. He has a film to make about a run of Christmas shows in Auckland; people are waiting for him. He can't simply not go.

'It's because of Canada really,' he murmurs later, when the two of us find ourselves alone in the kitchen. 'Remember I told you my dad took me there?'

'Yes,' I say. 'But why—'

'Dad was supposed to fly back to the UK with me,' he explains. 'I was four years old and only supposed to be out there for a two-week holiday. But then he decided he quite liked this dad lark after all – he had a couple more kids by then – and that all of his children should be together, in a kind of fantasy happy family way. And he phoned Mum to say I wouldn't be coming back.'

'She must've been horrified!'

'Yeah. And she had the shops by then – it was all taking off back here – and she had to get on a plane and come and fetch me and take me home. So,' he adds with a grim smile, 'you can imagine how well it went down when I told her I was moving to the other side of the world, of my own accord.'

I nod, taking this in. The festive fairy lights I've strung around the kitchen are filling the room with a soft golden light. Nick looks especially handsome tonight in a pale blue shirt and jeans, his hair freshly trimmed. I'll miss him more than I can begin to imagine, I realise now. 'But you were, what, in your late thirties then?' I ask. 'I know it would've been hard, but it wasn't *quite* the same.'

'Didn't make much difference,' he remarks. 'She was kind of . . . well, furious, I suppose. And it still surges up in her from time to time. But that's not the reason . . .' He breaks off and looks at me. 'I mean, it's not the only reason I'm coming back.'

I blink at him. The chatter and laughter from the living room seems to have faded away. 'You mean, for your next visit home?'

Nick smiles and shakes his head. 'No, I don't mean for a visit. I mean . . .' He blinks, and my heart seems to stop as those grey-blue eyes meet mine. 'I mean for good, Viv.'

I stare at him, barely able to take this in. 'You mean you're coming back to live in Glasgow?'

He nods. 'Yeah, that's what I've decided.'

350

'When?' I blurt out, not caring if I seem too eager.

'I'm not exactly sure,' he replies. 'There'll be a lot to sort out. But soon, hopefully.' And he smiles that smile that lifts my heart. 'Don't say anything yet, will you?'

I look at him in the soft, warm light, barely able to contain my joy. 'You want me to keep *another* secret from Penny?' I pull a mock-terrified face.

'Just for now,' he says, touching my hand, and then squeezing it. 'And please, never let her know I told you first.'

Chapter Forty

Wednesday, December 11

I haven't seen Penny at all since Sunday night. I have been busy with the aftermath of the show, starting to parcel up some of the clothes, which need to be returned – whilst trying to get my head around my own future. Hannah has asked to drop in for a meeting tomorrow evening, presumably for a debrief. I'm also keen to discuss how we might keep the public's interest up, after our big success. I suggested bringing Penny this time; after all, she's the expert on fashion, and the last thing I want is for her to not feel consulted.

'Perhaps next time,' Hannah said quickly. 'For this meeting, I'd like it to just be me and you.'

Thursday, December 12

I smile when I see the old-school Christmas decorations in the main open-plan museum office. With paper chains strung about, and several tiny tinsel trees perched on desks, the place looks almost homely. Back home, our decorations are a more full-on affair; Izzy insists on it, and I wouldn't be such a spoilsport as to rein her in. We have a large, real tree in place already, which Nick helped us to set upright and drape with lights, once it had been delivered.

'So, Penny says she's happy to come in and do a question-and-answer session with an audience,' I tell Hannah as she hands me a mug of tea.

'That would be great. I'm sure we could get more media coverage for that. You know, we're being featured in all the supplements this weekend, and there's been tons online already.'

'Yes, I've seen some of that. The photos of the show looked great.'

'The models were brilliant, weren't they? And Spencer did a fantastic job with the lighting!'

I grin with a surge of pride. 'Thanks, I'll pass that on to him.' I pause. 'You know most of the Girl Friday pieces were lent to us, don't you?' Hannah nods. 'Well, quite a few of their owners are happy for us to keep them on long-term loan, so I was thinking, perhaps we could set up a small collection here? A sort of capsule collection?'

'I think that's a wonderful idea. It would be a lasting legacy of the event.'

I smile. 'Can I ask you, honestly, do you think the museum has a future now?'

She looks at me, levelly, as if I have just asked a ridiculous question. 'I should think so, Viv. It seems we're the talk of the town now, and it's already had quite an effect on visitor numbers.' She smooths back her fine light brown hair. 'Of course you can never tell, in today's climate, what the future holds – but, yes, things are looking good for now.'

'That's so good to hear.'

A small pause settles over us. 'And what about you, Viv?' Hannah asks. 'How d'you feel about your job these days?'

'Oh, that's just a stopgap kind of thing,' I say.

'Really?' Her eyes widen in interest as I laugh awkwardly.

'Well, yes – a stopgap that's gone on for way too long. Half a decade in fact. But actually, working on the show here has been really useful for me too. It's changed everything, actually.'

'In what way?'

I exhale, wondering whether to hold back, or just to let it all out. 'I've been treading water these past few years,' I say. 'Not just with work but in all ways really. It's just happened. Maybe it was having a second child fairly late on or, um, other things in my life . . . but the show reminded me how much I loved my job, when I was younger. And it wasn't about the salary, or the recognition back then. It was just doing something I loved.'

She beams at me. 'I do know that feeling.'

'D'you feel like that, about working here?'

'I do,' she says firmly, 'and I know Isla does too. We all do. But I think we needed an injection of something new.'

'A Penny Barnett injection,' I suggest.

'Well, yes, Penny, of course. But you made it happen, Viv. You ran with the idea, and turned into a real thing, something entirely doable with virtually no budget at all. And look what's happened.'

'It's been brilliant,' is all I can think of to say. 'And it's also been a total pleasure. I wish everything I did felt like this. Work-wise, I mean.'

'Well, maybe it could,' Hannah remarks. 'Erm, would you consider taking on a role here, Viv?'

I blink at her. 'You mean . . . an actual job?'

'I do, yes. Well, a contract actually. A maternity contract . . .'

I look at her, not quite sure what she means. 'What kind of role would it be?' I ask. It's safer, I decide, than blurting out, *Are you pregnant?* to be met with a steely gaze, not that Hannah seems remotely steely, but it's not what an un-pregnant woman wants to hear. I've made that mistake in the past.

'It's the role of special exhibitions officer,' she replies, 'which basically means covering for me. It's a little while off yet. I'm hoping to work right through until May – but I'd like to have the right person in place well before that.'

I grin at her. 'You're going on leave? You mean, you're . . .'

'Yes, I am pregnant,' she says, laughing. I glance down, now seeing the small, neat bump beneath her loose grey cotton dress. 'I know it can be a dangerous thing to comment on. But yes, I'm taking a full year's leave, and the maternity contract will be for that year. And at the end of that . . .' She pauses.

'It doesn't matter,' I say quickly. 'I know you probably can't guarantee anything beyond that.'

She nods. 'I know. I'm sorry. It depends on visitor numbers, budgets – but I have high hopes for a great year ahead . . .'

'I'm definitely interested,' I say firmly, thinking: could I do this? Of course I could. Since the show, I've felt as if I can do *anything*.

Hannah looks delighted. 'Okay, so I'll set up a more formal chat – but it really is just that. A formality. After our Girl Friday event,' she adds, with a big, beaming grin, 'I think you've pretty much passed the test.'

Chapter Forty-One

Saturday, December 14

So Izzy is finally getting to see the eco-lodges up at Loch Fyne, as Andy is taking her away for the weekend. This time, with no Maeve's caravan trip to entice her, she is delighted to go. As for me, I am going on a jaunt today, with Penny and Nick.

He knows where we are going, but Penny doesn't. At least, she doesn't yet; we didn't want to risk her refusing to come. We've just told her we are going on a trip.

'This is ridiculous,' she says, rather crossly as the train pulls out of the station. We thought it would be more fun to travel this way; more of a mystery trip. Now I'm not sure it was the right decision. But it's not far to Lancaster – only two hours – and I'm hoping Penny will soon relax and just enjoy the journey. 'I don't like this "being taken" somewhere,' she says, turning to Nick to her left.

'Okay,' he says, catching my eye across the table. 'I can understand that. I'd probably find it a bit unsettling too.'

'To put it mildly,' she huffs.

The three of us fall silent. Penny, who's sitting at the window seat, gazes out at the fields. Rain trickles diagonally across the glass. Nick is alternately fiddling with his phone and trying, with limited success, to engage his mother in conversation.

'I'd love a coffee,' she announces, at which the two of us leap up, eager to escape for a few minutes.

'I'll get it,' I say brightly. 'Nick, d'you want anything?'

'Just a coffee for me too, please. Erm, in fact, I'll come and help.' He turns to Penny. 'Won't be a minute, Mum. Will you be okay?'

'For God's sake,' she exclaims. 'I'm not going to do anything, you know. I'm not going to get off at – well, whatever the next station is. And I'm not planning to throw myself from the moving train.'

'I'm glad to hear that,' he says with a smile.

'I don't need watching, you know. I'm not some confused old lady that you can't leave unattended for a few moments,' she adds sternly.

'No, we realise that,' I murmur. 'Sorry, Penny. The last thing we want to do is annoy you.'

'Just get me my coffee, darling,' she says, a little less crossly as she turns back to watch the rain.

She doesn't press us anymore, and by the time we return with the coffees, her mood seems to have brightened. Maybe she trusts us now, with surprises – or perhaps she's just enjoying the view of gentle sloping fields as she gazes out. The sky has brightened, and by the time we pull into Lancaster station the sun is shining brightly.

We make our way to the taxi rank. 'Beechwood Care Home please,' I tell the driver, and ten minutes later, we arrive. It's a well-kept Victorian house with immaculate gardens and benches set out around a lawn. Lynne, the deputy manager, is expecting us, and when she sees us climbing out of the taxi she beckons us over to the decked area.

There are patio heaters, and bunches of winter pansies on the tables, and residents are sitting around, enjoying pots of tea and cakes in the bright winter sunshine.

'This is Penny, Nick and Viv,' Lynne says with a smile, introducing us. She is a rounded, homely-looking woman in a smart blue tunic. 'We're just having tea. Would you like to join us?'

We hesitate, and I watch as Penny's gaze skims along the expectant faces of the residents. Someone pats a vacant chair, inviting her to sit down. An elderly man, who must be well into his nineties, brightens in recognition on seeing her face.

He wasn't too hard to track down, when I started on it. He has always been active in business, in fashion particularly, and the Girl Friday connection helped with my search.

'Penny?' he says, his voice catching.

She opens her mouth to speak and her eyes glint with tears as Nick and I step away. 'I think Penny will stay for tea,' I tell Lynne quickly, 'but we'll leave her for now.' And so we walk away, across the grounds, and when I glance back Penny and Saul are embracing. Nick takes my hand as the tears flow freely down my face.

Monday, December 16

Hi, how are things? reads Andy's text. I have just finished lunch in the work canteen. I haven't resigned yet; that'll be next week, when I have signed my contract with the museum.

All good, I reply.

Got time for a chat? he wants to know, so I call him. 'Just taking a break from packing,' he says. 'I'm moving tomorrow. So I just thought I'd see how you're doing.'

'I'm fine, thanks,' I say. 'So, where's the new place?'

This time, he gives me not only the full address, but precise instructions, in case I might have forgotten the numbering system that seems to apply to most flats: 'Flat 1/2. So that's first floor on the right.'

'What's it like?' I ask.

'Small, but nice, you know. Decent shared garden. I've just signed up for six months so I'm not committed beyond that.'

'Right.' Why is he supplying me with all this information? Last place, he wouldn't even let his daughter visit.

'You're really welcome to come over,' he adds. 'For coffee, I mean.'

I smile. 'Yes, I realise that, Andy. I didn't think you meant anything else.'

He clears his throat. 'Okay, well, I'd better carry on packing then . . .'

'Good luck,' I say.

'Thanks.' He hesitates. 'So, are you all ready for Christmas?'

I can't help smiling at that; it's the kind of thing someone would say when they're serving you in a shop. In fact, I do feel okay about this, our first Christmas apart in all the years we've known each other. Andy is heading up north to spend it with his parents, and has already asked, tentatively, if Izzy and I might consider coming too. I knew what he was asking really; if I might consider us getting back together.

I explained, without any feelings of irritation or sadness,

360

that that won't happen. But I have promised to call them on Christmas Day and I hope, genuinely, that they all enjoy their time together. As for Izzy and me, we are spending it at Jules, Erol and Maeve's this year. They tend to have a houseful and I know it'll be fun. Izzy is delighted.

'Viv,' Andy says now, 'if I send you a pic that I think's funny, you won't go mental, will you?'

'What kind of pic?' I ask.

'You'll see,' he says, and I can tell he's smiling now. So this is where we are, I realise now: at the sending-funny-pictures stage. Does this mean we can be friends? I'm not entirely against it.

We finish the call, and a few moments later the text pings in. It's a picture of me, pissed, glancing around furtively whilst stuffing an omelette under his windscreen wiper.

His caption reads: *Recognise anyone?*

Never seen that woman in my life, I reply with a smile.

Chapter Forty-Two

Tuesday, December 17

I used to make these lists all the time in my head. They helped somehow. One of them went like this:

Things Andy Moaned About
The unbuttered scone situation.
Parking at work.
Decline in loo paper quality.
The (imagined) cheesy smell in the wardrobe in Paris.
Midges.
My sweating.

But I no longer do that because we are okay, Andy and me. We are so proud of our kids, and I often remind myself that Spencer and Izzy are the result of us. And right now I am filled with happiness – not because I'm free of all of Andy's grumbling, but because it's a beautiful winter's day, and Nick is coming soon.

He leaves for Auckland tomorrow, with Penny; he is

taking her back with him for her first ever New Zealand Christmas. She is thrilled at the thought of sunshine and warm sand between her toes. She lives in Glasgow, after all.

We are having Bobby to stay for the duration of their trip. Or rather, Jules and I are; we have figured out a walking schedule. As I don't finish at Flaxico until Christmas, Jules will take him during the day. Izzy is delighted.

Then, in mid-January, Nick and Penny will come back, because he is moving home. Where will it lead? I have no idea. But right now my heart feels as light as candy floss as I answer the door.

I study Nick's lovely face for a moment, wanting to kiss him. And then I do, on the lips. I'd anticipated a quick peck but it's much, much more. My head spins as his arms wind around my waist. We are kissing, here on my doorstep, where anyone could walk by and see. Chrissie or Tim might arrive home with groceries, or their Christmas tree – I think they planned to fetch theirs today. Or Izzy could wander through and see us. But, for those minutes everything else melts away as we kiss, and it just feels so right.

We pull apart and he smiles. 'Well, is she ready?' he asks.

'Just about,' I say. 'She's very excited.' I run a hand over my hair and turn to the stairs, still feeling his kiss on my lips. 'Izzy?' I call out. 'Nick's here!'

'I'll get set up straight away then,' he says as we step inside.

So here we go.

'Welcome,' my daughter says, 'to a new episode of *Izzy Cooks!*' She beams at Nick, who's behind the camera, and at me. I keep glancing at him; I can't help it.

'Mum, are you watching?' Izzy says.

'Yes! Yes, of course I'm watching, love.'

Her gaze meets mine, and there's a flicker of what can only be her first eye-roll. Surely, those adolescent hormones aren't kicking in at eight years old?

'So, today,' she says, quickly regaining her focus, 'we are cracking the eggs into this bowl here. You can use three but for a really big one I like to use *four* eggs.'

She cracks them deftly into the glass dish. Nick catches my eye and we smile.

'And now we beat them lightly, not too much. You want them just mixed really, not frothy.' She grins. 'We already have our grated cheese here. Just ordinary, basic cheese.' I look at Nick again, who looks terribly handsome in his white T-shirt, freshly shaved. He has the sort of face you want to touch. I never thought I would ever want to do that again – touch a man's face, I mean, in that way.

But I do, and I know that when he and Penny catch their flight tomorrow, it's not the end. It's the start of something, for all of us.

Right now, I am a little edgy as Izzy heats the butter in the pan – 'Not too much!' she says with a smile – but we are close by and she has seen me doing this plenty of times. She has even done it herself. Not on camera, though; not being filmed, making a real cookery show.

'In go the eggs,' she announces. 'Now, as soon as they start to set, you need to get your spatula ready and drag the mixture to the middle of the pan, whirling it around. You want it to cook quickly. In with the cheese now . . .' She carries on, utterly unselfconscious, and tips it from the pan to the plate.

'And that,' she says, grinning right to camera now, another milk tooth gone, 'is how you make the *best* omelette in the world.'

The End

Acknowledgements

Huge thanks to Tilda McDonald, Molly Walker-Sharp, Rachel Faulkner-Willcocks, Sabah Khan and the entire fabulous Avon team. Thanks as ever to my wonderful agent, Caroline Sheldon, and to Wendy Rigg for the Seventies fashion angle and all-round David Essex-loving brilliance. A big shout-out to Tania Cheston for reading, checking and geeing me along, to Mary Fine (and Penelope) for schnoodle inspiration and to Jenny Tucker, Kath Brown, Susan Walker, Marie O'Riordan, Cathy Gilligan and all my wonderfully supportive buddies. Extra special thanks to Lisa Woolley-Band and Fiona Miller for the life coaching info (especially the standing-on-chair bit) and to all at Elise Allan's creativity coaching group (thank you Anne, Annie, Christobel, Mif and Helen!). Finally, all my love to Jimmy, Sam, Dexter and Erin, my fantastic family who somehow manage to put up with me.

Follow me on Instagram @fiona_gib
www.fionagibson.com

When the kids are away . . .

'Warm, funny and poignant' *Daily Mail*

THE MUM WHO GOT HER LIFE BACK

An empty nest has never been so much fun!

Fiona Gibson

The laugh-out-loud *Sunday Times* bestseller is back and funnier than ever!

Everyone has a last straw . . .

An unmissable novel, perfect for fans
of Milly Johnson and Jill Mansell.

What happens when The One That Got Away shows up again . . . thirty years later?

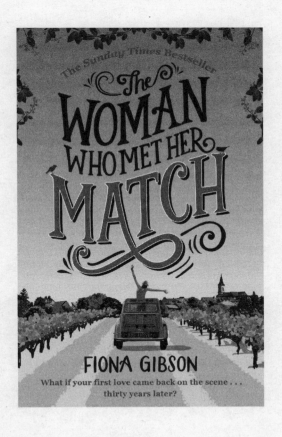

An unmissable novel from the voice of the modern woman!

Forget about having it all.
Sometimes you just want to
leave it all behind.

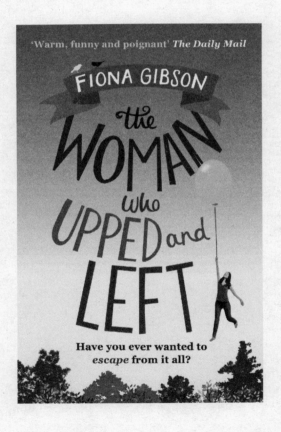

'Warm, funny and poignant' *The Daily Mail*

FIONA GIBSON

the

WOMAN

who

UPPED and

LEFT

Have you ever wanted to
escape from it all?

A warm, funny and honest read that's
perfect for when you've just had enough.

Midlife crisis?
WHAT midlife crisis?!

A hilarious read for fans of *Why Mummy Drinks*.